Leonid Yuzefovich

HARLEQUIN'S COSTUME

Volume 1 of the Putilin Trilogy

Translated by Marian Schwartz

ИНСТИТУТ ПЕРЕВОДА

AD VERBUM

Published with the support of the Institute
for Literary Translation, Russia

Glagoslav Publications

HARLEQUIN'S COSTUME
By Leonid Yuzefovich

First published in Russian as "Костюм Арлекина" in 2001

Translated from the Russian by Marian Schwartz

© 2001, Leonid Yuzefovich

Represented by www.nibbe-wiedling.com

© 2013, Glagoslav Publications, United Kingdom

Glagoslav Publications Ltd
88-90 Hatton Garden
EC1N 8PN London
United Kingdom

www.glagoslav.com

ISBN: 978-1-78267-029-2

Contents

Chapter 1. The Hapsburg Eagle. 10

Chapter 2. Polish Prince, Bulgarian Student,

                Serpent Tempter, Severed Head 27

Chapter 3. Hohenbruch's Rifle. 48

Chapter 4. New Characters. 60

Chapter 5. Two Stories from the Life of Ivan

                Dmitrievich, as Told by the Man Himself. 78

Chapter 6. Bite Marks Are Found 84

Chapter 7. The Appearance of Kerim-Bek 101

Chapter 8. The Weather Takes a Turn for the Worse. 119

Chapter 9. The Italians and Turks Get in on the Act 140

Chapter 10. A Night of Revelations. 149

Chapter 11. Disappointment All Around 165

Chapter 12. An Avenging Angel 181

Chapter 13. Among Ghosts. 195

Chapter 14. The Snake Bites Its Own Tail. 214

Chapter 15. The Gilt Worn Off. 240

Epilogue. 259

Prologue

Ivan Dmitrievich Putilin, the legendary Chief Inspector of the St. Petersburg police, came from New Oskol, a provincial town drowning in gardens in southern Kursk Province. Having lived half a century in Petersburg, he nonetheless retained the mild manners and accent of a Southerner, loved his cherry dumplings, and as he got on in years, dreamed more and more often of the chalk cliffs above the Oskol, only to awaken each time in tears, though he was never drawn back to his native lands. He found nature in the North more to his taste.

After retiring due to ill health in the spring of 1893, he left his apartment in the city to his son and settled in a house he had been fortunate enough to purchase at some point in the past from an elderly landed gentleman, a house complete with veranda and apple orchard, on the high bank of the Volkhov River. It was four versts from there to the nearest train station; on the other hand, the view from the cliff overhanging the river was so stunning and expansive that it made his heart ache. Here, in the village cemetery, lay Ivan Dmitrievich's wife, and here he lived continuously until his own death. Fate had given him another five and a half months.

Soon after his move, Ivan Dmitrievich wrote to his son: "I have conceived the notion of working up and publishing in the form of notes the most interesting material I have accumulated over the course of my career, to constitute something like a chronicle of crime in our Northern capital over the last thirty years. Would you please attempt to interest some reputable publisher in this project?"

By "reputable" he meant someone in a position to pay him well. Not a wealthy man, Ivan Dmitrievich realized that this was his only way of earning some small sum.

The memoirs of the great detective would naturally be quite saleable. A publisher was quickly found—more than one, in fact. Ivan Dmitrievich selected the most generous offer, took the advance, and sat down to work with enthusiasm. He put his archive in order, started a card file, compiled a detailed plan for his chronicle, and devised chapter titles and selected epigraphs for them—whereupon he got bogged down. He had thought it out to the tiniest detail, but as the plan accrued new points and subpoints listed under Roman and Arabic numerals, the picture of the past, which had been so blindingly vivid at first, faded. One morning, Ivan Dmitrievich was chagrined to admit that the more detailed his plan, the harder it was to turn into something bigger. He tried writing without any plan at all, but here, too, success eluded him. Coffee didn't help, nor did strong tea. Finally, an acquaintance to whom he had been complaining in his correspondence recommended as an assistant a literary man from the capital by the name of Safonov, the author of two novellas that had appeared in *The Russian Herald.* Ivan Dmitrievich and Safonov reached an agreement through an exchange of letters that for his labors Safonov would receive a third of the fee promised by the publisher, and in August Ivan Dmitrievich met his guest at the station four versts from his house. Safonov was an elegant strawberry blond in his late thirties, polite and neat. His luggage went on the cart while they themselves proceeded on foot. The weather was divine, not a cloud in the sky.

"What beauty!" Safonov was delighted.

"Yes, we do have marvelous spots," replied Ivan Dmitrievich proudly.

As they walked through the fields, in the distance they could see the river sparkling in the sun. Safonov sucked on a blade of grass.

"How long will it take us?" he asked, squinting in a business-like way.

"For what?" Ivan Dmitrievich didn't understand.

"For all of everything. How long will I be staying with you?"

"If I tell you one story a day, I think about a month."

"You can't manage two a day?"

"There are some of those, but very few. So count on a month."

"I thought we'd manage in a week."

"On the other hand, you'll be relaxing in the fresh air. We can hunt for mushrooms, and you can go fishing."

"And how do you intend to organize our working day?"

"Do you nap after dinner?" Ivan Dmitrievich inquired in turn.

"No. I don't have that habit."

"Nor do I. That means we can set to work this very day. I'll talk and you'll take notes. It's all very simple. For speed I advise you use a pencil—round, not faceted. Otherwise you're sure to get a callous on your finger."

"It's not all that simple. It will take me considerable effort to alter my style sufficiently so as to render it quite unrecognizable."

"And why is that?"

"I have my reader," explained Safonov, "and he shall grasp immediately by whose hand your memoirs were written."

They had their midday repast on the veranda, where Ivan Dmitrievich himself brewed coffee on a spirit lamp and poured each of them a cup. Then, after entrusting to Safonov the plan for his chronicle, he proposed the following:

"Choose what appeals to you. We'll start with that."

Safonov read the titles of the first three chapters: "Bestial Murder on Ruzovskaya Street," "Bloody Crime in Orlovsky Lane," and "Death on Liteiny."

"Rather monotonous," he noted after perusing the list to the end.

After that only the street names changed and the epithets varied: one murder was "nightmarish," another "frightful," and so forth.

"Alas!" Ivan Dmitrievich gestured helplessly.

Safonov sipped his coffee and, returning to the top of the list, asked, "Who was killed on Ruzovskaya?"

"The laundress Grigorieva."

"And in Orlovsky Lane?"

"The caretaker. Last name Klushin."

"Isn't there someone of rank?"

"Naturally. 'Death on Liteiny' is about Baron Frideriks from the Department of State Properties."

"Was he knifed or shot?"

"Neither. The murder weapon was tongs for splitting sugar."

"Red-hot?"

"Why would you think that?"

"I assumed he was tortured to death with the tongs."

"Heaven forfend! He was stabbed from behind in the darkness and that was that. Antique bronze tongs. They must have weighed a pound and a half."

Safonov wrinkled his nose.

"Didn't anyone ever use a dagger or a revolver? Are there any like that?"

"Yes, but then you have to choose one or the other: either a pistol and a caretaker or a baron and tongs. I am typifying and generalizing, of course," explained Ivan Dmitrievich. "Instead of a baron it could be a colonel and instead of tongs—whatever you like. Here, for example"—he pointed to the middle of the list, to "A Mysterious Crime on the Street of Millions"—"there's even one prince who was smothered with pillows."

"A prince?" Safonov perked up.

"Yes, Prince von Ahrensburg, the Austrian military attaché to Petersburg. Or rather, the military agent, as people said in those days."

"What days?"

"In 1871."

"Who murdered him?"

"Well, if I tell you right off, you'll lose interest in listening. Although . . ."

Ivan Dmitrievich left the veranda and went into the room. A minute later he returned holding a sheet of paper covered with writing.

"Here I have two epigraphs for the chapter. They'll set a certain mood and may possibly give you a hint."

"Why are there two of them?"

"The story is such that one does not suffice. In any event, I was unable to select one that did."

Here, Safonov began, guessing that the subject was an English bookstall, *the Golden Dreamer, and the Norwood Fortune Teller, were still on sale at sixpence each . . . with a picture of a young woman with a high waist lying on a sofa in an attitude so uncomfortable as almost to account for her dreaming at one and the same time of a conflagration, a shipwreck, an earthquake, a skeleton, a church-porch, lightning, a funeral, and a young man in a bright blue coat and canary pantalons.*

Indicated below was the author from whom this had been quarried: Charles Dickens.

The second epigraph was much shorter and fit on one line:

The envoy arrived, mute, bearing a deed unwritten.

"What is this? Where does it come from?" asked Safonov, having failed to discover a source citation.

"It's an ancient Russian riddle of unknown authorship."

"And the solution?"

"It refers to the dove who carried a branch—an olive branch, I believe—in his beak to Noah in the ark."

"And you think this will suffice for me to guess the solution?"

"I don't know. That depends on your perspicacity."

"All right," Safonov decided. "Tell me the story. Let's start with this prince."

From the glass of pencils on the table, ignoring Ivan Dmitrievich's advice, he chose a faceted one sharp enough to serve as a murder weapon and solemnly opened one of the fat notebooks bound in green leatherette that he had brought with him.

Safonov stayed on in the house with the veranda and apple orchard until mid-September and then, after returning to Petersburg, where from time to time he was pulled away by his newspaper job, he worked over his notes for a few more months. Only the next spring did the book come out, with the title, "Forty Years Amongst Murderers and Thieves," but Ivan Dmitrievich himself never did hold it in his hands. For two weeks in November 1893 he burned up with influenza with complications of pneumonia. He was buried beside his wife. The money from the publisher went to Putilin the younger, who did the honorable thing and paid Safonov his promised share.

During his lifetime, Ivan Dmitrievich had been an enigmatic figure. No newspaper reporter ever once managed to interview him. He preferred to do his job and keep his own counsel.

There were many legends that cast him as a policeman's Don Quixote, a Russian Lecoq, a fantastically accurate sharpshooter, a strongman who could bend horseshoes, a secret Old Believer, a converted Jew, even a repentant murderer who carried on his body certain distinguishing marks, but after the book Safonov wrote came out and went through several editions, the public was presented with an ordinary gentleman with luxuriant side whiskers, a man moderately honest, moderately clever, and moderately well educated. Gradually the legends about him were forgotten; the printed word had more power. The mystery dissolved, the aura surrounding Ivan Dmitrievich's name faded, and from here it was just one step to total oblivion.

Which was not long in coming.

It is difficult to judge whether Safonov was to blame for this or whether time simply demanded other heroes, but Putilin's name is not listed in the index of names for the century. It certainly belongs there, though, if only in connection with Prince von Ahrensburg's murder. The drama that played out on the Street of Millions on the night of April 25, 1871, threatened Russia with diplomatic complications so grave that they might well have altered the course of history. One must give Safonov's intuition its due, however; he had made a fortuitous choice. In setting forth the events of this drama he did allow himself, albeit for the benefit of the modest reader, to digress here and there from the actual facts, fabricating a point here and suppressing another there, but one of the notebooks in the green leatherette cover that has survived preserved Ivan Dmitrievich's story in all its original charm.

Chapter 1

The Hapsburg Eagle

That morning, as usual, Ivan Dmitrievich was reading the *Saint Petersburg Gazette* over breakfast. This was the only newspaper he took at home because it was the only one offered at official expense. His wife took great pride in this privilege, afforded, she believed, only to the select few.

Three-year-old Vanechka was already awake and pushing a gaily painted toy butterfly across the floor by its long pole. The butterfly had a tiny wheel under its belly, and its tin wings were supposed to flap as it moved, but only one did. The other hung there, limp.

"If only you'd fix it," his wife said. "There's just one nail to hammer in."

"I'll fix it, I'll fix it," Ivan Dmitrievich replied mechanically.

"When?"

"Tonight."

"You've been promising for more than a week. It's harmful for a child to play with freaks. It has a bad effect on the nervous system. I know from my own case. When I was a little girl almost all my dolls had an arm or a leg torn off."

"That's odd. I never thought of you as poor."

"That's not it. I later found out that my mother herself had secretly maimed them."

"Your mother?"

"Yes, she had all sorts of ideas when it came to my education—my moral education, mostly. She wanted me to learn to love my dolls even crippled. This was supposed to develop my sense of compassion. And what came of it?"

"What?" Ivan Dmitrievich inquired as he dove back into his newspaper.

"Have you forgotten my nerves when you and I were married? The least little thing and I was in tears. Simply a bundle of nerves."

Ivan Dmitrievich took this to mean that his son faced repeating her lamentable journey if the second wing wasn't fixed.

"How many sugars for you?" his wife asked, setting a glass of tea in front of him. "Two lumps or three?"

"Three."

"I'm asking again: three or two?"

"Two."

"Are you going to keep doing this?" she exploded. "Repeating my last word like a parrot? I can't have a conversation with you! Put away that fiendish newspaper! You have a sick stomach. I know because your breath was bad again this morning. Are you set on ruining your digestion completely?"

Ivan Dmitrievich put the newspaper aside and looked at the clock. He still had fifteen minutes.

Without touching his tea, he went into the storeroom, brought back a hammer and a tin can full of nails and took the butterfly from his son.

"What are you doing, Vanya?" His wife began to fret. "Aren't you going to drink my tea?"

What was in the glass was something which she referred to either tenderly as "my tea," or, with a note of pedagogic steel in her voice, "your tea," but which was in fact an herbal infusion concocted from a neighbor's recipe that included a small amount of real black tea, which his wife contrived to undermine and replace with herbs beneficial to the stomach.

"There'll be time, I'll drink it," said Ivan Dmitrievich, choosing a suitable nail. "If there isn't, I'll manage without your tea."

"Put away the hammer," his wife ordered. "Vanechka and I don't need these sacrifices from you. Isn't that so, my son? Tell your papa to give you back your butterfly and drink his tea."

"No!" Vanechka stamped his little foot.

Just then, the doorbell rang.

Walking out to the foyer, Ivan Dmitrievich expected to see one of his deputy agents making a routine stop at his apartment to find out whether he was needed, but instead he saw a young officer he did not know wearing the dark blue greatcoat of the Corps de Gendarmes—the secret police.

"Captain Pevtsov," he introduced himself. "Count Shuvalov sent me. His Excellency requests that you come immediately to the Street of Millions on a matter of utmost urgency. There is a carriage at your service, waiting downstairs."

"But what's happened?"

"You'll find out there. I beg of you, make haste."

"He still hasn't had his tea," his wife said in a booming voice, appearing from behind the door-curtain.

"If you please, Mr. Putilin. Explain to your wife who Count Shuvalov is."

"Count Shuvalov, my dear, is the Chief of the Third Section of the Imperial Chancellery and Chief of the Corps de Gendarmes," Ivan Dmitrievich explained, fully aware, however, that Peter Alexandrovich Shuvalov's influence extended well beyond even those prodigious posts.

"You must understand, madam." said Pevtsov. "This is an affair of state."

"And you, too, must understand. My husband has a sick stomach, and before he leaves he must drink his tea. This is no ordinary tea, as you are doubtless thinking. To the infusion I add St. John's wort, dog rose, a little chamomile—"

"All right, that's enough, enough," Ivan Dmitrievich stopped her and turned to Pevtsov. "Captain, why don't you go ahead without me. I'll be right along."

"May I inquire as to whether that will be soon?"

"Half an hour at the latest. I'll have a sip of tea and set out."

Naturally, it was not a matter of tea or even his wife. The reason for his delay was the following. As Chief Inspector, Ivan Dmitrievich would never allow himself to arrive at the scene of a crime without ascertaining in advance precisely what had transpired there.

After seeing Pevtsov out, Putilin finished his tea, put on his coat, and took his bowler off its hook.

"Don't forget your umbrella," his wife reminded him.

"Look out the window! Why do I need it?"

"It's still April and it's sunny now, but by evening that could all change. Is it so hard for you to take your umbrella for my peace of mind? If we were talking about your peace of mind I would."

They had this same conversation every morning, regardless of weather, and today Ivan Dmitrievich decided to demonstrate resolve.

"Leave me be. I'm not taking it," he said, attenuating his tone with a kiss.

His wife softened immediately and asked, "Shall I call the driver?"

"It's not worth it. I'll take a cab."

"That's always the way. You spare the horses but not yourself," she said, straightening her husband's tie.

Ivan Dmitrievich kissed her one more time and went downstairs. On the street, two cabbies raced up from opposite directions. Each morning since becoming Chief Inspector, Ivan Dmitrievich discovered at his doorstep one of the brotherhood, who considered it their great good fortune to have Putilin himself as a passenger. They would not take his money. Ivan Dmitrievich respected this small economy and without a twinge of conscience accepted the free ride—with one exception: he invariably paid the cabbies who were among his agents. With them he took no liberties.

He was superstitious and chose the droshky that of the two had guessed correctly and pulled up on his right. His plan was first to drive by the Bureau of Investigations, where they would certainly give him a full report, and then continue on to the Street of Millions.

"Where will it be?" the cabbie asked respectfully.

"Don't you know?" Ivan Dmitrievich got angry. "I see I should have taken your comrade's offer. He wouldn't have had to ask."

"I only ask, Ivan Dmitrievich, because perhaps you're not going to the bureau today as usual," the coachman said in justification. "The police—sure I know that."

"Why might I suddenly not be going to the bureau today?"

"I thought to Millions. They say that Austria envoy got his throat slit."

"Then take me there," Ivan Dmitrievich commanded. "You already know it all, so why ask?"

II

On the Street of Millions, opposite the barracks of the First Battalion of the Preobrazhensky Regiment, in front of a green, two-story, private residence, was a thick swarm of expensive carriages, official coaches, and landaus with imposing coachmen in their boxes. Here resided Prince Ludwig von Ahrensburg, cavalry general and military attaché of the Austro-Hungarian Empire. Ivan Dmitrievich had had the misfortune to make the man's acquaintance the previous autumn, when the brass door knocker had been swiped from his front door. At the time, the prince had created such a furor that the entire capital police had been run ragged searching for this treasure. For a couple of months they kept all the shops where antiques or metal scrap were sold under surveillance, but they never did find it.

On the back wall of one of the carriages gleamed the massive gold eagle of the Austrian Hapsburgs, two-headed like Russia's, but with slightly thinner feathers and long legs. This was the ambassador's carriage; Ivan Dmitrievich knew it well. It had stopped at a slight distance from the entrance, which meant it had arrived after the others. Hence it followed that the Austrian ambassador himself, Count Hotek, was alive, thank God, and it was the master of the house who had been killed.

In order to gauge the event more accurately, Ivan Dmitrievich took a stroll past the rank of carriages. Behind Hotek's stood a simple black barouche. He knew the coachman, who drove not just anyone but a grand duke, Prince Peter Georgievich Oldenburgsky.

On duty at the front door were two men in civilian dress. They were driving away gawkers and asking pedestrians to cross to the other side of the street, but they uttered not a word to Ivan Dmitrievich. He headed for the entrance. Suddenly, from off to the side, his deputy agent Konstantinov popped up and began mincing along beside him, whispering, "Ivan Dmitrievich, I've been watching for you here so that you would know why you were summoned."

"Get out," commanded Ivan Dmitrievich. "I already know without your help."

Konstantinov made himself scarce.

The front steps, the anteroom, the foyer, the hallway—it was a space without shapes or colors, only smells; there was no getting away from them. Something was burning off to the right. Ah, that would be the kitchen. Actually, even that innocent observation was superfluous for now. Ivan Dmitrievich walked toward the sound of muffled voices, looking straight ahead. Not knowing anything, not looking from side to side—that was the more reliable way. First you needed to establish a point of view, otherwise the details would obscure your gaze. The main thing was your point of view. Only a dilettante would goggle in all four directions, considering this a virtue.

The door opened with a nasty creak, and Ivan Dmitrievich walked into the drawing room, where it was bright from the epaulets and colorful from the embroidery on all the uniforms. Standing by the window was Count Hotek, who had already pinned a mourning rosette to his chest. Prince Oldenburgsky was saying something to him in German, and the ambassador was nodding with a look on his face that said he already knew everything the grand duke was going to tell him. Officers and officials were modestly holding up the walls as a threesome—Duke Meklenburg-Strelitsky, Minister of Justice Count Palen, and Mayor Trepov—paced back and forth past them. Shuvalov was not there.

Ivan Dmitrievich sidled in, cautiously, trying hard to make his bulky body as weightless as possible. No one paid him any mind. He took a comb out of his pocket, combed his hair, and then combed out his side whiskers in his habitual way. By the time he was forty they had grayed noticeably and lost their former softness so that they now stuck out to the sides, ruining the general contour. His whiskers demanded constant care, but Ivan Dmitrievich was beyond the point where he could shave them off. His fat bare cheeks would have required different facial expressions and thus a different tone for his relations with superiors and inferiors.

While he was combing his hair he heard Count Palen tell his interlocutor under his breath, "And why, one asks, are they forever forcing their Third Rome down our throats? The Third Rome! Has it been so long since we stopped calling ourselves the Holy Roman Empire? Less than a hundred years! The historian Soloviev told me that Ivan the Third borrowed the two-headed eagle from the Greeks so as not to lag behind the Hapsburgs, who simply appropriated it first. Now the moment we turn in the direction of the Balkans, the entire Viennese press starts howling that since we took our crest from Byzantium, we must be laying claim to the Byzantine legacy."

At that moment, Pevtsov separated himself from the group of gendarme officers standing by the opposite wall. Now Ivan Dmitrievich got a better look at him: tall, lithe, swarthy in a dullish way, with eyes an elusive color—maybe green, maybe gray, maybe yellow—that changed oddly depending on the time of day, the lighting, and the color of the wallpaper.

"Well?" he asked. "Do you know why you were asked to come?"

The very question held a tranquil confidence in the superiority of the Corps de Gendarmes over the police, therefore Ivan Dmitrievich responded accordingly.

"You are a naïve man, Captain."

"Why?"

"You hoped to conceal from me what the cabbies are already tittle-tattling."

The professional demeanor with which Pevtsov had been preparing to announce what had happened slid off his face, and he went into the bedroom. A minute later he looked out and crooked his finger, beckoning to Ivan Dmitrievich.

The faint buzzing of the drawing room shifted behind him and became almost inaudible. Before entering the bedroom, Ivan Dmitrievich allowed himself the satisfaction of looking over his shoulder. Five minutes before, no one had taken the slightest interest in him, but now everyone was looking at him alone. Only Prince Oldenburgsky and Duke Meklenburg-Strelitsky were still trying in tandem to make some point with Hotek, who looked as though he had long known that his emperor's military attaché would be murdered in St. Petersburg and had even given warning of this, but no one had believed him.

III

Prince Ludwig von Ahrensburg lay face up on the bed. His eyes were wide-open and staring, his face had darkened, and there were bluish spots near his Adam's apple, evidence that the Grim Reaper had paid his visit several hours before. The prince's black imperial beard, nobly streaked with gray, was disheveled, and his thinning hair was plastered to his temples by dried sweat. His stiffened fingers stuck out at a sickening angle, crooked in rigor mortis. His arms, crossed over his chest, were bound at the wrists with the twisted cord from a window curtain. The curtain on the right, closest to the bed, the one missing that cord, modestly shielded the dead body from the morning April light spilling in from the street.

"The doctor has already been here," Pevtsov whispered, forestalling Ivan Dmitrievich's question.

Standing beside Shuvalov, who had barely nodded to him when he entered, Ivan Dmitrievich inspected the dead man. His nightshirt was crumpled and stained with droplets of blood. One sleeve had been torn off and used to bind his legs at the ankles. Above the knees, the prince's legs had been tied together with a tourniquet of sheets, yet even in that position he apparently had continued to struggle. This was obvious from the way the featherbed dangled on the floor and from the corner of the blanket cover they had evidently crammed into his mouth.

"Mr. Putilin, how much time will you need to examine everything here?" Shuvalov inquired.

"Two hours will suffice, Your Excellency."

"Too long."

"I can keep it to an hour and a half."

"Also too long. Prince Oldenburgsky, Duke Meklenburg-Strelitsky, and Count Hotek have expressed a desire to view the scene of the crime. I cannot make them wait outside the door for another hour and a half."

"If they don't touch anything, they can come in now," Ivan Dmitrievich proposed. "I have no objection."

"He has no objection! You don't say!" Pevtsov fumed. "Can it be that you fail to appreciate the fact that we cannot show Hotek the deceased in such a state?"

"In no instance," Shuvalov supported him.

"Then how much time will you allow me?" Ivan Dmitrievich asked.

"Half an hour and not a minute longer. The examination will be carried out jointly with Captain Pevtsov. He has been assigned to conduct the investigation for the Corps de Gendarmes, so you will be working together. I beg of you, gentlemen, bear in mind that you are dealing with a matter of the utmost importance. The sovereign himself has commanded me to report news of this case to him on the hour. Begin, and I will immediately send in the valet who discovered the prince dead. While you are conducting your examination, he will give you a full accounting."

Scarcely had Shuvalov left when Pevtsov plopped down in an armchair with relief.

"To begin with," he said, "let us divide up the responsibilities. If we are to cut our route short, we might attempt to traverse it by starting simultaneously from opposite ends."

"How's that?"

"You will move from the obvious facts to the likely motive for the murder, while I will start in the opposite direction, from a likely motive to the facts."

And what, in your opinion, is the motive?"

"I have no doubt that von Ahrensburg's murder was political in nature. For example, the situation in the Balkans may have some bearing on it."

Ivan Dmitrievich got down on his hands and knees and looked under the bed. Kerosene from the broken table lamp had spilled on the floor. In fact, unimaginable chaos reigned throughout. The dressing table had been upset, the blankets and pillows scattered around the bedroom. One pillow had been ripped open and was all in feathers, and broken glass crunched underfoot. The prince had fought desperately for his life.

"You and I have only a little while," Pevtsov continued. "In the next few hours Hotek will be wiring Vienna, and in a couple of days the newspapers there will trumpet throughout Europe that foreign diplomats in Russia are getting their throats slit like chickens."

"That's probably the one thing they won't be writing," Ivan Dmitrievich replied irritably as he untied the knot in the sheet in order to free the dead man's legs.

"How poorly you know those hacks." Pevtsov snorted. "That is only the beginning!"

"No one is going to be writing about diplomats here getting their throats slit. You can rest assured."

"What makes you so certain?"

"Because the prince's throat wasn't slit. He was smothered."

Carefully, Ivan Dmitrievich turned the body from its back to its belly and showed Pevtsov.

"Convinced? There's not a scratch on him. Only bruises."

"Where did the blood on his shirt come from?"

"That's not his blood. Evidently he bit the hand of one of the murderers."

"You think there was more than one?"

"At least two. The prince was a wiry man. Just look at those hands! You could never tie someone like that up by the hands and feet alone. Unless . . ."

Ivan Dmitrievich fell silent.

"What? Say it," Pevtsov encouraged him.

"Unless at some moment he suddenly recognized his killer and lost the will to resist."

"Out of fear?"

"Not necessarily. He may have remembered having wronged that person."

"Shall we dispense with the Dostoyevskian speculation?" Pevtsov responded. "Don't forget, the deceased was a German, not a Buddhist and not a Russian intellectual. And tell me, on what is your assumption based? Why would he fail to recognize his murderer at first, start to resist, and then later suddenly recognize him?"

"Because it was dark in the bedroom, the lamp wasn't lit. If it had fallen and smashed when the wick was hot, that would have ignited the kerosene . . ."

Before Ivan Dmitrievich could finish his thought, the prince's valet appeared, having been sent by Shuvalov. He was a fat-faced, red-haired fellow with lashless fish-eyes.

"Were you the first to discover the prince dead?" Pevtsov addressed him.

"Just so, Your Honor, I did. He, you see, when he was going to bed he told me to wake him in the morning at half past eight."

The valet was bracing himself for a thorough accounting, but Ivan Dmitrievich interrupted him.

"You can finish your story later. For now, cast a proprietary eye about you. Is there nothing missing?"

After a painstaking joint search, Ivan Dmitrievich made a list of missing valuables on his notepad: "revolver (type unknown), silver cigarette case, French gold pieces (9-10)."

"Like these?" Ivan Dmitrievich asked in a whisper. He showed the valet a gold coin with the goatish profile of Napoleon III, Emperor of France, which he had found under the bed and concealed from Pevtsov.

He recalled in passing that this emperor had been the bitterest foe of his wife's favorite author, Victor Hugo. Recently she had bought Vanechka a plush goat and named it Esmeralda.

"Aha!" The valet nodded. "See from the side? They're as alike as two pins."

"Who?"

"Him"—the valet turned his eyes toward the deceased —"and him, on the ruble."

"It's called a Napoleon d'or," Ivan Dmitrievich said.

"What are you whispering about over there?" Pevtsov was beginning to fret. "What secrets are you keeping from me?"

"Oh it's nothing, nothing."

Ivan Dmitrievich returned to the dressing table, and while he was checking the contents of its drawers, Pevtsov reproached the valet.

"What is it about the doors in this house, my good man? Why do they all creak? Here they pass muster, just barely, but in the drawing room they screech like banshees. Are you lazy? Don't you oil them?"

"I do as I'm told," the valet said in his own defense. "When it came to the hinges, there wasn't any dissatisfaction."

"Off with you. We'll talk later," Ivan Dmitrievich told him, and after waiting for him to leave, he turned to Pevtsov. "Actually, Captain, I knew a moneylender once, and that son of the Jews strictly forbade his servants to oil the door hinges."

"He was afraid of robbers?"

"It's not just robbers people like that are afraid of."

The analogy worked. Pevtsov clasped his hands under his chin and pondered that thought, while Ivan Dmitrievich poured fat on the fire.

"Remember, the valet said the prince kept a revolver in the drawer of the dressing table by the bed. Why? Military habit? Or was he in fact afraid of someone?"

"Ah, yes." Pevtsov nodded. "I had thought of that myself."

"On the other hand" — Ivan Dmitrievich smiled at his game of cat-and-mouse — "his silver cigarette case has been stolen. How do you intend to link *its* disappearance to the situation in the Balkans?"

"We need to conduct a search in that Figaro's room. A suspicious fellow. . . ."

"Gentlemen, your time has expired," Shuvalov announced as he peered into the bedroom. "Thirty-five minutes have elapsed!"

Before going out, Ivan Dmitrievich cast one last look over the bed of Prince von Ahrensburg and noted one other odd circumstance. For some reason the dead man was lying with his feet pointing toward the head of the bed.

The bedroom was taken over by the valet and two ordinary gendarmes assigned to him as assistants. They laid the deceased out with a pillow under his head, having first rotated him 180 degrees. Then they pulled up his blanket and closed his eyes. From the drawing room Ivan Dmitrievich could hear a bucket handle clanking and a wet mop slapping the floor. Shuvalov had personally taken charge of the cleaning. This was a peculiar, purely Russian form of democratism, a leveling of ranks and estates: each man strove to do the other man's job.

One of the drawing room windows was set in a shallow, semi-circular niche. Standing there were Count Hotek and

Prince Oldenburgsky. Trailing the pungent smell of kerosene, Ivan Dmitrievich walked over to that window and pulled back the curtain. On the windowsill behind it he discovered an empty pint of vodka and a puddle of melted grease on a newspaper. He took a drop on his finger and licked it: butter.

"What is that?" Hotek, speaking Russian, asked with amusement.

"Your Excellency," Ivan Dmitrievich replied with a bow, "these are the facts with which I must begin my investigation."

The two gendarmes and the valet carrying the bucket crossed the drawing room in the opposite direction, after which Shuvalov, with the gracious gesture of a host inviting his guests to sit down to a well-laid table, proposed that those gathered proceed into the bedroom. Prince Oldenburgsky, Duke Meklenburg-Strelitsky, Palen, Hotek, and Adjutant General Trepov solemnly approached the bed, while the remaining uniformed folk crowded in the doorway. It occurred to Ivan Dmitrievich that if Shuvalov had had any notion of keeping this murder a secret, he had been overly hasty in bringing so many people here. Although, more than likely, they were all reliable men capable of holding their tongue.

"How horrid!" said Prince Oldenburgsky loudly.

Everyone nodded, although they had left the true horror—the horror of the unknown, the anticipation—behind in the drawing room, whereas here, in the tidied, shadowy room, looking at the deceased's face, whose dark blue spots the valet had managed to powder over, everyone ought to have been experiencing momentary relief. Death, thank God, looked perfectly proper.

IV

A quarter of an hour later, as he was escorting the Austrian ambassador to his carriage, Shuvalov spoke.

"It would be undesirable in the extreme for His Highness the Emperor Franz Josef, your Ministry of Foreign Affairs, and your General Staff to learn of the crime before we tracked down the perpetrator. I assure you, this will take us but a few hours."

Ivan Dmitrievich happened to overhear this conversation as he was studying the lock on the front door.

"My duty," Hotek replied coldly, "is to wire Vienna about all this immediately. I suspect this murder to have been committed by some fanatic from your so-called Slavonic Committee. True, that public is more active in Moscow than in Petersburg, but here too your press is filled with their howls about how we are supposedly oppressing our Slavic subjects. Evidently, these gentlemen felt their impunity and decided to move from word to deed. Their aim is to provoke a war between our empires."

"You exaggerate, Count."

"Not one whit. Today an attempt was made on my life as well."

"My God! How?"

"This morning, when I was riding past the Haymarket, someone standing behind a fence threw a stone through the window of my carriage." Hotek pointed. "It missed my head literally by an inch. There are witnesses. I fear poor Ludwig's death is but the beginning. I, or one of the embassy secretaries, could be the next victim. Baron Cobenzel, for example."

"I shall issue an immediate order for a guard at the embassy," said Shuvalov.

"I thank you."

"Whenever you go out you will be accompanied by a Cossack convoy."

"I dare hope you will not limit yourself to these measures," Hotek remarked.

With his footman's help he struggled up onto the

footboard, stopped briefly, caught his breath, and slid his withered, crane-like old body into the carriage, where another footman pulled him in.

"An eagle!" thought Ivan Dmitrievich, watching the carriage pull away.

Simultaneously, the thought flashed that given a successful conclusion to the case he might receive an Austrian as well as a Russian order. Wouldn't that be fine! His wife would be happy to boast to the neighbor women.

With that pleasant thought in mind, he continued his examination of the prince's residence. It was a two-story house whose entire first floor had been occupied by the prince and whose upper story was empty. Two hallways started at the antechamber and the foyer. One led off to the left, to the gentleman's quarters, and the second to the right, to the public rooms and the kitchen. Only the valet remained in the house at night, and he had a small separate room. The remaining rooms of the public half were locked, the coachman and cook's man lived off the courtyard, next to the stables, and the riding master and cook rented apartments in the city. All men. The prince was an old bachelor and did not keep a female servant.

Upon questioning these men, who were called into the drawing room one at a time, Ivan Dmitrievich was convinced of their innocence. They did not fidget, they answered his questions calmly and sensibly, no one expressed any suspiciously strong grief, and his instinct told him that this crowd had nothing to do with it. Pevtsov sat on the sofa in silence, listening but not interfering. Evidently, he intended to traverse the first part of his journey by his counterpart's side and only later race around and approach him from the other end.

That half of Prince von Ahrensburg's life, or rather, that third or even fourth, which he spent at home, was quickly sketched out. The prince was a worldly man, unencumbered by family obligations—much like his subordinates, for that matter. From time to time, he attended parades and demonstrations of marksmanship at Volkovo Field as well as maneuvers, though rarely, preferring the cavalry's, and that was the sum total of his affairs. In the afternoon he paid calls, in the evening he rested for an hour or two in his room, and he spent the night visiting or at the Yacht Club gambling. He usually returned shortly before dawn. Occasionally he brought a woman with him.

The previous evening, the prince had come home at about eight o'clock. He had napped until ten and then left for the Yacht Club. In those instances he always took his own horses, but not the riding master, and on the way back he hired a driver. He would let the driver go immediately. Yesterday he had returned after eleven, unharnessed the horses, and gone to bed. The cook's man, who lived at the residence, was already asleep by then; the riding master and cook had gone home to their families earlier in the evening. Only the valet was in the house.

The prince returned from the Yacht Club at five in the morning, as usual. He did not keep a doorman and carried the front door key with him. After helping the prince undress, the valet checked that the front door was locked (it was) and went to sleep in his little room. In the night he heard no noise or shouting.

"Drunk?" Ivan Dmitrievich asked.

"Bless me, no! I never touch it."

"Not you. The master."

"He did have a whiff about him."

Left alone with Pevtsov, Ivan Dmitrievich expressed his doubts. There was no way to get to the downstairs from the upper floor; that had been verified. The front door lock had not been forced, the service entrance was locked from the inside, all the glass in the windows was intact, and the frames were latched shut from the inside as well. How did the murderers penetrate the house?

"One night they stole up to the front door, pushed wax into the keyhole, and had a key made from the mold. It's very simple." Pevtsov shrugged. "The service entrance closes on an inside bolt, but not the front door. Did you notice?"

"I did."

"They anticipated everything. Send your men around to

the locksmiths. One of the masters may remember the client. What's wrong, Rukavishnikov?" Pevtsov asked the gendarme lieutenant who had entered the drawing room rapidly, his saber at his side.

Rukavishnikov held out a silver cigarette case with the von Ahrensburg monogram and pointed at the valet standing a little ways off.

"When we searched his room, we found this."

"The rogue swiped it, in the confusion. I told you!" Pevtsov exulted. "That's not what the murderers came for."

A tear rolled down the valet's face, and he started begging forgiveness, wailing:

"I swear by Christ our Lord, I took it, but that's all! Nothing else!"

"Silence! What is this sniveling?" Ivan Dmitrievich shouted at him. "Answer me, you fat little toad. Why did the prince tell you to wake him at eight thirty?"

"The Devil led me astray!" The valet sobbed. "I don't know anything!"

They called in the prince's coachman. He assured them on his oath that there had been no order to ready the horses for the morning.

"Apparently the prince was expecting someone," Pevtsov concluded.

This was perhaps the first thought he had had with which Ivan Dmitrievich could concur.

"Today, at eight thirty, nine at the latest, he was expecting a visitor," Pevtsov repeated, believing, evidently, that his perspicacity had not been fully appreciated. "Do you see? And now, Mr. Putilin, I shall take my leave and begin to act in accordance with my own plan."

Chapter 2

Polish Prince, Bulgarian Student, Serpent Tempter, Severed Head

Soon after Pevtsov's departure, a thoroughbred gentleman by the name of Lewicki, known to many of his friends by a different name, came to the Street of Millions to see Ivan Dmitrievich. To look at him, he was an aristocrat; in reality, he was a converted Jew and Ivan Dmitrievich's secret agent.

Once, long ago, at their first encounter, Lewicki had conveyed to Ivan Dmitrievich the words of his father, a cobbler from Lodz: "Every Jew is the son of a king." Lewicki passed himself off not as the son, naturally, but as the great-grandnephew of Stanisław August Poniatowski, the last king of the Recz Pospolita, who ended his days in Petersburg in 1798. Lewicki had in his possession certain genealogical papers to this effect that were evidently sufficiently incontrovertible to open the Yacht Club doors to him. There he played cards with the cream of the capital's aristocracy while simultaneously eavesdropping on the conversations of titled gamblers at neighboring tables and in the refreshment room, and whenever he had occasion to learn anything of possible interest to Ivan Dmitrievich, he informed him simply out of friendship. The latter, in turn, also exclusively out of friendship, would pay him something from certain police department funds over which he had complete discretion.

Unfortunately, Lewicki was a cardsharp, and ordinarily Ivan Dmitrievich showed cardsharps no mercy, since in his youth he himself had suffered at their hands. For Lewicki, however, he made an exception.

When at the Yacht Club, Lewicki could not fail to gamble, and when he gambled he could not fail to cheat, so Ivan Dmitrievich was forced to look the other way. Meanwhile, Ivan Dmitrievich never so much as hinted at their connection, especially since the time when Lewicki found himself in a tight spot and asked to be put on salary as an agent.

Actually, Lewicki often tried to shorten the distance between himself and his superior. He might slip into a friendly tone and start twisting the button on Ivan Dmitrievich's jacket, or he might stop by when Ivan Dmitrievich was out in order to drink tea with his wife and tell her the society news. In short, Lewicki hoped to advance from agent to confidant. Each time he tried, he received a slap on the nose from Ivan Dmitrievich, but he never lost hope and would merely try a new tack. Given his innate optimism, this was not hard.

Right there, in the drawing room, Lewicki drew up on the back of his restaurant tab a list of the ladies who had been linked to von Ahrensburg over the last two years. Though the list was rather long, it cannot be said that it gave Ivan Dmitrievich much joy. Inasmuch as Lewicki was basing himself primarily on chance meetings with the prince and his casual trysts, most of the ladies he characterized in such a way that it would scarcely be possible to seek them out in the big city.

For example: blonde, widow, likes tiny goose liver pastries.

Or: ginger-haired Jewess, has a poodle that looks like her known as Chuka.

Or like this: plump, jiggles as she walks (he had seen her from behind).

Or else he wrote the most utter muddle: "There was this girl." And nothing more!

"What's this you have for me here?" Ivan Dmitrievich bellowed. "What am I paying you for? What?"

"But look here, look!" said Lewicki, pointing a manicured nail at the very bottom of the list.

Indeed, last, under number nine, there was a certain Mrs. Strekalova, the wife of an official in the Department of Surveys, and there was even a location. He had written: "Kirochnaya Street, address unknown." Lewicki said that the prince had met her that autumn, during a walk on Krestovy Island. While they were swinging on the swings together and the husband was waiting down below, the deceased had arranged their first tryst. Ever since, if he had had other enthusiasms, they had been fleeting.

"What about these?" Ivan Dmitrievich ran his finger down the other numbers on the list.

"You were the one who told me to tell you for the last two years," said Lewicki.

Ivan Dmitrievich calculated that since autumn the love and jealousy of the ginger poodle's owner or the goose liver pastry fancier must have lost their homicidal power, like a spent bullet. Nonetheless, to clear his conscience, he decided to inquire as to which of these ladies had visited the prince's bedroom.

Lewicki commented reasonably that the prince, as a diplomat and a society man, guarded his reputation well, and in addition his career was far from over. That is, he might occasionally bring number three home, say, but only in the middle of the night and only when he was good and sauced, when a man throws caution to the wind. Usually, he visited his passions in their rooms.

They called the prince's coachman in, and he said yes, something had happened outside Poltava and he had driven the master to Kirochnaya Street, to a building with a green shop at ground level.

"Survey Department officials are often away from Petersburg," whispered Lewicki.

In passing it emerged that the prince's valet had previously served there, on Kirochnaya, and had taken up his current place only a month before.

"Before him it was Fyodor," said the coachman. "A good servant. Too bad, though—he started drinking. Smashed the Chinese teacups when he was soused. Hung the master's best frock coat in the courtyard to freshen it with a bit of breeze, but directly under a crow's nest. . . . Yes, and yesterday he came here, Fyodor did, to ask for his unpaid wages. Well, the master reminded him then and there of the coat and the cups. What was Fyodor thinking! You can't let them get away with things like that."

Be that as it may, that morning Ivan Dmitrievich had noticed that the prince's valet was much too common. The valets of titled personages are never that, and they do not covet cigarette cases. Apparently it was no accident that this fellow had moved his tent from Kirochnaya to the Street of Millions.

What a find! This was something to mull over.

"I remember what it sells! Wine!" said the coachman, explaining how to find the building where the prince's old servant Fyodor now lived.

By this time Ivan Dmitrievich's deputy Konstantinov had been let into the house and so was present at this conversation.

Ivan Dmitrievich looked at him and then at Lewicki and gave his instructions:

"Go over there and bring him back."

Insulted at this kind of order, Lewicki pursed his lips. Ivan Dmitrievich could see he would have to teach him a little lesson. That was quite enough of his face pulling. Lewicki would get used to taking orders or else. Just using the state's money to sharpen his whist-playing skills on princes wasn't going to cut it. And he could take that to the bank!

With Lewicki gone, Ivan Dmitrievich and Konstantinov went to the kitchen, where they fortified themselves with some cold roast pork that had been prepared for the prince's breakfast.

"There's no time to go home," said Ivan Dmitrievich, sucking on a piece of gristle, "otherwise no money could have made me eat this pig. It would be like wearing the dead man's trousers."

"Right you are," Konstantinov assented with a full mouth. "It's the last thing I'd do."

He was an old hand and he understood that standing up to his superior kept relations on a good footing, but he couldn't stand up to a new patron—he always agreed.

"Then don't eat!" Ivan Dmitrievich flew into a rage. "What are you sitting there for? Who do you think you are? A goat in a stable? Well then, off you go!"

Konstantinov disappeared, and Ivan Dmitrievich peeked into the room of the valet, who was sitting, downcast, on the suitcase from the bottom of which Rukavishnikov had extracted the silver cigarette case.

"I took it," the valet continued his agonizing thoughts out loud. "Who's going to pay me my April wages now?"

"They'll be paid," Ivan Dmitrievich promised. "His Excellency Franz Josef, Emperor of Austria and King of

Hungary, he won't leave it at this. Why don't you tell me why you didn't say you'd worked for the Strekalovs?"

"It's true." The valet nodded listlessly.

"Did the lady find you this place? Strekalova?"

"She did."

"And was she herself here often?"

"A few times."

"And what for?"

"I dare say you know as well as me. The departed was a prominent man, and she had the main thing, like all women—a proper crack."

"Fine. When you stepped outside this morning, was the front door open?"

"Uh huh."

"And the key?"

"Sitting in the lock on the inside."

"Last night, while the prince was resting, were there no visitors?"

"No."

"And the front door?"

"When the master's home, he doesn't lock it. Only at night. He puts the key on the little table in the hall."

"Wait up! Let's say you're here, in your room, and the prince is in his bedroom. How does he summon you?"

"There's a bell pull at the head of his bed. A tassel. And a little bell—there it is."

"Run down there," Ivan Dmitrievich ordered. "Pull it."

A minute later the little steel clapper trilled as it struck the brass palate. The bell was working.

"Why is it the prince didn't ring for you when they started smothering him?" asked Ivan Dmitrievich as soon as the valet returned.

The valet immediately grasped what they could accuse him of and let out an ugly wail.

"He didn't ring for me! Honest to God, he didn't! Do you believe me?"

"No. I don't believe you," said Ivan Dmitrievich, although he knew for a fact the valet was telling the truth. The rogue had taken the cigarette case, but he hadn't laid a finger on the prince. And he hadn't heard the bell, couldn't have heard the bell, because there wasn't any—bell, that is.

All this Ivan Dmitrievich understood perfectly, yet he repeated, "I don't believe you."

Let him suffer, the son of a bitch. It wouldn't hurt him.

And so, the poor prince had been turned so that his feet were facing the head of the bed on purpose, so that he couldn't reach the bell pull and call for help. This meant that one of the murderers had been in the prince's bedroom before and knew where the bell pull was.

The picture was gradually coming clear.

The murderers had entered the house between eight and nine that night, while von Ahrensburg had been resting and the front door had been open. First they had hidden in the foyer—behind the coat rack, perhaps—and after the prince left they made their way to the drawing room. They'd sat with their feet on the windowsill, behind the drapes. They'd had a little vodka. They'd bided their time, killed him, taken the key from the hall table, and left.

II

What information had guided Pevtsov such that, of all the Bulgarian and Serbian students studying in Petersburg, he chose three, who were then taken to the Street of Millions, and how he had studied their secret dossiers and card files, Ivan Dmitrievich never did find out. Gendarme secrets have no statute of limitations. Here even his deputy Konstantinov was powerless, and Konstantinov knew everything, up to and including what days of the week the chief of police slept with his young wife. For Ivan Dmitrievich this information was of purely practical significance. The preceding evening the chief would be as good as gold and would sign any papers. On the other hand, the following morning he was best given a wide berth.

In the drawing room, Pevtsov showed the students to the valet, who immediately fingered a thin, hook-nosed one with a mournful and distracted look.

"This one here came the day before yesterday."

They let the other two go but detained Hook Nose.

"Your name?" asked Pevtsov.

"Ivan Boyev. I'm a student at the Academy of Medicine and Surgery."

"Bulgarian?"

He nodded.

"So you see, Mr. Boyev, I know everything," Pevtsov announced in a tone such that even a child would realize he knew nothing at all. "The prince was expecting you today at eight thirty."

"Nine," Boyev corrected him ingenuously.

"Why didn't you come?"

"I overslept."

At that reply Ivan Dmitrievich let out a grunt.

"Well, brother"—he couldn't help himself—"that's exactly why you're sitting under the Turk to this day."

"I would strangle the Sultan with these very hands!" Boyev spread his fingers, which were long and slender like a pianist's, and slowly, breathing heavily from the strain, balled them into fists.

"Well now, well now." Pevtsov found this very interesting. "Show us!"

He carefully examined the Bulgarian's hands, searching for teeth marks.

"Yes, quite strong."

And he led him to the carriage waiting at the entrance.

Not another word was said, and Ivan Dmitrievich, as he had resolved, made no mention of either his conversation with the valet or the trunk. Meanwhile he should have spoken because the trunk was important. Though not very big, it was sturdy, had brass-plated sides and lid, and was screwed permanently to the floor in the study at all four corners. It was where the prince kept his papers. Upon examining this repository of military and diplomatic secrets of the Austro-Hungarian Empire, Ivan Dmitrievich was convinced that the intruders had attempted to open the trunk without the key—possibly with the fireplace poker, on which he had discovered fresh scratches. The brass on the edges of the lid was dented, but neither on the trunk itself nor anywhere nearby did he find any drops of blood. Evidently they had tried to break it open before the prince's return from the Yacht Club.

Pevtsov and the Bulgarian left, and in their place came Shuvalov. He was accompanied by the secretary from the Austrian embassy and two footmen, who hauled a long box out of the carriage and carried it into the bedroom. Ivan Dmitrievich did not realize immediately that this was a coffin.

The secretary was telling Shuvalov very matter-of-factly that the coffin would be caulked shut today, the cracks filled with pitch, as in cases of cholera, and then, through a special small hole, they would suck the air out from the inside to slow the decay, plug the hole with a cork, and ship the prince's body by rail from Petersburg to Warsaw to his family's estate.

After they had carried the coffin out, Shuvalov ordered Ivan Dmitrievich: "Get me an inkpot!"

Shuvalov was shackled to his hourly reports to the sovereign as a slave is to his galley oar. One stroke, then another. In the intervals there wasn't enough time to figure out where the ship was going.

A fat blob fell from the pen onto the report and spread over the salutation to the sovereign.

"Damn!" Shuvalov crumpled the paper nervously and threw it to the floor.

Ivan Dmitrievich went into von Ahrensburg's study, took another sheet from his desk, and returned.

"What are you giving me?" Shuvalov was angry. "How can I submit a report to the sovereign on paper like this? It's yellowed with age!"

"It was in the sun too long, Your Excellency."

"Then why did you bring it to me?"

'To show you that the deceased did not often apply himself to his writing."

"Don't engage in trifles, Mr. Putilin! I know as well as you that the prince did not compose verse or novels. Understand, if we do not catch the murderer by tomorrow, so many heads are going to roll that you certainly will not be long in your place. Or do you want to go back to being an inspector at the flea market again?"

Ivan Dmitrievich had begun his police career as assistant to the block inspector at the flea market, and now the threat from the chief of gendarmes did not frighten him so much as it tickled his pride. He was flattered that the all-powerful Shuvalov himself was initiated into the details of his biography.

"I would like to examine the contents of this trunk," said Ivan Dmitrievich.

"So would I." Shuvalov chuckled. "But there's no key."

"Did you ask the valet?"

"He doesn't know. Hotek and I searched the entire study and couldn't find it."

Shuvalov went over to the desk, took a fresh, unyellowed sheet from the middle of the paper stack, again dipped his pen, and again cursed. Instead of a drop of ink hanging from the pen there were the remains of a fly that had drowned in the inkpot. Ivan Dmitrievich cautiously removed it with two small leaves torn from the potted lemon tree, and Shuvalov began to write: a salutation and a few lines in which he easily fit what little news there was. Ivan Dmitrievich meanwhile examined the trunk once again. Depicted on the front were Adam and Eve. As yet serene in their nakedness, they stood flanking the Tree of Knowledge of Good and Evil; between them on the grass lay an apple around which coiled the scaly black body of the Serpent Tempter.

Ivan Dmitrievich thought about how the attraction between a man and a woman is merely a special case of the law of universal attraction, which Newton would never have discovered if, say, a pear had fallen on his head instead of an apple.

He shifted his gaze to the desk set and gasped. Lord, how could he have missed that before? The inkpot was in the shape of a bronze apple, evidently tasted already, inasmuch as the progenitors of mankind standing to its right and left, also cast in bronze, had now covered their shameful parts with awkwardly bent arms. Evidently the age of innocence, whose final fateful minute was stamped on the trunk, had only just passed. Eve was holding her slightly oxidized, greenish palm awkwardly, shielding herself below the belly, still unaware of the magical power of that gesture, honed since then by millions of bathers.

Ivan Dmitrievich squeezed the inkpot with two fingers, turned it, and with a few turns easily unscrewed it from the board. In the depression beneath it gleamed a key with a whimsical key-bit, a massive ring carved in the form of a snake biting its own tail.

"Amusing," said Shuvalov.

And once again, only now did Ivan Dmitrievich realize why the trunk's keyhole sat in the center of a big red rose with shiny, moist-looking petals. He slipped the key into the dark narrow slot framed by their shameless redness, thinking, What will be born of this coition? The lock clicked, and Ivan Dmitrievich threw back the lid.

Shuvalov was already standing beside him, peering over his shoulder. They saw a saber with a gold hilt and a watch set into the hand guard, honorary orders on little pillows, tiny jewelry boxes, small cases, a stack of banknotes, and more than a dozen letter bundles tied neatly with silk ribbons.

"'Ludwig, my naughty bearded boy,'" Ivan Dmitrievich read, "'all day today—'"

"And all from different women, Your Excellency," he said. "You see, the ribbons are different colors, and I don't think the colors were chosen at random. With age, bachelors become as sentimental as young ladies."

"Give me the key," ordered Shuvalov.

He slammed the lid, locked the trunk, pocketed the key, and moved toward the door, commenting imperiously in parting:

"I shall be at home this evening. Bring me your report."

Standing in the bay window, Ivan Dmitrievich watched Shuvalov's carriage pull away from the front porch and stop at the end of the block, where a quarter of an hour previously a drayman's wagon had smashed into the coach carrying Prince von Ahrensburg's coffin. Idlers were milling about and gawking and coachmen were cursing, but when the chief of gendarmes' carriage pulled up, silence fell at once. Thus roiling ocean waves are calmed when oil is poured on them from shipboard casks. Through the double glass of the closed window, Ivan Dmitrievich could feel the icy breath of power on his face. A master demanded obedience, but true power, supreme power, required naught but one thing: that it be remembered always, at every waking moment. Genuine power was like love. Forgetting it was akin to treason.

Von Ahrensburg's death had frightened many people because the murderers had smothered a foreign diplomat a stone's throw from the Winter Palace, as if they had clean forgotten that power's existence. This was difficult to believe. Things like that don't happen, particularly in Russia. No, thought Shuvalov, the criminals forgot nothing. They remembered, my friends. Of course they remembered! That was why they had killed him.

III

Ordering the driver to halt, Shuvalov flung open his carriage door and beckoned to the embassy secretary escorting von Ahrensburg's body.

"Mr. Secretary, I beg of you to convey this to Count Hotek personally."

The snake was wound around his index finger; the key from the prince's trunk hung for a second above the crowd and then fell into the secretary's open hand. A man wearing an official's greatcoat and standing close by followed him with a quick, tenacious gaze.

"Oh yes," Shuvalov remembered. "Be so kind as to tell me your name."

"Baron Cobenzel."

"Cobenzel?"

"Shall I spell it for you, Your Excellency?"

"Cobenzel, Cobenzel. Have you ever been introduced to me?"

"I have not had the honor."

"Why do I know that name?"

"One of my ancestors came to Moscow as an ambassador from Regensburg, to see Ivan the Terrible. He is mentioned in Karamzin."

Shuvalov immediately lost all interest. He said goodbye and left, and the carriage carrying the deceased's body also prepared to move on, but at that moment, for the first time in a day, the sun peeked out from behind the clouds. Squinting blissfully, Cobenzel decided there was absolutely no need for him to accompany the coffin to the embassy. The footmen would manage without him. He told them to continue their journey themselves and he himself strolled across Palace Square, passed under the arch of the General Staff, and emerged on Nevsky. It never occurred him to be wary of anyone in broad daylight. He failed to notice the man in the greatcoat tailing him.

On both sides of the avenue flowed an elegantly turned-out crowd. No one here was thinking about Prince von

Ahrensburg's death. Life went on, and fifty paces from a pastry shop's wide-open doors the aroma of roasted coffee wafted temptingly under his nose. In the window, Cobenzel saw a tiny room decorated in the German resort style. He entered. Couples sat at three of the four tables, and at the fourth was a well-dressed man of middle age with a florid, thoroughbred nose. This was the agent Lewicki, who had considered it beneath his dignity to head directly where Ivan Dmitrievich had ordered him to go. He was sipping his hot chocolate with such pleasure that Cobenzel, who himself was incapable of strong feelings, envied him.

"If you please, monsieur." With a royal sweep of his arm. Lewicki indicated the chair opposite.

Cobenzel sat down, ordered coffee and a pastry, asked the owner for a piece of paper, took out a pencil, and with mixed feelings, dominant among which, I suppose, was vague gratification, began to dash off a letter to his wife, who had gone to Vienna for Easter. At one time, she had had an affair with Ludwig von Ahrensburg, and now, without making any direct allusions, God forbid, he wanted to express his sympathy to her in such a way that she would appreciate his, Cobenzel's, magnanimity.

"A letter written in pencil is like a conversation under one's breath." Lewicki smiled.

"Is that a Russian saying?" asked Cobenzel.

Lewicki laughed out loud.

"Are you a foreigner?"

"Yes."

"But your Russian is superb."

"Thank you for the compliment. The fact of the matter is that our family has been linked to Russia for over three hundred years. One of my ancestors was an envoy from the Holy Roman Empire to the court of Ivan the Terrible."

"Oh ho!" Lewicki was intrigued. "And do you know what he died of?"

"There is a legend that the Tsar ordered that his hat be nailed to his head when he refused to remove it before the Tsar's throne. That, however, is a lie. The Poles fabricated that."

"The Poles? Why the Poles?"

"For political reasons. To provoke a quarrel between Moscow and Vienna."

"Is that so? Curious. Actually, I did not mean him."

"Who then?"

"Ivan the Terrible. Do you know anything about the causes of his death?"

"I have read Karamzin," said Cobenzel modestly.

"Karamzin is a pack of lies," Lewicki declared. "Now let me tell you . . . "

The man in the greatcoat sitting at the corner table glanced cautiously in their direction, listening in on their conversation.

"Once," Lewicki recounted, "after the Tsar had eaten a heavy meal, Boris Godunov proposed that they do battle at chess, so they sat down to play. Boris, being a brunet, was a cunning man, that's a historical fact. You see, he had acquired the following habit. He would pick up the knight and use it, say, to scratch the back of his head, then think better of it and move his bishop. That is against the rules, of course. Well, eventually the Tsar got sick and tired of this and he said, 'Whichever one you pick up, you son of a bitch, whichever man, that's the one you move!' 'I wasn't picking him up, Your Majesty.' He was purposely trying to rile him and make him lose his temper. The Tsar, naturally, out of pride, said, 'Who are you arguing with, *villein*? Move your knight!' Godunov would not give in; he hadn't been picking him up, and that was that. He swore to God, the beast, that he had never laid a finger on that knight. It was a bald-faced lie, and he even nodded to the witnesses. 'They'll back me up,' he said. 'They'll tell you the whole truth.' But the boyars who had been watching the game, they were Godunov's accomplices, they were in on the conspiracy. They fell to their knees, beat their brows on the floor, and wailed, 'Your Majesty, don't have him punished. You were tempted! Boris, your slave, he never picked up the knight!' At this the Tsar trembled all over. His eyes popped out, and he started some real shouting: 'Move your knight!' At that, the blood rushed to his head, he wheezed, and he died. Which is normal at that age, especially after a heavy meal."

Cobenzel made no reply. He didn't know whether to rejoice at the tyrant's demise or condemn the method by which the conspirators had brought him to his death.

"Now that, to my mind, is clean work," said Lewicki. "Not like smothering someone with pillows in his bed at night."

"You . . . you mean Prince von Ahrensburg?"

"True, he wasn't playing chess, that wasn't his nature. But he was quite fond of cards. And he was reckless, may he rest in peace! If a smart cardsharp had picked up on him, he could have given him a heart attack. If someone had slipped that cardsharp five hundred or so, he would have made an all-out effort. But the murderers were paid thousands, I dare say. People don't know the value of money, by God!"

Cobenzel still hadn't written the letter to his wife, but he didn't feel like lingering at this table any longer. He paid his bill and went out into the vestibule, where he dawdled and then hesitantly opened a door, in the hope of finding what he was looking for behind it. Damp wafted up, and a gloomy staircase with jagged stone steps led downstairs, into the darkness.

The man in the greatcoat, who had come out after him, inquired, "Do you need the closet, sir?"

"Yes." Cobenzel nodded, embarrassed.

"It's this way."

"You know, somehow . . ."

"Let's go, I'll show you."

The earthen chill of the grave wafted up from the cellar, nothing else. Sniffing, Cobenzel was hesitating in the doorway when suddenly the stranger came up right behind him and with a strange insistence gave him a small shove toward the stairs. That gave Cobenzel a fright. He jumped to one side, pushed the glass door with the little bell, and ran out onto the noisy, sun-drenched avenue.

IV

Lost in thought as he stood by the window, Ivan Dmitrievich was letting his gaze follow Shuvalov's carriage when a deputy of his by the name of Sych—"Owl," in Russian—entered the drawing room without knocking. There was a little dance to his walk and he was smiling enigmatically, as if he had a dandy little surprise in store for his superior. Stumbling in behind him was a policeman carrying a sack, which he was holding out well in front of him.

"A most important clue, Ivan Dmitrievich!" said Sych, beaming. "If you would permit me a little newspaper."

He took the top copy from the stack of fresh papers newly delivered for the prince and was about to put it on the table but for some reason thought better of that and spread it out on the lid of the grand piano. Then he instructed the policeman:

"Let's have it!"

The policeman untied the sack, applied its mouth to the newspaper, and carefully lifted it up, shaking it lightly. Left behind on the piano was something round, yellowish-blue, and awful, which Ivan Dmitrievich did not immediately recognize as a severed human head. He shut his eyes. A spasm clutched his throat as the burning acid of vomit came up.

"Here it is, Ivan Dmitrievich! We found it," announced Sych with a barely restrained grin.

On his gaunt, mustached face could be read the delighted awareness of a job well done.

"Why did you bring that here, you blockhead?" Ivan Dmitrievich howled, struggling to overcome the nasty feeling in his throat.

Sych was saddened.

"Oh! I thought I would please you."

"Just who do you think I am?" Ivan Dmitrievich's hackles were up. "Some monster? Genghis Khan? Dracula?"

The head rested on the newspaper facing the window. Small, dark, and wrinkled, it had one ear torn off and was surrounded on all sides by the piano's indifferently majestic shine. Inexpressibly pathetic in its posthumous solitude, deprived even of its body, it evoked neither horror nor disdain but rather a feeling like the one Ivan Dmitrievich's deceased mother-in-law had attempted to encourage in his wife when she tore off the arms and legs of her daughter's dolls.

Meanwhile, Sych was recounting how this morning, at six o'clock, policemen passing down Znamenskaya Street, near a tavern, saw this head on the ground, picked it up, and took it to the station. There it lay of no use to anyone until Sych, who had stopped in utterly by chance, happened to notice it.

"Well, and what was the purpose in dragging it here?" asked Ivan Dmitrievich wearily.

"Word is they cut off the Austrian consul's head. I thought this was it."

"Whose word?"

"People's."

"Where?"

"Everywhere. I, for one, heard it from the water carrier."

Ivan Dmitrievich heaved a sigh. Oh yes! The streetlamps were barely lit and the talk was already wreaking havoc on the entire Austrian diplomatic corps: the ambassador had had his throat slit, people said, and the consul's head had been cut off. The clerk at the tobacco shop where Ivan Dmitrievich slipped out to purchase some tobacco confided in him that students were knifing Austrians. Why? The clerk knew that as well: so that our sovereign would quarrel with their king. There would be war, the sovereign would leave Petersburg at the head of his entire army, and then the students would rise up. The deuce take it!

Could someone be purposely spreading these rumors? Ivan Dmitrievich glanced toward the piano. The head seemed a harbinger of impending chaos. He didn't want to examine it, but out of the corner of his eye he noticed, nonetheless, that it was a man's, with a beard and mustache.

"Take it away. The newspaper, too," Ivan Dmitrievich ordered and then pulled up short. "No, wait up. You say you found it near a tavern on Znamenskaya?"

"Yes."

"There are a lot of them there. Which one?"

"The Three Giants, Ivan Dmitrievich."

"Take it away and show it to the waiters. If they recognize it, report back to me immediately."

"Yes, sir."

The policeman, who hadn't uttered a word this entire time, opened the sack and held it up to the piano while Sych, without touching the dead head, started pulling the newspaper toward the edge of the piano lid and then dropped it right into the sack.

When it finally fell in, Ivan Dmitrievich took the Napoleon he had found under the prince's bed out of his wallet and held it out to Sych on his open palm.

A happy smile spread across Sych's face.

"Is that for me? Oh, Ivan Dmitrievich, you spoil me!"

"Not a damn thing for you! You're way ahead of yourself."

"What are you taunting me for, then?"

"Take a good look at it so you'll remember. This is a French gold piece, and on it is Emperor Napoleon III. Can you remember that?"

"So?" said Sych in a bored voice.

"So this," Ivan Dmitrievich ordered. "Hustle over to Znamenskaya, and after you've settled things with the chief, go around to the churches and ask whether anyone has ordered a prayer for the dead using money like this."

Then he strode toward the door, opened it wide, and called out:

"Konstantinov!"

Konstantinov, who was lounging around in the hallway waiting for his favorite superior to trade his anger for kindness, appeared instantly.

"Do you see?" Ivan Dmitrievich showed him the same Napoleon.

"Yes. I'm not blind."

"What kind of answer is that? Is your nose out of joint?"

"What do you think! I've been standing guard here with you since morning and not had a single bite, and you drove me away from the table over nothing at all."

"All right, we'll settle that later. Right now, step lively and go around to all the taverns. Try to find out whether anyone paid their tab today with a coin like this. First look in on Znamenskaya. Do you remember the taverns there?"

"The Hut, Old Friend, Kalatch, Fisherman's Retreat, Three Giants, Tidbit," Konstantinov rattled off the list.

"Here, take this piece and hide it. Show it, but don't let anyone else hold it. If you manage to find out anything useful, it's yours."

Ivan Dmitrievich uttered that last sentence only after Sych and the policeman had left the drawing room with the sack.

Much later, in Petersburg, as he was going over his notes, Safonov reached the episode with the severed head and was struck by the word "newspaper." The next day he went to the reading room of the Imperial Public Library, where he asked to be brought several newspaper files of twenty years' vintage, with issues from late April to early May 1871. For accuracy he wanted to compare what was written about the murder of Prince von Ahrensburg by the press of the day with what Ivan Dmitrievich had told him. Safonov was amazed to discover, however, that none of the capital newspapers had reported anything at all about a crime on the Street of Millions on April 25 or the days following.

Meanwhile, in setting forth the events of those days, Ivan Dmitrievich had complained that it had been impossible to leave the prince's residence without bumping into a reporter with an eye to asking him some idiotic question.

All this was strange to say the least. After quickly skimming through the newspapers, Safonov began examining them more carefully in the hope of discovering at least some tiny item on the Austrian military attaché's death.

The first columns were all taken up by lengthy correspondences about the battles outside Paris. The insurgents were beating off the attacks of the Versailles forces, Fort Issy was being handed back and forth, and a balloon filled with Commune broadsides had ascended over the city, but due to a lack of wind all the broadsheets fell on the proletarian suburb of Saint Antoine, which had no need of socialist propaganda. The groundless assertion of one Berlin weekly that General Dombrovsky, virtually the most popular of the rebel generals, was a Russian by birth was rejected with indignation. No! Although he was a Russian subject, he was a Pole.

What else were the newspapers writing about those days?

In England a proposal to give suffrage to women was rejected by Parliament, with 151 votes in favor and 220 against.

In Odessa, a three-day pogrom against the Jews ended. Jews were calling for a boycott of drinking establishments where the pogrom-makers gathered. Students locked up the Golden Anchor tavern and wouldn't let customers in. The police dispersed the students.

In the preceding week in Petersburg, 89 cases of cholera were registered.

During a stroll through the Demidovsky garden, Mademoiselle Gandon danced the cancan on an open stage and was taken to court for violating public decency. At the trial, a witness, a lieutenant colonel of the gendarmes by the name of Foch, denied the accusation, saying, "Gentlemen, what indecency can we be talking about if the dance was performed in a man's suit of clothes? After all, there was nothing to see!"

A deserter by the name of Ivanov was arrested for forging tokens for the public baths used by the common folk and taking other people's clothes.

Beaver hats, kangaroo fur coats, anti-hair loss agents, steam furnaces, mineral waters, and so forth. Advertisements.

The weather was changeable, although the river had already broken up. The Northern spring. The last columns were dotted with announcements about dachas for rent. Here, too, were the funeral borders of the obituaries, but the sought-for name was not to be found among them.

Only at the door of his home did Safonov realize that in 1871 the new censorship charter had not yet been passed, and every issue of every newspaper was checked by the censors before being sent to the printer. Naturally, everything untoward was deleted. Shuvalov had evidently given the appropriate instructions, and not a single item about the tragedy on the Street of Millions ever slipped into print.

Meanwhile, the censor shamefully overlooked the following fact. On April 25, *The Saint Petersburg Gazette* assured its readers that it was twelve degrees Celsius in the capital and sunny, whereas *The Voice* insisted on a temperature close to zero with rain and wet snow.

Chapter 3

Hohenbruch's Rifle

Ivan Dmitrievich stood at the window finishing the last of his sandwiches with the white chicken meat that sat so easily on his stomach and that his wife provided him with so religiously. Suddenly the front doorbell rang. A minute later the valet showed a new visitor into the drawing room. A young man in a military uniform, he introduced himself accordingly.

"Lieutenant of the Preobrazhensky Regiment . . ."

Ivan Dmitrievich missed the name but treated the appearance of such a guest with understandable interest. The barracks of the Preobrazhensky Regiment were located directly opposite the von Ahrensburg residence, and the guards there or the duty officer might well have something important to report about the prince's murder.

"You, I take it, are Mr. Putilin?"

"The very same."

"Chief Inspector of Police?"

"For the time being, yes. Please sit down."

The lieutenant sat down and examined his interlocutor guardedly with his clear and light gray but almost glassy eyes, like the eyes of sharpshooters, ambitious young men, and aging drunkards who have known better days.

"Did you know," he inquired at last, "that our army is being outfitted with a new type of rifle?"

"Alas," Ivan Dmitrievich shook his head. "I am a civilian. I don't even care for hunting. Fishing's more to my liking."

"The old muzzle-loading rifles are being refitted using the system of the Austrian Baron Hohenbruch," explained the lieutenant. "So that they breech-load."

By way of a visual demonstration, he tapped his finger just below the spine of the bronze Eve on the inkstand.

"From here. Do you see?"

"Very interesting," said Ivan Dmitrievich. "You came here to tell me this?"

The lieutenant peered quickly into the bedroom and the study and only then, convinced that no one was eavesdropping, began his story about how that winter he had been assigned to a special detachment conducting trials of the new weapon. Present at the trials were Hohenbruch himself and a certain Cobenzel, also a baron, minor riffraff attached to the embassy. Before the midday meal they fired the Hohenbruch rifles and afterward a different shipment was brought in, manufactured according to the designs of Russian gunsmiths, and—now this was very strange!—all of the second set yielded a much worse result for accuracy and speed of firing than the earlier trials. No one could figure it out. The inventors were tearing their hair out, practically crying, and the inspectors shrugged contritely. As a result, Prince Oldenburgsky, who had seemingly just happened to attend the trials that day, recommended arming the infantry with the Hohenbruch rifle. Only on the way home, when they were returning to the barracks, did he, the lieutenant, realize that his soldiers smelled of vodka!

"And they hadn't gone off drinking of their own volition!" the lieutenant related. "After the meal, it turns out, Hohenbruch and Cobenzel called them over to their carriage and served each one nearly a full glass. As if to celebrate how well the rifle had performed in their hands. That was why my brave lads were loading more slowly and aiming worse after dinner."

"Oh my, that's not good," said Ivan Dmitrievich indifferently.

"Keep listening. The next day I submitted my report to the War Ministry, but they wouldn't give it a chance for some reason. I wrote a report to Shuvalov, with the same result. Hohenbruch is one thing, he's a private individual. But Cobenzel, that provocateur, not only wasn't he punished but he was actually promoted, he became embassy secretary. Not only that, but it was the deceased master of the house where you and I, Mr. Putilin, now find ourselves who secured him that post. Doesn't that make you think?"

"Not yet."

"What if I told you that, in the autumn, von Ahrensburg went hunting with Prince Oldenburgsky, Cobenzel, and

Hohenbruch? And that all of them were armed with these very same rifles? Quite a remarkable coincidence."

"Is the rifle at least good?" asked Ivan Dmitrievich.

"It's not bad."

"Then what's the matter? So be it."

"Well, there is better." The lieutenant began to fidget. "I shall tell you without false modesty, I myself proposed a superb model. I labored over it for three years, perfecting it. A straight-line action firing pin! Can you imagine? A spiral spring! Give me a piece of paper and I'll draw it."

"No need," said an alarmed Ivan Dmitrievich.

On this subject he knew only what his father-in-law, a retired major, went on about over doleful Sunday family dinners. The rifle, or rather, the Russian rifle, he considered to be a special accessory to the bayonet, which, as we know, is a wonder, no matter what you say about bullets. Among the chief virtues which this minor accessory should possess, his father-in-law proposed two: thickness and heft to the rifle butt's neck. The thicker the neck, the harder to split it with a saber, when the infantryman defending against a cavalry attack raised his rifle over his head. And the weapon's weight developed endurance among the lower ranks. If a rifle was too light, the soldiers became spoiled.

The lieutenant jumped up and started pacing up and down the drawing room.

"My model's aim is accurate to fifteen hundred paces!" He was practically shouting. "Hohenbruch's is only good to twelve hundred. In mine the shell ejects automatically. It does! In his, it's pushed out by hand. The Austrians themselves rejected his system, but we adopted it. Why?"

"Maybe it's cheaper to refit the old rifles that way?"

"Hah! They could economize somewhere else."

"Or von Ahrensburg took a bribe from Hohenbruch. As military attaché he had entrée to the upper spheres and could be helpful."

"On the contrary," said the lieutenant. "The idea was the prince's, and Hohenbruch was merely his instrument. As was Prince Oldenburgsky, who was, actually, an unwilling instrument."

"I really don't understand," Ivan Dmitrievich confessed.

"Oh you. . . . I'm certain the prince had a secret assignment from his government to contribute to the weakening of the Russian army. The situation in the Balkans is such that sooner or later we will be fighting there, and not just the Sultan but Vienna as well."

"You really are obsessed with that situation in the Balkans."

The lieutenant lowered his voice.

"Someone had to prevent von Ahrensburg from carrying out those plans."

"Do you mean his murderer?"

"I beg you not to use that word in my presence!"

"Because?" Ivan Dmitrievich did not understand.

"Not a murderer. No! An avenger."

"However, it was not you, I hope, who took your revenge in such a brutish manner?"

"I will tell you frankly, the thought did occur to me. And not to me alone, I think."

Ivan Dmitrievich pricked up his ears.

"Who else?"

"Many honest patriots."

"Do you know them by name?"

"Their name is legion!" said the lieutenant gloomily. "You, Mr. Putilin, can no longer refuse to conduct an inquiry. I do not condemn you. However, I must warn you not to display excessive zeal."

"What are you talking about? I do my duty."

"Your duty is to serve Russia!"

"And I do. I guard the peace of my fellow citizens."

"Citizens are peaceful in a powerful state," the lieutenant objected, "and not in one whose army is equipped with Hohenbruch's rifles. Tell me, may I hope that von Ahrensburg's avenger will not be captured?"

"No," replied Ivan Dmitrievich firmly. "You may not."

"I challenge you to a duel!"

"And I do not accept your challenge." Ivan Dmitrievich smiled calmly.

"Is that so?" With a sudden cat-like movement the lieutenant grabbed him by the nose. "Fool policeman!"

Ivan Dmitrievich's nose felt like it was being squeezed in a vise, and he didn't have the strength to free himself and break away from the pitiless hand. The pain and humiliation brought tears to his eyes. Ivan Dmitrievich was heavyset and in a fight would have crushed the lieutenant, but he could not overpower the lieutenant's iron claw. He waved his fists in the air, trying to hit his offender and punch him in his impudent freckled nose, but the lieutenant held him at arm's length, and his arm was the longer.

"Remember me! Remember me well!" he kept saying, cruelly twisting the nose cartilage.

Ivan Dmitrievich was already starting to sniffle.

Then he used the tried and true weapon of the weakest—his teeth. He contrived to scrape the lieutenant on the hand, right at the base of the thumb, where there is a convenient bulge for biting known in chiromancy as the Mount of Venus. Its meatiness attested to the lieutenant's great talents in that field where the deceased prince might have proved him a worthy opponent. Both of them, alive and dead, evidently possessed the magic key to trunks, boxes, and cases whose keyholes are surrounded by the red petals, wet with night dew, of the queen of flowers, the rose.

Ivan Dmitrievich could not boast of such a remarkable key, but he did have strong teeth. Cursing, the lieutenant let go Ivan Dmitrievich's nose and with his left hand took a handkerchief out of his pocket, pressed the bleeding wound, and when he heard footsteps in the hallway slipped away to the front door. On the threshold he nearly collided with Pevtsov, who watched him with a look of amazement and then with no less amazement espied the red nose and tear-filled eyes—from the pain—of Ivan Dmitrievich.

"Who was that fellow?" asked Pevtsov.

"Oh, some madman."

"I thought he was your agent."

"That's rich! We don't keep agents like that."

"Why did he come here?"

"To pour out his soul. He was telling me what a swine Prince von Ahrensburg was."

"And he brought you to tears?"

"This?" Ivan Dmitrievich dabbed at his eyes with his handkerchief. "From laughter. A hilarious fellow. So, what did your Bulgarian tell you? Boyev, I think it was?"

"He told us a thing or two," Pevtsov replied pompously as he took a seat. "As your job requires, I suppose you know of the Slavonic Committee's activities."

"You mean there's something blameworthy in its activities? As far as I know, the organization was created at the authorities' initiative and enjoys the highest patronage."

"You exaggerate. In the upper spheres the attitude toward it is ambivalent, but in this case that is immaterial. Here is the point. A month ago the Slavonic Committee collected donations to benefit the Bulgarians who had fled Turkish violence for Austria-Hungary, and von Ahrensburg agreed to redirect the money as intended."

"Why did he do that?"

"He was hoping to gain the support of certain influential persons in Petersburg who sympathize with the Slavonic movement. Hotek did not approve his scheme but the prince nonetheless secretly accepted the money and issued a receipt. At some point Boyev appeared on the horizon. He apparently had contrived to have some of the donations redirected to the needs of the association of Bulgarian students in Russia. The day before yesterday, Boyev came here for the money, but von Ahrensburg refused to give him the sum agreed upon unless the Slavonic Committee drew up all the financial documents afresh. Their next appointment was made for today, at nine o'clock this morning, but Boyev never showed."

"Why?"

"He says he came late, when they weren't letting anyone in the house. He says he'd been studying for an exam the night before and fell asleep at dawn, so he overslept."

"And what did the search turn up?"

"Nothing of any importance. No bite marks were found either."

"Did you examine his arm to the elbow?"

"To the shoulders. Then we made him undress to the waist and examined his entire torso."

"And you let him go?"

"On the contrary. We locked him up in the guardhouse."

"For goodness' sake! On what grounds?"

Pevtsov smiled.

"I am laying out the bare facts for you, Mr. Putilin, and keeping my conclusions to myself, otherwise you will inevitably drive the results of your own investigations to fit my suspicions."

"You think so?" Ivan Dmitrievich was insulted.

"Yes, but through no fault of your own. You will agree that there is a vast difference in status between the police and the gendarmes, a fact of which you, for all your talents and ambitions, cannot help but be mindful. My idea has more value than yours not because I am more intelligent but because of who I am. I would not like to influence you with the authority of our department."

As if to lend significance to this thought, the clock on the wall struck five.

"Then explain to me, if you will," asked Ivan Dmitrievich, returning the conversation to the territory of bare facts, "why the prince invited Boyev to his home at what was for him an ungodly hour. After a wakeful night at the Yacht Club, he might have made the appointment with him a little later."

"The prince did not want his meeting with Boyev to become known. As a rule, at nine and even ten o'clock in the morning he was still asleep, so surveillance on the house would have been posted for sometime around noon."

"He was being watched?" Ivan Dmitrievich was thunderstruck. "By whom?"

But Pevtsov quickly back-pedaled and cut him off.

"Excuse me, Mr. Putilin, there is no reason for you to know that."

"A secret affecting Russia's state interests?"

"Precisely."

"In that case," Ivan Dmitrievich faltered, but decided to proceed, "I advise you to turn your attention to the Preobrazhensky lieutenant with whom you nearly collided in the doorway. I don't know his name, unfortunately. On the other hand, I do know that this fellow invented some magical rifle that was rejected by our bureaucrats in the Ministry of War."

By the time the clock had struck a quarter past five, Ivan Dmitrievich had recounted the story about Baron Hohenbruch's intrigues, also without drawing any conclusions. The facts and nothing more.

"Yes, it is curious. But why aren't you yourself pursuing this lieutenant?" asked Pevtsov warily. "Why are you yielding him to me?"

"Politics are more in your line, Captain. Not for us to be sticking our noses in there! We know our place."

"Are you mocking me?"

"Maybe a little," Ivan Dmitrievich admitted. "But seriously, I truly do believe that you would deal better with this. My profession is catching criminals, not those gentlemen who kill their like out of the noblest of political convictions."

"Fine." Pevtsov nodded. "Thank you for the information. However, in my opinion you are intending to conceal from me one highly important circumstance."

"Which is?"

"The severed head. My men were talking with your agent, by the name of Sych, but couldn't get much out of him. Actually, that is why I came here, in order to learn in more detail about his visit. What did he report?"

"All kinds of nonsense. Supposedly they chopped off the Austrian consul's head and he, you see, had found it."

"Fine agents you have." Pevtsov chuckled.

"He's the only one I have like that. I'd get rid of him, but I feel sorry for him. He has a brood of seven chirping on his bench."

"What your Sych said is absurd, naturally, but it is still a link in one long chain. I am forming the definite impression that someone is trying to sow panic in the city."

"But whose head is it?" Ivan Dmitrievich inquired. "Did you ever find out?"

"It's no one's head."

"How can it be no one's?"

"It's from the anatomical theater at the Academy of Medicine and Surgery. Yesterday a student, Nikolsky, bet his friends a bottle of Champagne that he could spirit the head out unnoticed, and imagine, he did. He got drunk and scared the ladies with it and then abandoned it right there on the street."

"There's a scoundrel for you!" Ivan Dmitrievich was indignant. "Did you arrest him?"

"We'll get to that. The story isn't as simple as might appear to the casual eye."

Pevtsov went over to the window, rapped loudly on the glass to attract the attention of his driver, and signaled that he was about to come out.

"Where are you going?" asked Ivan Dmitrievich.

"Why, where do you need to go?"

"Kirochnaya."

"Well, I can't take you there, but I can drop you halfway."

Ten minutes later they had driven under the arch of the General Headquarters, turned, and were riding down Nevsky. Suddenly the shouts of cabbies and coachmen rang out and there was a continuous whoosh of rubber tires, like the fizzle of beer foam settling in mugs. A buoyant, elegant crowd was flowing down both sides of the avenue, noisily, as always happens during the first warm evenings of spring, when the very air is suffused with the promise of a change for the better.

"Do you feel it?" Pevtsov's voice was sullen. "An unnatural, feverish excitement everywhere."

Ivan Dmitrievich cleared his throat.

"It's springtime. Even a block of wood could get excited."

The carriage boasted springs, and its smooth rocking disposed one to candor.

"Springtime, you say? Why is it that what comes to my mind for some reason isn't some Russian Pan with his pipes but you know who? Mikhail Bakunin, strange as that sounds in this kind of weather. Have you heard of him?"

"The socialist?"

"Yes, the socialist, the émigré. Revolutionaries from all over Europe bow down to him. He's like their Pope. In his opinion, you won't get anywhere with this bunch." Pevtsov indicated a group of students near a notice kiosk. "Mama's boys, softies, afraid of blood. They should be recruiting riff-raff and criminals into the secret societies. He has a scientific name for that scum: the rogue element. Used to be, they just killed and robbed, but now, don't you know, they're going to do the exact same thing but backed by a theory that aims to provoke unrest among the public. Then the socialists will have an easier time seizing power. The way they did in Paris."

Ivan Dmitrievich thought that an idea like this could only occur to someone who had never set foot inside a real thieves' den, and only the same kind of person could believe in the possibility of making it come to pass.

"If you suspect that von Ahrensburg fell victim to this theory," he said, "it's worth looking into that pint of vodka."

"What pint of vodka is that?"

"Remember, this morning I found it in the drawing room behind the drapes, on the windowsill? A Bulgarian would probably have preferred wine."

That gave Pevtsov pause. For a while they rode in silence, then he ordered the driver: "Stop! I turn right here and you go straight. Climb out. Good luck."

II

On his way to the Fontanka, to see Shuvalov, who needed material for his reports to the sovereign, and later, while seeking out the Preobrazhensky lieutenant pointed out by Ivan Dmitrievich in order to tug at that thread just in case, Pevtsov continued his mental journey—from the obvious cause to the likely facts.

Although Boyev had not confessed to von Ahrensburg's murder, suspicions had not been lifted from him. Pevtsov assumed that he had made his way into the prince's residence that night for the purpose of absconding with the entire sum collected by the Slavonic Committee, not just a part of it, intending to use that money to purchase weapons for the Bulgarian insurrectionists. There were grounds for such a conclusion. According to the Slavonic Committee's chairman, Boyev had told him many times that the best way to help the refugees suffering from Turkish attacks was to exact vengeance. He knew the money was in the trunk, but he hadn't been able to open it, and even under the threat of death the prince had not told him where the key was hidden. As a result, Boyev and his accomplice, who was evidently the man whose hand the prince had bit, had to be content with the revolver lying on the dressing table and a dozen French gold coins.

Pevtsov had concealed his conclusions from Ivan Dmitrievich so that, if his suspicions were confirmed, he would not have to share the laurels with him, but Putilin had guessed it all himself. Not that they were very complex deductions.

However, there was something else Ivan Dmitrievich did not know. Nikolsky, the medical student who had stolen the head from the anatomical theater, had been arrested that afternoon. They had nabbed him the moment he showed up at the lodgings of Boyev, who was by then in the guardhouse. Pevtsov had ordered surveillance on the apartment, and, as it turned out, not in vain.

When Pevtsov arrived, he asked Nikolsky five questions:

1. Had it been his idea to remove the head from the

Academy of Medicine and Surgery and then abandon it on the street, or had he acted at someone's instigation?

2. Might any of his comrades have provoked him and bet him on it?

3. Where had he spent that night?

4. What was his relationship to Boyev?

5. On what business had he come to his apartment?

"I promise that if your answers are sincere," Pevtsov had told him, "your action will have no consequences. Otherwise you will surely be blacklisted."

Nikolsky took this promise to heart, nonetheless he answered that he had stolen the head exclusively out of his own idiocy, had spent the night with his older sister Masha, and had come to Boyev's to ask him for half a ruble to get drunk because they were friends and studying together.

There was something in the very artlessness of these explanations that set Pevtsov on his guard.

Pevtsov ordered Nikolsky to remove his jacket and roll up his sleeves. He carefully examined his pudgy white arms. Nikolsky stood there paralyzed with fear. The procedure was even more terrifying because he could neither discern its meaning nor find the courage to ask.

Discovering no trace of Prince von Ahrensburg's teeth, Pevtsov set the scoundrel free but put two gendarmes dressed in their special clothing on his tail.

The fright sobered Nikolsky up completely, and he walked quickly. The tails moved after him, separately, down either side of the street. Soon the entire trio dissolved in the crowd on Liteiny without a trace.

Chapter 4

New Characters

After covering a block along Kirochnaya Street, Ivan Dmitrievich halted in front of a massive, once prosperous, now dilapidated building with a green shop on the ground floor. Here, as the prince's driver had asserted, resided the personage whose name followed the last number, number nine, on Lewicki's list.

He had no trouble clarifying at the caretaker's lodging precisely which apartment was rented by the Strekalovs. He walked up to their floor and rang. The maid opened the door. A minute later the mistress of the house came out into the vestibule, where Ivan Dmitrievich was waiting for her, and when she heard his name and position, said, "Come another time. My husband is away."

"It is you I need, madam," replied Ivan Dmitrievich.

They went into the drawing room. With the gesture of a commander determining the site for a bivouac, she pointed to a chair for him and herself sat down on a padded Turkish stool upholstered in colorful quilting and festooned with uneven fringe—evidently her own handiwork.

On the wall hung a photograph, the portrait of a doleful, fat-cheeked man wearing the dress uniform of the Department of Surveys. Beneath the photograph were two crossed sabers.

"What campaigns did your husband take part in?" inquired Ivan Dmitrievich politely.

"He did not take part in any."

"Then why the sabers?"

She did not reply but wrinkled her nose, and this grimace of hers, performed out of purely feminine, or rather maidenly even, contempt, was more eloquent than any words could have been. Only now did Ivan Dmitrievich appreciate the particular figure of this woman. There was something accomplished and solid, cast, in her powerful neck, her strong arms that moved with such captivating languor, her straight back and small head with its tight knot of black hair. And something masculine at the same time. It was the beauty of a cast iron cannon, which Russian grammar so wisely assigns to the feminine gender. Such a woman, having such a husband, might very well fall in love with Prince von Ahrensburg, once a dashing cavalryman, a hero of battles with the Italians and the Alpine campaigns.

"Let me change seats," said Ivan Dmitrievich, rising from his chair and sitting in an armchair with his back to Strekalov's portrait. "The conversation is going to touch on such matters that I would rather not see your husband's eyes in front of me."

"I don't have much time," Strekalova interrupted him. "I'm expecting guests for dinner."

"There won't be any guests today," replied Ivan Dmitrievich.

"What do you mean by that?"

"Madam, please don't misinterpret this . . ."

He began in a roundabout fashion, but he would need to stun her all at once, in one fell swoop, and then see. He did not have the heart to tell her right away, though.

"I have never questioned a woman's right to dispose freely of her own affections. Especially if doing so inflicts no damage on a marriage. However, I do not approve of Russian beauties who give their hearts to foreigners. This reminds me of the duty-free export of valuables."

"I am not a valuable, and you are not a customs officer. What do you need from me?"

"You see . . ."

"Oh, I think I can guess." Strekalova began to laugh with relief. "Lord, calm yourself! My husband has no inkling. And even if he did! You have only to take one look at him."

Ivan Dmitrievich cast a quick sidelong glance at the portrait.

"No, take a good look! Well? Would such a man dare challenge Ludwig to a duel? You're afraid of a diplomatic scandal, isn't that it? Calm yourself, Mr. Detective, there will be no scandal."

"Prince von Ahrensburg is dead," said Ivan Dmitrievich softly. "He was killed last night. In his bed."

The maid had evidently been listening behind the door because she ran in immediately. Together they were barely able to lift Strekalova up and drag her over to the sofa. She gave no sign of life. With this swoon, noiseless and bottomless, the former life in her came to an end, and now a new life had to be born and find strength.

To his question of where her master was, the maid replied that the master had spent last night and the night before at Tsarskoye Selo, on official business. She was wailing, fluttering like a broody hen around her lifeless and prostrate mistress, holding a glass of water in one hand and a napkin in another and unable to bring herself to put either object to use. Ivan Dmitrievich told her to wipe her mistress's temples and hold a scented candle, if they had one, under her nose.

Supposedly in search of that candle, he opened the door of the sideboard, where he saw tiny porcelain teacups, thick platters with chipped edges, and a paper attached to the side with a spell against cockroaches. Among the glasses of various sizes, like orphans, loomed a pint of Madeira with a small twig sticking out of it. A notch on it marked the level of the wine, so the servant would not take any. The same kind of twig had been stuck into a jar of jam, on which Ivan Dmitrievich noted five or six notches. Evidently, after one of their rare Belshazzarian feasts, when the spouses helped themselves to an entire saucer of cherry or gooseberry jam apiece, the master took his knife and noted how much remained. The sideboard doors creaked, like the doors of that moneylender who wanted to hear at night whether the maid was trying to steal the treasures hidden there.

Ivan Dmitrievich closed the sideboard and surveyed the room one more time. The cheap wallpaper with the traces of claw marks, the decrepit sofa with the bedbug spots, the greasy armchair dating from the Crimean War, the handmade stool. The furnishings of an annual salary of five hundred. And of course, the canary by the window. The cloth cover had been turned back from the cage, and the bird was singing, rending the soul with its eternal longing for another life.

The nauseating smell of onions cooking in grease came in waves from the kitchen. Naturally, the maid, did the cooking as well.

It made no sense to resume the conversation, but Ivan Dmitrievich did not feel he could leave the apartment until Strekalova had revived. She was staring at a single point on the ceiling, which had not been whitewashed in a long time, a point where the crack in the plaster snaked along like the plumage of a cuirassier's helmet.

"The prince once served in the cuirassiers," recalled Ivan Dmitrievich.

On the street he hailed a cab and went to the Fontanka, to see Shuvalov. It was long since time to report to him on the progress of his investigation. But what was he to report? That this woman had loved the prince and the swoon was genuine? That the canary in the cage was singing of love?

The cabbie, recognizing the chief inspector, asked cautiously, "Will there be war?"

"With whom?"

"I don't know. People are saying all officers have been ordered to report back from leave to their regiments. Is that true?"

"What else are people saying?" inquired Ivan Dmitrievich.

"Oh, all kinds of things. For instance, I heard they let a live pig loose in the house of the Turkish envoy. Under their Basurman law there's no worse insult than that. They're saying some monk brought it in a sack and dropped it into the rooms through a window. The envoy went straight to the Winter Palace, to the sovereign, but he wouldn't give the monk up and had him hidden someplace safe. I don't want to know anything about it, he says."

When they stopped at a corner to let a coach pass, Ivan Dmitrievich heard a wall clock chime seven times through open first-floor windows.

It was still quite bright outside. The late April nights were almost white under a cloudless sky, but the routine of the great city's life could not bend to the capricious play of light in the firmament. It chimed seven, and on a signal from the Municipal Duma's tower a pale scattering of gaslights began emerging on the streets.

"The way I understand it," said the cabbie, "if they don't

give up the monk, the war's going to be with the Turks."

That morning all these rumors had started flowing of their own accord, and now they had joined the same channel as Pevtsov's suspicions.

II

Shuvalov was sitting in his office composing his next report to the sovereign. Had the Tsar read them with the same intensity with which they were written, these reports would have become the most exquisite torture. Thus do the Chinese drip water on the shaven crown of the criminal's head. The man goes mad in anticipation of the next drop.

"Thank God, that's the last for today," said Shuvalov, entrusting his opus to the duty officer. "The sovereign has deigned to exchange hourly reports for daily ones. The next is due tomorrow at noon. I hope by then we shall have something to report."

"Why noon specifically?" asked Ivan Dmitrievich. "Couldn't it be a little later?"

"No, it couldn't. That is the rule, and rules must hang over us like a sword of Damocles. Without rules, there can be no order in Russia."

Shuvalov had three clocks in his office: on the wall, on his desk, and standing on the floor. Ivan Dmitrievich noted that they all told a different time.

"I'm not sure the sovereign is going to gather very much from my reports," said Shuvalov, stretching in his chair, "but they have done me personally a fine service. I have penetrated more deeply into the essence of this case and have realized that Pevtsov is right. The murder was painstakingly prepared. One needs to find the courage within oneself to admit that the prince fell victim to someone's clever intrigue."

After listening to the story about the bell pull in the princely bedroom and about Ivan Dmitrievich's visit to Kirochnaya he began to get angry.

"Love, jealousy, wounded pride. All these petty, mundane little passions we police are accustomed to dealing with explain nothing here. You are investigating a crime of state importance, and you must approach it with other measures."

"Your Excellency, I merely wanted to say that von Ahrensburg was killed by someone who had been in his bedroom before and knew about the bell pull," Ivan Dmitrievich tried to vindicate himself. "As it is, it is nearly imperceptible, especially in the dark. It would never have occurred to someone entering the bedroom for the first time to turn the prince so that his feet faced the headboard."

"I allow that, although anything can happen by accident, in the heat of battle. But why have you latched onto this Strekalova? It was not she who bound her lover hand and foot and smothered him with pillows, was it? Why would she?"

"And her husband?" Ivan Dmitrievich reminded him.

"What about her husband?"

"He might have murdered out of jealousy."

"But how would he have found out about the bell pull? Or do you think he brought his own wife to her lover's bedroom?"

"He might have found out some other way."

"What other way?"

"I don't know yet."

"Confound it all!" Shuvalov swore. "What are these Spanish passions seething in your imagination? We aren't in Seville."

"Recently I read an article in a medical journal," said Ivan Dmitrievich. "The author proves that in Petersburg girls mature earlier than in Berlin and London. At approximately the same age as Italian girls."

"And this is apropos of what?"

"Apropos of the Russian's temperament."

"You think I don't want to believe that the prince was smothered by a cuckold of a husband, a jealous lover, or his own valet, tempted by a silver cigarette case?" said Shuvalov conciliatorily. "I'd like nothing better. But you have to understand, I can't. Foreign diplomats don't just get killed so unceremoniously, especially in Russia."

"The fault is mine, Your Excellency. Whom do you suspect?"

"There's the rub. No one specific. Unless it's the agents of some Polish conspiracy, assuming such a thing exists."

"What do the Poles have to do with this?"

"Before setting out for Lombardy, for the war between

Victor Emmanuel and Napoleon III, the cavalry division von Ahrensburg commanded was billeted in Krakow. He may have done something to insult the Poles, and they are a vengeful nation. Krakow belongs to the Austrians, and meanwhile it was there, in Galicia, that Count Hotek once began his service."

"Judging by his name, he's Bohemian," remarked Ivan Dmitrievich.

"That is immaterial. Servants of the empire have no nationality. I was led to thinking about the Poles by the fact that an attempt was made on Hotek's life today as well. He nearly died."

"Well, that's hardly likely. It's very hard to sling a rock through a carriage window and kill someone."

"How do you know that?" Shuvalov was amazed. "Who told you about that?"

"No one. The rumor has gone around," replied Ivan Dmitrievich evasively.

"Astonishing! Everyone knows everything and even more than there is in fact to know. Hotek was informed by some provocateur, for instance, that it was we who had secretly sent the murderer to von Ahrensburg's."

"Who is 'we'? You?"

"Yes, we. The gendarmes. Can you imagine?"

"And the reason?"

"The prince was allegedly linked to Austrian and French journalists and was supplying them with fabrications about our government's secret intentions. Slanderous, naturally."

"Did he in fact supply them and was he so linked?"

"I'm not ruling that out, but right now something else worries me more. Someone, apparently, is striving by any and all means to undermine the sovereign's confidence in the Corps de Gendarmes and in me personally."

All the while Ivan Dmitrievich was listening, a single question danced on the tip of his tongue: Who had been watching von Ahrensburg's residence? Should he ask or was it not worth it? No, better not to ask. Pevtsov had refused to speak of this, citing state secrecy, and Ivan Dmitrievich couldn't help but feel that he had sat down to a table with players who had divvied up the winnings and losses in advance. In that situation the most sensible thing was to play small and not stick his neck out, assuming he couldn't throw his cards down on the table altogether and get the hell out.

"Hotek is behaving provocatively," said Shuvalov. "He doesn't trust me and he's threatening to raise the issue of admitting the Austrian gendarmerie to the investigation. I was compelled to tell him rather sharply that Russia's honor would not permit that."

"Rightly so, Your Excellency!" Ivan Dmitrievich offered his fervent approval, suddenly realizing that Russia's honor, which had never been the object of his daily concern, depended upon how quickly he could find von Ahrensburg's killer.

"And that isn't all," complained Shuvalov. "Hotek presented us with a demand that we declare the Slavonic Committee outside the law and hinted that, if we refused, serious diplomatic complications between our powers might ensue."

"What does that threaten? War?" Ivan Dmitrievich was alarmed.

"Well, for now that is highly unlikely, although in the more distant prospect anything is possible. In Vienna there are influential circles close to the government which are prepared to exploit the incident on the Street of Millions to fan anti-Russian hysteria. How it will all end, God only knows."

As always in moments of agitation, Ivan Dmitrievich began twirling his right side whisker into a little tail. His wife had attempted in vain to disabuse him of what was in her eyes a horrid habit. None of it made any sense, but the thought of the bell pull rather reassured him. All he had to do was pull it and this whole monstrous nightmare would fall apart at the seams, like Harlequin's costume.

Ivan Dmitrievich had seen a costume like that a very long time ago at a street performance on Stone Island. He had been supposed to track down, arrest, and escort out of Petersburg a Mogilev Jew by the name of Lazershtein, a common street actor who had not wanted to convert but had preferred to playact in the capital rather than Mogilev, in order to earn a little extra, don't you know. They had offered an Italian farce, and Lazershtein had played Harlequin. During the performance he ruled the stage, entertained the public, and ordered poor Pierrot about until, brought to the point of despair, Pierrot found an imperceptible thread in his tormenter's costume and pulled it. At that, Harlequin's costume, virtuosically sewn from rags with one single thread, fell to pieces. To the laughter of the audience, left standing there, amid a heap of multicolored rags, was a naked Lazershtein, all skin and bones, his circumcised disgrace barely covered.

Shuvalov rose and began pacing up and down his office, from corner to corner.

"Perhaps I'm overtired today, but I have a strange feeling."

He rubbed his temples with his fingers martyrishly.

"It seems to me. . . ."

And again a pause.

"What, Your Excellency?" Ivan Dmitrievich tensed, feeling with his skin that a crucial point was about to be made.

"It seems to me," Shuvalov finally spoke, "that the rumors of von Ahrensburg's death began to spread even before he was murdered."

III

Back out on the Fontanka, Ivan Dmitrievich felt in dire need of a shot of vodka. He turned into the nearest tavern and sat down at a table. The proprietor of the establishment immediately recognized his esteemed guest and himself sprang forward to serve him.

"A shot of vodka and some pickled mushrooms," Ivan Dmitrievich ordered brusquely, as he examined Ceres with her horn of plenty depicted on the wall.

Fanned out before her were fantastic Southern fruits such as had never seen the inside of this third-rate tavern, where soaked peas were considered the ultimate delicacy. Ceres was smiling at the customers invitingly. Each one of her breasts must have weighed a good six pounds.

Before the billiard players in the corner could play two balls, his order came.

"What, Ivan Dmitrievich, a little tired are we?" asked the tavern keeper sympathetically as he placed the pickled mushrooms, which out of respect for his guest he had put in a china sugar bowl, on the table. "Well, God is merciful. Find the evildoers and the Austrian emperor will give you an order."

"Even you know?" Ivan Dmitrievich gave him a mournful look.

"We're no worse than anyone else. If others know, so do we."

"Have you heard about the pig?"

"That was today. But about the prince getting murdered, that I knew yesterday."

"What?" Ivan Dmitrievich was surprised.

"We have a lively place here. I find out all the news first," the tavern keeper boasted. "Well, after you, naturally."

"What rot is this? How could it have been yesterday? He was killed last night."

"I understand politics," the tavern keeper conceded. "Let the people think it was today. Or else tongues will start wagging that the police are asleep and couldn't catch a mouse."

"Wait up. Who told you it was yesterday?"

"There was a pair sitting here last night, discussing something between them. Over there, in the corner. I listened in. Prince Antsburgh kicked the bucket, they said."

"Last night?" Ivan Dmitrievich asked again, helplessly.

"Not a soul's going to hear it from me, Ivan Dmitrich. Silence! I understand politics. But when you get your order, please come here for your banquet. I'll set all the tables in the room. I have some nice Kama sterlets and wine straight from France. We order it in bottles," the tavern keeper lied inspiredly.

Ivan Dmitrievich lifted the lid and stabbed a mushroom pensively with his fork.

Shuvalov had said that rumors of the prince's death had begun to circulate in advance of his actual death. Now this assumption did not seem mad at all but rather was starting to drive him unbearably mad. What did this imply? The prince played cards and drank wine at the Yacht Club, rode home and went to bed, but he was already dead at the time, and many in the city knew it.

That afternoon Konstantinov had found the driver who had taken the prince home the night before. He had left the club at three in the morning but hadn't arrived at the Street of Millions until nearly four because the horse had not been itself. It had been obstinate and had whinnied as if it were afraid of something, so it had taken them a whole hour to get there. Does that mean even the horse guessed it was pulling a dead man?

Nevertheless, he still could not credit the idea of conspirators. A slave to experience, Ivan Dmitrievich knew all too well that the most cunning conspirators were chance and passion.

"No," he answered the tavern keeper's question of whether to pour him more and finally lowered his arm with the empty glass, which had frozen in mid-air. "How much do I owe you?"

"Not a thing. When they give you your order, come see us. We'll celebrate and I'll add this glass to what your guests eat and drink."

"If you say so." Ivan Dmitrievich was not about to argue. "But you do have fine agarics!" he praised, stabbing one more mushroom with a fork.

"Wait just a moment. I'll put them in a little jar for you right away!" the tavern keeper rejoiced. "Take it with you."

"Don't."

"Why not? You get home, you'll eat it."

"All right. Only just a few!" Ivan Dmitrievich cautioned him.

In wait for the promised jar, he went over to the billiards table in the corner and, somewhat torpid from the vodka, stared at the green field. One of the players jabbed his cue and the ball he hit skipped overboard and crashed to the floor. Ivan Dmitrievich picked it up and put it back on the green field. The ball rolled ponderously, slowly, as if it were returning from another life. Having crossed the fateful line and spent time beyond the edge of the known world, it saw all the clicking and clacking here as vain and foolish. This ball helped Ivan Dmitrievich imagine Strekalova regaining consciousness after her swoon and surveying the setting of her daily life with perplexity: the stool, the crossed sabers under her husband's portrait, the canary in the cage, the twig in the jam jar. Whosoever faints has dwelt in heaven alive, and henceforth none of this is for them. Why should she stay there? Here she was getting dressed and leaving her building. She's summoned a cabbie and gone . . . where? To the Street of Millions, naturally. The valet there was her man. How could he not let his former mistress in?

The tavern keeper ran up with the jar. Checking to make sure it was tightly closed, Ivan Dmitrievich stuck it in his pocket and stepped out into the deserted evening street.

Meanwhile, delivered to Shuvalov was the report he had requested that morning from the archive of the Ministry of Foreign Affairs about when and under what circumstances exactly which foreign diplomats had ever had occasion to die a violent death in Russia.

It turned out that in the entire thousand-year history of the Russian state, only a few such instances had been counted, the last of them under Grand Duke Vasily Ivanovich, father of Ivan the Terrible, when in 1532 a Crimean courier, Devlet-murza, had been murdered. From that time and up until April 25, 1871, things had gone more or less smoothly.

The circumstances of Devlet-murza's death were as follows.

Sahib Girey Khan had sent Devlet-murza to Moscow with an official document in which he threatened to "mount his steed" and "bring my saber to the outskirts of Moscow" if the tribute, which Moscow preferred to refer to as a "token of good will," arrived in Bakhchisarai "with diminishment." After crossing the steppe frontier, Devlet-murza and his suite arrived in the border town of Borovsk, where he was met by Vasily Chikhachev, the son of a boyar, who had ridden from Moscow as the official envoy. He presented the courier with a fur coat and invited him to be his guest in the town. They sat down to eat, and that was when it all happened. After drinking "mead, cherry and boiled," the conceited murza, "who had no desire to listen to the sovereign's names standing," that is, he refused to stand when Chikhachev proposed a toast to the health of the "great sovereign, the Grand Duke Vasily Ivanovich" and began enumerating his titles. At first Chikhachev simply indicated to the slow-witted courier that "at the sovereign's names he, dog that he was, was not fit to sit," but the courier insisted. Persuasion being to no avail, the envoy, who evidently had had opportunity to sip some of the aforesaid mead, lost his temper and began acting "impolitely." What was meant by this laconic formulation in the official document of the day was not explained in the report, but it was not hard to guess. All in all, as witnesses reported to Moscow, "evil was done," as a result of which the Crimean courier "remained no more in life."

Chikhachev's further fate was unknown to the report's compilers, however they did know that a year later, when the Russian ambassador, Fyodor Begichev, arrived in the Crimea, Sahib Girey "did him shame, did sew his nose and ears shut, and baring his body, did lead him around the bazaar."

Stowing this report away in his desk drawer, Shuvalov thought that, thank God, no retribution of that sort threatened the Russian military attaché in Vienna.

IV

Since becoming Chief Inspector of Police in the capital, Ivan Dmitrievich had not taken part personally in any raids or pursuits, but he had made an exception to this rule about ten days before the crime on the Street of Millions. That day—or rather, that night—he, Sych, and Konstantinov had been sitting in ambush outside one of the portside warehouses. It was somewhere there, in the harbor, as anonymous well-wishers had secretly informed them, that the elusive Vanka Pupyr, an escaped convict, bandit, and murderer, cached his stolen goods. Catching him had become a point of honor for Ivan Dmitrievich, and he was not counting on his assistants, who were spineless against this devil.

Pupyr was the scourge of Petersburg. The fur coats and hats, watches, and rings torn off of people in the streets now numbered in the hundreds, but what was more, on his nocturnal paths they had found three dead bodies, all three with fractured skulls. Pupyr armed himself with a kettlebell. The victims who had survived swore that the terrifying weight—a cannonball with a handle, to look at it—was neither iron (which it was) nor bronze but gold, which Ivan Dmitrievich naturally did not believe. But he did know this: at the glint of this kettlebell, sable hats flew off heads of their own accord and rings that had not left fingers for decades slipped off as easily as if they'd been soaped.

Pupyr was cruel, clever, and cautious. He always plied his craft alone and he had no accomplices, which made him hard to catch. Many people thought he could not be caught, for he knew every police agent by face. Dressed in fancy beaver coats, but carrying revolvers in their pockets, over the course of several weeks, night after night, they roamed the dark lanes, pretending to stagger and bawling songs like drunkards. They even lay down on the ground, as if they had stumbled and gone to sleep before they could reach home, but not once had Pupyr risen to the bait. Poor Sych, after lying in the snow for two hours, caught a chill in the vicinity of his groin and became impotent, whereupon his wife started stepping out with her neighbor the cobbler, but Ivan Dmitrievich did not let his agent come to grief. He put that cobbler in lock-up under some pretext or other and held him until the danger had passed.

That night, while they were lying in wait, Sych had been very afraid of catching a chill again. He grumbled and said it was time to leave, the sky was already growing light in the east. But they didn't and sat there freezing to no avail, as it turned out. Just as dawn was about to break, a familiar figure flickered in the distance. Although Ivan Dmitrievich had never seen Pupyr before and had pictured him only from the stories, he immediately recognized his short-legged, long-armed silhouette, which had appeared to him in his dreams.

"Halt!" shouted Ivan Dmitrievich, leaping out of the ambush and pretending he was pulling out a revolver, such as he had never carried in all his born days.

Pupyr started to run, bobbing and weaving, expecting to be shot in the back.

Konstantinov and Sych had weapons, but Ivan Dmitrievich did not order them to fire; he wanted to capture this Herod alive. All three rushed off in pursuit and half an hour later had Pupyr up against the brick wall of a storehouse in the wharf district.

Ivan Dmitrievich and Konstantinov approached him from the right and left along the wall, and Sych, toying sinisterly with his revolver, came at Pupyr head on. Pupyr cast a hunted eye around, but holding to his thievish ways kept his face covered with his silk kerchief.

Directly in front of him, hoisted on a winch, hanging fairly high off the ground, upside down, was a large, eight-oared tender. That afternoon it had evidently been tarred and caulked and then raised up on jacks, so it would not block the way to the storehouses.

Of the three, Sych was especially angry at Pupyr for his conjugal disappointments. In a lather, he strode forward and ended up under the tender before Ivan Dmitrievich could let out a warning cry. At that very moment, Pupyr kicked the winch stopper, and the tender came crashing down, burying Sych.

Pupyr ran and broke free of the ambush, but Ivan Dmitrievich did not himself make chase, nor would he allow Konstantinov. Under the tender, Sych, crushed, was wailing in an ungodly, heart-rending voice. The two of them were barely able to overturn the heavy boat. Sych crawled out on all fours, green from the fright he'd had, but alive and unscathed. Convinced that he was whole, an angry Ivan Dmitrievich gave him a good clip on the back of his head and cursed roundly. It no longer made sense to pursue Pupyr.

By then it was dawn. Ivan Dmitrievich strode sullenly along the shore beside Konstantinov, and behind them, keeping his distance just in case and wheezing contritely, minced Sych. That was when they saw an Italian steamer, *Triumph of Venus,* moored at one of the piers. She had arrived the day before from Genoa with a shipment of oranges and lemons.

The red, white, and green flag of the Kingdom of Sardinia fluttered on her mast, and her smokestack was painted the same colors. On the pier, arm in arm with ladies of dubious appearance, stood three or four tipsy students, who had evidently rolled into the harbor straight from a night of revelry. They were hollering at the top of their lungs, "Viva Garibaldi!" In response, a tiny sailor, who looked like a chimp, tossed them fragrant orange fruits from the deck. The students laughed and treated their girlfriends to the oranges. Konstantinov caught a couple, too, for himself and Ivan Dmitrievich. For Sych, naturally, he broke off not a single section.

"Somehow the freight seems out of season," Safonov expressed his doubts, setting aside his pencil and kneading his fingers, which had fallen asleep.

"I don't know." Ivan Dmitrievich pouted. "I'm telling it just the way it was. You don't have to pick at my every word."

But Safonov was already off and running.

"Not only that," he said, "but in the last episode of your story I noticed one blatantly inauthentic detail and one anachronism. May I point them out?"

"Go right ahead. Point them out."

"Why was the tender that dropped on Sych hanging on jacks upside down? Usually for repairs boats are hung in the opposite position, right side up."

"Are you a sailor?" asked Ivan Dmitrievich sarcastically.

"No, but I've read a lot of seafaring writers. Staniukovich, for instance."

"Fortunately, the men who hung that tender hadn't read Staniukovich and had hung her the wrong way. Otherwise there would have been nothing left of Sych but a wet spot. Would you prefer that?"

"God forbid! I think he'll still come in handy."

"Quite true. And what kind of anachronism is there? Where did you see that?"

"In the name of the schooner. It seems too decadent. *Triumph of Venus,* isn't that right? I won't argue, a ship might have been given that name in our day. But twenty-odd years ago? Hardly."

"My dear man," Ivan Dmitrievich smiled condescendingly. "You reason like a Russian, but the schooner was Italian, don't forget that. Twenty-odd years ago is exactly the length of time by which we lag behind Europe."

Then he concluded:

"All in all, on April 25, 1871, this schooner was still moored in port and being unloaded."

"And that's it?" asked Safonov, disappointed, not waiting for him to continue.

"For now."

"There's something I don't understand. What does this have to do with von Ahrensburg's murder?"

"You'll understand. All in good time," promised Ivan Dmitrievich.

Just a few days later, while analyzing the composition of Ivan Dmitrievich's stories, Safonov managed to perceive their unique aesthetic. Ivan Dmitrievich worked like an artist who scatters smears, blots, spots, and lines on the canvas before a bewildered audience, in apparently random fashion, and then, with a flick of the wrist, suddenly pulls them together into a single whole and blinds his viewers with the instantaneous revelation of his intent, concealed hitherto in chaos.

Chapter 5

Two Stories from the Life of Ivan Dmitrievich, as Told by the Man Himself

It had grown dark on the veranda and they had brought out a lamp. Midges swarmed around it. Ivan Dmitrievich stood up and walked behind Safonov, who was bent over his notebook, writing feverishly. Putting his hand on Safonov's shoulder, he said, "Enough. Let's take a short break. Would you care for more coffee?"

"I'd prefer tea."

"Then tea it is."

While Safonov finished writing from memory the pursuit of Pupyr, embellishing as he went, inserting expressions like "the damp Petersburg fog" and "peering around with haunted eyes," the samovar came to a boil.

"Drink," suggested Ivan Dmitrievich, placing a cup in front of him and moving the wicker sugar basket toward him, "and in the meantime I'll tell you a story."

"Does it have anything to do with Prince von Ahrensburg's murder?"

"Indirectly. It's about a crime whose victim was a foreign diplomat in Russia. But don't write this down. Enjoy your tea. Have a biscuit."

"Why shouldn't I write it down at least in brief?"

"The story is such that I would not want it included in the book. Readers might get the wrong impression of the police in general and me in particular. Actually, at the time I was still quite young. The matter occurred under our sovereign Nicholas Pavlovich. I did mention, I think, that I began my service as an inspector at the Flea Market, didn't I?"

"Yes." Safonov nodded.

"But during the Crimean War they transferred me from the Flea Market to the Apraxin Market, moreover with a promotion, as deputy precinct inspector. The Apraxin inspector at the time was Sherstobitov. Have you ever heard of him?"

"No."

"People have forgotten him now, but in those days the man was quite famous, an extraordinary mind. He had an apartment right there, next to the market. He would sit in his damask robe for days on end playing ballads on the guitar, but he knew every last detail whenever anything happened and could unceremoniously hound a man to death. But he liked me! Once he called me in and said, 'Well, Ivan Dmitrievich'— he always styled me by my name and patronymic, even though I was young enough to be his son—'it's Siberia for you and me for sure!' 'Why Siberia?' I asked. 'Because,' he said, 'a silver tea service belonging to the French ambassador, the Duc de Montebello, has gone missing, and our sovereign emperor Nicholas Pavlovich has ordered Chief Inspector Galakhov to find the service without fail. And Galakhov has ordered you and me to find it, "And if you don't," he says, "I'm going to have you carted off to the back of beyond."' 'Well, we can worry about the beyond in good time,' I said. 'Let's give it a try. We might even find it.' We started searching. We went around to all the Petersburg thieves, but no, none of them had stolen it. Less than happy about this affair, they conducted their own search, better than ours, and reported back: 'We're ready to take the icon off that wall, but we didn't steal that tea service!' What could we do? Sherstobitov and I thrashed around, and thrashed around, got the money together, and ordered a new tea service from Sazikov."

"How did you know what the old one looked like?"

"The Frenchmen had kept the drawings, and Galakhov had given them to us so we would know what to look for. In short, we prevailed upon Sazikov to make it quickly, and after he presented us with the new tea service, we took it to the fire station. The firemen grazed it with their teeth, to make it look as if it had been in use, and we presented the service to the French and waited for our rewards. Only suddenly Sherstobitov called me in. He sat there looking so sad, and his guitar was hanging on the wall. 'Well, Ivan Dmitrievich,' he said, 'it looks like we'll be going to Siberia after all.' 'How's that?' I asked. 'What for?' 'Galakhov called me in to see him today, and he stamped his feet and used some very bad words.

"You and Putilin are tricksters," he says. "You got me into hot water!'"

"Aha!" said Safonov, pondering, "a poor likeness?"

"No, that wasn't it. It turns out, the sovereign saw Montebello at a ball at the palace and asked him, 'Are you content with my police?' The duke replied, 'Quite content, Your Highness. Your police are unexampled. This morning they brought me my stolen tea service, although late the previous evening my valet admitted that he had loaned the very same tea service to a certain foreigner. He even presented me with the receipt, so that I now have two tea services.' All this Galakhov told Sherstobitov and Sherstobitov me. He said, 'It's off to Siberia with you, Ivan Dmitrievich.' 'Maybe yes and maybe no,' I replied, 'but it is a nasty business.'"

"What year was that?" asked Safonov.

"The very same year, my friend, that Nicholas Pavlovich and the same Napoleon on the gold piece vied for the keys to the temple of Bethlehem. First we had them, then the Sultan handed them over to the French, our sovereign demanded them back, and the Sultan dug in his heels, and we refused to yield as well. In Paris they set the dogs on all of us, there was the scent of war in the air, and now this tea service on top of it all. In short, Sherstobitov and I decided to take action. We sent someone to find out on the sly what the ambassador was doing. It turned he was leaving to go hunting with the Austrian ambassador. Aha! We immediately went to see a merchant friend of ours who had sewn the livery for the French embassy and knew all the servants there. We asked him, 'When's your saint's day?' 'In half a year.' 'Could you celebrate it two days hence and invite all the servants from the French embassy? All the refreshments are on us.' This merchant's establishment was at the Apraxin Market, so how could he refuse Sherstobitov? It goes without saying, he agreed, and we put on such a ball for him, even the sky was hot. The French all had so much to drink, they had to be delivered to their houses in the morning, so while they were out celebrating, Yasha the Thief went to Sherstobitov's apartments. There was a man for you! What a soul!" Ivan Dmitrievich recalled, touched with emotion.

"A heart of gold, mild, obliging, and when it comes to agility, I've never met another like him in my life. God rest his soul! At about three in the morning he brought us a sack, you see. 'Please count it,' he said. 'I think that's all.' We started counting—two extra monogrammed spoons. 'What's this for, Yasha?' we said. 'Why did you take two extra?' 'I couldn't help myself,' he said. Well, the next morning Sherstobitov went to see Galakhov, indignant. 'For goodness' sake, Your Excellency. There never were two such tea services. There was and is only one. The French are a flighty nation, and you just can't believe them.' The next day the ambassador returned from his hunt and saw there was just one tea service, and the servants were all green from drink and banging their heads instead of the doors into the doorjambs. He dropped the whole matter and never said another word."

"That's a story out of the past, fairy tale times," Safonov said after he'd stopped laughing. "I advise you to include it in the book anyway. It will make your figure more vibrant."

"Do you think they'd let something like that into print?"

"They print worse than that and nothing happens. The world hasn't stopped turning."

"The fact that the police were consorting with thieves doesn't bother you?"

"Who doesn't know that?"

"Indeed," Ivan Dmitrievich hesitated, "maybe it does make sense to include this story, but only after the chapter on the Street of Millions crime. The closer to the end of the book, the better."

"Why?"

"The reader first has to get to know me as a serious, responsible man concerned with the well-being of society. After that we can recall the sins of his youth. You do know how important first impressions are."

"But what about the chronological principle you're insisting on?"

"That's right! In that case we won't include it. To hell with it!" decided Ivan Dmitrievich. "We've had our fun, now back to work."

II

At supper he recounted for Safonov another episode from his youth, this time a tragic one.

This was again at the Apraxin Market, where he had been pursued for some time by an odd petitioner who would show up at the station, or stand guard outside the building where Ivan Dmitrievich lived and then right in the middle of the street fall to his knees and embrace Ivan Dmitrievich's boots. Ivan Dmitrievich would drive him away without the least pity because this muzhik's request was quite unthinkable. A quit-rent serf from somewhere outside New Ladoga, he had got it into his head, don't you know, that God had singled him out to be an executioner.

At first Ivan Dmitrievich wouldn't even talk to him, but one day his curiosity got the better of him. How did this come to pass? What was behind it? He lifted him up from his knees, took him to a tavern, and there got the following story out of him. A year before, robbers had slit the throat of this muzhik's wife. They were soon caught, convicted, and whipped in public, and either they had an inexperienced executioner or he had been bought off, only the murderers walked away from the lash on their own two feet. "That very day," related the muzhik, "I prayed for my dead wife, and a sign appeared to me that I should become an executioner and punish all assassins to the full extent, right like." He had made a lash and practiced for an entire year without going to the bathhouse or cutting his hair, and he had achieved such terrible artistry that with five blows he could shatter a brick in a stone wall. That was when he nailed his hut closed, came to Petersburg, and offered his services to the police. The good people there pointed out Ivan Dmitrievich to him.

That day, at the tavern, Ivan Dmitrievich told him, "I can tell from your eyes that you would never last."

The man got back down on his knees and swore on his dead wife. As a result, Ivan Dmitrievich yielded and petitioned Galakhov on his behalf. And what happened? After the first execution they carted the criminal directly to the cemetery and the executioner straight to the insane asylum. There the hapless man died a year later, but while he was still alive Ivan Dmitrievich would occasionally visit. Each time he brought along a child's toy whip, and during their stroll together through the hospital garden the madman would loudly proclaim a sentence against some poplar or birch. "Steel yourself, for you shall feel my wrath!" he would shout in a terrible voice, like a true executioner, tottering up to the tree, and he would start lashing it with his whip until he passed out. Then, for a long time after, he would be quiet and docile.

"I felt to blame for this unfortunate man and did what I could to try to redeem my guilt, to ease his sufferings," Ivan Dmitrievich concluded.

After this he returned to the crime on the Street of Millions:

"Here my error threatened misfortunes of a different scale. Later our former ambassador at the court of the Emperor Franz Josef told me that when the wagon with von Ahrensburg's coffin arrived in Vienna, there was a rowdy demonstration at the train station. The tone was set by the prince's comrades-in-arms, veterans of the Italian campaign, who carried the coffin through the streets of the Austrian capital. The orchestra played the Radetzky March and the crowd broke a window in the entry of the Russian embassy, but the police made no arrests. Persistent rumors going around army circles said that the prince had fallen at the hand of an assassin sent secretly by the gendarmes.

Chapter 6

Bite Marks Are Found

Outside the tavern, Ivan Dmitrievich hailed another cab, and en route to the Street of Millions, where he was counting dearly on finding Strekalova, he stopped in at home to reassure his wife. She always began to worry after eight o'clock if he had not been home yet. In those instances it was worthwhile giving her advance warning.

"My God, Vanya, how I've missed you!" said his wife impulsively, hugging him right there in the vestibule. "Did you miss me, too?"

"I did, I did."

"Then kiss me."

Relenting, throwing caution to the wind, Ivan Dmitrievich kissed her on the lips. She recoiled immediately.

"Have you been drinking?"

"My word of honor, just one glass!"

"Then please don't try to assure me that you won't take to drink, be hounded out of service for drunkenness, and die like a beggar somewhere. I know very well that you are at no risk of this, but it is spring right now, and in spring all chronic illnesses are exacerbated. It is right now that you must be especially attentive to your stomach. Is it really so hard to keep to a diet, if only until the end of May?"

Listening meekly as a lamb, Ivan Dmitrievich realized that the pickled mushrooms were off limits for him, and it would be safer not to take the jar out of his pocket. There would be no end to her shouting.

"Why do I do it, I ask myself?" continued his wife in a doleful voice. "Why, like a fool, do I try to prepare everything dietetic for you? Why do I brew you St. John's wort and dog rose?"

"One," Ivan Dmitrievich showed her one raised finger. "One glass."

"Enough for all my labors to go to hell in a handbasket."

She should not have said that. After that phrase, which was repeated on a nearly daily basis, Ivan Dmitrievich felt released of any moral obligations.

"Enough!" he cut her off, removing his coat and proceeding to the washroom.

His wife ran after him, lamenting.

"You're not a little boy anymore. It's time to give your stomach serious thought! If you fall ill, what will we live on? You married and fathered a son, so please think about your stomach. This is your duty to me and little Vanya."

He had no choice but to put his arms around her and give her a real kiss to calm her down.

Fifteen minutes later, after a wonderful bowl of scalding hot fish soup, Ivan Dmitrievich sat down on the floor with his son to build a house out of blocks, but before he finished he stood up.

"You shouldn't do that," his wife said disapprovingly. "You're teaching the child that he doesn't have to finish something he has started."

This homily enjoyed no success. Ivan Dmitrievich was already in the vestibule.

"You're leaving again?" his wife was alarmed.

"Yes. You have heard, no doubt, that the Austrian military attaché was killed."

"Where would I have heard that? Little Vanya and I have been sitting home all day."

"Well, now I'm telling you. He was killed, the investigation was assigned to me, and I have to go."

"At this time of night?"

"There's nothing to be done for it. That's my job." Ivan Dmitrievich had uttered the magic word, whose magic, however, had ceased to have its usual effect on his wife of late.

"But when will you be back?"

"In a couple of hours. If I'm detained, don't you wait up for me. Go to bed."

"I will," said his wife ominously. "If you come back in more than two hours, don't get in bed with me. I'll make up the sofa for you in the parlor, just in case. When I'm woken up in the middle of the night, my head aches the whole next day."

Her head aches! This was something new, but he was in no mood to delve deeper. Ivan Dmitrievich picked up his bowler, went outside, and got into the droshky whose cabbie he had told to wait by the front door.

II

It was dark by the time he reached the Street of Millions, and the lamps had been lit in people's homes. From a distance Ivan Dmitrievich could tell that there was someone in the prince's drawing room. The windows there were warmed by a meager, disturbing yellow light suggesting the barest hint of domesticity.

The tower on the roof reminded him of a cuckoo clock. The little doors seemed just about to open, and then out would pop the iron bird's head. It resembled the clock on the nursery wall in his own apartment, whose cry pointed out to little Vanya the fleeting of time, which still did not frighten him, and marked both the routine of meals and bedtime's implacable approach.

He walked up the front steps and rang. The valet opened the door and at the sight of Ivan Dmitrievich began imploring him right at the threshold.

"For God's sake, don't say anything to her about the cigarette case!"

This meant that his former mistress was already there.

Ivan Dmitrievich moved down the hallway in the direction of the drawing room.

"Please do me this kindness and don't tell her about the cigarette case," whined the valet, trailing behind. "She has a heavy hand. She'll beat me."

From the drawing room, through the open door of the bedroom, he could see the outline of a female figure. Strekalova was standing motionless over the prince's neatly made bed, a bed of love and death. Black hair, black dress. Her loose jacket was tossed carelessly over the arms of a chair, but a shawl, blindingly white on its backdrop of mourning, remained on her shoulders. With one hand Strekalova was tugging its ends across her breast, as if trying to ward off a deadly draft gushing up from below.

Ivan Dmitrievich couldn't help it. He pitied women when they wrapped themselves in a scarf or shawl like this. It was a pose that signaled a woman's vulnerability and constant anxiety—over a child's illness, a husband's late return, an evening's solitude. His wife knew this weakness in him and exploited it with some success.

Long ago, back in the days when a jar of pickled mushrooms offered as a bribe would have seemed an insult only blood could avenge, Ivan Dmitrievich had often given thought to his own funeral. In the first few years after his wedding, he was very much afraid that his wife would follow his coffin dressed carelessly, tear-stained and disheveled, with hairpins poking out from under her hat. At the time he had explained to her that a real woman must take care with her appearance in front of her dead beloved. The more powerful her grief, the greater her attention to her shoes, dress, and hair. Herein was manifested her true love, not in her tears or her hand wringing.

Judging from how Strekalova looked, she was a real woman, and her love was not subject to doubt. But her mourning dress sat rather too easily on her. Where had she obtained it? Had she perhaps sewn it in advance?

As he entered the drawing room, Ivan Dmitrievich could not help but notice the door howl like a wolf on its unoiled hinges, but Strekalova did not even turn around. This noise was nothing in comparison with the silent wail residing in her breast.

"Whosoever faints has dwelt in heaven alive," Ivan Dmitrievich recalled. During her swoon her soul had flown there and fallen face down before the throne of the Almighty, pleading for her beloved, and now Prince von Ahrensburg's soul, the anemic soul of a soldier, gambler, and lady's man, was scrambling up the approaches of Purgatory, saved by this woman's intercession.

Only when Ivan Dmitrievich coughed several times behind her did she notice him.

"Oh, it's you."

"I realize you would like to be alone, but it is not within my powers to afford you that opportunity. I am here in my official capacity."

She interrupted him.

"Have you found his murderer?"

"Not yet."

"And you won't."

"You don't think so?" Ivan Dmitrievich was stung.

"I'm certain of it. And if you do find him, you won't arrest him."

"Why?"

"You'll be too afraid."

"I'm Chief Inspector of Police. What am I to be afraid of?"

"You're not that mighty. You'll be afraid. You will."

The beginning of the conversation was quite promising, but Ivan Dmitrievich decided not to push his luck.

"Fine." He nodded. "Let's set that conversation aside for the time being. But tell me, did the prince have enemies?"

Strekalova squinted ironically.

"Look at me carefully," she told him in the same tone Ivan Dmitrievich had used two hours before to order her to look at her husband's portrait. "Well? Do I look like a woman capable of falling in love with a man who had no enemies?"

"My fault," said Ivan Dmitrievich flirtatiously. "Allow me to kiss your hand as a sign of forgiveness."

He pressed his lips to the graciously extended but cold fingers and once again, now without being told, examined Strekalova's face carefully.

"My dear departed mother taught me to beware of men with cold hands and women with hot ones."

Strekalova pressed her palm to her cheek to check its temperature.

"What is that supposed to mean?"

"I have confidence in you and I'm counting on that confidence being returned."

He had to make this woman understand that he was not a little boy. A mite of informality would not harm and might, in fact, promote their mutual understanding. Ivan Dmitrievich unbuttoned his jacket with intentional gravitas, insolently tossed her jacket on the bed, and sprawled in the armchair. However, as he was seating himself, he accidentally grazed Strekalova with the flapping hem of his jacket. The jar in his pocket struck her hip.

"What's that you have there?" she asked suspiciously.

Ivan Dmitrievich decided there was nothing to be gained from telling the truth. A man carrying a jar of pickled mushrooms on his person is scarcely capable of catching a murderer.

"This?" He slapped his pocket with an unperturbed look. "It's a revolver."

"Loaded?"

Ivan Dmitrievich shrugged, as if to say, Foolish question. For the first time, Strekalova looked at him with respect but then immediately gestured in despair.

"It won't do you any good. You'll be afraid anyway."

"Then tell me straight out!" Ivan Dmitrievich could not contain himself. "Who is the murderer? Do you know?"

"You'll be afraid, you'll be afraid," repeated Strekalova, like a wind-up toy. "As sure as sure can be."

"Recently we took into custody the head of an office in the Ministry of State Properties. I had established his guilt in the poisoning of his maid, who was pregnant by him."

"Perhaps," said Strekalova indifferently. "But when it comes to this, you'll be afraid. And even if you aren't, no one will allow you to bring charges against Ludwig's murderer. To say nothing of arresting him."

As always in moments of agitation, Ivan Dmitrievich's hand tugged at his right side whisker and twisted it into a little tail. Lord, could Hotek actually be right?

Ivan Dmitrievich cast a sidelong glance at Strekalova, who seemed to be waiting for objections from him, counting on them. He was supposed to tell her, No, I won't be afraid, I'll do everything in my powers. Could the gendarmes actually be complicit in the murder? There's no smoke without fire, that's their logic. The three clocks, all telling different times, seemed like a sign of Count Shuvalov's triple essence: he was three individuals in one. Each of them went about his business without reporting to the other two, living in its own time.

"I think I can guess who you have in mind," said Ivan Dmitrievich. "Answer me just one question. Were his subordinates watching the prince's house?"

"So you know everything?" Strekalova was astonished.

"Everything."

"Then let's be frank. Yes, the count set his men on Ludwig because he feared and hated him."

"Well, my pigeon," thought Ivan Dmitrievich with compassion, "if you lifted a hand against Shuvalov himself, dear, there would be no allies to be found. Your womanly charms notwithstanding!"

"So because of him . . ."

Ivan Dmitrievich fell silent, incapable of saying the Chief of Gendarmes' name out loud.

"Because of him," he continued, "you had to leave this house before it was light?"

Strekalova did not answer right away, not knowing, evidently, whether to rejoice that the inspector was so well informed or to hate him for that niggling but thorough knowledge so demeaning to her feminine pride.

"Yes," she admitted after a pause. "I left here early in the morning, sneakily, like a maid leaving the master's son, but I'm not ashamed of it. Do you hear me? I'm not ashamed! I loved Ludwig, and he loved me. Yes, he did! Do you hear me?"

"I hear you, I do. Don't shout."

"The problem was that Ludwig was a diplomat and he had to take care over his reputation. Otherwise he would never have become ambassador. Ludwig was even forced to let his doorman go because he had informed on him."

"And his valet," added Ivan Dmitrievich.

"No, his old servant drank too much, and I suggested he take mine instead. But he slept through the whole thing, the pig!"

Sitting on the bed, Strekalova smoothed the cover with the palm of her hand, though there wasn't a wrinkle on it as it was. Then she looked up at Ivan Dmitrievich.

"Well then, are you going to expose the murderer?"

He did not answer.

"You're frightened, so you won't. That fiend—"

"Just don't name names!" Ivan Dmitrievich interrupted her hastily.

He heard a lone wolf howl mournfully for his sweetheart, shot by hunters. It was the door from the hallway into the drawing room creaking open. Then he heard Pevtsov's voice.

Ivan Dmitrievich left the bedroom, shutting the door behind him, and saw that Pevtsov had not come alone. With him was the Preobrazhensky lieutenant, who turned out to have been on duty for the battalion, so Pevtsov had not had far to go, just across the street.

"Such is the nature of our job, Captain! It gives us no rest," complained Ivan Dmitrievich without even looking at his offender.

Then he returned to the bedroom, while Pevtsov and the lieutenant remained in the drawing room to talk.

Two conversations were going on simultaneously in the two rooms.

Pevtsov: "Do you think Prince von Ahrensburg could have been killed by anyone to whom Russia's might is dear?"

Lieutenant: "Their name is legion."

Ivan Dmitrievich: "Please keep your voice down."

Strekalova: "You're already afraid."

Ivan Dmitrievich: "Let's get back to the person of whom we were speaking."

Strekalova: "He wanted to defile Ludwig before the sovereign. Make him out to be a degenerate, a gambler, a drinker."

Ivan Dmitrievich: "Wasn't he?"

Strekalova: "It must seem odd to you that I fell in love with this foreigner. But I swear, his money did not interest me. He was a real man, a true knight, such as I had never seen. He fought in Italy, he fell into a gorge with his horse. He fought duels eight times. All the policemen on duty saluted him, whereas my husband, when he returns a little tipsy from seeing friends, can't remove his hat too readily before every single policeman he sees. He's afraid of his superiors, afraid of driving fast, of geese, colds, and my colorful attire, of dreams on Thursday night, cholera, and war with the English because British ships at sea might suddenly fire upon our Kirochnaya Street."

Pevtsov: "Where did you spend last night?"

Lieutenant: "With a lady."

Pevtsov: "Her name?"

Lieutenant: "How dare you? I do not answer questions like that."

Pevtsov: "Fine. Why is your hand bandaged?"

Lieutenant: "I scratched it with a ramrod."

Pevtsov: "Be so kind as to remove the bandage. . . . That's it. In my opinion, these are teeth marks."

Lieutenant: "I completely forgot! I hurt my other hand with the ramrod. Here a dog nipped at me."

Pevtsov: "A dog?"

Lieutenant: "A little ginger poodle. Called Chuka. A sharp-toothed wretch!"

Pevtsov: "Interesting little dog. She seems to have human teeth."

Strekalova: "When my husband wanted to please me, he would bring home half a pound of dried apricots. And at night, when he wanted to incline me to caresses, he would whisper tenderly in my ear that I and I alone had been able to open his eyes to the healing properties of cherry jelly. Ludwig would say that because of me he was beginning to understand and love Russia. But he was a diplomat, after all! The love of this man could have far-reaching consequences. It could end his career. He was foretold an ambassador's chair, and I will admit honestly that sometimes it seemed, when I had my arms around him, that I myself was party to major policy. I even had a dream of converting Ludwig to Orthodoxy."

Ivan Dmitrievich: "Was your husband jealous?"

Strekalova: "He never suspected a thing. I hope you have no interest in the pretexts I used for the occasional nights I did not spend at home."

Ivan Dmitrievich: "And were you jealous of other women?"

Strekalova: "That doesn't matter now."

Ivan Dmitrievich: "I need to ask the valet a few things. Please, summon him."

Strekalova (rising and moving toward the door): "Just a minute."

Ivan Dmitrievich: "Why go anywhere? He's in his room."

Strekalova: "Well, I'm not going to shout! He wouldn't hear in any case."

Ivan Dmitrievich. "You don't have to shout. There's a bell."

Strekalova: "Where?"

Pevtsov: "Be honest, who bit you?"

Lieutenant: "Why should you care? Maybe it's the trace of a lover's passion!"

Pevtsov: "And maybe you were trying to shut someone's mouth. To keep him from calling out for help."

III

Hanging to one side of the princely bedstead was a large painting depicting three naked Italian ladies standing against a backdrop of Vesuvius. They were holding tiny pitchers that would have only held enough water to brew tea, but the Italians were preparing to bathe from them. Here it was, the much-vaunted European cleanliness!

The bell pull, yellow like the wallpaper, ran along the wall and behind that picture. Only the very end stuck out below, lost in the filleted curves of the picture frame and almost imperceptible from the side. Strekalova surveyed the bedroom distractedly but couldn't find it.

Ivan Dmitrievich had already realized that the valet was not guilty of anything. Why should he drag the prince away from the headboard? Let him ring as much as he wanted.

Now he could lift suspicion from Strekalova as well. "Poor thing!" thought Ivan Dmitrievich.

This woman had been put out early in the morning, like a loose woman, without breakfast even, since if breakfast had been served in bed she would have known about that rope. The prince would have risen reluctantly in his linen, yawning, and escorted his lover no farther than the drawing room doors. Then, after drinking his coffee, he would have luxuriated in bed, gazing at his naked Italians and comparing their charms with the charms he had just had at hand (if you took a little off here and made that curve a little deeper), while she walked down the street all alone, shuddering from the morning chill, as her own former servant watched her from the window with a vile grin on his ugly face.

"You know," said Strekalova. "Back in his youth, it was foretold that Ludwig would die in his own bed. A Gypsy told him that. The murderers would never have been able to do it had it not been for that prediction. He remembered it and gave up."

"The coffin may not have been sent to the station yet. Go to the embassy and say goodbye," suggested Ivan Dmitrievich.

"The embassy? Never!"

"I'll tell you a story that might console you. Last spring my dear mama fell out of her sledge and hit her head on the ice. We had given up hope that she would survive. But no, she recovered. She saw the next world and came back. 'Well,' I asked her, 'How is it, Mama, is it frightening to die?' And she said to me, 'Oh, it's so sweet!' she said. 'It was as if they were wrapping every fiber of my being in velvet.' Maybe it was like that for the prince."

Ivan Dmitrievich felt sorry for women in general. Not for any particular reason, simply because they were women, although usually people feel sorry for small, ethereal ones, not ones like Strekalova. Right now, though, this mighty, cast body seemed helpless and weak. She had suffered quite a blow.

"Do you have evidence against the prince's murderer?" he asked.

She shook her head.

"Alas!"

"Well," Ivan Dmitrievich lingered over the word, "then what are we talking about?"

"You're the detective!" She looked at him with forced coquetry, and he heard capricious little notes in her voice, as if she were talking about a trifling favor. "Expose him!"

"And then what?"

"I'll go all the way to the sovereign with the evidence. And I promise not to mention your name."

Expose the Chief of Gendarmes? It was an insane scheme.

"Do you like me?" asked Strekalova all of a sudden, patting her hair with a pathetic playful motion. "Help me take revenge."

"And what then?"

"I shall be yours."

"I have a wife," said Ivan Dmitrievich hoarsely.

At that moment a heart-rending cry reached them from the next room.

"Why it was he who scratched me!" the lieutenant howled. "He did! Your friend! Putilin!"

Ivan Dmitrievich leapt into the drawing room.

"Admit it!" the lieutenant rushed toward him. "It was you who bit me. Why don't you say something? Was it or wasn't it you?"

"Or perhaps Prince von Ahrensburg?" said Pevtsov.

"Look at this! See this?" The lieutenant made a famously obscene gesture. "You want to make a Russian officer your scapegoat? Are you trying to curry favor with the Austrians?"

"Listen here, Lieutenant," said Pevtsov conciliatorily. "You can't hide from us anyway. Go on over to your battalion, calm down, and consider your position. I'll be waiting for you here."

"You can wait until hell freezes over!"

"In that case I'll come for you myself."

"I'll throw you down the stairs!" promised the lieutenant.

"I won't be coming alone. Rukavishnikov!"

The subaltern loomed up at the threshold with his saber at his side.

"And I" —the lieutenant was incensed— "I shall raise my platoon of brave fellows!"

"I would not advise it," said Ivan Dmitrievich.

"Aha!" The lieutenant turned to face him, shaking his bitten hand. "So you left me this marking on purpose? Scoundrel!"

He bared his saber with a clank and slashed an x in the stuffy air in front of him. Then he lopped the top off a potted lemon tree.

Ivan Dmitrievich observed these martial exercises with equanimity.

"Defend yourself!" the lieutenant exclaimed, his blade upraised menacingly.

Ivan Dmitrievich spread his arms helplessly.

"With what?"

He felt well protected by his own lack of weapon.

Rounding the table behind which sat the speechless Pevtsov, the lieutenant ran Rukavishnikov up against the wall, emitting a faint squeak in the process, tore his saber from its sheath with his left hand, and hurled it all the way across the drawing room at his foe. But Ivan Dmitrievich gave no thought to catching it. He ran into the bedroom, slammed the door behind him, and met Strekalova's reproachful look.

"You do have a revolver," she reminded him.

By now the lieutenant was holding a saber in each hand. One of them he wanted to thrust into his enemy's hand in order to have the lawful right to strike him with the other. He kicked the door, and when he jumped back, intending to strike at it with his chest, Ivan Dmitrievich warned him.

"Be careful! I have a revolver."

Pevtsov quickly recovered, winked at Rukavishnikov, and the two of them piled on the lieutenant from behind, taking away his sabers and twisting his arms behind his back.

Once the danger had passed, Ivan Dmitrievich emerged from his siege.

"How about it, brother?" He winked at the lieutenant. "You see what happens when you snatch at noses!"

"Scoundrel!" The lieutenant hawked up a quantity of saliva, but Rukavishnikov managed to force his head down so that the spit landed not in Ivan Dmitrievich's face but on the tip of his boot.

"You can lock him up in the pantry," advised the valet, who had run in at the noise. "There aren't any windows there."

The threesome (Ivan Dmitrievich did not help) dragged the lieutenant down the hall, but it was not so easy stuffing him into the pantry.

"Judases!" he hollered, straining hard, clutching at the door jambs. "Where are you taking me?"

Pevtsov wheezed and did not respond, realizing that further discussion was pointless for the time being. He had to regain his patience.

Meanwhile Ivan Dmitrievich returned to the bedroom, where Strekalova greeted him like a long lost friend.

"Don't grieve." She stroked him tenderly on the shoulder. "Later you'll challenge him to a duel. Do you actually suspect this officer?"

"No. We have our own scores."

Ivan Dmitrievich felt rather awkward—not because of the lieutenant, no, the fault was entirely his, but because this was not the most appropriate time for settling personal scores.

"I'm going to lie down," Strekalova leaned back on the pillows, not in the least embarrassed by his presence, exactly as if what she had promised him had already come to pass. "You can send him a challenge later," she said. "I feel sorry for you. I saw what it cost you to restrain yourself and not fight him."

"Yes," mumbled Ivan Dmitrievich.

"Does this mean you need to live in order to expose the murderer? Or am I wrong? Give me your hand. . . . Ludwig had short fingers, too. These are the fingers of a real man. The count's are slender, long, and yellow, like noodles. . . . I would like to be left alone. You go on. Go on."

Tenderly, she made the sign of the cross over him and turned to the wall.

It had grown dark. In the drawing room, Ivan Dmitrievich turned up the lamp wick, the flame flared brighter, there was the smell of kerosene, and the rose petals around the trunk's keyhole gleamed wetly. The shadow from the swinging lampshade ran across the bronze Eve and over the porcelain naiads on the mantel. They looked as if they were all curtseying at the same time, greeting Pevtsov as he entered.

"Give me your hand," Pevtsov said, whistling merrily. "The case is closed!"

"You think so?"

"It's closed. Closed! Oh, he took us for simpletons and tried to buy us off with his candor. Here I am. Do your worst. . . . Hohenbruch! Hohenbruch!" Pevtsov taunted the lieutenant. "A true fanatic! And apparently slightly touched. Imagine what he accused you of! Eh?"

"What if I did bite him?"

"You?" Pevtsov gave a laugh. "Now you can joke. Who, by the way, is the personage in the bedroom?"

"She was in love with the prince."

"A formidable woman! And how did he cope with her in bed?"

"Desist, Captain!" Ivan Dmitrievich turned on him.

"Enough of this! We'd better agree on the share each of us is taking in this case. The suspicions are yours, the evidence mine. Agreed?"

"I should think just the reverse."

"So be it." Pevtsov treated this clarification casually, not penetrating to its essence. "We must celebrate our success. I believe we'll find something warming from the master of the house. He was not a total loss in that respect."

Pevtsov went out to the kitchen, on the way poking his head outside and sending one of his gendarmes to report to Shuvalov, and brought back an opened bottle of sherry and two glasses.

"Please join me, Mr. Putilin!"

That morning Ivan Dmitrievich had himself eaten some of the prince's pork without a glimmer of conscience, but now he felt he did not have a right to drink the owner's sherry.

"Don't be bashful," Pevtsov invited him. "The deceased would have been happy to treat you on this occasion."

Seeing that his companion was dragging his feet, he drank down one glass of the wine, raising his glass jauntily to his own reflection in the mirror as he said, "Hussar style!"

Ivan Dmitrievich recalled that gendarme officers received the highest salary in the army—on a par with the hussar or cuirassier wage—and he cursed privately. As if you had something to drink to! Parasites.

"Drink," Pevtsov laughed, pouring himself a second glass. "Or do you think your guardsman won't confess? That he's going to say at the inquiry that it was you who bit him? Have no fear, I'll take care of that. The main thing for men like this is for their deed to be appreciated. They're all itching to be martyrs. You tell them, I personally respect your gesture, but the law . . . And case closed. They have a weakness for sympathy, the devils. You just have to let them dig their own graves. Hear that?"

The sound of dull blows reached them from the pantry.

"Fanatics. They always confess," concluded Pevtsov with the professional confidence of a hunter of souls. "For instance, Boyev has already confessed."

Ivan Dmitrievich's hand reached once again for his side whisker.

"What's that? The Bulgarian?"

"The very same."

"Impossible!"

"He confessed like a perfect dear," confirmed Pevtsov.

IV

At this same time, Shuvalov, having been informed by Pevtsov of the criminal's capture, had sent the duty officer to the Austrian embassy, to see Hotek, and himself had made ready to leave for the Street of Millions. All the circumstances of the case would be clarified more readily at the scene.

Hotek gathered his things quickly, and both counts set out simultaneously.

Hanging from the ambassador's carriage was a yellow lantern, whereas Shuvalov's lantern glass was tinted blue. The carriages bowled along through the city, the two lights, one gold and one blue, implacably approaching one another, and ultimately pulled up at the two-story residence on the Street of Millions simultaneously.

The ambassador was escorted by a Cossack convoy, without which Hotek now did not go anywhere. One Cossack galloped ahead of the carriage, two behind, and the Cossack captain alongside, even with the door.

Shuvalov also sent a courier to Grand Duke Peter Georgievich and Prince Oldenburgsky but decided to bide his time and send his final report to the sovereign in the morning.

On a turn his carriage nearly knocked a solitary pedestrian off his feet. It was the agent Sych. Previously he had served as a stoker at the Church of the Resurrection at the Volkovo cemetery, so he knew the ways of religion, which was why Ivan Dmitrievich had sent him specifically around to the churches to look for the Napoleon and sent Konstantinov to the taverns.

Ivan Dmitrievich assumed that the murderer was unlikely to risk going to a big cathedral like St. Isaac's or Prince Vladimir's. Sych had been instructed not to poke his head in there but rather to be sure to stop in at the smaller, poorer sanctuaries. He had done exactly this—all, unfortunately, to no avail. Not only that, but things were moving slowly inasmuch as Sych was making his way from church to church on foot. The official money issued him for a cab he had given to his wife that afternoon when he had stopped in at home for dinner.

Chapter 7

The Appearance of Kerim-Bek

Two or three years prior to this, a file containing secret documents had gone missing from the office of a prominent official, a department director in the Ministry of Foreign Affairs. The ministry had searched for a couple of weeks to no avail and eventually had been forced to report the loss to Chancellor Gorchakov. The lost papers concerned the political situation in the Balkans, and clever minds had suspected Austrian or Turkish spies.

Two more weeks passed. Late one evening, a young ministerial official from the same department whose director had lost those documents was walking his spitz along the quay when suddenly he noticed a stranger ahead of him carrying the stolen file. He recognized it immediately by its clasp, which glinted in the moonlight, but there was no one to summon for help on the deserted quay. Stealing up behind the stranger, the official deftly snatched the file away but was unable to detain him and the spy escaped, leaving at the scene of the struggle the top hat which had fallen off his head. That was when it was decided to resort to the services of the police.

Ivan Dmitrievich had a conversation with the department director in his office. The director said, "Naturally, Mr. Putilin, now I suspect this official. He evidently wants to earn merit with me in this way, and I am going to have to reward him because I have no evidence against him. If you can find any, I would be in your debt."

They passed into the room where his subordinates sat. Ivan Dmitrievich asked him not to name the hero who had restored the stolen papers, saying that he would determine that for himself, and he did. A minute later he pointed confidently to an official of about thirty with a prematurely balding pate.

At this they brought in the top hat with the cracked lid and holey lining that had been dropped by the spy. Ivan Dmitrievich twirled it in his hands and then with a sudden motion planted it on this official's head. Convinced that the top hat fit him perfectly, he said, "Case closed."

The poor man began sobbing and confessed to everything. The other officials rushed to take the top hat away from one another and examine its insides. They thought that the owner's name had been left on the lining, that he had written it there and forgotten to expunge it, but they found nothing. Moreover, no one could understand how the confession had been so easily obtained. After all, the size of a top hat is not exactly evidence sufficiently conclusive to make a guilty head droop. Ivan Dmitrievich never did explain to anyone that what had helped him expose and convict the criminal were his quill pens.

On this official's desk he had seen a wooden cup filled with ordinary goose quills. They all had bare stems, and at the tips their feathery edgings were trimmed in the shape of little hearts. Ivan Dmitrievich had seen exactly the same kind on the desk of the department director. The other officials did not trim their quills at all or trimmed them differently. Two people in the entire department trimmed their pens identically, and it wasn't hard to guess who dreamed of emulating whom.

The confession was obtained in the following manner. When the top hat was poised on this official's head, Ivan Dmitrievich took one such pen out of the cup and poked its little heart through the crack between the crown and the bottom. How much did it weigh, this pen? How many pathetic ounces? Nonetheless, its weight forced the guilty man to lay his head on his desk and cry. He had seen his reflection in the mirror and been horrified. The old top hat, crowned with a goose quill with the idiotic little heart at the end was emblematic of his soul, so miserable in its vanity, like a clownish likeness of a hussar shako.

He cried, which meant the soul inside him was not yet dead. Ivan Dmitrievich removed the top hat and ran his palm over that balding crown sympathetically. A balding man senses the ominous flight of time more acutely; in his day Ivan Dmitrievich himself had experienced similar emotions, which are especially dangerous as one's youth wanes, but he had found the courage not to surrender to them. That may have been why his hair stopped falling out.

He recalled that story now looking at Pevtsov, who was standing in front of the mirror and trying very hard to lay three hairs across his bald spot; they had been disturbed in the process of hauling the lieutenant off to the pantry. One of his epaulets had been partially ripped off, and one button had torn off, taking with it a scrap of fabric. The lieutenant had sold his freedom dearly.

"As for our Bulgarian," said Pevtsov, "I nonetheless forced him to confess to von Ahrensburg's murder. Not that that matters now."

"How do you mean?" said Ivan Dmitrievich, upset.

Pevtsov jerked his head in the direction of the pantry, where the captive lieutenant continued to rant and rave.

"The perpetrator has been caught and I can reveal to you my method. By knowing the general political situation in Europe and the Balkans, I gain the ability to anticipate the separate individual events in which this situation manifests itself."

It was almost pitch dark outside. The gas lamp by the front door had gone out, though a tiny blue moth was fluttering its little wings impotently over the jet. The windows were dark in the Preobrazhensky barracks, and the guardsmen had gone to sleep without a duty officer.

"I was perfectly honest with Boyev," Pevtsov related. "I behaved like a gentleman. I said, 'You may not be guilty. I quite allow that.' I explained to him that Russia cannot quarrel with Vienna right now because soon she will have to fight the Turks. Any clashes between our powers would play right into the Sultan's hand, because then it would be harder for us to extend a helping hand to our Bulgarian co-religionists. Yes, I was more candid with him than Count Shuvalov was with the sovereign. I said, 'Hotek has already sent a dispatch to the Emperor Franz Josef, and we have held it back at the telegraph office, but only until tomorrow morning, unfortunately. The murderer must be found today; tomorrow will be too late. The dispatch will go to Vienna and the consequences are unpredictable.' I expressed my sincere doubt that he had in fact murdered the prince. I simply said, 'If you truly do love your long-suffering homeland, my friend, the duty of a patriot calls upon you to accept the guilt in any case. The sheep on his right hand,' as I told him, 'and the goats on the left!'"

Ivan Dmitrievich leaned his chest against the table and the sherry splashed over the glass's rim.

"And what did Boyev say?"

He knew the answer, but he wanted to hear it from the lips of the man who would reject a jar of mushrooms, of course, but who could take a living soul without blinking.

"He agreed on one condition."

"Which is?"

"That we pass him off as a Turk."

"Good Lord!" escaped from Ivan Dmitrievich.

"But why are you so amazed? I myself was about to suggest just such a scenario. If he is guilty, this is the best way for him to retain the sympathies of the Russian public for Bulgarian émigrés. If he isn't, he gets a marvelous opportunity to convince public opinion yet again of Constantinople's perfidy."

"And what do you think? Is he or is he not guilty?"

"Actually, I have noted several quirks in his behavior. Here's an example for you. When we had already agreed upon everything, I said to him, 'Let me send some wine to your cell so you won't be bored. Which kind do you prefer, white or red?' He looked at me askance and said, 'In Bulgaria there are a thousand songs about red wine—and only one about white. Do you know how it begins?' 'How am I supposed to know?' I replied. He looked at me again and said, 'Oh, white wine, why aren't you red?' Now, though, since we've caught this lieutenant, I'm prepared to lift suspicions from Boyev. His sacrifice is no longer required."

"And you would have had the conscience to accept it?"

Pevtsov frowned.

"A man with a conscience can be a citizen without one. But this matter is in the past now, which is why I told you the story. Thank God, it won't be necessary. We can forget it."

Ivan Dmitrievich was silent.

Pevtsov poured the sherry he had not drunk back into the bottle and then returned it and the glasses to the bookshelf.

"You're right, Mr. Putilin, it is too soon to celebrate victory. After all, we still don't know who stood behind the murderer. And anyway, the situation in the city is such that in the next few days we must be prepared for anything. Do you know, by the way, that as of last night officers from both gendarme divisions will be spending the night in the barracks?"

A month before, at this very hour—although then twilight had fallen earlier—Ivan Dmitrievich had seen a wolf running down Nevsky. It had been deserted, and he was returning home from work when he saw it. His wife, though, had her doubts when Ivan Dmitrievich told her the story, and at work not a single person believed it, although they nodded, said yes, and oohed and aahed. He could tell from their eyes that they did not believe him. Indeed, how could a wolf come to be on the capital's principal thoroughfare? But he was! The Evil One had brought him. It was a real wolf, too, not a dog. A wolf's tail, a wolf's fur and paws, and a yellow wolfish glint in its eyes. It had trotted, in no hurry, down the quiet nighttime street, as if it were trotting through the forest, mangy and much too dirty for a werewolf—a natural-born wolf. The most frightening thing of all was seeing how cheerful its expression was, as if it were in search of entertainment, not gain.

Had the wolf been set loose on purpose to run through the city? To frighten the inhabitants, sow panic, undermine confidence in the authorities? Gibberish!

At Pevtsov's instruction, the valet had dusted off the piano and was now using a damp cloth to wipe off the leaves of the lemon tree damaged by the enraged lieutenant. A disturbing coziness descended upon the house.

To Ivan Dmitrievich, whose nerves were frayed and could be set off by the least little thing, his route through the drawing room seemed endless. Meanwhile, all of four steps delivered him to the bedroom.

Strekalova was lying with her face to the wall. Asleep? Or reminiscing? Not that it mattered. Suspicions and revenge had been set aside for later and she had perched at the edge of the bed, as she had doubtless lain with the prince, for fear of disturbing him with her large body and not even stirring when Ivan Dmitrievich covered her legs with her jacket. Suddenly he felt like kissing this woman, on the cheek or the back of her head, innocently, the way people kiss a sleeping child. Pity for this woman, who had raised her hand against the all-powerful Count Shuvalov, made his heart ache. He had always fallen in love with unfortunate women; for him love began not with admiration but pity. But how could he help her? Where were the clues? So what if the gendarmes were watching the prince's house; that didn't prove anything.

Again, for the umpteenth time, Ivan Dmitrievich glanced at the bell pull. Here it was, its gilded tail. Of course, a stranger might not have discerned it, especially in the dark. If he had, he would have cut it off in advance and that would have been the end of it. No, the murderer knew about the bell. . . . All of a sudden Ivan Dmitrievich was pricked with the presentiment that when the criminal was finally caught he, Putilin, should not expect any gratitude from Strekalova. Ordinary human gratitude, not the kind she had promised, which no decent man would accept. She would come to hate him yet, Ivan Dmitrievich, more, perhaps, than the murderer himself, because she thought her beloved a great man responsible for the fate of Europe and in his death saw the consequence of these destinies. Whereas he was quite ordinary, her prince. He sat at his desk rarely, at the card table more often, and everything about this case was simple.

They think they are standing on the seashore, whereas before them lies a pond. They imagine the wind's trace on the water, betokening a storm, whereas it is nothing but a pond-skater that has drawn a path gliding along the shore. There are no storms on ponds, but if all the water were to surge over that pond-skater, dragging with it Bakunin, the Turkish Sultan, the anarchists, the Pan-Slavists, the Polish conspirators, the officers of both gendarme divisions, and God knows who else, then even in this muddy puddle a wave could rise up that would wipe away everything in its path.

"Where are you going?" inquired Pevtsov lazily.

Without answering, Ivan Dmitrievich moved quickly toward the pantry, threw the bolt, and flung open the door. The prisoner hobbled out and reached tentatively for Ivan Dmitrievich's face. To a bystander it might have looked as if the lieutenant had spent long years in captivity, gone blind from the darkness, and was now attempting to recognize the features of his liberator by feel. In fact, he was trying to grab him by the nose again but thought better of it when Ivan Dmitrievich invited him into the drawing room.

"Well, what is it?" asked Pevtsov. "Did you remember who bit you?"

"To tell the truth, it was I who bit him," replied Ivan Dmitrievich

The lieutenant leapt toward the sofa and grabbed his saber. Raising it menacingly but holding it blade flat rather than blade forward, he evidently was considering whether or not to whack one of these two flatways on the back of the head.

Pevtsov jumped back, hand over fist, toward the study door so that he could hide there at any moment, but Ivan Dmitrievich stayed where he was.

"Scoundrel!" Pevtsov shouted at him. "Do you know what false testimony will get you?"

"No, Captain! It's the truth! But he was the first to do me injury. What would you have me do? I'm a civilian and not in the habit of fighting duels."

Ivan Dmitrievich related what had happened.

"Idiot!" shouted Pevtsov when he finally understood. "What a time to pick for settling scores! Do you know what Hotek suspects our Corps of? Tomorrow his dispatch will go out to Vienna, and he and Shuvalov may be here at any moment. What are we going to tell them?"

"The truth. There's no need to sacrifice innocent lambs, just find the murderer."

"You won't," the lieutenant predicted. "He's one of the people, and he's returned to the people. The people will hide him."

"And you're going the same place, you dimwit." Ivan Dmitrievich was rueful. "Get going. We'll sort this out ourselves."

The lieutenant pondered this, trying to decide whether he should take offense or let it go (he was rather limp after sitting in the pantry), and he was inclined to think that there was no point sticking his nose any further in this business.

"There will be war," he promised nastily as he sheathed his saber. "And then you'll think of me."

He was still padding down the hall when Pevtsov, standing over the sofa where Ivan Dmitrievich had calmly sprawled out and hanging over him like a decuman wave prophesied in a fierce whisper:

"I'll have you falling on your knees before me, you buffoon!"

II

The lieutenant dragged himself despondently across the street to the barracks' gate. The sky on that northern April evening held its light in abeyance. It was the time of year when people are still in the habit of going to bed early, as in winter, but cannot fall asleep right away, and the languor of thousands of bodies pulses through the city in an odd and troubling way.

In the barracks, Baron Hohenbruch's mongrel spawn bristled in stacks. Fresh grease glistened wetly on the breach mechanisms, and the barrels were neatly crammed with wooden plugs. The lieutenant glanced with hatred at these crutches. Someday their place would be taken by another rifle whose sole exemplar he had placed at home between two mirrors, so as to revel in the spectacle of their infinite likenesses, in ranks, like on report, receding into the distance.

The lieutenant unbolted the battalion chapel, lit a candle, and dropping to his knees, began to pray. Yes, he had murdered Prince von Ahrensburg in his thoughts. He had murdered him every night, but right now he begged forgiveness not for this sinful intention but because he had been too weak to accept the blame. After all, he could have given a speech at trial and it would have been in the papers.

The chapel was on the second story, and the floorboards were warm from the heating pipes that ran underneath them.

By an effort of will, the lieutenant called to mind the vague image of the unknown avenger and began praying for him to be delivered of his persecutors. A child's riddle surfaced in his memory: the lock is water, the key is wood, the hare has run away, and the fisherman is drowning. The meaning is this: that Moses struck his staff on the sea and the waters parted, the Jews were saved, and the Pharaoh drowned. The lieutenant had never seen this man, and he did not know him by name, but he prayed for his soul's salvation, this man whose sin of vengeance cast a mere shadow on his angelic purity. Kneeling in the empty and resonant chapel, the lieutenant pictured this soul as a white hare dodging as it raced to the sea. The pharaohs were catching up with him, stamping their boots.

"Help him, Lord," whispered the lieutenant.

The candle flame flickered and was put out by a sudden draft.

This sign could have been interpreted in various ways, but the lieutenant decided immediately that his plea to the heavens had been found wanting. He had no right to this kind of intercession because he had shown cowardice and given up, even though fate itself had indicated he should suffer for Russia's truth and might.

The lieutenant did not relight the candle. He left the chapel, went over to the window, and saw a carriage pulling away from the princely residence. The lantern in front flickered and was lost from view.

In the carriage, alone, like a lord, sat Junior Lieutenant Rukavishnikov. Pevtsov had sent him to the New Admiralty guardhouse. Languishing there was the unfortunate Boyev, who had already come up with a new name for himself. Now he was Kerim-Bek, the Sultan's secret agent, who had slit the throat of Bulgarian medical student Ivan Boyev and commandeered his documents. Kerim-Bek had come to Petersburg on secret assignment from the Sultan to murder the Austrian ambassador, the consul, or at least the military attaché in order to sour relations between Austria-Hungary and Russia, for accord between them threatened the integrity of the Ottoman Empire. The cowardly Kerim-Bek had chosen the easiest option and ended Prince von Ahrensburg's life.

"Kerim-Bek," repeated Boyev, trying to lend his mild and distracted look an expression of Asiatic cruelty.

"Kerim-Bek" was the name of the Turkish officer who had been billeted in their house twenty years before. Fat and cheerful, this Turk had walked around the village slashing the skirts of the women he met with his yataghan. His favorite pastime had been firing small shot at dog weddings.

The carriage came to a halt at the guardhouse, and Rukavishnikov ran in to see the chief of watch. At that moment Boyev was questioning the Tatar guard through his barred window about the details of the Muslim confession. The guard whispered in reply:

"No eating pork."

At the Corps de Garde, sabers, swords, and daggers confiscated from arrested officers were hanging on the marble columns all around. The chief of watch led Rukavishnikov past them and down the hall. The officers in their cells were sleeping on pallets brought them from home, but there was no one to bring a pallet for Boyev. After clarifying the matter of pigs, he lay down on his bare, filthy mattress, which was spattered like a hyena, and began recalling his native village. The mountains, the vineyards, the girls walking from the spring with their jugs. At best he might get there only after hard labor and Siberia. He thought about his native village, and strange though it seems, even that fat Kerim-Bek, who had aroused mortal hatred in his childhood and later, he now recalled almost with tenderness, as a part of that life to which he must say goodbye forever. Forgotten by everyone, rotting away under a stranger's name, Boyev lay perfectly still on the stinking mattress, feeling how decisively this name was crushing his soul and squeezing out his paltry conceit, to say nothing of the turmoil and the filth, so badly it hurt, but leaving behind his memories of childhood and his love for his native land.

Keys jangled on an iron ring, and the lock clanked. The gendarme subaltern entered the cell along with the chief of watch.

"Kerim-Bek?" he asked. "By order of Captain Pevtsov, follow me!"

They went out and climbed into the carriage, and the driver whipped the horses.

And there, where they were going, under the lighted windows of the house on the Street of Millions, a man, fat-cheeked and thick-lipped, wearing a greatcoat with the tabs of the Department of Surveys, was dawdling on the sidewalk. At last, summoning all his courage, he walked up the steps and rang the bell.

III

The blood-spotted bandage the lieutenant had torn off his bitten hand was lying under the table in the drawing room. It lay there as a sign that everything visible has a secret meaning. When he heard the bell, Pevtsov kicked it under the sofa with his boot and hurried to the door. Ivan Dmitrievich followed behind, in no hurry. There was no point rushing; from the cautious, weak tinkling of the bell it was not hard to guess that this could not be Shuvalov.

The valet, heading them off, opened the door. A man wearing the uniform of the Department of Surveys blinked in bewilderment.

"Senka? You, you son of a bitch?"

"Me, master."

"Look who you're serving nowadays! Oh you!"

The new arrival flicked the valet across the nose and only then noticed in the distance Pevtsov's epaulets and Ivan Dmitrievich modest gray jacket.

"What do you want?" asked Pevtsov rudely.

"I humbly beg your forgiveness." The visitor bowed and scraped. "I have urgent need of His Grace, so to speak."

"Come in," Ivan Dmitrievich invited him. "Mr. Strekalov, if I'm not mistaken?"

"How do you know me?"

"I am Putilin. Chief Inspector of Police."

Ivan Dmitrievich led the dumb-struck Strekalov to the prince's study, inasmuch as in the drawing room his voice might be heard by his wife. He submitted without a murmur. As he entered the study, Ivan Dmitrievich released the trip latch and deftly slammed the door in Pevtsov's face.

"I must have an utterly private conversation with His Grace, so to speak," mumbled a frightened Strekalov.

"Prince von Ahrensburg is dead," said Ivan Dmitrievich. "He was murdered last night by persons unknown."

Strekalov covered his mouth with his open hand.

"It was not I." His voice was hoarse through his fingers. "Mr. Putilin, it was not I!"

"Why did you come here?"

"I have . . . I had a conversation . . . of a purely personal nature. . . ."

"Answer me! Or I'll have you arrested."

Strekalov had been holding his hand in his pocket and from there came the cautious rustle of paper being crumpled.

"What do you have there? Give it over!" ordered Ivan Dmitrievich. "Well?"

A piece of paper crumpled into a ball and ripped along the edges—another minute and Strekalov would have ripped it to bits. A letter. The sense was this: Mr. Strekalov, your spouse has been perfidiously seduced by Prince von Ahrensburg, the Austrian military attaché, and you, Mr. Strekalov, if you treasure your honor, must take vengeance on the seducer. Let the cuckold strike him in the chest with his horns, and they will fall off. . . . There was no signature.

"It was not I," whined Strekalov. "I did not strike . . ."

According to him, the postman had brought the letter the day before yesterday, and since then it had been lying in the maid's room. Just an hour before, upon his return from Tsarskoye Selo, Strekalov had read the letter and rushed immediately to the Street of Millions—to challenge the prince to a duel and at the same time to verify whether or not Katya was here.

"Katya, I see," noted Ivan Dmitrievich, "Ekaterina. . . ."

He surveyed the cuckold. He did not resemble a raging bull. What kind of duelist could he be? He imagined himself in his place. What would he do? Well, he would drive his wife out first thing, that was clear. Then he could use the lieutenant's method: grab his nose, the scoundrel's nose! In public! And that would put an end to the prince's career. Who needs a diplomat going around with a crushed nose?

However, Strekalov was scarcely capable of even such an action. Why had he come? And suddenly the light went on.

"How much did you hope to get from the prince in recompense?" asked Ivan Dmitrievich.

"I?"

"So you wouldn't create a scandal. . . . Ten thousand?"

"Good God!" Strekalov was horrified.

In his fury he seemed to be rejecting not the idea itself but merely the amount of the demand.

The door was flung open. It was Pevtsov, who had obtained the key to the study from the valet, opened the lock from the outside, and now strode toward Ivan Dmitrievich.

"That, gracious sir, I will not tolerate!"

Without replying, Ivan Dmitrievich looked at Strekalov threateningly, holding the letter by the corner with two fingers, like a dead bird by its wing.

"And you believed this pasquille? This slander?"

He flung the letter aside contemptuously, taking note, however, where the sheet of paper fell.

"Your spouse is guilty of nothing. Hurry home and get down on your knees before her. On your knees, and beg forgiveness for insulting her with your suspicion!"

"I haven't insulted her. She wasn't at home."

"And the lady in the prince's bedroom?" interjected Pevtsov. "That sturdy brunette. Is that not she?"

'Katya? She's here?" exclaimed Strekalov, trying to run out of the study after Pevtsov.

He raced to the foyer, but wheels and hooves were already rumbling at the entrance.

"Ekaterina!" Strekalov called out meekly.

Ivan Dmitrievich held him back by the sleeve.

"She has not been here! The captain is toying with you. Go to the kitchen, and after His Excellency passes through here, go home quietly. Step lively!"

Receiving a shove in the back for greater speed, Strekalov dashed down the hallway obediently.

Ivan Dmitrievich had time to make sure the bedroom door was tightly shut before Shuvalov walked into the drawing room with Pevtsov, who was explaining that they would be bringing the criminal in any minute. Lagging a little behind was the Chief of Gendarmes' adjutant.

"Congratulations, congratulations," said Shuvalov, interrupting Pevtsov. "Tomorrow to my report—my final report, thank God—I will attach a petition for your promotion. You shall be a lieutenant colonel. How old are you?"

"Thirty-four, Your Excellency."

"How about that, Captain? Not bad, a lieutenant colonel at thirty-four, is it? I think Hotek will see to getting you an Austrian order."

"I will not accept a reward from someone who has insulted our Corps."

"I am delighted to hear that. Then we will give the little cross to Mr. Putilin. You, I trust, will accept it?"

"Yes," Ivan Dmitrievich shrugged. "If they give it."

"Now tell me everything exactly as it happened," ordered Shuvalov.

"You see," Pevtsov began mumbling, "there have been a few changes. You and I need to speak alone. Shall we go into the study, Your Excellency?"

When they returned five minutes later, not a trace remained of the Chief of Gendarmes' philosophically playful mood. To Ivan Dmitrievich he had one thing to say: "The flea market!"

Hotek had already entered the drawing room. Bald, long-faced, and gaunt, something halfway between a deck chair and a gigantic grasshopper, he nodded to Shuvalov and surveyed the others with an expression of vile omniscience on his powdered, aged face. He seemed to know some dirty secret about each one of them. A great power that extended from the Alps to the Carpathians and had, as did Russia, a two-headed eagle in its crest, a symbol of its power over East and West, the homeland of waltzes and the nationalities question, at the slightest provocation baring its rusty sword with the martial carelessness of aged empires—this power had entered in the person of Count Hotek and sat down on the sofa, dousing Ivan Dmitrievich with such a chill that he considered it best to move away.

"I am obliged to state the following," pronounced Hotek with the haughty deliberateness of a grandee that always irritated Ivan Dmitrievich in public speeches by official personages.

This deliberateness was supposed to demonstrate that not only the meaning of the words uttered but the very fact of their utterance as well merited attention and respect.

"Naturally, Count, I have every confidence in you," continued Hotek after a pause, "however, an ambassador's confidence has as its limit his monarch's honor. I shall not cross this limit by so much as an inch. I need to hear the confession from the murderer's lips myself."

"And so you shall," Shuvalov assured him.

The cracked glass in the window began to whimper from the clatter of hoofs, and the horses by the porch, upset, began to neigh. It was Rukavishnikov delivering Boyev. Holding his bared saber at his shoulder, Rukavishnikov led the prisoner into the drawing room. All of a sudden it got very quiet. Boyev pressed both arms to his chest in Oriental fashion and silently greeted those gathered according to all the rules of etiquette accepted in some Bukhara bazaar, or so it seemed to Ivan Dmitrievich.

Pevtsov assumed a dignified air and viewed the work of his own hands with delight. After admiring him for a moment, he snatched one of the chairs and placed it to one side.

"Please!"

Without looking at anyone, majestically and indifferently, like a sacrificial animal prepared for the slaughter and given a potion to drink so that it will not kick and spoil the holiday, Boyev crossed the drawing room and sat down. Rukavishnikov stood behind him, never lowering his saber.

When he was already sitting on his chair, Boyev at last recalled the greeting he was supposed to utter upon entering, and he said quietly, *"Salaam alaikum."*

No one responded.

Hotek listened dispassionately to Pevtsov, who was singing like a nightingale, recounting who the murderer was and why he had committed the crime. An agent of the Sultan who had slit the throat of a Bulgarian student, and so forth. Listening to this raving, Ivan Dmitrievich consoled himself with the thought that Boyev was expeditious, a temporary means. Later they would release him and perhaps even reward him for his service.

The Bulgarian was already answering Pevtsov's questions—in Russian but with an accent that might well be taken for Turkish. Yes, that was all correct, and he, Kerim-Bek, was prepared to confirm this under oath.

"You will swear in court," said Pevtsov hastily.

He had not envisaged, somehow, that he might have need of such a thing as a Koran.

"No, let him now," commanded Hotek.

"Your Excellency!" his adjutant addressed Shuvalov. "The caretaker in our building is a Tatar. If you allow me, I'll dash out!"

Consent was given, and the adjutant ran outside, jumped into the carriage, and raced off to get the caretaker's Koran.

Pevtsov continued the questioning. After several fencing lunges that reminded Ivan Dmitrievich of exercises with a stuffed dummy, he wielded the final, mortal blow:

"And so, do you admit that you are guilty of the murder of Prince Ludwig von Ahrensburg?"

"I admit it. I killed him."

"Well, Count? Did you hear?" asked Shuvalov gloomily.

Leaning on his cane, Hotek rose, walked over to Boyev, and with an unblinking gaze stared at the bridge of his nose.

"Was it you who threw the rock at me?"

"A fanatic!" said Pevtsov.

Emboldened by this exclamation, Boyev nodded obediently. At the same moment, Hotek put his right foot forward and thrust his cane deftly and cruelly into Boyev's stomach, like a rapier.

Shuvalov half-rose.

"Have you no shame, Count!"

"It is you who have no shame," replied Hotek with the same regal delay after each word, as if it was not he who had just knocked the wind out of a man with his stick. "Where were your gendarmes? I could have been dead and lying in a coffin, too, like Ludwig."

Hunched over, Boyev was still trying to catch his breath. Ivan Dmitrievich felt that he, too, was gasping for air. His ears were ringing from hatred and a lack of oxygen. Through the ringing, from afar, came the conversation between Shuvalov and Hotek. They were squabbling tediously over whose court Kerim-Bek should appear before, the Russian or the Austrian.

"My sovereign is definitely going to insist," Hotek stressed.

"And my sovereign," replied Shuvalov, "in turn shall demand . . ."

Ivan Dmitrievich retrieved the bottle from the bookshelf and poured Boyev a little sherry, but he silently pushed away the hand with the glass because true believers, after all, do not drink.

"Oh, white wine, why aren't you red?" Ivan Dmitrievich quoted in a whisper.

Chapter 8

The Weather Takes a Turn for the Worse

Evening was shifting into night. The city was growing quiet.

The clock on the Municipal Duma's tower struck eleven times. Konstantinov counted the strikes and spat angrily at his feet. He was bone weary after making the circuit of a great many drinking establishments of every rank, from elegant restaurants with Gypsy choruses to modest but neat German beer halls, from famous taverns where writers and university professors celebrated their jubilees to miserable pubs that lacked even names. Napoleon III's golden profile had flashed under the gazes of footmen, doormen, and waiters, in the radiance of crystal chandeliers and the glow of kerosene lamps, candles, and oil lampions that stank of blubber, only to plunge back to the bottom of his pocket.

Meanwhile Konstantinov's own agents, Pashka and Minka, two vagabonds who did jobs for him in return for food, darted in and out of lodging houses and various market haunts. Ivan Dmitrievich had given no such instructions, but Konstantinov had decided to demonstrate some initiative, reckoning on the promised reward. Tucked into Minka's shirt was a piece of paper with an image of that same French gold piece. Unable to draw, Konstantinov had simply laid a piece of paper over the coin and run a pencil across the paper sideways until an impression resembling the stamping came through. "A Napoleon!" Konstantinov said gravely as he entrusted his artwork to his agents.

Alas, fortune failed to smile on any of the three. That evening, thirsty souls had paid with everything under the sun, including holey boots and sworn oaths, but not a single Napoleon. In one small, clandestine cellar where thieves gathered, someone had fingered Konstantinov as a police agent and he had had to hightail it. Elsewhere, a railroad contractor on a bender had tried to talk him into dancing naked with a pig for twenty-five rubles, and in a third some woman of questionable virtue whom Konstantinov had never seen before in his life had started shouting about how he had promised her silk stockings but had tricked her, the scoundrel. Konstantinov barely shook free of her and was ready to wash his hands of the whole affair and go home to bed. Many establishments were already shutting down for the night, but a light burned in the windows of a tavern by the name of America, and voices could be heard inside. Out of a sense of duty he decided to make one last attempt, so he went in, revealed his treasure to the waiter, and then, after receiving the usual reply, decided to sit down at a table to catch his breath and have a shot of something for the sake of the sleep that was in his immediate future.

The waiter made the rounds of the room, collecting money from customers. Suddenly he darted over to Konstantinov with a conspiratorial look and flicked a round gold piece with the familiar goatish profile down on the oilcloth.

"Where did you get that?" Konstantinov gasped.

"From that one there," the waiter reported in a terrified whisper, pointing to the corner.

There, all alone, a young, fair-bearded fellow of twenty or so was drinking his wine and finishing his sheep's brains and peas. He was wearing an oddly cut jacket, very tight and short, and the tails of a red neckerchief had slipped out from under his collar.

Konstantinov rose and crossed himself. His fingers were trembling. It was time to call upon the Archangel Michael, who delivered men from tremors, the way he'd been taught by Minka, who knew how to drive away drinking tremors with a prayer. To accomplish what he was contemplating, Konstantinov would need a steady hand.

"I'll circle around from the back," he told the waiter quietly, "and as soon as I grab him, you come over and punch him in the neck. Got it?"

"Aha."

"He'll go limp right away."

To show what he meant, Konstantinov gave himself a light punch to his tensed Adam's apple and then started maneuvering around the room, feigning an interest in the lithographs hanging on the walls. Depicted in one of them was a female savage dressed in a skirt of palm leaves, carrying a spear, and riding a tortoise—America. Her breasts jutted out to the sides, pointy, like a witch's.

Fairbeard finished his wine and was about to stand up, but Konstantinov prevented him. He boldly grabbed the fellow from behind, digging his chin into his shoulder, and tried to drop him back down on the chair. The waiter ran up, hit him where he'd been told—and punched Konstantinov in the eye. Fairbeard broke free, punched Konstantinov again for good measure, this time in the ear, and started upsetting chairs as he made for the exit. Konstantinov was right behind him.

He had been so sure the waiter would join the chase and even hail the whole gang from the tavern to follow, but a minute later, looking over his shoulder as he ran, he discovered he was pursuing the criminal alone. The street was deserted, and only three lamps in four were lit.

"Stop!" Konstantinov shouted without any particular hope and was amazed when Fairbeard heeded his call and stopped.

Not only did he stop, he started walking toward him, first slowly, then faster and faster. There still wasn't a soul around. Fairbeard was coming closer and closer, his fists windmilling. "He's going to kill me!" Konstantinov thought, and he tore off in the opposite direction, as fast as his legs would carry him.

Now he was the one running away. He was the one being chased. They ran a block in this order. Konstantinov was hoping to dodge into the America, but they had already locked up, and no one responded to his cry for help. Gasping for breath, he turned right, where there was a police booth that for some reason was empty. He had failed to lure his pursuer into a trap. They ran past it. Fairbeard was about to overtake him. His boots were thudding closer and closer, louder and louder. Not once did he call out, or swear, or curse, which made it even more terrifying. Summoning up his last strength, Konstantinov picked up his pace, but by then Fairbeard was only two steps away. He thrust his arm forward and with the palm of his hand slapped Konstantinov between the shoulder blades.

This is a well-known method for stopping someone running. You don't grab him from behind or hold him back but just the opposite—you give him an extra shove in the back. His feet can't keep up with his lurching body, the man loses his balance, and he falls.

That's exactly what happened to Konstantinov. He literally flew through the air a few paces and then slid forward on his paunch, his buttons rasping over the cobblestones, and finally rammed his nose into the curb. Blood dribbled down his lip, and Fairbeard, without even kicking his fallen foe, as Konstantinov, huddled in fear, had expected, straightened his neckerchief, turned on his heel, and ambled off. A receding whistle, a gentle Neapolitan tune, flitted like a butterfly between the stone giants until it was whisked away by the wind.

II

Night had moved in imperceptibly, and Shuvalov told Hotek that Prince Oldenburgsky, informed of the criminal's capture, would likely not be coming at such a late hour.

"That's only natural," Hotek replied with squeaky irony. "Why indeed should one alter one's agenda over such a trifle as the murder of a foreign military attaché?"

Shuvalov maintained a silence that was broken by Pevtsov's ingratiating voice. Addressing first one count and then the other, he began saying that now that nothing else threatened the good relations between the Winter Palace and Hofburg, it was time to agree on further action. The Turkish provocation was certain, yes, nonetheless it would be unwise to trumpet it all over Europe and thus throw down the gauntlet to Constantinople. In view of the current situation in the Balkans, such a political step would be premature. Therefore, rather than hand him over for public trial, they should lock Kerim-Bek up in a fortress.

Ivan Dmitrievich realized that Pevtsov did not have total confidence in his protégé and was fearful either of publicity or of lawyers' tricks.

"You may well be right, Captain," said Shuvalov, and he glanced inquiringly at Hotek.

"This could never happen at home in Vienna," Hotek replied, "but in Russia everyone is accustomed to maintaining silence, and the suggestion makes sense."

"He could be confined in some monastery," Pevtsov interjected.

"No." Hotek shook his head. "You must hand the murderer over to us."

"You?" Shuvalov was surprised.

"Not to me personally, of course. We will place him in Zielle Castle."

Ivan Dmitrievich listened but could not believe his ears. What if they never did find the real perpetrator? What then? His poor namesake was done for. In time they might release him from a monastery's dungeons, but from the castle at Zielle—not a chance in hell. He'd be buried alive.

"But the law. . . ." Shuvalov was about to begin.

"Cease and desist, Count," Hotek interrupted him. "Have any of you intelligent men noticed that the severity of Russia's laws is redeemed only by the nonbinding nature of their enforcement?"

Ivan Dmitrievich looked at Boyev, who had straightened up from the cane blow but had not taken his arms away from his stomach. The stubble that had grown in the last day was even more distinct on his pale face.

"Your Excellency," said Ivan Dmitrievich, cleverly looking right between the two counts, so that neither could tell which of the two he was addressing. "Will you permit me to ask the perpetrator a few questions?"

His calculation paid off. While Shuvalov was mulling it over, Hotek replied in the affirmative.

Smelling a rat, Pevtsov attempted to protest, but in vain. The Austrian envoy was one of those men who never changed his mind once it was made up.

"Let him ask," he smiled indulgently. "I know the police. In Petersburg, Vienna, Paris—they're all the same everywhere you go. These idlers find a dead dragon, cut out his tongue, and present it as proof that they have vanquished the monster."

Ivan Dmitrievich smiled as well—guiltily, as if admitting the truth of those words—and then walked over to Boyev.

"Mr. Kerim-Bek, would you be so kind as to tell me how you were able to penetrate this residence last night?"

Boyev gave Pevtsov a look of distress.

That afternoon, an officer of the gendarmes, having made the rounds of locksmiths with the key they had found in the front door lock, reported that one locksmith had recognized his handiwork and recalled the customer, who turned out to be Prince von Ahrensburg, a fact Pevtsov had failed to mention. He hastened to explain about the wax mold, and Boyev assented: "That's right."

Ivan Dmitrievich continued his questioning. He asked, Pevtsov answered, and Boyev assiduously repeated his answers. Eventually, Hotek began to suspect something, as Ivan Dmitrievich had supposed he would.

"Who is being questioned here, Captain? You or him?" He was angry. "I would ask you to go out in the hall."

"Your Excellency, do you have the right to give me an order?" Pevtsov asked respectfully.

"Count," said Hotek, turning toward Shuvalov. "Order him to get out."

"Get out," Shuvalov said through clenched teeth.

Swaggering, Pevtsov got out, and only then did Ivan Dmitrievich ask his main question: "Where exactly did you strike the prince?"

Hotek was sitting with his back to the door, which Pevtsov had left ajar so that he could peek through the crack and prompt him with gestures. He gripped himself by the throat, but it was dark in the hall, and Boyev, misreading his movements, answered:

"I stabbed him in the chest. . . . With a dagger."

Hotek's face darkened, and pale pink flakes of powder became visible on his forehead and cheeks. He was just about to start shouting, spraying saliva, stamping his feet, and dashing Pevtsov (who had come running in) over the head with his cane. But no! With a mild, all-knowing smile, he took a step toward Rukavishnikov and clapped him on the shoulder:

"Put your saber down, fool."

"Don't!" Boyev spoke quickly. "I killed him! I, Kerim-Bek. . . . By Allah, I swear!"

"But will you take an oath on the Gospels?" asked Hotek. "Will you kiss the cross?" And again, grabbing his cane, he raised its tip menacingly.

To his credit, Shuvalov quickly recovered. With a shout and bulging eyes he promised Pevtsov he'd place him under arrest and demote him to private for this deception. Then he took Hotek by the arm: my deepest apologies for this most shocking surprise.

Coldly moving away, Hotek nodded to Ivan Dmitrievich.

"I am extremely grateful to you."

"As am I!" Shuvalov readily chimed in. "I thank you for your service from the bottom of my heart." He gave Ivan

Dmitrievich a friendly embrace as he guided him toward the door. "A good night to you, Mr. Putilin! You have earned it honestly."

A ceremonial handshake, Shuvalov's hate-filled eyes, and a whisper: "The flea market!"

And one more equally decimating, incinerating look — Boyev's—aimed not at Hotek or Pevtsov and Shuvalov but at him, Ivan Dmitrievich.

The door slammed and he was left in the hallway.

From the drawing room came Hotek's squeaky voice.

"Forgive me, Count, but I am increasingly convinced that you and your men are complicit in Ludwig's murder. What is this pathetic farce with this Kerim-Bek person? Do you realize who you were intending to deceive in my person? I, however, am not one to hold a grudge and am prepared to keep all that has transpired to myself. Here are my conditions. First, the Slavonic Committee must be disbanded and its leaders deported from Moscow and Petersburg in three days' time. Second, an honor guard from the Preobrazhensky Regiment must accompany the coffin with Ludwig's body all the way to Vienna. Third . . .

Ivan Dmitrievich blood ran cold as he listened. Could Hotek be making such obviously unreasonable demands on purpose in order to have grounds for breaking diplomatic relations?

In asking Boyev that last question, Ivan Dmitrievich had not intended to fool Shuvalov and was not fooling himself; he knew what awaited him. Yes, the flea market. He was prepared. If it came to that, he would chase down drunkards, separate scrappers, and make sure cooking fires weren't lit on cold nights in unsuitable places and pipes weren't smoked just anywhere. In short, he would do the simple and honest work no great city can do without. Here he would have his monk's schema, his desert. His small arena in the very center of St. Petersburg—his hermit's plot. No fear, no medals. A clear conscience and the joys of family life. He had merely wanted to save this Bulgarian, and now look what had happened.

Ivan Dmitrievich pictured his friend the lieutenant in the somber ranks of the Preobrazhensky Regiment as they marched through the streets of Vienna behind the prince's coffin to a hail of apple cores. Now a rotten egg flies from the crowd and smashes into the order on his chest. Turning pale, he reaches for his saber and commands his men: "Follow me, boys!" And what then?

Maybe the wolf that had run through the capital that night a month before, maybe that was an omen. Maybe he had trotted down Nevsky so calmly because in fact there was no such boulevard in that location anymore. The city lay in ruins, destroyed by enemy artillery, deserted, like on a night in times of cholera. Maybe this was how Vienna, Moscow, and Prague looked now. The wolf feared nothing for there was no one to chase him away. He was hunting cats and feral pigs. His production allotment stretched from the Municipal Duma, where the rusty brown poodle Chuka had been blown to smithereens, all the way to Nikolaevsky Station. Its boundaries were marked by rivulets of urine. The wolves had divided up all Petersburg among them, and here and there a new administrative division coincided with the old boundaries between police precincts.

Wars don't just start between great powers, and the visions were only make-believe, ludicrous really, but they left Putilin with a dreary sense of the duality of existence. He, Ivan Dmitrievich, could be flung out the door like a pup, yet he felt as though Europe's fate were riding on him.

Listening to Shuvalov's incoherent attempt at explaining to Hotek that this was impossible, unthinkable, Ivan Dmitrievich took another stab at unraveling the thread of his reasonings. The prince had clearly been killed by someone close to him. They had tied him up to get him to say where the key to the trunk was. The trunk with the snake-ring latch. The prince did not tell them, though, because he was looking at one of his own and simply could not believe that someone on his side could kill him.

"Fifth," Hotek dictated his conditions (Ivan Dmitrievich had missed the third and fourth), firmly sweeping aside all objections, "I demand that the investigation of this case be assigned to the Austrian secret police."

All this excitement had exacerbated Ivan Dmitrievich's cold, but he was afraid of giving his nose a good blow and being discovered and put out on the street, so he blew very gently into his handkerchief, like the cook's son invited to join the master's children for their Christmas party. The moon appeared off and on in the tiny hall window, behind low, ragged clouds. The weather had taken a turn for the worse, and the wind had come up. Ivan Dmitrievich regretted not listening to his wife and leaving his umbrella behind. No doubt she was agonizing over this now!

The door creaked. He pressed up against the wall and a band of light spilled out of the drawing room but did not touch him. Boyev emerged and wended his way despondently toward the foyer. Ivan Dmitrievich did not call out to him.

A week before this he and his wife had been to the theater, to see a Russian operatic production, *Napoleon III at Sedan*.

The music struck up and the curtains parted. The Emperor bade farewell to his Andromache and went off to war, and then the action shifted to the Prussian camp. The Germans rolled an enormous cannon out on stage, loading it, moreover, not with an iron ball but with a ball cast in pure gold, and the chorus began calling on heaven that this shot, fired blindly, might with God's help find and lay low the Emperor of the French.

The orchestra rattled the chandeliers, but Ivan Dmitrievich was listening to his four best agents—whom he had rewarded for their service with free tickets to the theater—wheezing behind him, disgruntled. They had been counting on a different sort of reward, but they had also been afraid not to come.

The German cannon went off with a bang. "Fire into the bushes and may God find the culprit," whispered Konstantinov.

The Germans reached after the flying ball, and the lights went out. When they came back up they were illuminating the French camp, where the cardboard ball wrapped in gold foil had come crashing down. Zouaves in baggy red trousers picked it up and brought it to Napoleon III.

"Has the Sun fallen to the ground?" he wondered.

"No-o-o, no-o-o, no-o-o," the Zouaves sang in reply, explaining what was what.

Then, resting his foot on the ball, the Emperor launched into a mournful aria.

"Why?" he asked. "Why has the Almighty led death away from me? Why did He not accept my golden sacrifice? Or is it that there, in the eternally streaming ether, they know my heart, eaten away by my thirst for truth and good?"

"And my heart, too," thought Ivan Dmitrievich, gazing out the tiny hall window at the smoky edges of clouds drawn across the moon. "Do they know? There, in the eternally streaming ether?"

III

Only late that night did Sych reach the Volkovo cemetery and the Church of the Resurrection, where he had once served as stoker. The sanctuary was closed, but next door, in the little house where his old friend Savosin the sexton lived and traded in candles, lamps, and lamp oil through the church, there was a light in the window. Sych knocked and was recognized, let in, and favored with conversation.

They talked about life in general and about how, in particular, policemen were issued boots and a uniform by the state to last a certain length of time.

"And the fabric!" Sych boasted. "So sturdy, you could bounce billiard balls off it. The officers are jealous. I'll come see you tomorrow in my uniform and you can feel."

"They're the state's—not yours," Savosin replied. "The state gives you something, you see, and takes something else away. You'll have your uniform, but in that length of time there'll be nothing left of your boots but the uppers."

"Hey, just look what boots!" Sych took offense. "They'll wear like iron."

He started twisting and turning his foot, displaying the heel, the sole, and the drawing of the tuck.

Savosin meanwhile had gone back to counting his daily take. He was sorting coins, and copper and silver stacks of varying thicknesses and heights started rising on the table. At this, Sych finally remembered why he'd come, and he asked about the French gold piece.

Rummaging around in his drawer, Savosin took out a gold coin with the profile of Napoleon III.

"This one?"

"Exactly!" Sych grinned. "Give it over!"

In response Savosin made a tight fist around the coin, saying, "Leave a pledge."

"Have you lost your mind? What pledge do I have to give you? I'm the police."

"I won't give it to you without a pledge. We know your kind."

Sych was about to take the coin by force, but he glanced over at Savosin's offspring sitting in the corner, a healthy lad with a cheeky mug, thought better of it, and asked, "How much?"

"Twenty-five rubles."

"It's not even worth that much!"

"All right, twenty," Savosin relented.

After extensive haggling, they agreed on fifteen rubles in banknotes, but all Sych had with him was a half-ruble coin.

"Can I leave you my watch?" he offered in despair. "It's a good watch."

Savosin examined it and shook his head.

"Terrible watch. Leave something else."

"You monster! What, my jacket? You'd have me take that off? My cap?"

"Take it all off, that'll do it. The boots, too," Savosin commanded, pulling out from under the table a pair of old felt boots and a warm but sloppy jacket, an old woman's *katsaveika*.

Muttering dire curses, Sych undressed and pulled on the felt boots but refused the *katsaveika*, took the coin, and hurried off to the Street of Millions. He knew that on tough cases Ivan Dmitrievich remained at the scene of the crime late into the night.

Fortunately, he came across a cabbie right outside the cemetery fence. Sych recalled the precious half-ruble and called out, "Hey, Vanka!"

The cabbie didn't stop, just reined in his horses slightly, looking warily over his shoulder at the odd fellow dressed in only a shirt and felt boots who had come running through the cemetery gates.

"Street of Millions. I'll give you half a ruble," Sych promised excitedly, forgoing any bargaining, although, had he been so inclined, even at night he might have haggled him down to twenty kopeks. Thirty at most.

"And you have it on you, that half-ruble?"

"I do, I do. Have no doubt."

"Show me."

Sych showed him.

"Money in advance," said the cabbie, still driving at a walk.

With his left hand he took the half-ruble and with his right, at the very same moment, he whipped his horses and the cab sped off, disappearing around the corner. Sych tried to give chase but soon gave up.

With nightfall the air had chilled off, and an icy wind had blown in from the islands. The clouds' smoky edges drifted across the moon. Sych, wearing just a shirt, strode quickly down the street, thinking with secret relish how he would catch cold and fall ill and Ivan Dmitrievich would come see him at home, sit down on his bed, and say, "Sych, you never spared yourself or your health, therefore I forgive you Pupyr. I'm going to make you a deputy agent like Konstantinov."

In the air was the smell of imminent snow.

IV

Leaving the noisy streets behind, the student Nikolsky trekked down a dirty, unpaved lane, past blackened fences and wooden houses. At first they had balconies and annexes and were roofed in iron and stuccoed to look like stone, then came more modest ones faced in rough boards in a herringbone pattern, and finally came a row of simple log houses, more like huts, occasionally with a torch's reddish glow in the tiny windows. Here Nikolsky became harder to follow. To keep from being spotted in the same guise all the time, Pevtsov's detectives turned their coats inside out. These were special coats that could be worn either way: the right side was black, the wrong side a mousy brown.

Recently, yielding to his subordinates' entreaties, Shuvalov had allowed officers in the Corps de Gendarmes to appear in public in this designated dress, as their service required, but only if it was standard issue. He strictly forbade any get-ups that made it easier to get lost in a market crowd, for example. He considered that kind of masquerade inadmissible and harmful. Pevtsov had tried in vain to change his mind.

It was dark by the time Nikolsky walked into a small, low-slung, shingled house. A candle had been lit in the window, and through the partly drawn calico curtains the detectives could see a miserable rented room: a couch with a ragged blanket and no sheets, shredding wallpaper, and books scattered all over the floor. Nikolsky picked one up, leafed through it, and tossed it in the corner. They could see his silhouette in the next window over, where a kerosene lamp burned and a bald old man in a vest was dressing a dog pelt that lay on the table in front of him.

There were no streetlamps nearby, so their black coats melted into the darkness along with the blackened logs. The senior detective dug a rotten rag out of the round hole in the wall where the shutter pin went and put his ear to the hole.

Gradually, after a rambling conversation about kerosene and money not paid the last month for the room, a story began to unfold that, according to the old man, would be instructive for a future doctor like Nikolsky. The old man told him about the village of Evtyata, in New Ladoga District, Novgorod Province, where a rich muzhik by the name of Potapych had lived with his wife and mother-in-law. Due to advanced age, the mother-in-law had gone completely blind and could neither keep a house nor housekeep, but she still gobbled up more than her share, and Potapych, thoroughly sick of this, decided to see her off to the next world. He gathered poisonous toadstools in the forest, cooked them up, and served them. She ate, praising them. She was blind! She ate them and nothing happened. The next day Potapych fed her the toadstools again, and again nothing happened. She devoured them, relishing every bite. The third day, as he started sprinkling them into the pan, she walked up and screamed, "What are you cooking up for me, you son of a bitch?" The old woman was on to him.

"So what? So what if I am studying to be a doctor?" Nikolsky asked angrily. "What was the point to that story of yours? What's the conclusion?"

"The conclusion is this," the old man explained. "The toadstools there are good for you!"

Struck by this conclusion, Nikolsky went back to his room, lay down, and closed his eyes.

"He's asleep," one of the detectives whispered appreciatively.

"Without ever putting anything in his belly?" the other objected.

And indeed, five minutes later, Nikolsky suddenly jumped up, threw on his coat, went out, and with a quick step headed back toward the city center.

V

The front door slammed. Boyev left.

Ivan Dmitrievich was still standing in the hall, and in the darkness Junior Lieutenant Rukavishnikov, who had been sent to the kitchen for a drink of cold water for Shuvalov, crashed into him.

Pevtsov poked his head out of the drawing room at the noise.

"Hold onto him," he ordered.

Rukavishnikov had already recognized the man he had run into, but he obeyed without a murmur. He was Pevtsov's myrmidon. Konstantinov was Ivan Dmitrievich's deputy. There was a big difference.

Pevtsov dug his long filed nails into Ivan Dmitrievich's wrist.

"The flea market?" he hissed. "As inspector? Not likely! Sweeping up garbage is more like it."

He and Rukavishnikov led Ivan Dmitrievich to the front door and out on the steps, where Pevtsov gave him a stiff shove from behind. Ivan Dmitrievich went flying down the stairs and landed hard on all fours.

"No one saw anything," said Pevtsov mockingly.

That was the truth. The counts' coachmen were sitting on their boxes with their backs to them, the Cossack escort had taken shelter from the wind around the corner. The rising wind trumpeted down the Street of Millions, drowning out every other sound. A vision flashed before Ivan Dmitrievich of his wife, weeping, pawning her wedding ring, and his son Vanya asking her to buy a toy train and her being unable to because she had no money. And then a blinding vision of the police coachman Trofim leading his horses, Gaiety and Gryphon, out of his courtyard.

Everything had come crashing down, drowned out by this wind. He had no business here anymore. Pevtsov and Rukavishnikov were gone. Ivan Dmitrievich felt for the bell pull in the air, grabbed on, and rose to his feet. He wiped his palms on his trousers and dusted off his pants, then he climbed the stairs and peeked into the foyer, where the prince's greatcoat stirred all by itself on its hook, as if the deceased's spirit had had a mind to put on his old clothes. And what of it? If the prince, still alive the night before, had in fact already been dead, then if he was dead he might well be alive. It was stark raving lunacy!

Ivan Dmitrievich didn't know that Strekalov had never gone home and was hiding under the greatcoat, so he shook his head, chasing out the hallucination. The greatcoat fell still. Rukavishnikov hurried from the kitchen with the drink of cold water for Shuvalov. Trying not to make a sound on the tile floors, Ivan Dmitrievich stepped back onto the front porch, where he found the Preobrazhensky lieutenant, who clicked his heels:

"Mr. Putilin, arrest the avenger. He stands before you!"

Under no circumstances could he let this man into the drawing room. "Blast you both!" thought Ivan Dmitrievich, referring to Pevtsov and Shuvalov. He sat down on the top step and patted the space beside him.

"Have a seat. Let's talk."

From the drawing room, muffled by the windows, spilled the gentle melody of a waltz; the keys told the story of the beautiful blue Danube. This was Hotek, who, having presented Shuvalov with his ultimatum, had sat down to the piano.

The lieutenant listened and lamented. God forbid they should have to force the Danube with Hohenbruch's rifles. He pulled his flask out from his greatcoat.

"How about a swig, after all?"

They drank straight from the flask, like adversaries in a window niche, but instead of butter they had pickled mushrooms with it, each extricating a mushroom with his fingers. Then Ivan Dmitrievich sealed the bottle up again and stuck it back in his pocket. Who knew what life would bring or what you'd be eating with your vodka?

"They're bound to give you a medal for me, and here you're being stingy with those nice mushrooms," the lieutenant reproached him.

Ivan Dmitrievich replied that he wouldn't accept a medal. "The true cross? You wouldn't?"

"No. It would burn a hole through my chest."

"Then listen." The lieutenant was moved. "Go over to my rooms tomorrow." He told him the address. "My batman will give you my rifle. My beauty! You can go hunting, the sweetest of occupations. And at the trial you can tell everyone how well it fires."

Ivan Dmitrievich was touched as well.

"Allow me to embrace you, you dimwit!"

They embraced, and the lieutenant vowed that after he died, when he was in heaven and Ivan Dmitrievich was in hell, he, the lieutenant—his word as an officer!—would intercede for him with God, and if his entreaty failed, he himself would abandon heaven's tabernacles and go to hell, so that there at least they could be together, inseparable.

"It's time!" He stood up. "Let's tell everyone."

Ivan Dmitrievich stood up, too, letting him go first, when a strange figure appeared at the end of the street.

"Look! What's that over there?"

The lieutenant took a good look. Floating toward them — rapidly, and, what was most striking, utterly without a sound, like a ghost, a couple of feet off the ground, swaying in the night air—was a blurry white blot.

Half a minute later it was close enough for Ivan Dmitrievich to make out a head on top and below, under the blot, legs. Agent Sych, vindicating his name—"Owl"—was flying soundlessly down the street dressed in only his shirt. The next moment it became clear why his footsteps had not been heard on the cobblestones. He was wearing felt boots.

"Who swiped your clothes?" Ivan Dmitrievich asked briskly. "Not Pupyr, I hope? And where are your boots?"

"I left everything as a pledge," Sych gasped, breathing heavily. "At the Church of the Resurrection." He held out his fist, opened it, and smacked his lips sweetly, blissfully. "For this here!"

Still not believing this fantastic good fortune, Ivan Dmitrievich first tested the coin with his teeth. Gold! He embraced Sych and kissed both his cheeks.

"Good work! You're a hero. . . . Who gave you this?"

"Savosin the sexton."

"And who gave it to him?"

The lieutenant listened with interest but said nothing. He didn't know what this was about, thank God, otherwise he would have declared that he himself had bought a candle for this gold piece at the Church of the Resurrection.

"Someone. I think," Sych stalled as he realized with horror his mistake. The gold had blinded him. "Someone was generous with it. I think."

"Idiot!" Ivan Dmitrievich began hollering like a man possessed. "Run back! Ask him who gave it to him. What kind of . . . Why are you standing there?"

"Give me the coin or else the fifteen rubles' pledge," said Sych, almost in tears.

This was the final straw for Ivan Dmitrievich:

"Listen to that! He wants fifteen rubles! You find out first."

"Running there and back all naked . . . I'm sure to catch my death."

"A fool's feet are always warm. Well?"

Sych snorted and sulked and then very deliberately, dragging his felt boots, wandered off to execute the order. He was hunched over, and his shoulder blades poked out resentfully underneath his shirt.

"On the double!" commanded Ivan Dmitrievich.

Sych twitched but did pick up the pace, though he did not start running, which took all his courage.

Then Ivan Dmitrievich, recalling his own provincial, weed-filled childhood, stuck three fingers into his mouth. His wild, highwayman's whistle rollicked down the Street of Millions. The ambassador's, the gendarmes', even the Cossacks' horses, which were inured to everything, shied and neighed, the lieutenant took a step back, the Cossacks dashed out from around the corner, and Sych himself took a great leap and flew headlong toward the Volkovo cemetery.

At that moment the drawing room piano fell silent, stopping short of a bar. A woman's piercing scream penetrated the double window and burst out on the street. Ivan Dmitrievich recognized Strekalova's voice.

"Murderer!" she cried. "Murderer!"

That meant she had woken up, come out of the bedroom, and seen Shuvalov. Ivan Dmitrievich was horrified, since it was he who had awakened her. Idiot! Why had he whistled? What now awaited this woman who had dared called the Chief of Gendarmes a murderer? Prison? A convent? A madhouse? This was not the time to ponder, though. Ivan Dmitrievich rushed to her assistance with the lieutenant at his heels.

Chapter 9

The Italians and Turks Get in on the Act

Blood was dripping from Konstantinov's nose, but not all that freely. He got back on his feet. His bottom coat button had been ripped off and his knees were muddy. The eye the tavern waiter had punched so accurately had begun to swell, but otherwise he was all right.

He felt for the gold coins in his pocket and was relieved to ascertain that both were where they belonged. To the first, found by Ivan Dmitrievich in the prince's bedroom, had been added one more identical to it. Konstantinov had no plans to return it to the waiter; this would be his penalty for the bodily harm inflicted. The two Napoleons clinked reassuringly.

Clouds feathered the sky, and a northerly wind was blowing snow around. It was hard to imagine the almost summer-like sun that had warmed the air so recently. Konstantinov gathered a little snow from the curb and applied it to the bridge of his nose. The bleeding stopped completely. He wanted to search the pavement for his coat button but quickly thought better of it. He had to hurry because his offender was getting away, whistling a cheerful Neapolitan tune and threatening to drop out of sight altogether.

Konstantinov ran after the whistle like a gopher.

Snowflakes of spring, wet and fragile, melted on his brow and cheeks, but the snow kept falling, and the wind was turning it into a real blizzard. Fairbeard was striding forward calmly, his broad back disappearing and then reappearing in the snowstorm. Konstantinov did not lag behind. He stole along the walls of buildings, hid behind water pipes, and dove into gateways, trying not to violate the rules of outside surveillance Ivan Dmitrievich had laid down for him. From time to time he would press one of the Napoleons to his battered eye as he walked, but he could tell that wasn't going to help. The waiter had had a heavy hand.

Streets, canals, bridges. The ice had broken up on the Neva; he could hear the rumbling in the darkness. Fleecy white clouds were rolling by, and the piles by the embankments were listing. Konstantinov realized that Fairbeard was headed for the port. Soon they passed a barrier, then storage sheds, shops, warehouses, and very rarely a lit but moribund streetlamp. "It was right around here we were just chasing Vanka Pupyr," Konstantinov remembered.

Past enormous mounds of coal, stacks of logs, sacks piled high, empty boxes, and some clever wire cages—God only knew what they shipped in those contraptions—they moved toward the berths. Fairbeard sprang up a ramp to a small sleek vessel with a long, thin, samovarish smokestack and vanished among the deck structures. Konstantinov could barely make out the snow-obscured Latin letters on the side of the boat: *Triumph of Venus.*

An hour later he was at Ivan Dmitrievich's apartment talking to his wife.

"Why are you asking me where he is?" she fumed. "I should be the one asking you!"

"Well, if he's not here, I'll leave."

"And just where are you headed? To a wife nearby?"

"What wife? I'm going to look for him."

"Walking or riding?"

"Riding what? A gray wolf?" Konstantinov was good and angry now, too. "You can't get horses at the office. They're always out, or not fed, or not shod, and the kopeks our brother in the treasury gives out for cabs won't get you far."

"In that case go into the courtyard and rouse our driver. Do you know where our driver lives?"

"Yes."

"Tell him to harness the horses and bring Ivan Dmitrievich home if you find him. My husband spares the horses but not himself."

"I don't think so. I'm better off on my own two feet," said Konstantinov.

No matter how much he would have liked to take the carriage, he knew he'd get a hefty crack on the ear from any chief for that kind of brass.

Then at least take him something to eat."

To this Konstantinov agreed. He accepted the linen bag of sandwiches and hurried off to the Street of Millions, hoping to catch Ivan Dmitrievich still there. If he wasn't at home that night, there was nowhere else he could be.

II

After dinner, Baron Cobenzel, who had taken a modest brick house on Vasilievsky Island, went down to his half-basement, where he had set up a firing range. He hung a fresh target, adjusted the lighting, and then selected one of the dozens of polished cases lying in a special cupboard. He removed, inspected, and loaded a pistol, thinking as he did so about what penalty to exact upon himself should the accuracy of his aim not achieve his established threshold. Actually, this rarely happened. He easily extinguished a candle with a bullet and could hit a balloon dancing in a fountain stream, and if he had an audience he willingly performed other tricks of this sort. He had also mastered an absolutely fantastic trick: by choosing the angle of fire very precisely, he could make a bullet (a round one, naturally) ricochet off water, but for some reason that sleight-of-hand, although it required exquisite artistry, never impressed people very much. Just as there are poet's poets, Cobenzel had become a marksman's marksman. In all Petersburg, only a few officers—plus Baron Hohenbruch, a famous gunsmith who himself was incapable of hitting even a watermelon at ten paces—were capable of appreciating Cobenzel's art.

Cobenzel had begun target practice when he was eleven and his father died in a duel. However, he never did challenge the murderer to a duel and shoot him. Very quickly Cobenzel discovered that he was incapable of firing at a live target. His eyes would begin to well up straightaway, his breath grow short, and his hands tremble. Later Cobenzel saw in this Divine Providence. The Almighty, having rewarded him with a marvelous feel for weapons, had taken care that this gift could not be used for evil.

Bang! As expected, the bullet tore the paper at the very center of the black square. Unusual though today had been, Cobenzel nonetheless intended to meet his evening quota of seven shots.

After he had fired the last, he took a five-kopek coin and placed it over the tears in the target. This time two were not covered by the copper circle. Not knowing whether to be vexed or to consider it natural, that Ludwig's death had thrown him off balance, Cobenzel set about cleaning the pistol, at which point a courier arrived from Hotek. He reported that the gendarmes had captured the murderer and that the count himself had left for the Street of Millions and had ordered Cobenzel to go to the embassy and wait for him there, so that they could compose a detailed report together upon his return.

At the embassy, lights were lit in all the windows, and bands of illumination leaked out around the draperies, which had been lowered in mourning. By the entry stood a guard, a Russian soldier with a rifle that had yet to be refitted according to Baron Hohenbruch's system. Cobenzel sprang to the sidewalk and noticed that next to his was another carriage from which had emerged a heavy, mustachioed man wearing a red fez.

"Monsieur Cobenzel," he said in French. "How good that I found you!"

This was Yusuf Pasha, secretary at the Turkish embassy. A year before they had been introduced at some diplomatic reception but had not exchanged as much as ten words since.

"Monsieur Cobenzel, could you spare me half an hour?"

They ascended the stairs together and passed through the hall, where in flickering candlelight Ludwig's closed black coffin could be seen on a table. At its head stood the embassy chaplain holding a prayer book. Cobenzel ushered his visitor into his office and shut the door.

"Did it not seem to you that the guard in front of the entrance had a suspiciously pure-bred face?" asked Yusuf Pasha. "In my opinion, that is no soldier but an officer wearing a different uniform."

"All the more reliable a guard," said Cobenzel.

"But what if it is a gendarme placed there to keep an eye on you?"

"We have nothing to hide from Count Shuvalov. If he takes no pity on his own men, let them freeze."

"Yes, simply horrid weather," Yusuf Pasha concurred. "I was recently in Constantinople and returned by sea, via

Italy. The apple trees are in blossom there now. A marvelous country. So sad your emperor lost it. In Genoa I embarked on an Italian ship, *Triumph of Venus.* Can you imagine a Russian or German vessel with such a name? That would be absurd."

The north wind that had blown in as night fell shook the windows in their frames, and the heavy draperies billowed. Somewhere in the embassy's depths, a window made a banging sound as it flew open. Papers touched by the draft fluttered on his desk.

In his office, which he had dreamed of occupying long ago but had in fact moved into only half a year before, Cobenzel was transformed beyond recognition, as he himself was very much aware. Looking at him in the mirror was a stranger's face, different from the face in his mirrors at home. At times he felt that here he could even fire at a live target.

"You and I are of the same rank," said Yusuf Pasha, "so I shall permit myself to get down to business without further pleasantries."

Cobenzel silently twiddled his fingers, showing that he had no intention of making the first move.

"Monsieur Cobenzel, are you aware that extremely bizarre—no, I would put it even more bluntly—monstrous rumors are spreading through Petersburg about a provocation allegedly carried out against our embassy? They're saying some monk stole up to the window of the ambassadorial apartments and released a live pig inside."

"A pig?"

"You know, of course, that Mussulmen consider this animal—"

"Amazing!" Cobenzel interrupted him. "Three hundred years ago, a very similar story was told about Ivan the Terrible. Briefly, it went like this. The Tsar sent the Sultan a brocade bag embroidered in gold and decorated with precious stones, but when they opened it to take out the rest of the gifts, the bag turned out to be stuffed with dried pig manure."

"Is that true?" Yusuf Pasha asked with interest.

"Of course not. Myriad legends circulated about Ivan the Terrible. Why, did they really release the pig?"

"Of course not."

"Then, forgive me, but what is upsetting you?"

"People are saying that this monk has been taken into hiding at the instruction of the Russian authorities."

"People say all sorts of things."

"But a wild rumor like that doesn't just come out of nowhere! Someone undoubtedly took care to see it spread around the capital."

"To what end?"

"You really don't understand?"

"No."

"The investigation is being pushed strongly toward the notion that Prince von Ahrensburg was murdered by our agents, with the intent of sowing discord between Emperor Alexander and Emperor Franz Josef. This rumor benefits only those who arranged the prince's murder."

"And you suspect someone?"

"Yes," Yusuf Pasha replied in a firm whisper. "The pig rumor was spread in order to drown out the other, true rumor. Which is that the deceased had connections with Russian revolutionaries abroad. You must understand me correctly, Monsieur Cobenzel, but people are saying that the prince, at the behest of your government, which is trying to weaken Russia, supplied money to conspirators in Petersburg itself. Now you judge for yourself whom his death served."

"Forget about the pig and all the rest," Cobenzel tried to calm his visitor. "The gendarmes have captured the murderer."

"So quickly?" Yusuf Pasha could not hide his disappointment.

"This does not please you?"

"What a thing to say! And precisely who is he?"

"I don't know yet. The ambassador will return and tell all."

"This is very, very, encouraging news," said the Turk sourly.

"Even if Count Shuvalov has assigned us a gendarme in another guise"—Cobenzel nodded out the window, in the direction of the guard pacing in front of the entry—"I'm prepared to forgive him these minor ruses. He has a right to them since it was his men who captured the criminal the very same day."

Yusuf Pasha rose.

"In that case, you will forget our conversation."

"I cannot promise you that, but I shall try."

Cobenzel rose as well and, as protocol prescribed, escorted his colleague to the middle step of the front stairs. Here he remained, while Yusuf Pasha, descending the bottom three steps, made for his carriage.

"By the way," he said after he had climbed onto his seat. "I know, Monsieur Cobenzel, that you are a superb marksman. Baron Hohenbruch was telling me about you. He is a good friend of yours, apparently, is he not?"

"Yes, we are friends."

"In a few days our experts are going to be conducting trials of his rifles. If you will allow me, I shall send you an invitation. I hope you will afford us the pleasure of admiring your art, about which such wonders are told."

Yusuf Pasha bowed in farewell and tapped the driver on the back as the carriage moved off. Cobenzel, abandoning protocol, quickly ran down the stairs and walked alongside.

"You have acquired the rifle patent from Hohenbruch? For the Turkish army?"

"In any event, he has proposed that we do so."

"But how could that be? The Russians have bought his system. He does not have the least right!"

"Baron Hohenbruch made such improvements to it that it is now a different system." Yusuf Pasha bowed once again, and a minute later his red fez disappeared around the corner.

Cobenzel stood for a while in the brow-chilling wind and then returned to the embassy. Startled again by the draft, the candle flame beside the coffin wobbled. In the hallway one of the windows had been pushed open by a squalling gust. The trees were very noisy, and their bare branches sliced the air with a plaintive whine.

Cobenzel proceeded to his office feeling a sudden, soothing composure wash over him. If he had fired right now, the coin would have covered all seven tears. Yes, Ludwig had had to die, that was his destiny. Otherwise how could he have looked Prince Oldenburgsky and the generals from the Ministry of

War in the eye? Ludwig had been prone to a variety of sins, but a lack of honor was not among them. He had used all his influence to help Hohenbruch settle his model on Russia, and now his friend had decided to make even more money off of the very nation with whom the Russians would be at war in the near future—the Turks.

A steady, melodious murmur came from the hall. The chaplain was reading from the prayer book.

"Such was his destiny," Cobenzel told himself as he gazed into the mirror.

Chapter 10

A Night of Revelations

The prince did not let Strekalova spend the night, as a rule, but on the rare occasions when he did, he asked that she leave early in the morning. He himself fell asleep immediately after their lovemaking, and she usually did not sleep but lay beside him as quiet as a mouse admiring her sleeping lover. If she did doze off, then it was not for long, with the thought he might suddenly awaken in the middle of the night, light the lamp, and see her with her mouth hanging open unattractively in her sleep and a trickle of saliva on her pillow. In addition, her husband was always accusing her of snoring.

That night, though, all these worries dropped away, and she fell into a profound sleep. Very weak, she slept so soundly that she slept through the arrival of Shuvalov and Hotek, the visit of her own spouse, the questioning of Boyev, and the banishment of Ivan Dmitrievich. In vain had he fretted thinking he had awakened her with his highwayman's whistle. Any such sound—be it a whistle, a shout, or the wail of unoiled door hinges—wove harmoniously into her nightmares, but the moment Hotek sat down at the piano and began to play Strauss, the tender melody burst into her dream. A startling dissonance.

Ivan Dmitrievich might have recalled how recently at their Sunday family dinner his father-in-law had told the story about the defense of Sevastopol, when, having grown accustomed to the artillery cannonade, he no longer awoke at the thunder of French cannons. You could fire a rifle right in his dugout, and he would sleep without stirring. His batman knew only one way to quickly awaken his master should the need arise: sing a soft lullaby in his ear.

More or less the same thing happened with Strekalova: the tender strains of the waltz forced her to open her eyes. She lay there briefly, coming around, then got up and cautiously opened the door, looked through the crack, and saw her enemy.

When Ivan Dmitrievich and his lieutenant flew into the drawing room, Strekalova, standing in the bedroom door, was no longer shouting but speaking in the pathetic sing-song of a mechanical doll that is winding down, softer and softer.

"Murderer, how dare you come here? Scoundrel, how dare you—"

Pevtsov was prying the fingers of her left hand off the door jamb, and the right was stretched out in front of her, pointing, trembling not at Shuvalov but at the other count—Hotek.

Strekalova's cheek was disfigured, like a prisoner's brand, by a red mark—the traces of the crumpled pillowcase.

Ivan Dmitrievich froze at the threshold. Just that morning there had been a line drawn between insanity and common sense, a boundary complete with striped poles, customs officers, and a border guard, and now none of that existed.

"You again?" shouted Shuvalov when he saw Ivan Dmitrievich. "Get out!"

Pevtsov attempted to push Strekalova back into the bedroom, but he couldn't get the better of her.

"Captain," Shuvalov could not restrain himself, "where are you dragging her?"

"There." Pevtsov pointed.

"Why? Throw this madwoman out! What is she jabbering?"

"Stop," Hotek imperiously intervened. "I have to know who she is."

"This woman loved the prince," said Ivan Dmitrievich.

Shuvalov rolled his eyes.

"Oh, Lord! That's all we wanted!"

"Count," Hotek addressed him, "I hope you are cognizant of whom she is insulting in my person?"

"Murderer!" Strekalova exclaimed with new energy.

"There, you see. Are you really incapable of guarding me against such insults?"

"What's wrong, Captain, can't you overpower the woman?" asked Shuvalov menacingly.

Pevtsov grabbed Strekalova by the waist to tear her away from the jamb, but she herself easily pushed him away, took a step toward Hotek, and tore the mourner's rosette from his chest.

"You should be ashamed to wear this!"

At that, her fingers opened slackly, and the black velvet flower fell to the floor. The cat dashed out at it from under the sofa, took a sniff, and turned away, twitching her whiskers contemptuously. No one said a word.

"Pick it up!" Shuvalov finally bellowed.

Strekalova shook her head, and fat tears spurted from under her instantly swollen eyelids.

Pevtsov picked up the rosette and handed it to Hotek with a bow. Hotek carelessly slipped the flower into his pocket, saying, "I must demand the arrest of this lady. I personally will be present at the interrogation."

Pevtsov ran into the hall and a minute later returned with Rukavishnikov.

"Take her away!" Shuvalov commanded him.

"Yes sir, Your Excellency. Where?"

"The fortress."

"No." Ivan Dmitrievich shielded Strekalova.

"What's that?" Shuvalov exhaled, breaking off into a wheeze.

"I will not allow—"

Pevtsov and Rukavishnikov exchanged glances and made straight for Ivan Dmitrievich, but next to him appeared his new friend, the Preobrazhensky lieutenant. He had nothing to lose. He drew his saber from its sheath and brandished it at them with a fierce grunt--*whish-swish*—and turned to face Shuvalov.

"Your Excellency, it is I who took vengeance upon Prince von Ahrensburg!"

"Be careful!" warned Pevtsov, reluctant to get any closer.

Shuvalov staggered back, and the lieutenant, taking a step forward, put his lips to the blade and extended the saber to him.

"Here is the weapon of my sacred vengeance."

A cloudy patch from his breath spread over the blade. When it had contracted, faded, and only the trace of the kiss remained on the metal, Shuvalov cautiously accepted the saber, not knowing what to do with it next.

"Enough of this farce!" Hotek exploded. "Your actors are all well and good, but why didn't you get around to explaining to them that Ludwig was suffocated with pillows?"

"Believe me, Count . . ."

Strekalova cast an imploring look at Ivan Dmitrievich:

"You did promise me, didn't you?"

"What"

"To find his murderer."

Before he could respond, a wild howl let up.

"Katya! Katya!"

After that brief howl, the door banged open, and into the drawing room rushed Strekalov, who had not gone home as he had been told and had been eavesdropping the whole time in the hall.

He ran past the Chief of Gendarmes as if he were a pillar and grabbed his wife by the arm.

"It was I who killed him! I!"

The murderer had as many heads as a hydra. One head—Boyev—Ivan Dmitrievich had cut off; the next, the lieutenant's, had fallen off of its own accord; but now it had grown a third—round, with puffy cheeks and greasy curly hair. Little horns could easily have been lost in them, the sole weapon of a deceived spouse.

"Strike your offender in the chest with your horns and they will fall off," Ivan Dmitrievich recalled. The letter lay in his pocket, already spread out and smoothed.

"And who are you?" challenged Shuvalov.

"It is I, Katya. I!" Strekalov repeated, paying not the slightest attention to him, and holding his wife firmly by the hands.

"Don't believe him!" she exclaimed. "This is my husband. He is incapable of this. Fool! Go home."

Strekalov let go of her wrist.

"Oh, you don't know me, Katya. Take a good look, I'm capable of it, aren't I? Look me in the eyes! You may be looking at me for the last time."

She took a few steps back:

"No, I don't believe it. No."

"Take a good look! I'm going to Siberia because of you!"

Gasping, Strekalova squeezed her husband's temples with the palms of her hands.

"You?" She rose nearly an entire head above him.

"I," said Strekalov. "After all, you are my wife. Because of you, I have taken this sin on my soul."

Powerful hands pushed him away and he flew to one side, getting tangled up with Ivan Dmitrievich, but immediately, with surprising agility, he unfolded his slack body, the body of an overfed boy, and spun on his heels, even attempting to click them, quite like the lieutenant ten minutes before.

"Arrest me, Mr. Putilin. I'm ready!"

His face was calm, his fat lips compressed.

Strekalova rushed toward him and impetuously pressed his curly pate to her breast.

"Oh!" she wailed. "I'm a foolish woman! Forgive me!"

No one said a word. Strekalov calmed down and started stroking his wife's back, and then lower than the back, more and more boldly, as if there was no one around, just the two of them.

"Don't cry, Katya," he said. "Don't cry, darling. They won't give me hard labor, just deportation."

"Count, you've heard all you needed," said Shuvalov without any particular confidence, addressing Hotek.

"And you'll follow me to Siberia," advised Strekalov. "I'll never hold it against you, honest to God! We'll get ourselves a goat, and you'll knit downy scarves. All is lost! Just you and I. Hear me, Katya?"

"My poor boy!" she sobbed. "Poor both of us. What have I done!"

Her body was too tight for her soul, and her dress for her body. The seam down her back had split. Ivan Dmitrievich saw a white stripe, pathetic and defenseless across the black silk. He felt like running his finger over it tenderly, but one glance at Strekalov and he immediately remembered the twig in the jam jar. Or did he really not understand anything? What Siberia? What goats? What downy scarves, for that matter? The Zielle dungeon, that's what awaited him. And what could he do? If the maid had told the truth and he did in fact spend last night at Tsarskoye Selo, witnesses could be found. And if not? Simultaneously he was bothered by the thought of the person who had taken the Napoleon stolen from the prince to the Church of the Resurrection.

Strekalova was fiddling with her husband's hair. Her fingers were running freely through his tight curls. No horns there.

To distract himself and rest his gaze on something unrelated, Ivan Dmitrievich looked at the cat. Fluffy, with a dandy's socks on his hind legs, it was walking slowly on its way with that special expression on its face that always arouses respect for this beast, as if it knew exactly where it was going and why at any given moment.

Meowing, the cat moved toward Strekalova, brushed under the hem of her dress, and began to stir there, underneath, in the hot twilight. It got quiet. Ivan Dmitrievich noted that everyone, even Hotek, was watching the edge of her mourning skirt, poked out by the cat's tail, sweep over the floor, with the kind of faces that said this swaying was the day's crowning glory, as if they had gathered here for just this.

"Your Excellency," the lieutenant reminded him resentfully and now without his former insistence, "I was the first to confess!"

"You can just keep quiet now," Ivan Dmitrievich ordered him.

He walked over to Strekalova and touched her shoulder:

"Ekaterina . . . I don't know your patronymic."

"Fyodorovna," said Strekalov sternly.

"Ekaterina Fyodorovna, you are not at all to blame for the prince's death. Your spouse is lying."

"You're lying?" she looked at her husband hopefully.

"No, Katya, don't get your hopes up."

"He's deceiving you. But a lie like this demands much more courage of a man than it takes to commit murder."

Ivan Dmitrievich had said what he was supposed to say. The man who has sacrificed himself wins a woman's life in reward, and the wise man can console himself with the awareness of a duty fulfilled. Thus God has laid down that for courage of the heart one gets his due more fully than for strength of mind, and this is proper, otherwise the world would cease to exist.

"Deceiving her?" Hotek repeated. "Do you have proof?"

The question's very tone fully convinced Ivan Dmitrievich that this man had far from any interest in the speedy capture of the perpetrator. Only in such an ambiguous situation could he dictate his will to Shuvalov.

"I swear it! I killed him!" shouted Strekalov when he came to his senses.

"That's not true," said Ivan Dmitrievich, addressing Hotek. "Mr. Strekalov spent last night in Tsarskoye Selo. His alibi is irreproachable. There are witnesses."

The lieutenant decided to take advantage of the ensuing pause.

"Look!" he shoved his palm with Ivan Dmitrievich's teeth marks on it under Hotek's nose. "The prince bit me when I was covering his mouth."

There, at the top of the sacrificial altar, both he and Strekalov, for the first time in their lives, perhaps, had experienced destiny and freedom, and they had no desire to climb down. Unseen, Boyev walked up to them and stood by their side. Three men who had voluntarily sacrificed themselves in the name of love—for their Homeland and for a woman—and were standing shoulder to shoulder in the middle of the drawing room. Ivan Dmitrievich gazed at them with admiration but without tenderness. Tenderness softens you, and right now he needed a hard heart.

"The insane asylum," said Shuvalov fatefully. "Come, Count, arrest them both in any case."

"This won't change anything. My ultimatum remains in force," replied Hotek.

"Would your sovereign truly approve of such actions? In my opinion you're risking—"

"Have no fear, I know the thoughts of my sovereign better than you."

Hotek walked toward the chest, took from his pocket his wallet with the Hapsburg eagle embossed on the leather in gold, and from the wallet the snake-key.

"Did Mr. Cobenzel give that to you?" asked Shuvalov as a subtle reminder that he could have studied the trunk's contents of the trunk in detail but had not done so.

Nodding, Hotek inserted the key in the lock between the rose petals but could not turn it.

"The other way around," Ivan Dmitrievich suggested artlessly. "Nubbins up."

"Ah, like this?" Hotek turned toward him and immediately shifted his glance to Shuvalov. "You mean you opened it without me?"

"Believe me—"

"Even if this is a simple lack of tact and not political espionage, as I suspect, this curiosity is going to cost you dearly. I shall report it to Chancellor Gorchakov."

"We only wanted to test whether the key fit," Ivan Dmitrievich stuck his neck out again.

"Go away!" Shuvalov spoke in a strangled whisper. "Captain, take him out immediately! I'll deal with him tomorrow."

"You gave yourself away, Count." Hotek chuckled. "Now I see that the only honest man in your company is this policeman."

"And do you realize who you are insulting in my person?" asked Shuvalov.

"The comparison is inappropriate. I embody my sovereign here, whereas you merely serve yours."

Once again Pevtsov was about to approach Ivan Dmitrievich, but the lieutenant, taking the saber from the windowsill where Shuvalov had abandoned it, swung the dully gleaming blade significantly.

"A murderer on the loose," said Hotek, "my own life in danger, and all the more do I have grounds for stating the following. If by tomorrow noon the demands I have issued have not been met, I am starting to make preparations to leave Petersburg."

Thus, without ever opening the trunk, he put the key back in his wallet, crossed the drawing room, and grabbed the door knob.

"I implore you, wait another twenty-four hours!" Shuvalov asked.

This request was so humiliating that Ivan Dmitrievich forgot about his own offenses. The almighty Chief of Gendarmes seemed ready to collapse on his knees before the Austrian envoy.

"Tomorrow noon," Hotek repeated imperiously.

Reddening, Shuvalov tore at his uniform collar. A hook flew off and clicked like a hailstone on a window pane.

Hotek decided it was time to leave and that he had already witnessed this outrageous spectacle for far too long. "If chaos could have a single center, such as order has," he thought, "then the midpoint would have to be here, on the Street of Millions. And then, in expanding circles—Petersburg, and Russia. Here you have it, that persistent Russian chaos of which the departed Ludwig used to say that this element of life, with all its inconveniences, brings Russians closer to the primordial foundations of existence, to those times when spirit and matter, light and dark, good and evil, were inextricable. A repulsive chaos whose westward movement must be halted no matter what."

Hotek grabbed the door knob, but next to his long, slender, yellowish fingers lay Ivan Dmitrievich's stubby fingers, as puffy as dumplings.

"One moment, Count."

Holding the door with his left hand to prevent the envoy from leaving, with his right he snatched out the letter Strekalov had received, unfolded it, and with a provocative lack of ceremony brought it up to Hotek's face.

"Recognize it?"

"What does this mean?"

"Madam was right," said Ivan Dmitrievich. "You are the murderer!"

He expected anything and was prepared to continue if Hotek in response had simply shrugged his shoulders, but the envoy's nerves had evidently snapped. Ivan Dmitrievich had barely pulled away his hand and the letter when Hotek made a grab for it.

An angel passed over the drawing room.

Suddenly hurried steps thundered down the hall and in walked Shuvalov's adjutant. Under his arm was the holy book of the Prophet Mohammed.

"I brought it, Your Excellency! He can swear," he reported loudly, glancing around in perplexity at the drawing room, where new faces had appeared, and not finding Kerim-Bek among them.

But Shuvalov had forgotten about the Tatar porter long since.

"What are you pushing at me?"

"The Koran. For oaths Turks rest two bared sabers on top of it."

"You're going to drive me mad!" Shuvalov howled.

He gave the distraughtly blinking adjutant a shove and strode toward Hotek:

"For God's sake, forgive me, Count! I'll have this scoundrel taken away to the insane asylum immediately."

By attempting to grab the letter, Hotek had given himself away, which is what Ivan Dmitrievich had wanted to say but hadn't been able even to open his mouth: Strekalova had pressed him to the wall at full tilt. There was the stupefying smell of hot feminine perspiration and perfume. She wanted to kiss him? Alas! Her hand fished around in his jacket, feeling the pocket and the tapered jar of mushrooms. "She's looking for my revolver," Ivan Dmitrievich thought. "To shoot Hotek." Everything happened so quickly that no one else understood what was happening, nor did he have time to. Pulling out the jar, Strekalova stared in shock at her trophy, as if some stranger were showing her this object and she could not guess its meaning. Her fingers squeezed its glass sides in an iron grip, and only her index finger scratched the lid incoherently—solitary and helpless, it kept trying to find the trigger. When her finger calmed down, Strekalova heaved a long half-sigh, half-wail, threw up her hand, and threw the jar at her feet. The shards and splashes of brine spilled like shot, staining the furniture and wallpaper and spattering the walls. A brown puddle pooled on the floor around the broken glass and a pitiful mound of slimy dark brown caps.

II

Ivan Dmitrievich had Strekalova sit in an armchair and spoke to her gently.

"Come, dear, why don't you tell me the whole thing properly, from the very beginning, just as it happened?"

Her words, spoken a few hours before, still rang in his memory.

"Ludwig had expected an appointment as ambassador. . . . The count set his men against Ludwig because he feared and hated him. . . . The count wanted to defame Ludwig, portray him as a degenerate, a gambler, a drunkard."

"To be honest, my dear," said Ivan Dmitrievich, "I didn't understand immediately which count you were referring to. At first I thought that—"

He sensibly did not utter Shuvalov's name out loud but turned to him when he asked, "Mr. Putilin, we would all like to know the grounds for your accusation."

"Logic, Your Excellency. The most elementary logic. At its base I lay the circumstance that surveillance had been established over von Ahrensburg's home."

"How do you know that?" Shuvalov was astonished.

"From Captain Pevtsov. True, he refused to explain to me whose men were watching the deceased prince, but I was able to penetrate that mystery independently. It was Count Hotek's men, am I right?"

Shuvalov scowled.

"And who informed you of this?"

"Mrs. Strekalova. After analyzing a thing or two she said, I arrived at the conclusion that in Vienna, at the Ministry of Foreign Affairs there, von Ahrensburg was expected to become the ambassador to Russia, that is, to take Hotek's place. Hotek, however, had no wish to resign, and in order to defame his competitor, he collected a compromising dossier on the facts of his personal life. A banal but winning array: cards, wine, and women. Hotek bribed the prince's porter, demanding written denunciations from him against his master, and sent his own man to spy on the house where we now find ourselves," said Ivan Dmitrievich, concluding the first segment of his thoughts.

Now he did realize that the Gendarmes had had nothing to do with this, although they had known about the rivalry and had been reporting to Chancellor Gorchakov, apparently, so that he could decide whom he would prefer to see in the role of Austrian ambassador to Russia—Hotek or von Ahrensburg. Depending on who was shown favor, Shuvalov, one would think, was supposed to help one of the two bring down the other. There it was, the state secret that Pevtsov had been trying to uncover!

"Not that long ago," continued Ivan Dmitrievich, turning now not to Shuvalov but to Hotek, "you, Count, learned of the existence of Mrs. Strekalova, and it occurred to you to use her in your intrigue. You sent an anonymous letter to Mr. Strekalov in order to provoke a scandal and duel between the deceived husband and your rival. Then, you reasoned, von Ahrensburg definitely would not be the ambassador! So you sent this letter and waited, but unfortunately, without effect. You thought Mr. Strekalov was simply too cowardly, and finally you decided upon an extreme measure. Last night your men suffocated the poor prince, who had the misfortune to constitute competition for you in the diplomatic arena."

Naturally, during this monologue Hotek had not been mute. At first, actually, underestimating the danger, he had merely grinned crookedly and reminded Shuvalov about the psychiatric clinic where this detective should be put, then in a menacing tone he had begun asking whether those present were sufficiently aware of whom these insults flung at the plenipotentiary representative of Emperor Franz-Josef were resting their full outrageous weight upon. The response was silence. In a rage, Hotek jumped up and made a desperate dash for the exit. He did not succeed, whereupon he began shouting and waving his cane at Ivan Dmitrievich, but after the cane was taken away from him, he shrank into himself, grew quiet, and sat calmly in a corner of the sofa.

"The key to the front door," said Ivan Dmitrievich, addressing him, "you had taken long ago temporarily from the prince's doorman, whom you had bribed, and had had a copy made. And the rumors about how the murder was political in nature were also your work. It was you who spread them, Count."

"How?" Hotek rasped out.

"Last night, when the prince was still alive, your men went around the taverns and told tales of his death. Simultaneously, you spread a rumor about how an attempt had been made on your life as well. As for the half-shtoff of vodka I found on the windowsill, your men left it there with the contrary goal of suggestion to the investigation that there had been tramps in the house, convicts. As if to say it was they who had stolen the Napoleons."

"Why both then?" Shuvalov had his doubts. "In my opinion, either it's politics or it's crime. Why both?"

"The calculation," explained Ivan Dmitrievich, "was that the Gendarmes would work on the political murder and the police on the criminal, and given our mutual antipathy, I'm sorry to say, we would start throwing spanners into each others' work."

Again he shifted his gaze to Hotek.

"And so your conscience would not torment you too badly, you decided to turn your crime to the benefit of the fatherland and obtain a ban on the activities of the Slavonic Committee. Your other demands were made to give you something to rescind if your principal demand was met."

Ivan Dmitrievich paused and then concluded. "I dare say that you justified yourself with the famous Latin saying, 'The good of all is the highest justice.' By ridding yourself of your rival, you may have imagined that you were thereby working for the good of the empire. I must disappoint you, Count. This saying is true only if the person achieving the common good by criminal means does not himself join those who benefit by this action."

Hearing out the final points of the accusation, Hotek tried with pathetic irony to curl his disobedient lips, but his gaze had gradually become glassy, and his senselessly staring eyes were fixed on a single point on the empty wall.

"Admit it. After all, this is your handwriting," said Ivan Dmitrievich, pointing to the letter Strekalov had received.

Hotek twitched and made a second attempt to snatch the letter. It was as unsuccessful as the first; on the other hand, it proved conclusively that this document had been written by his hand.

Powder was flaking off the Austrian envoy's face, which was damp from a cold sweat. Like a scrofulous little boy, his forehead, cheeks, and chin were peeling. Unable to grab the letter, he staggered and collapsed back down on the sofa. His tongue would not obey him and a lisping gurgle burst from his mouth.

"Your Excellency, will you need my help in drawing up a summation for your sovereign?" Ivan Dmitrievich asked Shuvalov.

"Hey?" the man came to his senses.

"He did write this letter! He did!" Pevtsov was triumphant. "I saw his dispatch at the telegraph office. It's the same handwriting, Your Excellency!"

Ivan Dmitrievich could feel Shuvalov trying his utmost to force the indecent exultation that filled him to the brim into the bounds of decency. The abyss that had gaped before him so recently had suddenly turned inside out and blown up into a mountain. He was standing on its summit, gazing down victoriously on Hotek far below, small and no longer frightening.

"They're going to find out in Europe, aren't they?" said Shuvalov quietly, and casting aside convention was the first to laugh.

At this, everyone exploded in laughter. Shuvalov's adjutant threw his head back and there was silvery water splashing in his throat. The captain was dancing in place with excitement. Laughing, Pevtsov playfully nudged Ivan Dmitrievich with his shoulder and winked, as if to say, just look at what can happen in our business! Let us forget, my friend. Strekalov, too, giggled, to keep up with the others, only his wife did not join the general merriment, and Ivan Dmitrievich himself was silently aloof. If it is true that one can judge a man's merits from the woman he loves, in this case Strekalova, then the deceased prince could not have been so bad that a mad carnival would be organized on his grave.

Shuvalov evidently began to feel awkward as well. He raised his hand:

"Your attention, please!"

"Attention, gentlemen! Attention!" Pevtsov chimed in.

"I am addressing all those present without exception," Shuvalov announced, surveying the drawing room. "I advise all of you most insistently to remain silent about what you have learned here. This is a secret affecting Russia's interests. Anyone who makes it public will be arrested on a charge of treason."

"Aha," Ivan Dmitrievich reasoned, "that doesn't work out so badly! After all, one could blackmail not only Hotek but the Austrian government, and before you know it, Franz-Josef himself. A murderous ambassador! A disgrace throughout Europe, a scandal."

"Well, I'm going to tell everyone!" Strekalova declared with tears in her voice. "Why on earth should I conceal the truth? Let everyone know who the murderer is!"

Shuvalov gave her a significant look, but she stamped her foot and continued shouting.

"I'm going to tell! I am! Do what you want to me, I'm not afraid!"

"Nor am I, nor am I!" Strekalov supported her. "Do you hear, Katya?"

"You heard me, gentlemen," paying them no attention, without raising his voice, Shuvalov concluded. "I do not intend to repeat myself. If someone does not understand, we will discuss this elsewhere. Captain!" He turned to Pevtsov. "Drive this audience out of here."

"Yes sir, Your Excellency!"

"How am I supposed to drive them out?" the captain was at a loss.

"On their ear," said Shuvalov.

The captain, still clutching the bared saber, finally decided to insert it into its sheath, but his fingers were trembling and he couldn't land the blade into the slit until Strekalov came to his rescue.

"Come along, brother," the captain clasped his arm and sighed. "They don't need us."

"Katya, where is your coat?" asked Strekalov solicitously but at the same time sternly, as befits the head of a family.

Without waiting for her answer, he strode into the bedroom, took his wife's douillette, returned to her, and pulled her toward the exit by the hand. She submitted reluctantly, like a child who would really rather stay where she is. Shards of the broken jar crunched under her shoes and the mushroom mess squished. Her mourning hem lapped at the threshold one last time, and the white arrow—the open seam on her back—sped off into the darkness.

Ivan Dmitrievich did not get so much as a backward glance, and Strekalov, as he was shutting the drawing room door behind him, cast a perfectly indifferent look over him. Having broken his horns off on his own chest, he proudly bore his lightened head and led his wife by the arm, which she did not try to take away. And the captain, although he had long been prepared to flee from heaven to hell for Ivan Dmitrievich's sake, said not a word to him in parting.

Chapter 11

Disappointment All Around

The clock had struck midnight long since and Hotek was still not back. In anticipation, Cobenzel had gone outside several times. A fantastic April storm was raging over the rooftops, and the Neva seemed to be making noise on all sides, as if the embassy were located on an island. He couldn't help but think of the terrible Petersburg floods.

Cobenzel returned to his office, giving the dozing doorman a nudge as he passed. The bustle of the day had calmed down. The servants were sleeping wherever they did and the councilors had dispersed to their homes. It was quiet; the chaplain's voice had also stopped talking. In the silence and emptiness you could hear the bare branches of the trees scraping against the windows at particularly strong gusts of wind. To ward off sleepiness, Cobenzel decided to drink a cup of coffee, but he couldn't find anyone capable of satisfying this particular desire. He managed to locate the duty courier, who had snuggled up on the small sofa next to Ludwig's coffin. Cobenzel ordered him to go to Hotek's apartment and find out whether he hadn't gone straight home from Millions. Half an hour later the courier returned and reported that no, he had not come home, and his wife had begun to worry. Cobenzel circled the room some more, trying to stay as far away from the coffin as possible, and finally he realized that he simply could not bear the uncertainty. Why shouldn't he go to Millions, actually? Ultimately, as a friend of the deceased, he had a right to know all the circumstances of his death. That is what he would tell Shuvalov and Hotek if they were displeased by his visit. Subordination? The Devil take it! What kind of subordination can there be at one o'clock in the morning? Wasn't it natural that he was worried? Hotek still hadn't returned, although he had promised to be at the embassy soon. Yes, he had the Cossack convoy with him, but anything could happen on this mad night.

Cobenzel went to tell the coachman to bring the carriage around, but he was nowhere to be found. Cobenzel wanted to call the courier, who had only just been to Hotek's apartment, for help, but the man had taken the precaution of moving off the little sofa, where he had been found once already, and lain down somewhere else. Where exactly, Cobenzel did not know.

Cobenzel put on his coat and estimated the distance to Ludwig's house. Not that far, and there was no danger of missing Hotek—there was only one way. He opened the drawer and put the miniature French pistol in his pocket—just in case Vanka Pupyr attacked. This bandit's deeds had given rise to so many rumors in Petersburg that it was not considered shameful to discuss them even in society drawing rooms. He hoped that if their paths crossed his finger would not refuse to pull the trigger. Even if he fired in the air. Dead silence reigned all around. As through an enchanted castle whose mistress has stuck her finger with a spindle, Cobenzel passed from his office to the front door, walked down the steps, and strode boldly in the direction of the Street of Millions.

II

People said Vanka Pupyr was a werewolf and at night he prowled the city in his wolf's guise.

Ivan Dmitrievich had been hunting for him since Christmas but had seen him up close only once, when Pupyr had lowered the boat on that bungler Sych. Pupyr was squat and short and unusually broad of chest, with long arms, short legs, and no neck whatsoever. When he came out to ply his trade, he usually tied a kerchief around his head, and this time Ivan Dmitrievich could see only his eyes above it—small, abominably blue, and piggish. A wolf was the last thing he resembled. A man capable of turning into a gray brother had to be sinewy, yellow-eyed, and predatory of glance and habit. Ivan Dmitrievich suspected that Pupyr had intentionally spread these rumors about himself so that he would not be recognized on the streets. As those who had been his victims recounted, they feared the werewolf with the soundless approach, whereas Pupyr tromped loudly as he approached. Like a block with paws hanging below his knees.

About five years before, he had been arrested for murdering a soldier at the state wine shops and had gone to jail, escaped, and turned up in the capital that winter. However, neither Ivan Dmitrievich nor his agents knew that Pupyr, once he amassed a little money, was planning to move permanently to Riga and there open a tavern featuring Russian cooking. He had learned somewhere that these taverns enjoyed the protection of the Riga police chief, who felt such establishments served the state good and promoted the empire's unity. It took a lot of money to carry out this plan, both for the tavern and to bribe the clerks and get a passport, but Pupyr was reluctant to rob anyone's house or store; this was hard to do solo, and he had no wish to get mixed up with anyone, so he plied his trade on the streets. However, the fur coats and hats torn from passersby were getting to be more and more trouble to sell. Occasionally he had gold or gems. Any jeweler would buy them and not ask where they came from.

The last few days, knowing that Ivan Dmitrievich had abandoned all his cases and was hunting only for him, Pupyr had not gone out to ply his trade and had sat almost without break at his mistress's, the scrawny, flat-chested, and meek laundress Glasha. He kept his stolen goods at her place, where he caught up on his rest after his sleepless nights.

Glasha lived in a wood cellar, for a ruble a month renting a corner with a ventilation pane that was walled off from the firewood by a board partition. She had welcomed Pupyr in without knowing anything about him, in December, during the fierce frosts, when, dressed in rags and blue in the face, his ears in scabs, he had asked to spend the night in the laundry, next to the furnace. She had brought him home, fed him, and warmed him out of pity. Down on his luck, she'd thought. But then she found out he was a murderer. How could she love a murderer? He gave her silver earrings, and Glasha threw them down the latrine. She wouldn't take the stolen scarves from him. She even slept separately, on the floor. Pupyr instilled horror. Even dogs, seeing him, put their tails between their legs. "I smell like a wolf," he would say. He had no hair on his face or his body, but he had such a thick hide that the bedbugs couldn't bite through it. At night, lying sleepless, Glasha would weep and pray that this devil would not return. Foul murderer! It was terrifying to live with him but even more terrifying to think of driving him out. He'd kill her! And at the thought of informing the police, her tongue simply failed her: he would escape hard labor and kill again. She didn't even say anything to her friends at the laundry, she was so afraid.

Sometimes, after eating, he would tell her things about Riga, where Germans lived and Finns, another neat little nation, and there were some Russians there, and everyone lived cleanly, not like Glasha, and swept their floors every day, everyone had felt floor cloths and shook them out in special places, not just anywhere. Generally speaking, he loved cleanliness and reproached Glasha for her filthy way of life. He always had three rags hanging on a line: one for his hands, another for cups, and a third for something else, and God forbid they got confused. These rags sent a wave of desperate sorrow rolling over her and made her want to howl like a wolf herself.

Pupyr had not gone anywhere the last few nights but had lain on his cot with his eyes open, napping during the day, and from time to time he would start singing about some battalion commander who was "Oh, a chief, a commander" and "did not sleep or doze and trained his battalion." Sometimes he would get up and fire the stove red hot, after which he would take off his shirt and sit there bare-chested. Returning home after midnight, Glasha would smell his smell, which put a nasty, bitter taste in her mouth. The one good thing was that their lovemaking had ended. Pupyr didn't have much need for a woman's love.

"Aglaya," he would say when Glasha came in from the laundry, "they're going to bury you in a washtub, not a coffin. And instead of a cross they'll stick a felt boot in the ground."

This made her feel uneasy every time he said it. If she wasn't careful they really were going to be knocking together a cross for her grave because she harbored this Satan.

Glasha had stayed away from her cellar for several days, spending the night in the laundry, on the ironing table. Just before dawn she would wake up all of a sudden and decide that she would do it, she would go to the police.

She knew who to see.

About three weeks before, Pupyr had dragged Glasha by the hair so she wouldn't be stubborn, tricked her out in someone's squirrel coat, the very first loot he hadn't been able to sell, forced her to tie on a fluffy scarf torn off some merchant's wife, and dragged her to Nevsky by force—to promenade like everyone else. Glasha walked with him arm in arm, not feeling her feet under her she was so ashamed and frightened. In each lady they met she imagined the owner of the coat or scarf. Pupyr strode grandly alongside in his glossy telescoping top hat and his coat with fur collar and eagle buttons—a real gentleman. From time to time he would bow to one of the passersby. Some looked at him in amazement, and some thinking they had failed to recognize an acquaintance and ashamed of this, responded with exaggerated courtesy to his bow and tipped or raised their hat. They walked along sedately. Pupyr was again flapping his gums about Riga and about how he was a useful man for the sovereign because he stole fur coats not idly but for the future good of the state. As they were strolling they met a man with long side whiskers visible even from behind. "The chief of detectives," said Pupyr. "He's been trying to catch me, the sly fox. The hell he's going to!"

Early in the morning, awakening from her own tears on the ironing table, Glasha resolved to go to the police that day and find the man with the side whiskers. Come what may. But the day passed and she failed to go anywhere. She tried to justify herself by saying that she would bring the police and Pupyr would be gone—having left, without waiting for her, and taken all his goods with him. How would you prove then that you hadn't been deceiving them? They would arrest her and cart her off to prison. Glasha pictured this scene so clearly and repeated it so many times in the clouds of hot steam, talking to herself, that he was gone, run away, the monster, that by evening she believed this was how it was. She flew home as if on wings. She descended to the cellar and indeed: her little hut was locked. With a beating heart she rummaged under the hopsacking where they put the key and clicked the lock open. Empty! She rushed to the shelves and howled at her impotence, at the vain hope that had instantly blown up in her chest, like a bubble in a fish, ripping her heart from her body and her body from the earth—and burst. All of Pupyr's shirts, which she had laundered, all his underpants, all his neckerchiefs and handkerchiefs were lying on shelves in neat stacks. She poked her head into his hiding place among the firewood, where it smelled of lost furs. All his loot was here, which meant he would be back.

Glasha scooped water from the bucket, drank, her teeth chattering on the edge of the ladle, and moaned thinly in despair. The cold ran down her throat and she calmed down a little. She looked in the place where Pupyr kept his kettlebell and chain. His notebook with culinary recipes for his future tavern lay there, but the kettlebell was gone. Glasha felt her legs giving way. If he murdered one more person today, she could never be forgiven. No, she couldn't! You can't pray away your sin.

She ran outside and was lashed by a fine net of snow. The lights went out in the house and only the entry windows looked in the darkness like partitioned yellow wells.

III

Prince von Ahrensburg's coachman explained in detail and even drew it on a napkin: turn into the gateway behind the tavern and there you would find a two-story annex, you go upstairs . . . But Lewicki, who had been instructed to bring the prince's former servant Fyodor to Millions, had not found him at home. He wandered nearby for half an hour, spat on the whole thing, and went to a friend's, where he played forfeits with the ladies, cheating only rarely, by force of habit. In the end, he lost a couple of times on purpose. The first time he had been sentenced to sitting on a Champagne bottle, and then they'd told him to act out the Greek orator Demosthenes, that is, give a speech of praise to the mistress of the house with a handful of sunflower seeds in his mouth. Lewicki managed to do both and just after ten o'clock went to get Fyodor again. But his kennel was empty as before, the door locked.

Lewicki went out into the courtyard clicking the sunflower seeds from his speech in his pocket. It was getting cold and the wind penetrated to his bones. With a wave of the hand he strode decisively as far as the gateway, stood there a little while, and was about to shout out to a passing cabby, but at the last moment stopped himself after all. It was dangerous to leave without carrying out his instruction. Ivan Dmitrievich might not forgive that and it was not that easy to justify yourself to him.

Lewicki knew that his secret boss was merciless toward cardsharps. The sight alone of cards with an imperceptible scratch made by a needle drove Ivan Dmitrievich into a fury, but an exception had been made for Lewicki, inasmuch as he played with those cards at the Yacht Club, with aristocrats, who saw in him a descendant of Polish kings. Ivan Dmitrievich believed that the losses incurred by his titled partners were even beneficial, like bloodletting for medicinal purposes, and so turned a blind eye. Actually, at any moment he could have seen quite well with that eye, so that Lewicki was careful not to anger him. He would have to suffer and wait. There was nothing to be done for it.

Glancing from side to side to see whether this damn servant, whose features had also been described by the coachman, was coming, Lewicki decided to wait until eleven and then leave. At eleven he gave himself until eleven-fifteen, then until half past, and then until a quarter 'til, but at twenty minutes before midnight he could stand it no longer and headed for the Yacht Club.

The chandeliers burned hot there, and the gambling was in full swing at the tables. Lewicki gave a shudder, drank down some warmed wine at the sideboard, and here Ahrensburg's friend walked up to him, the Austrian Baron Hohenbruch, with whom the prince often went duck shooting.

In fact, he was no more a baron than Lewicki was a Polish prince. Each knew this about the other, but they held their tongues.

"Listen," Hohenbruch asked, puffing on his cigar, "wasn't it you who saw the prince home yesterday?"

"I just took him outside and put him in a cab," replied Lewicki.

"And came back?"

"No, I took another cab."

"What did the prince say to you in parting?"

"I don't recall. Nothing special."

"I beg of you, try to remember. Those may have been his last words."

Lewicki thought a moment.

"He said . . . I think he said he should have put a ten of hearts on the first hand."

A stout officer in a blue gendarme uniform came floating up silently from behind his back. It was Lieutenant Colonel Foch, or so he introduced himself. The three went to a free table with a green cloth where they were joined by one other blue officer somewhat younger. Foch ordered Champagne and two decks of cards, but he was in no hurry to begin play. With these gentleman Lewicki had to be on his guard, and he decided it would be best not to replace the official decks. A conversation got under way around von Ahrensburg's death in connection with the current political situation in Europe. Like Shuvalov, Foch suspected Polish conspirators of the prince's murder.

"I remember," said Hohenbruch, "the words spoken by

Frederick the Great about a certain Polish gentleman. I can't vouch for their accuracy, but the sense was that this gentleman was capable of any foul deed for the sake of ten chervontsy, which he would then toss out the window."

"It's to the Poles' advantage to make our sovereign quarrel with Franz-Josef," said Foch. "If there is a war, they're hoping "to take advantage of the general turmoil to revive the Recz Pospolita."

The other officer was silently shuffling the cards but for some reason was in no hurry to deal.

Yes," agreed Lewicki, "there are in Polish society those irresponsible elements, although in their great majority—"

"Nonetheless," Foch interrupted him, "let us imagine for a minute that Poland has once again gained her independence."

"That is impossible," said Lewicki.

"But if it were so. . . . Is there any chance you might occupy the Polish throne?"

"Well," Lewicki smiled, flattered, "I don't know. It's hard to predict."

"But even the slightest?"

"If you like."

Lewicki took the deck away from the officer and with the natural grandeur incumbent upon a pretender to the throne dealt the cards, picked up his own, and out of habit opened them in a narrow cardsharp's fan:

"Well now, gentlemen."

But none of his partners touched his cards.

IV

Once, while taking a stroll on Krestovy Island (not far from the Yacht Club, actually), at an outdoor puppet show where Ivan Dmitrievich had stopped by with his son Vanechka, he saw a woman-hydra with three heads. It had been simply done. In the half-dark a piece of black material had been stretched over the platform, and in front of it, facing the audience, stood a busty mademoiselle wearing an over-gilded leotard, and over her shoulders, to the right and left, through slits in the fabric, two other girls poked their kissers through. Thus, a hydra.

During the hours Ivan Dmitrievich spent in von Ahrensburg's home, now and again he recalled that puppet show freak. All day, the murderer had been growing false heads on his invisible body. They moved, made faces, and winked, but the real one was lost in the gloom along with the body. True, the gold Napoleon Sych had brought had shed a glimmer of fragile light on it. You could make out a thing or two.

With a respectful bow, Ivan Dmitrievich returned Hotek his cane. Hotek latched on to it but did not have the strength to brandish it and for some reason his tongue would not obey. Mumbling furiously, the envoy moved from side to side with firmly compressed, bloodless, old man's lips. He seemed to be trying with all his might to suck his last saliva from his dried out mouth in order to spit in Ivan Dmitrievich's face.

"How do you feel, Count?" Shuvalov inquired solicitously. "Shall I call a doctor?"

Hotek struck the tip of his cane on the floor forcefully—once, twice. The rug he was beating passed under the piano legs, and the muffled ringing of piano strings filled the drawing room.

Ivan Dmitrievich watched him with alarm. Had he had a stroke?

"It's all right," continued Shuvalov calmly. "You'll go home right away. You'll get into bed and calm down. I highly recommend a hot foot bath. We can talk tomorrow. If you're well, I'll expect you in my office before noon."

Hotek mumbled something inarticulate again, but no longer furiously, rather sadly and eerily, like a calf at the slaughterhouse gates catching a whiff of his brothers' blood.

"We'll meet as you suggested," said Shuvalov. "Tomorrow at about noon. Only now you, Count, will be coming to see me."

And he repeated with pleasure, "Tomorrow at about noon."

"I don't think he has any need of a Cossack convoy," Pevtsov interjected.

All this time he had been circling near Hotek, like a jackal by a dead lion, leaning over him, examining the withered yellow hands clasped on the knob of his cane. "He's looking for bite marks," Ivan Dmitrievich imagined.

"You are correct, Captain," Shuvalov agreed merrily. "There's no one to fear. Unless the dead man's ghost decides to wreak vengeance on his own murderer. But in that case the Cossacks will be no help."

"I'll tell their captain," Pevtsov volunteered.

"Yes, they can remain here."

At Shuvalov's sign his adjutant and Rukavishnikov took Hotek under the arms firmly, although respectfully, lifted him from the sofa and led him outside. The envoy did not balk more out of courtesy. He climbed into his carriage willingly. The door slammed and the driver waved his whip. Standing by the window, Ivan Dmitrievich followed, not without satisfaction, the two-headed Hapsburg eagle that adorned the Polish carriage sink to one side, straighten, and toddle, battered, down the Street of Millions waddling duck fashion, from wing to wing. The golden wings and the crowns on the two heads flashed and were lost in the darkness.

"Well now, Mr. Putilin." Shuvalov smiled. "You will not be seeing an Austrian order now. If you have the Anna, I will petition for a St. Vladimir."

"I do not have an Anna."

"Don't worry, you will. And a Vladimir, too, in time. After all, your deal gave us the trump ace. An ambassador-murderer! Isn't that something? What a fellow! I don't think you quite realize what this bodes for us. Tremendous success! I'm looking forward to our sovereign's emotions tomorrow morning when he reads my report. My hands are itching to write as soon as possible."

In a few strokes Shuvalov sketched out this prospect: Franz-Josef would be promised the entire matter consigned to oblivion, that his diplomats would not be disgraced, and Russia would be assured Vienna's support in all aspects of its foreign policy, even in the Balkans.

Ivan Dmitrievich allowed him to finish and asked, "So you mean the prince's murder was to our benefit?"

"Naturally, naturally," confirmed Shuvalov. "Therein lies the entire trick."

"But let us say, Your Excellency, that you had learned of the murderer's intentions in advance. Would you have prevented him?"

"How dare you ask His Excellency such questions?" Pevtsov was irate.

"Don't get excited, Captain," said Shuvalov peaceably. "My adjutant has not yet returned, the three of us are here, and today is the kind of night that we can go ten minutes without ceremony. I will answer you honestly, Mr. Putilin: I don't know. This question of yours is a fateful one. Isn't it? In general, it makes no sense to answer questions like this theoretically. In theory a man thinks that he should act one way, but when it comes to practice he acts the other way around. Here it depends on what God puts in his heart."

"But in any case you now intend to conceal the murderer's name from the public?"

Shuvalov frowned.

"I explained the plan to you. Did you not understand?"

"An excellent plan," Ivan Dmitrievich agreed, "but the murder of a foreign military attaché cannot go unsolved. Who are you thinking of naming in the criminal's place?"

Shuvalov got upset, like a child who has had his new toy taken away.

"Yes, I did lose sight of that."

"We'll find someone," said Pevtsov. "There are three who've already volunteered."

"Correct," Shuvalov took heart. "We'll definitely find someone."

"I'll find someone," promised Pevtsov.

"And you shall be a lieutenant colonel. I do not go back on my word, Captain."

"Lucky man!" thought Ivan Dmitrievich enviously. "For some reason the good of the state invariably coincides with his, Pevtsov's, personal advantage no matter the situation." Climbing to lieutenant colonel rank, he confidently led Russia to the heights of glory and might. It had all worked out quite the opposite way for Boyev, the lieutenant, and Ivan Dmitrievich himself.

"But we have no need of witnesses," Pevtsov reminded him. "We should remove this insane lieutenant from the Guards and send him to some distant garrison. We'll put such a scare in the Strekalovs that they won't dare say a word."

He measured Ivan Dmitrievich with an appraising glance, as if figuring what to do with him, but he did not express any thoughts on this score.

Shuvalov was silent. Evidently he was tormented by doubts.

All of a sudden it dawned on Pevtsov:

"Your Excellency, why the excessive complications? We already have the murderer's substitute!"

"Who exactly?"

"Why, this Figaro! The prince's valet. He stole the cigarette case, there's a clue. He won't wiggle out of our hands!"

"But if there's a trial, Vienna might call him as a witness," Shuvalov objected reasonably. "They don't have fools there either. They'll say, 'What are we talking about, gentlemen, if the murderer has been found and convicted?' We're not going to get anything out of them then."

"There's no hurry for a trial. First we'll prove Hotek's

guilt and suggest that the Austrians sign all the necessary agreements in exchange for keeping the secret, and then we'll take the case to court."

"You want to condemn an innocent man?" asked Ivan Dmitrievich.

"It's not good to steal, either," said Shuvalov. "Let him serve a little and we'll get him out under an amnesty. We'll give him some money and let him plow the land somewhere in Siberia! Look at that ugly puss! He's fattened up here."

"Yes!" Pevtsov suddenly remembered. "Give me the letter."

"What letter?" Ivan Dmitrievich pretended not to understand.

"The one Hotek sent to Strekalov."

"Oh that. . . . Why do you want it?"

"We'll make a copy and send it to Franz-Josef," explained Shuvalov. "Let him read it."

"Your Excellency, the point is . . . You see . . . In short, I'm still not entirely convinced that it was Hotek who strangled the prince."

"How's that?" Shuvalov was stunned.

"It's a conjecture. A guess. . . . There are counterarguments, too."

"That is irrelevant," Pevtsov interposed. "With this kind of evidence we can prove anything we like. Give it here, the letter."

Ivan Dmitrievich fell back toward the door. The matter had taken an unexpected turn. What had they conceived? Make a fool of all Europe? It wouldn't work. Rise like a falcon and plummet like a stake in a grave, like Hotek. He felt sorry for the ginger Figaro, too. That lad had never laid eyes on a plow. He'd be lost in Siberia.

"Where is the letter?" Pevtsov pressed.

"Listen to me, Your Excellency! I admit I accused Hotek to make him withdraw his ultimatum. After all, something had to be done! Russia's honor—"

"Give me the letter!" shouted Pevtsov.

"I beg of you, hear me out!" Ivan Dmitrievich began quickly, clutching the pocket where the ill-starred letter lay. "I've already picked up the trail of the real murderer, but

I need time to catch him. A day perhaps, or two, but Hotek gave us until tomorrow noon. What else could I do? I wasn't thinking of myself!"

"You weren't?" Pevtsov lost his temper. "And how much do you hope to fleece out of Hotek for the letter? Ten thousand?"

"Lord!" said Ivan Dmitrievich, almost in tears. "I would rather rip it up right now. Right in front of you."

"Just try it!" Shuvalov threatened.

"Come to your senses, Your Excellency! What are you doing? Don't take Hotek as an example. You've seen how that ends. I swear, I'll find the murderer!"

"You'll keep quiet," Shuvalov spoke slowly. "And you'll get your Anna. With a bow. Your murderer is beside the point for us. We need Hotek. Do you understand? Give me the letter."

Ivan Dmitrievich looked around. Rukavishnikov and the adjutant were entering the drawing room and behind them a gendarme lieutenant colonel he didn't know.

"Foch?" Shuvalov was surprised. "What's happened?"

The man went up to him and began whispering about something. Ivan Dmitrievich was able to make out: "Apparently you were right . . ."

"And where is he?" asked Shuvalov.

"At the entrance in his carriage," replied Foch. "Captain Lundin is with him."

"Rukavishnikov! Don't let him go!" Pevtsov ordered, noting that Ivan Dmitrievich was cautiously backing up toward the door.

The way out was cut off, and navy uniforms surrounded him on all sides: a general, a noncommissioned officer, and three officers. Pevtsov was coming closer and closer. Ivan Dmitrievich did what Strekalov had attempted to do—as if by chance, with an absent-minded gesture, lower his hand into his pocket and without moving his shoulder or elbow, without changing his expression, with just his fingers, he began destroying the damn missive, rip it up, crumble it to dust. To hell with them!

The door to the bedroom was open, and in the blue light of the dying streetlamp the naked Italian ladies in the picture turned very blue. Foch was examining their chilled charms with interest.

Pevtsov came right up to him.

"The letter!"

Ivan Dmitrievich pulled out a handful of paper scraps and threw them at his feet.

In the ensuing silence everyone suddenly noticed that the prince's clock was silent. The pendulum hung motionless; the arrows indicated a quarter past midnight though it was already two thirty.

Pevtsov crawled on the floor gathering the scraps, appealing to Shuvalov indignantly, but Shuvalov made no reply, gazing on Ivan Dmitrievich with consternation. His consternation was so great that it fractured his fury, vexation, and disappointment, all his emotions. What did he want? What did he expect? He was the spawn of chaos, this detective with the disheveled side whiskers, he was impossible to understand and apparently impossible to get rid of, just as it was impossible to lay a whirlwind of dust low with a bullet.

Ivan Dmitrievich, mortally terrified, bit his fist in horror, and the insane thought flashed through his mind that if he just clenched his jaw a little harder they could just as well use that mark to accuse him of the prince's murder.

Chapter 12

An Avenging Angel

On the veranda of the house with the apple orchard, the clock said it was more or less the same time as it had on the Street of Millions when the lieutenant and Strekalov spouses left it.

It was the dead of night.

"Shall we go to bed and wrap this up tomorrow?" suggested Ivan Dmitrievich. "You must be tired."

"That's quite all right, I'm used to working at night," replied Safonov. "Brew a little coffee and finish your story. The murderer has been caught, which means the end is nigh. I realize that according to the laws of composition a stormy apotheosis is supposed to be followed by a lyrical diminuendo, but I hope it won't be too long."

The spirit lamp flared up. Five minutes later, filling the cup with grounds at the bottom left over from the previous portion one more time, Ivan Dmitrievich said, "Put down your pencil, drink your coffee in peace, and in the meantime I'll tell you a story."

"Is it connected somehow to von Ahrensburg's murder?" Sazonov fretted.

"To be honest, not very."

"Then better leave it for later."

"No, better right now," said Ivan Dmitrievich firmly. "It's a sad story, but it tunes us to a certain key and will help you to perceive all that follows properly."

When he became chief of detectives, Ivan Dmitrievich moved to a new building where, on the same stairwell, someone named Rosshchupkin was renting an apartment, a childless widower of about sixty, a good-natured tippler and horse lover and the owner of some decent land in Tula Province. Every fall Ivan Dmitrievich was invited to his estate to hunt and each time he declined, but once, having quarreled with his wife, he up and went. About fifteen guests had gathered: three of Rosshchupkin's nephews, former comrades from his regiment, neighbors of the estate, and various hangers-on. While the entire company was exterminating hares, Ivan Dmitrievich gathered mushrooms, and in the evening, at the table, when they sat down to eat, Rosshchupkin told them the following story.

Thirty years ago or so before, he had served in the Kingdom of Poland and had brought back a marvelous Barella hunting rifle (inasmuch as Ivan Dmitrievich barely knew where to squeeze to make a rifle fire, he did not recall what exactly made it so fine). Rosshchupkin had bought it in Warsaw, by chance. The rifle had been tempting as well because soldered under the trigger was a copper plate with the initials of its former owner engraved on it—IPR, which coincided down to the last letter with his own: Iakov Petrovich Rosshchupkin. As proof he showed his guests the case left from the rifle, which had on it exactly the same kind of plate. By then the rifle itself had been lost, not having lasted a year. Either he had forgotten it at some roadhouse, or else he had dropped it in a field when he was drunk, or else it had been stolen. He had searched for the lost object for a long time, promised the finder a large reward, and eventually gone to see a Gypsy. She dealt the cards and foretold that the rifle would return to him without fail. Rosshchupkin rejoiced and gave her ten rubles, but she wouldn't take the money. She agreed to five, but she would not take a red note. He was amazed. Why? So the Gypsy told him: "Because, my dear, the rifle will return to you on the day of your death."

"But you know, if that bitch had taken the ten rubles," said Rosshchupkin, concluding his story, "I wouldn't have believed her for anything!"

A year after that hunt he died.

Ivan Dmitrievich and his wife attended the funeral, and his old servant informed them in neighborly fashion of the following. The owner of a weapons shop where Rosshchupkin numbered as a longstanding and most profitable client had sent several rifles over to Rosshchupkin's house with his shop assistant for him to choose. Rosshchupkin picked them up one after the other, hefted it, shouldered it, and suddenly — crash! — dropped the rifle on the floor, staggered, and turned white. That night he did indeed die, although he had not been ill, and that morning had been healthy and in good spirits.

They drank vodka and ate their *kutia*.[1]

Ivan Dmitrievich asked the servant whether the rifle had been returned to the shop, and learning that no, it had not been returned but was still at the house, went to see it. They were all new but one was old with a worn buttstock. Ivan Dmitrievich picked it up and saw under the trigger a plate with three Latin letters: "IPR."

Meanwhile, little by little, the guests had begun to forget why they had gathered. Someone was strumming his host's guitar, someone else wanted to play cards immediately, someone else yes was snoring face down on the table, and the Rosshchupkin nephews, now tight, were inviting all gathered to hunt on their uncle's Tula estate, which had now become theirs.

Ivan Dmitrievich watched them patiently and indulgently, as he would small children. Let them! It was better they didn't know the terrible truth. Not everyone can tolerate it without going mad.

Again he went to the room where the rifles lay. A price tag was attached to each one by a thread. The Barella, the messenger of death with a box of walnut, had cost twenty-five rubles. Ivan Dmitrievich gave one of the nephews a twenty-five ruble note, took the rifle home, and hung it over his bed as a permanent memento mori.

In the morning, rubbing his puffy eyes, he stared at the rifle for a long time, not understanding where it had come from. At last he remembered. He had bitter morning-after saliva in his mouth, and he regretted the twenty-five rubles. Cursing, Ivan Dmitrievich was all set to take the rifle back when episodes from yesterday's funeral, certain words and glances, began to

---

1 A boiled grain pudding with raisins and honey, often served at funeral repasts.

filter through his headache. Something about them had put him on his guard and burned his memory, like a scratch left by a fleeting and forgotten half-guess.

He removed the Barella from the wall and examined it carefully. On the left barrel, on the underside, he discovered a discreet factory stamp with the date of manufacture: "11.1868."

In the clear morning light, Ivan Dmitrievich saw a nice new but assiduously worn plate with the traces of fresh scraping, a copper plate with initials that was thicker and brighter than it should have been, and unnaturally bright green, and he recalled the eldest of the Rosshchupkin nephews and the grimace of instant sober fear on his drunken face: he had been watching Ivan Dmitrievich walk through the dining room carrying the rifle.

There was a trial. At the trial Ivan Dmitrievich appeared as a witness and gave a speech after which the jurors said as one: Yes, they're guilty. The eldest had been in charge, but the nephews had made common cause and had asked the unsuspecting owner of the firearm shop to send their beloved uncle this Barella among other rifles. The nephews were sentenced only to deportation from Petersburg; it proved difficult to class their crime under an article of the law. The Tula inheritance was seized for the treasury.

Unlucky Iakov Petrovich had been avenged, and the talk died down, but all his life Ivan Dmitrievich remembered the morning when he'd been sitting on the bed holding the rifle. In the evening, at the funeral, he had been frightened to think that there was such a thing as fate, but in the morning he was even more frightened to think that there wasn't. After all, if there is such a thing as fate, that means someone is thinking about you and you are no longer alone in the world.

Alas, though, you are!

II

Prince von Ahrensburg, once a dashing cavalryman and fine swordsman, had always driven around Petersburg hell for leather on lathered horses, which gave him pleasure, but Hotek, who did not like to go fast, considered it the heavy burden of the envoy of a great power. Inhabitants of the capital had to see him as constantly rushing and to worry, and to ask each other what had happened. Only to a reception at the palace did he proceed unhurriedly, gravely, careful not to let fall the dignity of his emperor by excessive haste.

Now the streets were empty and there was no one to gawk or be alarmed, but the coachman, fighting sleep, as usual set the horses at a gallop. On the disgusting pavement the carriage was tossed up, and down, and then up again and sideways. The night-time city, bereft of people and powdered with snow—and this was April!—rushed past like a nightmare in stone. Hotek looked out the window. Later, recalling the stone that flew through the carriage near Haymarket, he sat farther back in his seat.

A few minutes later he calmed down and his thoughts acquired clarity. The carriage was rocking, and he had to dig his feet into the floor and hold on with his left hand to the edge of the cushion and with the right to the strap hanging from the ceiling, and the tension of his body gradually pulled his soul out of its stupor.

Yes, he had written the letter to Strekalov, but there was no signature there, or seal, and the handwriting—that wasn't proof. He had spent the entire night at home, the servant would confirm that. He had been taken by surprise, like a little boy, and most shameful of all had been the sudden onset of muteness, his furious aglossia, in which Shuvalov could espy an admission of guilt, his wordless and thus even more obvious despair. However, this intrigant would pay cruelly for having seen Count Hotek lowing like a cow. Tomorrow at around noon? As you wish. His majestic bearing, the smile on his lips, the complete imperturbability. The melodious clinking of spoons on porcelain, and the question: Where is the criminal? Oh, you don't know? *Punch* is running a cartoon: "Russian blind man's buff. Chief of Russian Gendarmerie catches Austrian military attaché's murderer in Petersburg." In it Shuvalov, blindfolded, is attempting to catch foreign ambassadors—British, French, Spanish, and Turkish—running in different directions. Their sojourn in Russia was becoming unsafe. Tomorrow they would be warned of this. Today, that is.

But did Shuvalov really believe in his own innocence? Hardly. He was being cunning, choosing his moment.

The horses' spleens were going pit-a-pat, and Hotek was about to shout to the coachman to take it easy but changed his mind. It was safer this way. Anything might happen. He didn't have a convoy.

Naturally, he had hated and despised Ludwig. How could he not? That degenerate, gambler, and drunk an ambassador? Could such a man be entrusted with the empire's fate in the East? A nobody and idler, at least dead he could serve the emperor! A fine diplomat he'd be if he didn't exploit the man's death.

In order, one by one, Hotek recalled the points of his ultimatum and lightly snapped his fingers to mark out the principal one. Actually, now two of them were principal: the ban on the Slavonic Committee, which was inciting Czechs, Slovaks, Croatians, and Rusyns to rebellion against Vienna; and the punishment of that scoundrel of a detective as an example. Actually, there was no point trying him because that would attract attention, but he had to be drummed out of the service and banned from residing in the capitals. The swine! And that vile female, that column of sweaty flesh with rostrum-breasts! How could a man capable of a liaison with a woman like that have the right to be ambassador? No taste, no sense of measure. . . . Hotek clenched his fists. Why hadn't he thought to accuse her of Ludwig's murder? He was a grasshopper compared to her; she would have had no trouble strangling him in bed. She wouldn't even have had to strangle him! She could have crushed him with her monstrous body, the way a remiss mother in her sleep crushes the infant sleeping by her side. Shuvalov ought to have implied that this woman was on his payroll. So, they wanted to construct their policy on the blood of an Austrian diplomat, did they? It wouldn't work! Tomorrow he would show them, the scoundrels! They would not be strutting like peacocks for long. Nonetheless, he felt uneasy at the memory of the powdered, dark blue spots on Ludwig's neck. He wished he could be home right now. A hot evening bath? Not bad either. Shuvalov was right about that.

A brief muffled wail cut through the thunder of hooves. Something heavy and soft, like a sand bag, struck the front of the carriage and tumbled to the ground. Hotek retracted his head into his shoulders and grimaced.

The driver shouted.

The mighty blow—like a sable slashing his chest—threw him from his box, smacked him into the front of the box, and threw him onto the pavement. He rolled head over heels across the chipped paving stones and stopped when he bumped into the curb. The horses shied, and the left wheels went up onto the sidewalk and caught a pillar. The axle cracked. The carriage listed and flung Hotek back and forth. His shoulder bashed the door open and he fell to the ground, but at that very moment the horses got up and everything worked out more or less well.

Hotek lay briefly on the wet pavement regaining his senses. The thought flashed that this accident would be another trump in his hands during his conversation with Shuvalov. He raised himself up on his elbows. The street, covered here and there with patches of spent snow, was empty. The buildings with their darkened windows were lifeless.

"Come here! Help me!" called Hotek.

No one was rushing to his assistance so he would have to take charge himself. He drew his knees toward his torso and sat up. He moved his arms and shook his head. All whole.

Suddenly the only one of the three closest streetlamps that had been burning, weekly but evenly behind him, went out. The blue gleam languishing in the puddle died. That same second broken glass rained down on the stones. Hotek turned around and his throat was seized with horror. Someone awful, with a black blotch instead of a face, was running up from behind.

The driver lay motionless a few steps away and there wasn't another soul around. Hotek gathered all his courage and tried to stand to meet death standing, as befits the ambassador of a great power. Only his feet for some reason just wouldn't obey.

The running man approached. From below he seemed huge. What he was wearing, Hotek didn't have a chance to see; his gaze was clouded by tears. He looked like death, nothing but eyes and a head around which, quickly flaring up, a yellow fillet had appeared, a flickering golden halo like they draw on saints in Russian icons. Over him he saw a flickering angelic radiance and his fear left him and a strange warmth surged through his body. Hotek realized with relief that the most terrifying part of this was behind him. He was already dead and with the eyes of his soul he was seeing the lop-sided carriage, the wheel that had come off, the horses, the moon. His soul was rushing toward where his Divine messenger was waiting for it, outlined in a circle of gold, racing toward him amid the clouds and snowy swirls streaming beside him. Light, having abandoned the prison of the flesh, but having nearly achieved its goal, it palpitated in despair. So terrible were the eyes of this angel—two dark holes with a chill at their bottom, so evenly and plaintively did the air feeding the flame whistle next to him, as if it were streaming down from mountain peaks, fanning the pitiless countenance of the heavenly messenger, that Hotek guessed: before him was the Avenging Angel.

He screamed and fainted.

III

The student Nikolsky walked into the entryway, went up the dirty stairs, which stank of cat, and rang at an apartment on the third floor. Here lived Pavel Avraamovich Kungurtsev, a correspondent for *The Voice,* a liberal newspaper, which Pevtsov's spies learned after waking up the porter, whereupon they considered their mission accomplished and dispersed to their homes. In view of the late hour, they decided that the results of their observation could be reported to Pevtsov the following morning.

Tormented by bad presentiments, Nikolsky had come to see Kungurtsev to ask for a relative's advice; Kungurtsev's common-law wife was his cousin Masha. A man of broad views and one of the capital's most honest and talented pens, as Nikolsky's besotted cousin insisted, Kungurtsev listened attentively to the story about the head stolen from the anatomical theater and said, "You're a pig! What kind of doctor will you be? If you don't respect dead flesh, you can't cure the living."

"I was drunk," Nikolsky defended himself.

"And where is this head now?"

"Damn if I know. . . . The gendarmes took it."

Skinny, clear-eyed Masha tirelessly poured tea and cut sausage and pitied her cousin because he would be booted out of the Medical-Surgical Academy. She advised him to find the head and give it a humane burial.

"I don't have the body," said Nikolsky gloomily.

Masha started to say that tomorrow he needed to buy it from the anatomical theater and bury it with the head. If he didn't have the money, she was prepared to donate the sixty rubles she'd set aside for a new winter coat.

"You know, my dear," Kungurtsev made a disgruntled face. "I know a thing or two about materialism, and I believe you need a coat more than he does a shroud."

Nikolsky sniffed guiltily. He felt like the worst scoundrel.

"You booby!" Masha struck her cousin on the forehead with her hot teaspoon and sobbed, looking at her husband. "I don't need that coat either!"

Kungurtsev shrugged. Reasoning out loud, he had attempted to find at least some sensible explanation for the strange fact that a gendarme officer, moreover an officer of considerable rank, a captain, had taken it into his head to investigate the theft of an dead unidentified head from a jar of formaldehyde. What deviltry was this? After all, that head was probably from some tramp without family or tribe, a drunk who had frozen outside long since or fallen under the wheels of a coach.

"Especially since he has to bury him in a humane way," said Masha angrily.

"Were there any wounds to the head? Was the skull intact?" asked Kungurtsev.

"I didn't notice. Why?"

"A thought occurred to me. Maybe it was Pupyr and his kettlebell. Maybe they're looking for Pupyr since the police don't seem to be capable of it."

"Oh no, it was quite intact," said Nikolsky, slurping his tea.

"I can get through next winter in my old one," Masha interjected again.

"Wait up!" A sudden conjecture dawned on him, and Kungurtsev took away Nikolsky's glass of tea. "You say they picked you up at that Bulgarian's, your friend's, right? Just so! And this afternoon they took him over to Millions. Took him under guard, I saw it myself. Maria, that means they suspect your cousin of murdering the Austrian military attaché."

"Lord!" she said, horrified. "From bad to worse!"

"Why were they asking about the head?" Nikolsky was dubious.

"Did you steal it? Did you go around to the taverns with it? Did you abandon it on the street?"

"I was drunk."

"That is irrelevant. Consequently, you're capable of killing a living person. There's a certain logic here, I can't argue."

An explanation had been found so Kungurtsev calmed down. The further fate of this ne'er-do-well relative was of no interest to him. He began talking about how that afternoon, on Millions, he had tried to interview Chief of Police Putilin.

"I ring and a servant opens. This ginger beast. He says, 'I have orders not to let anyone in!' Well, I gave him a ruble and passed into the drawing room without any interference. I look and this famous detective is sitting there all alone and twirling his shopman's side whiskers around his fingers with a thoughtful look."

"What's going to happen to him now?" Masha interrupted, putting her arms around her cousin's shoulders.

Kungurtsev waved his hand disdainfully, as if to say, Nonsense, they'll sort it out. In any event, he imperceptibly moved the box with the set aside sixty rubles in it farther behind the books.

"How naïve we are!" he continued. "We would like to see in this detective a veritable Russian Lecoq. Give us a Lecoq! But this Lecoq's face looks like it was hacked out by an axe, and a dull axe at that. What good is he to us? Look at the enigmatic figure they've found. I don't understand how anyone can write about him at all. Just a little while ago he performed a Herculean feat and caught some retired soldier who forged tokens for common bathhouses and absconded with other people's underpants. What kind of a plot is that? Well, apparently he was walking from bathhouse to bathhouse and scrubbing himself, naked, among the muzhiks. So they caught him. And we start shouting, 'Lecoq! Lecoq!' People in Europe would die of laughter. I think what this is all about is . . ."

Masha brought her old winter coat out of the storeroom to show that it was still perfectly good. Talking nonstop, Kungurtsev scraped his nail across a fur cuff that was worn down to the leather and poked a finger first in one hole and then another.

"Here's what I think this is," he said. "Russian thieves and murderers are hopelessly mediocre people, and in order to catch them you need someone just like them. Like cures like, fight fire with fire. That's where the shoe pinches. Putilin is the embodiment of mediocrity, therein lies the secret of his successes. Quite relative successes, I must say. Here they go killing Prince von Ahrensburg, and what happens? Masha, you know my political convictions, you know how I feel about the gendarmes, but in the investigation of this case I am laying bets on them. Cases like this are nuts too hard for the likes of him to crack. This requires imagination and a developed intellect. Education, at a pinch."

"If you're going to write about the murder for the newspaper," said Masha, "mention our Petenka and say he has fine morals and his comrades respect him."

"As if I could!" Kungurtsev grinned wryly. "Lieutenant Colonel Foch has already gone around to all the editorial offices and ordered them not to print a word. Pfah! People on every corner are chewing the fat, but we can't write. Oh no! God forbid you might start thinking that the gendarmes cooked this up and now don't know how to disentangle themselves. I once had the dubious honor of visiting Count Shuvalov in his office. You won't believe it, Mashenka! Three clocks, and each showing a different time."

Appearing before Putilin, Kungurtsev recounted, he had stunned him instantly with questions: Were revolutionaries, Italian Carbonari, pan-Slavists, Geneva émigrés, or agents of the Polish Rada mixed up in the murder? Or maybe the recent maneuvers, the construction of the new battleships, the reequipping of the army? Did Mr. Putilin conjecture the possibility of a political provocation on the part of Constantinople? What about suicide? Had that possibility been ruled out entirely?

"Other correspondents would have relished the details of the crime," said Kungurtsev. "Don't feed them bread, let them paint the bloody sheets. But I always try to understand the underpinning of events."

"What do the Carbonari have to do with this?" asked Nikolsky.

"A few years ago von Ahrensburg fought in Italy. People say he was not on his best behavior with the prisoners, and the Italian secret societies have a long reach. . . . But this Lecoq wasn't about to listen to me. I ask him, 'Mr. Putilin, are you informed of the fact that the secretary of the Turkish embassy, Yusuf Pasha, is recently returned from Istanbul? That for some reason he traveled there via Odessa, as usual, but sailed home from Italy, on a Genoan steamship?' And do you know how our detective reacted? In your whole life you'll never guess! He asked me how much money I'd given the servant at the door. I told him ten rubles."

"Ten rubles?" Masha was aghast. "But before you said it was a ruble."

"Yes, it was, it was," Kungurtsev reassured her. "I purposely told him that. As if to say, look what expense I'll go to in order to have a chat with you. And he said to me: 'You're lying. You gave him a ruble, no more, and you could have gotten by with twenty kopeks.' And that was the entire conversation! You see what kind of problems interest him. Lecoq indeed!"

"What's that?" Masha, listening, raised her voice. "It sounds like people shouting outside."

"That's me running my finger over the window," said Nikolsky. "I'm writing a certain word."

"What word?"

"A secret word. Boyev taught me. Haiduks carve it into trees."

"You're our Haiduk," Kungurtsev grinned wryly. "You're mixed up with that Bulgarian. If they drum you out of the academy, where will you go? I'm not giving you money, so don't count on that."

"I'll treat the blind," said Nikolsky, "with fly agaric."

"Someone's shouting again. Don't you hear it?"

Masha went over to the window, but the wide cornice kept her from seeing what was going on outside.

"Oh no! They've smashed the streetlamp!"

"No surprise," commented Kungurtsev. "Remember what happened in the fall when they started putting booths up with fire alarms on the streets? A week later there wasn't a single glass left intact. Night falls—and false alarms. The fire chief was moaning and groaning. I'm not talking about the streetlamps. Every last drunk comes across them. The nastiest enemies!"

"The White Nights are nearly here," said Nikolsky.

Masha knelt by the windowsill, pressed up to the window, and nearly fell when she staggered back: a shot rang out on the street and the echo reverberated as it struck the windows.

"Don't touch it!" Kungurtsev shouted at his wife, seeing

her attempt to unseal the ventilator pane that was caulked shut for the winter.

While Kungurtsev was dragging Masha away from the window, Nikolsky rushed to the vestibule, dashed out onto the landing, and clattered down the stairs. Startled cats leapt from corners and raced upstairs in silent leaps, to the attic.

"Petya! Where are you going? Come back!" his cousin shouted after him.

He did not reply. Yes, he had defiled the dead head, but now he would save a live one.

He pushed the entry door open with his chest and ran outside. There was a white moon in the clearing sky and the wind had died down. On the right, about twenty paces away, Nikolai saw the tilted carriage with the dull gold Austrian eagle. Next to it a man lay on the ground and another was leaning over him. Hearing steps, he straightened up.

"I am Baron Cobenzel, secretary of the Austrian embassy. Do you live here? This is our ambassador, Count Hotek. We must take him inside."

Chapter 13

Among Ghosts

Captain Lundin led Lewicki, who had taken tremendous fright, into the drawing room. The previous week he had used marked cards playing with Prince Oldenburgsky and Duke Meklenburg-Streletsky, who from time to time sat at the table with him out of respect for his genealogy, and now there was a suspicion that the business had been revealed. The worst part was that he had not had time to dispose of the decks of cards in his pocket, and they would be found in a search.

Lieutenant Colonel Foch, spreading the sweet smell of Champagne wherever he went, began setting out a new scenario for Shuvalov: a war between Russia and Austria-Hungary was to the advantage of the pretender to the Polish throne because it would lead to a weakening of both powers that shared the Recz Pospolita, and then. . . . Ivan Dmitrievich listened, incapable of uttering a word. The raving went on and on, like a whirlpool. Suddenly his own name came up and bobbed on the surface like a float: Putilin. Just a little later, again: Putilin, Putilin. This was Captain Lundin reporting to Shuvalov that this afternoon Lewicki had for some reason come here, to the Street of Millions, where he had had an appointment with Chief Detective Putilin.

"Why did they meet here on such a day, not just anywhere but at the scene of the crime? What secret business do they have?" Lundin expressed his own misgivings.

As for Foch, like the lieutenant colonel he looked on things more broadly and more deeply.

"Your Excellency," he said, "we have all lost sight of the fact that the Poles soon will be marking a sad anniversary for them."

"Which?" Shuvalov interrupted.

"Next year it will be one hundred years since the first partition of Poland by Russia, Austria, and Prussia. There are bound to be hotheads prepared to shed sacrificial blood on the altar of this anniversary."

Not listening, Lewicki butted in, hastening to report something about cardsharps, whom he had supposedly always beat with candelabras himself. Yes, with candelabras, on their ugly, ugly faces! Foch grinned sinisterly. A brilliant conjecture seemed just about to rise up out of this raving and blossom like a double bloom: he, Ivan Dmitrievich, conspiring with Lewicki, had strangled von Ahrensburg in order to provoke a war with Vienna, restore the Recz Pospolita to its 1772 borders, and as a result make for himself a brilliant career and become chief of the secret police under the Polish king. Why not? In fact, this was altogether in the Lewicki style.

"Why there he is. Putilin!" Foch said in amazement, as if he had just noticed Ivan Dmitrievich. "Now we can ask him."

Shuvalov's left eyelid twitched.

"Now we can ask him," said Foch gently, "just what they were meeting about here, tête-à-tête, my dear fellows. Eh?"

"What is wrong with you?" Shuvalov roared suddenly, bringing his fist crashing down on the table. "Are you drunk, lieutenant colonel? Have you hit your head? What pretenders? What are you jabbering about? Get out of here!"

"Your Excellency," Foch began trying to defend himself, "you yourself, Your Excellency, were speaking of Polish conspirators."

"Out!" Shuvalov raged, pressing the disobedient eyelid with the palm of his hand.

Foch and Lundin were swept out of the drawing room as if by the wind, only their sheaths clattered against the doorjamb. Lewicki whisked through the door behind them, and behind him, Ivan Dmitrievich, who had decided to use that moment to take to his heels as well. An astonished Rukavishnikov did not try to detain him. Thank God! Jostling in the front door, all four tumbled onto the front steps, where the Cossacks of the convoy were still smoking their nose-warmer pipes, and only here, coming to their senses, did Lundin and Foch head sedately toward their carriage. Lewicki turned tail in one direction and Ivan Dmitrievich in another, for fear of a chase; after all, Shuvalov and Pevtsov naturally would never forgive him the shredded letter. He was about to take a running start, crawl over the fence, and leave by way of back alleys, and he had already grabbed hold of a cold iron point when he remembered Lewicki. Where was he, the bastard? Where had he gone? They hadn't had time to talk!

No one seemed to be following him. There was silence. Ivan Dmitrievich returned to the corner of the house and while hiding behind the downspout cautiously surveyed the street. It was deserted. The pretender to the Polish throne had vanished, dissolved in the gloom. Even his steps were not to be heard. The black oilcloth top of Shuvalov's carriage, wet from melted snow, gleamed in the moonlight like a grand piano. Lieutenant Colonel Foch and Captain Lundin had also vanished, as if they had never been there, as if they had been woven out of thin air, out of the putrid Petersburg fog—ghosts, bogies whose every question, as his dear mama had taught him when he was a child, had to be firmly answered just one way: "Come back tomorrow!"

Away from this house! And as quickly as possible. Or he himself could lose his wits looking at them.

Ivan Dmitrievich shuddered and turned up his coat collar. It was time to catch the real murderer. Even if no one—not Shuvalov or Pevtsov, not Hotek, not Strekalova—needed him, this murderer, he still had to catch him, otherwise his own life lost all meaning.

He could hear Shuvalov storming around the drawing room. The Cossacks were laughing among themselves, and their captain was tweaking his mustache in irritation. He was tired of hanging around outside with nothing to do, but there had been no orders.

Ivan Dmitrievich listened a little while and started down Millions following an already marked out, well-contemplated route, but fifty paces later a breathless Konstantinov came flying toward him. Literally the next minute Sych, too, was delivered up, now wearing his boots, coat, and cap. Resentful of his beloved chief, he had not been in much of a hurry and had run home to dress and swallow a nice mouthful of hot water.

Out of breath, Konstantinov recounted his adventures in detail and enumerated the features of his pursuer: tall, healthy, a biscuit-colored beard.

Sych reported that someone of the exact opposite appearance—short, emaciated, and clean-shaven—had bought candles from the sexton Savosin.

Listening to both of them attentively, Ivan Dmitrievich looked at the windows where Pevtsov's silhouette shone through the curtains. That was quite a blow to my back just now, the bastard! And the main thing was, Pevtsov had seen Ivan Dmitrievich fall down on all fours. The memory of the wet pavement awoke in his hands and knees. And what for? No, that kind of thing cannot be forgiven.

"This is for you, Ivan Dmitrich. Your wife sent it," said Konstantinov, pulling a linen sack of sandwiches out of his coat.

Ivan Dmitrievich gave it a sniff.

"Chicken again?"

"I don't know."

"All right. And where's the coin?"

"Your promise!" Konstantinov reminded him. "One is mine now. You just promised. Don't you remember?"

"I remember everything. Give."

"Which one?"

"Both."

Konstantinov sighed and took out the Napoleons: one full-weight, the other thinner, with a worn profile. The coinage dates on them were different. The first, found under the princely bed, was stamped during the defense of Sevastopol but looked brand-new. The second was minted the year before last, but it was already rubbed and worn. Why hadn't these coins been in the trunk at the prince's? Had he received them from someone or had he wanted to give them to someone, since he had put them in his dressing table drawer? And why, for all that, had a revolver been there as well?

Ivan Dmitrievich jingled the Napoleons and tossed them in his open hand thoughtfully. At last he made up his mind. Returning them to Konstantinov he gave his instructions.

"Go into the house and show them to Count Shuvalov. Tell him what you just told me. Word for word. But not a word about having seen me."

Sych obeyed his chief sadly. No, he was not going to be an agent. After all, he wasn't being sent to report to Shuvalov. That meant Konstantinov's news would be more important.

But Konstantinov was not the least bit pleased.

"But how can that be, Ivan Dmitrievich!" he objected. "What for? Why should I give them up, and to those parasites? We'll manage ourselves. We'll put a call out to our lads—"

"Hop to it," Ivan Dmitrievich repeated.

"No," said Konstantinov in a weepy voice. "Beat me, do what you want, I won't!"

Without a word, Ivan Dmitrievich turned him around and kneed him lightly in the back, sending him on his appointed route.

Konstantinov meandered as ordered, muttering. "Now they'll get the rewards, they'll get everything. But what about us? You run around all day long, like a dog . . ."

Ivan Dmitrievich waited for him to walk up the front steps and then went around the corner so that he could not be seen from von Ahrensburg's house. There he untied the sack. There were three sandwiches, all with lean Finnish cheese. He divided them almost equally: he took two for himself and gave one to Sych. He took a bite and began to wait impatiently for further events, trying to convince himself that this would not take long.

The wind began to die down, and he could hear the noisy Neva breaking up in the distance.

Taking the sandwich, Sych immediately forgot about Ivan Dmitrievich driving him all the way to the Church of the Resurrection in just his shirt. He had nothing against him. What of it, what if Konstantinov was sent to see the gendarmes? On the other hand, he had bread and cheese, so there! And Ivan Dmitrievich wouldn't give it to him for nothing, oh no. Sych held the sandwich in his hand with care, as if it were the finest jewel, and could not bring it to his mouth. His heart was singing: he'd earned it, he had!

"Eat," said Ivan Dmitrievich. "What are you looking at!"

Sych took a bite and was ecstatic.

"Honey, not cheese! It simply melts on your tongue."

"It's not too lenten?"

"If anyone tells you that, Ivan Dmitrich, don't believe him."

They were silent, and then Sych asked, "Why are we standing here, Ivan Dmitrich? Are we waiting for someone?"

No answer was forthcoming, and he was frightened that he had poked his nose where agents weren't supposed to, even trusted agents, and decided to open an unrelated conversation.

"That man there, on the coin, how would he be related to that Napoleon?"

"Only through Adam."

Ivan Dmitrievich took out his watch and clicked the cover open. Aha, it was getting to be four. . . . Twenty-four hours ago at this time Prince von Ahrensburg had opened his front door, locked it from the inside, put the key on the little table in the front hall, and gone to his bedroom, where his valet had begun to pull off his boots, and the pair sitting on the windowsill behind the curtain had held their breath. Ivan Dmitrievich tried to imagine himself sitting on that windowsill. His numb feet had pins and needles. He pictured that and there he was—sitting and waiting. He whispered to his mate: "What if he doesn't tell us where the key is?" And his mate answered with just his lips: "He will." He couldn't hear him, and he couldn't see his lips in the darkness, but he got the idea. The lamp was burning in the bedroom, the light penetrated to the drawing room, and there was a bloody patch of light on the wall cast by the copper side of the prince's trunk. Neither knife nor nail had been able to open it. They had attempted to pry the top off with the poker, but that hadn't worked either.

In the morning, Ivan Dmitrievich had examined the windowsill and now he once again mentally ran his palm over it. No crumbs, which meant they hadn't been eating bread. In that case, why had they taken butter? It was an odd snack.

The sky would be growing light soon, but the echo was still muffled but strong in a night-time kind of way. He shifted from foot to foot, but he had the feeling someone was nearby, hiding behind the buildings.

When as a sixteen-year-old lad Ivan Dmitrievich had first found himself in Petersburg, he had been struck by the echo there. In his hometown, a person's step and voice had nothing to strike, nothing to bounce off; everything was soft, wooden or thatch. But here there was stone all around and walls to the sky. What was echoing? Where did it come from? There was no telling.

"We're waiting for something, after all, Ivan Dmitrievich!" began Sych, breathing raggedly. "We're not hiding here for nothing, after all. We're standing here in ambush, after all, and I'll never forget it to my grave that we're together. That you offered me cheese. . . . You trust me, Ivan Dmitrievich! Tell me, what are we waiting for?"

"Wait a minute," said Ivan Dmitrievich. "We'll be going soon."

"Where to?"

"The Church of the Resurrection."

Not believing his own good fortune, Sych said, "So it wasn't for nothing, it turns—"

"Shh!" Ivan Dmitrievich moved him around the corner and slapped him on the back of the head so he wouldn't peek out.

The front door slammed. Shuvalov stepped onto the steps, followed by Pevtsov.

"The Italians, Your Excellency," he said loudly. "Of course, the Italians!"

Behind his back Shuvalov's adjutant began explaining something to the Cossack captain who had run up and who, listening, nodded with comprehension. Konstantinov was hovering nearby. One of his eyes had begun to well up, but the other was wide open and shone like the eyes of a society beauty who had used atropine drops before a ball. Either the general excitement had been conveyed to him, or else he had forgotten his greed and had a foretaste of pure joy: seeing his bearded offender having his hands tied.

"That is what I thought, as well, the Italians," said Pevtsov soothingly as he helped Shuvalov on with his greatcoat. "However, I have not found any evidence. They hate the Austrians the way the Bulgarians hate the Turks. They were under their thumb for so many years. Your sleeve, Your Excellency. . . . And Prince von Ahrensburg did fight in Italy. According to my information, he did not show himself quite as a knight. He burned down a village."

"Indeed?"

"Alas! And he executed prisoners. The Italians had to take their revenge out on him. A vendetta!"

"Garibaldi himself probably sent them," said the adjutant deferentially.

"No," the Cossack captain objected with somber confidence. "It was the Pope."

"You and the convoy—follow us!" Shuvalov ordered him as he climbed into his carriage.

Pevtsov sat next to him and immediately after the adjutant squeezed in with the Koran under his arm. Konstantinov climbed on the box to show the coachman the way, and Rukavishnikov leapt onto the footboard at the back.

The Cossacks had already saddled up. A minute later the entire cavalcade had vanished at the end of the street, having splashed Ivan Dmitrievich with slush from its wheels and hooves.

He squeezed Sychev's trophy—the Napoleon from the Church of the Resurrection—harder in his fist. The two brought by Konstantinov had led Pevtsov and Shuvalov onward, to the harbor. The French emperor, bowing to the will of Ivan Dmitrievich, had drawn them their route with his goatee.

"Gallop away," he thought. "Sheep on the right hand and goats . . ."

He told Sych to wait outside and he himself went up the front steps and rang. He asked the valet who opened the front door:

"Where's the cat?"

"What?"

He was not thinking very clearly due to lack of sleep.

"The cat."

It was found in the kitchen, sitting on the table sniffing a dirty saucer. Ivan Dmitrievich thrashed his cat Murzik by the whiskers to enforce discipline if it jumped onto the table, but he had no intention of educating this cat. He grabbed it by the scruff of its neck and moved down the hall. Near the doors leading from the drawing room to the bedroom, he lifted his captive to the door hinge and thrust it face first straight at it.

The cat hung there apathetically and quietly, like a pelt on a hook. Ivan Dmitrievich had to change tactics. First he scratched it behind the ear and petted it, trying to reassure it, and once again stuck its nose there. The cat started sniffing with interest and twitching its whiskers. Aha, it licked it!

That afternoon Ivan Dmitrievich had tasted the hinge but hadn't come up with anything. His tongue, burned daily by hot tea, vodka, and tobacco smoke, had long since lost its sensitivity. Women were more delicate, they could taste and smell because they didn't drink or smoke, and there was no point being hypocritical by reproaching them for gluttony, a love of French perfume, and Turkish rubbings. Everyone loves what he is capable of appreciating, but you couldn't make Strekalova lick the door hinges! Actually, the cat was more reliable. An animal, no pretending. Although even so it was clear that one of the murderers had studied the prince's apartment and knew it like the palm of his hand. He knew about the bell pull and knew that the doors creaked. Now Ivan Dmitrievich could picture the scene in all its details. While the prince was relaxing in the evening, the criminals had entered the house and left the door to the drawing room open. That door didn't creak or howl. In order to penetrate to the bedroom later from the drawing room without making any noise, after the owner's departure for the Yacht Club they greased that door with butter.

Ivan Dmitrievich let the cat go, gratefully petting it in parting. Good work! It had given him irrefutable proof that the murderers had not had a previously worked out plan but had improvised. Otherwise, they would at least have brought along some vegetable oil.

He moved into the bedroom and pulled out the dressing table drawer. Here had lain the Napoleons. Next to him, dozing right on his feet, stood the valet.

"These coins," Ivan Dmitrievich asked him, "did someone give them to the prince or what?"

"He won them at cards. The day before yesterday he went to the Yacht Club and that's where he won them. He's usually a loser. He's not very lucky. But this time he arrived pleased as punch. 'Take a gander!' he says. He took one out of each pocket and threw them into the drawer. Clink, clink!"

"Who was he playing with, do you know?"

"Yes, he has a friend. Baron Hohen . . . Hahen . . ."

"Hohenbruch?"

"Uh huh. The next day the Polish secretary came here on some business and the master was boasting to him. No sooner did he leave then that's all I heard: king, queen, and two aces in a pair."

"Were they speaking Russian?"

"Why would they? German."

"And you understand?"

"I should say! My mother's a Finn and I've spent my whole life among gentlemen. I used to live in Riga."

Ivan Dmitrievich did not have a chance to ask him about the revolver. Someone outside was pounding loudly on the window. He saw Sych's face pressed up against the window, his nose squashed. Sych was making scary eyes, working his mouth silently, and signaling that Ivan Dmitrievich had to run out to see him right away.

He scrambled up the front steps shouting:

"Disaster, Ivan Dmitrievich! The Austrian ambassador was attacked right in the street!"

"I know, I know. They cut off the consul's head and let a pig into the Turkish embassy through a window. I know everything!"

At that moment a voice rang out behind him:

"Your agent is telling the truth. I'm the one who told him everything."

Ivan Dmitrievich turned around. Alongside a droshky that had evidently just driven up stood his good friend and block supervisor Sopov.

"Is he alive?" asked Ivan Dmitrievich quickly. "Answer me! Is he alive?"

"For now. A young student reached him and took him into an apartment."

Who was to blame that Shuvalov sent Hotek home without a convoy? Ivan Dmitrievich felt a chill just below his belly. He pushed Sopov toward the droshky, jumped in himself, and ordered the cabby: "Drive!"

Sopov hopped on when it was practically moving.

"A rope had been drawn across the street," he recounted. "The driver was thrown from his box and his face was all scraped up. He hit his head and doesn't remember a thing. Like a bit of fluff! They were hurrying on ministerial . . . I was walking nearby and heard it—crash! Shooting—"

"But you said it was a rope!"

"We assumed."

"Who did you report to?"

"No one. I came to you right away."

The night watchman's clapper was banging behind the buildings, as if to ask, "Who are you? Who are you? Who are you?" The moon was clouded over. Water was dripping from the roofs.

In the light of the streetlamp an advertising pillar splashed with fresh mud flashed by: Shuvalov and his suite had only just sped by.

II

One Cossack was galloping ahead of the carriage, two behind, and the captain to the side, by the door.

They needed to hurry. Konstantinov had reported that this morning the *Triumph of Venus* was sailing home. The dockworkers had told him.

The shaking nearly knocking his head into the ceiling as he jolted between Shuvalov and his adjutant, Pevtsov laid out his ideas for them. He had come to the conclusion that the murderers had been aided by some Russian socialist. Bakunin, he was keeping company with Mazini now, you see, and with the Carbonari in the south of Italy, and had a longstanding score with the Austrians, having spent time in their prison. Could it have been he who incited the Italians to take their vengeance out on von Ahrensburg? He decided to exploit their feelings and use the murder of a foreign diplomat to drum up ferment in society. He always had the leavening at the ready: the brigand element. Look at what was going on in Paris! The commune! Why not set one up in Petersburg, too?

"Still it's strange that it's the Italians," said the adjutant. "I saw them outside Sevastopol. I was still a cadet. Sickly but full-throated devils in battle! Oh, and they sang! At night, sometimes, I'd crawl toward their trenches and listen. I'd be lying in the grass chewing on a blade. I'd sprinkle it with powder instead of salt and chew, listening to them sing. The stars above me. As easy as pie to pick me off with a bullet and I'm lying there, fool. I wouldn't do that now."

Interrupting, Pevtsov reasoned further. Undoubtedly the Carbonari had resorted to the assistance of Petersburg criminals. Otherwise nothing was likely to have come of it. In a foreign city, not knowing the language. . . . But understandably the convicts didn't have a word of Italian, either. Consequently, there was an intermediary. A Russian or a Pole. Maybe a Jew.

"I think it's the emigrant who hired on as a sailor on the *Triumph of Venus*," said Pevtsov. "He was the one sitting in the America tavern."

"Why do you think that?" asked Shuvalov.

"We know, Your Excellency, that Italians consider vengeance a sacred matter. Murder—yes. Even from around the corner or at night in bed—fine, as you like. Nobility is no obstacle. In this regard they remind me of our Caucasian mountaineers. But robbing, that's quite another matter. The Napoleons were pocketed by their accomplices. By the way, the half-shtoff of vodka found on the window attests in favor of this scenario. Italians would have preferred wine."

In the pause the adjutant attempted to continue his own story.

"But they have a weakness for song, too, you know."

"Stop interfering!" Pevtsov elbowed him in the side. "It's simply good fortune, Your Excellency, that this fellow with the black eye, this Putilin spy, brought the coins to us and not his superior. He would have done something clever, chosen his moment. Have you already decided what to do with him?"

"With whom?"

"Putilin. The only thing I can't understand is whether he's crazy or having us on? To accuse the Austrian ambassador of murder without proof!"

"First, Captain, I have to decide how we're going to defend ourselves to Hotek."

"Very simply," said Pevtsov. "We'll arrest Putilin or drum him out of the service. There's your defense."

"Outside Sevastopol, I'm telling you, there was a case," the adjutant butted in. "Some company commander of ours gives an order: 'All right, boys, crank up "Nochenka," and put all you've got in it!' What a scoundrel. He picked up the rifle himself and went to the parapet. I was with him. Our little soldiers started singing, it brought a tear to my eye. We looked and the Italians were already poking their heads up from the trenches like ground squirrels. They were listening. The commander whispered to me, 'Fire, fire!' He went 'bang!' and took out their officer. But I couldn't. My arm wouldn't rise."

"And thank God," said Shuvalov. "Because I'm listening to you and thinking, Am I really going to have to find myself another adjutant?"

The driver tugged on the reins with all his might. The horses neighed and the carriage came to a halt. The Cossack captain tapped the window with his whip.

"Some female. Crawling right under the wheels."

Shuvalov opened the door and the young woman rushed at him, her scarf slipping onto her shoulders, disheveled, with a look of madness.

"Your honor, Pupyr! He's right around here."

Tears were streaming down her face.

Shuvalov tried to pull the door shut, but the woman grabbed on with both hands and wouldn't let go. The Cossack captain began easing her away with the horse's breast, explaining, "You need to go to the police. Go to the police."

"I'm not afraid for myself, your honor! I've been living with him. He won't do anything to me."

But the Cossack captain, not listening, was turning his horse. The blue lamp on the front of the carriage winked and was lost to sight, blocked by the backs of the convoy.

To the harbor, and quickly! The *Triumph of Venus* was already getting up steam and the flame was dancing in her firebox.

Near the gate at the entrance to the port, a sleepy soldier from an invalid detachment ran toward them.

"Raise it!" Konstantinov shouted at him from a distance in his general's voice.

With trembling hands the invalid lowered the rope, freeing the end of the gate. The sturdy iron weight attached to the other end pulled it down, the striped cross-bar flew up with a creak, and when the carriage, barely slowing down, dashed under it, Konstantinov, who was sitting on the box and didn't duck in time, had his cap knocked off.

He half-stood to get a better look at the road at a glance. With his hair blowing and his face burning in the wind, he pointed out where to go, shouting, "To the right! And right again. . . . Where are you going? Grrr! What hand do you cross yourself with, you dolt?"

At last, in the light of daybreak, Konstantinov made out a familiar silhouette by the shore. He imagined his nostrils catching the faint smell of oranges. He saw the elegant outlines of the ship's sides, its mast with its ropes fluffy with snow, the dim light on the forecastle, and the long smokestack decorated with the national colors of the Kingdom of Sardinia—red, white, and green. Smoke was issuing from the smokestack, and an engine was knocking below decks, but the ramp had not been taken up yet nor the anchor raised.

III

Ordinarily Pupyr plied his trade near the harbor, in whose saving labyrinths he could always hide from pursuit. Someplace there he also hid a portion of his loot, which was more convenient for selling it to sailors from foreign ships. Glasha knew about this and spent an hour and a half wandering through the neighboring blocks. She rambled down empty lanes, roamed in dark corners amid dustbins, stealthily followed the clientele wending their way home from the drinking establishments, choosing the better-dressed ones because those were the kind Pupyr most often hunted. A few times, in hopes of attracting his attention herself, she started singing high-class songs in a drunken voice. Let him think some reckless miss had run away from her husband with her ridicule, gold earrings, and hundred notes between her breasts, slipped there by some passionate admirer. Alas, all in vain.

The storm died down after midnight, the snow melted on the ground, which had warmed up in the last week. Her boots were soaked through, but Glasha wasn't thinking about that. What did it matter now?

But after all, not even a year ago she had been hoping for a groom: she had locked a big padlock over the Neva, and that night she had put the padlock and key under her pillow. The women at the laundry said that then in her dream her intended would come and ask for a drink of water. You just had to say, 'My lock, your key.' When morning came, the water carrier Semyon Ivanovich, a good man and a widower , had come. Waking, he had gazed on her and treated her to nuts. Oh, but no! She had to go get mixed up with a murderer. And he had been so wretched, so raggedy, his ears all scabby. After three months his face had rounded out. He was going around the taverns, writing in his notebook how to bake a pie with sturgeon jowl and one with catfish tail. And why hadn't she said anything, fool that she was? What was she afraid of? A fool, a terrible fool. Lord! Could there be anything on earth worse than living with him? How many souls she had on her conscience! And if he sinned against anyone today, you couldn't pray that sin away. It would be time to lay hands on herself. There was only one thing left: find the man with the side whiskers, and then into the Neva. Lord!

Glasha rushed through the streets, and a moment came when she suddenly felt he was somewhere there, that Satan, nearby. The dogs in the yards gave him away. First one mongrel, then another, started yelping pitiably and apprehensively, and then they all let up a howl at once. They had caught the wolf scent off Pupyr.

Twice Glasha ran up to policemen on duty and called on them to search for Pupyr, implored them and wept, but the first one was frightened off and the second started playing with her, grabbing her skirt, her breast, threatened to run her in for prostitution if she didn't please him. Glasha just barely beat him off. She even stopped a general's carriage, but the general wouldn't hear of Pupyr, nor would the mustached officer on the horse, though she got down on her knees before him. Sitting on the wet pavement, Glasha watched the horsemen move off and the horses' docks with their neatly cropped tails dance merrily, and she howled, rocking from side to side. A terrible thought turned her soul to ice: could Pupyr actually be someone the sovereign needed, since no one cared to catch him? Maybe he hadn't been just jabbering?

The clock on the Neva tower struck four. She stood up and wended her way home.

As she approached her building, she noted a faint light escaping from below, from the cellar. The light shuddered in the ventilation pane, and her heart sank: she had let him slip. There he was. Back.

A puff of smoke—people were lighting stoves here and there. Glasha lingered in the courtyard, distraught, not knowing what to do, whether to go or not, and she saw the light in the window go out. When she came to, Pupyr was in front of her. She looked at him, shrinking out of habit and not realizing immediately that for the first time she was looking him in the eye without fear.

"Where were you?" asked Pupyr.

Glasha shrugged and waggled her dirty hem bravely but didn't answer. She sniffed: he smelled of cologne. What was she afraid of? What about him was wolfish? A fur-collared officer's greatcoat, his boots scrubbed in front, and dirty heels. And his arms! Like an ape's! He could put a shine on his boots without bending over.

"Gone deaf have you? Where were you, I asked!"

She started to laugh.

"I was following you!"

"Me?" He goggled. "What did you see?"

"Everything! I saw everything!"

Glasha laughed, but for some reason tears were running down her cheeks.

"What did you see?" Pupyr asked quietly.

She wiped her tears and with great pleasure spit in his loathsome face, at the same time clutching his hair and shouting,

"Here he is! Arrest him!"

Pupyr ripped her hand away along with a tuft of his own hair, but he couldn't cover her mouth.

"Good people!" Glasha exclaimed lightly and joyfully, turning around. "Here he is!"

With his right hand Pupyr grabbed her across her stomach and with his left roughly crushed her lips, then he lifted her up and dragged her toward the service door.

On the third floor a window frame scraped and someone's bald head hung down over the cornice.

Glasha beat Pupyr off, tore the collar off his coat, scratched him on the neck, and gave a cry she thought was piercing but in fact came out a puny, rasping bleat. Pupyr dragged her down the stairs leading to the cellar and flung her like a sack on the stone steps. She struck the wall, sobbed, and fell still. Outside it was quiet. Listening closely, Pupyr ran downstairs, to his cache among the firewood. First he got out his luxurious leather trunk, lying in wait for his journey to Riga, then he flung the wood aside and dug out the box with the money, rings, earrings, and crosses, put it into the trunk and, after a moment's thought, jammed two sable hats in there, too. He tossed his notebook of culinary recipes for his future tavern in on top. The rest of his goods he would have to leave here. If Glashka came to her senses, she would thank him for it.

He clicked the lock and even now this brisk, merry click with which the curved steel pins on the chest interlocked reverberated sweetly in his heart with its promise of another life. He felt like giving it another click but didn't, of course. He ran back toward the stairs and saw Glasha staggering but standing at the top and trying to open the door.

His kettlebell reached her at the threshold and fetched her up right on the temple. She sat back down on the step and through the ultimate pain saw him coming, Semyon Ivanovich, the water carrier, a good man and a widower, coming for her on his barrel.

Tearing himself away from his notebook, Safonov asked, "This laundress's surname didn't happen to be Grigorieva, did it?"

"How did you know?" Ivan Dmitrievich was amazed.

"And did she live on Ruzovskaya Street?"

"Entirely correct. How did you find out?"

"Your turn to guess," suggested Safonov, with a little laugh.

"Beats me. Of course, they did write about her in the newspapers, but have you really retained the memory of both the murdered woman's surname and her street? You were just a child at the time."

"A gymnasium boy in my last year," Safonov clarified. "Actually, at the time I didn't read the newspapers, on the other hand today at dinner I read the chapter outline of your notes with the chapter, 'Bestial Murder on Ruzovskaya Street.' You went on to explain that this referred to the laundress Grigorieva."

"Ah yes," recalled Ivan Dmitrievich, "but in the course of the telling I decided to describe her death not in a separate chapter but in connection with von Ahrensburg's murder. That would be more proper. Judge for yourself. Who cares about some laundress? On the other hand, interweave her, poor thing, into some political intrigue, which is what I've done, and people are certain to read it. Please, put in her full name: Aglaya Grigorieva."

"I will later."

"No, do it now, so my mind can be at rest. I owe her a debt. Had I caught Pupyr sooner, she might still be alive."

"If you think about it, Sych is the most to blame," reasoned Safonov.

"We're all fine ones."

Ivan Dmitrievich recounted that he allocated the money for Aglaya Grigorieva's funeral out of the detective police's secrets funds and he himself followed her casket on foot, along with Sych and Konstantinov, naturally. They buried her at Volkovy Cemetery.

"On the way back we stopped at a tavern to remember the deceased," he said. "We had a drink and I picked up my empty glass, squeezed it in my fist, and crushed it like an egg. When I spread my fingers there wasn't a scratch on my hand. Well, that cheered me up right away."

"Why?" Safonov did not understand.

"It was a sign, I thought."

"A sign of what?"

"How dense you are! It meant she'd forgiven me, there" — Ivan Dmitrievich raised his eyes to the veranda ceiling — "in the ever-flowing ether."

After a pause he continued.

"By the way, at the funeral I met that Semyon Ivanovich, the water carrier. He was the one who revealed to me the secret of the first attempt on Hotek's life."

"When they threw a rock at him?"

"Yes, and this is what happened. The night before, Hotek's driver had purchased feed for the embassy horses at Haymarket and had slipped one of the merchants a forged banknote. The merchant went to the embassy to complain and they tossed him out on his ear. That's what Semyon Ivanovich told me. He's one of the boys at Haymarket, he knows everything. Basically, the next morning the offended man saw his offender as he was driving Hotek to the Street of Millions and in the heat of the moment launched a rock at him from behind the fence, but he missed. The rock went through the carriage window, and that's the whole story. I must say," added Ivan Dmitrievich, "I'd imagined something like that from the very beginning."

Chapter 14

The Snake Bites Its Own Tail

Swaddled up to his neck in a lap rug, Hotek lay on the sofa in Kungurtsev's apartment. Next to him sat Nikolsky. Like Cobenzel, having dragged the ambassador to the apartment and daubed the bruises on his arms with iodine, he thought he had done everything possible to save him. Kungurtsev himself had already managed to array himself in his frock coat. Nervous, he didn't know what to do with himself, and in anticipation of important personages arriving from the Ministry of Foreign Affairs he drove his wife off to change clothes.

"They're coming," he said in a tragic whisper, "and you, my darling, are perfectly slovenly."

"Just a minute, just a minute," Masha replied, simultaneously brewing fresh tea, opening a bottle of Cahors, and applying a cold compress to Hotek's brow.

In the next room the ambassador's driver, about whom she also had to concern herself, was moaning.

Cobenzel was pacing back and forth for fear of missing the moment when one of the two was in a condition to recount all the details of what had transpired.

They had already run out for a doctor, but when he had examined Hotek he had found no injuries on him and diagnosed a deep faint caused by the nervous shock and ordered that he not be disturbed and then he'd gone to tend to the driver.

"Sir, your duty is to be alongside His Excellency," Cobenzel reminded him several times.

The doctor said, "I'm coming."

But he wasn't.

In the vestibule, guarding the door, sat the porter, and crowded on the staircase were the neighbors, roused by the turmoil. A gentleman wearing a fox fur coat thrown over his robe was showing all comers to the window of his apartment on the fourth floor, directly above Kungurtsev's apartment, and showing them the rope stretched across the street. As long as the snow didn't melt, there was a good view of it from that height against the white background. Those who had been outside explained that one end of the rope was tied to a streetlamp and the other to a rounded iron fork set into the building wall that grasped the stem of the waterspout. They were reluctant to remove the rope before the police arrived, so two volunteers with lamps stood downstairs to make sure no one else was its victim. In the entryway doors kept slamming, and the inhabitants gathered on the landings. From time to time a hysterical female voice was heard crying that there was going to be a war and entreating someone named Alexander Ivanovich not to sleep but to run to the telegraph office and immediately send a telegram to someone named Lelechka in Carlsbad telling her not to start out for Russia with the children tomorrow.

"That's odd," said Cobenzel, addressing Kungurtsev. "I sent that policeman to the duty officer for the Foreign Affairs Ministry, but no one has come from there yet."

"A-a-ah!" the driver hollered in a nasty voice on the other side of the wall and fell silent.

"It's the doctor fixing his dislocated shoulder."

That very moment the long-awaited bell pealed.

"Masha!" hissed Kungurtsev. "Quickly! That one, the black. With the poufs. And don't forget your brooch!"

Tugging at his coat as he went, he hurried to the vestibule. The porter had opened the door wide, and across the threshold stepped Ivan Dmitrievich. He entered alone; Sopov and Sych remained in the entryway.

Seeing Putilin rather than Chancellor Gorchakov, Kungurtsev calmed down.

"Oh, it's you. Well then, come in."

Nikolsky stood up, and Ivan Dmitrievich took his seat next to the sofa, gazing in terror at Hotek's white pointy-nosed face.

"Your Excellency."

The other man was silent. His lowered eyelids were motionless, the blue vein swollen on his forehead looked like it was just about to burst through the dry and thin old-man skin.

"Wouldn't you like some tea?" cooed Masha, leaning over him like the child she didn't have. "Some nice hot tea."

Ivan Dmitrievich moved her hand holding the cup away.

"Don't you see he's lost consciousness?"

"No no," she said. "The ambassador gentleman has already come around. He just doesn't want to talk to anyone. Clearly he's gone through something horrible. I was feeding him Cahors from a spoon, and he swallowed it."

Ivan Dmitrievich stood and walked over to the window. The short piece of rope illuminated by the light from a lower window pierced the darkness like a rapier. Across the way, recently completed construction and an as yet uninhabited building stretched the length of the block. On this side of the street there was the single apartment building. To the right of it was a small garden, then the long two-story building of a boys' grammar school—empty, naturally, at night. To the left stretched a vacant lot cleared for construction. The place for the assassination had been chosen with uncommon success. You could scarcely find better in the middle of the capital.

"Gentlemen," requested Ivan Dmitrievich, "please be so kind as to tell me your names."

"Pavel Avraamovich Kungurtsev," said Kungurtsev. "*Voice* correspondent. If you recall, this afternoon I went to see you on Millions. And this"—he faltered, inasmuch as Masha was his common-law wife, they had not registered, and he let her untangle herself from her position herself.

"I believe you and I saw each other recently as well," said Cobenzel.

Only now did Ivan Dmitrievich notice that there was one more person present in the room. He recognized the secretary of the Austrian embassy, who had arrived on Millions with the coffin. The name cited by the Preobrazhensky lieutenant surfaced in his memory.

"Cobenzel?"

"Baron Cobenzel. Is it true you have found the murderer of Prince von Ahrensburg?"

"Yes."

"And who is he?"

"I'm sorry, I cannot tell you that right now. You'll find out tomorrow."

"Tell me just one thing. Has he been arrested?"

"Yes," Ivan Dmitrievich lied, anticipating events.

"Isn't there some mistake here? Who then carried out the attack on the ambassador? I thought I was firing at the same person—"

"You fired at him?" Ivan Dmitrievich interrupted.

"How's that?" Cobenzel was amazed in turn. "No one told you anything?"

"We heard a shot," Kungurtsev confirmed.

"First a cry," Masha clarified, "then a shot."

"Are you sure? Not the other way around?" asked Ivan Dmitrievich.

"First he tapped his finger on the window," said Kungurtsev, nodding at Nikolsky. "Remember?"

"No, I heard—"

Ivan Dmitrievich turned to face Cobenzel.

"Tell me everything just as it happened."

"In my opinion you're losing precious time."

"Briefly, then."

"If you like." Cobenzel shrugged. "But all responsibility rests on you."

And so, that evening Hotek had asked him to stay at the embassy and wait, while Hotek himself went to the Street of Millions. Upon his return they were supposed to compile the report for Vienna together. However, after midnight Hotek was still not there, and Cobenzel began to worry and ultimately decided to meet him halfway. . . . Why on foot? Everyone was asleep and he couldn't find the driver. He took along his pistol—

"Do you always carry a weapon?" Ivan Dmitrievich cut him off again.

"This is starting to resemble an interrogation." Cobenzel frowned. "Generally speaking I am not a lunatic and am not accustomed to roaming the city at night. But you know you have been powerless to catch this infamous Pupyr. . . . I was walking past the school when I heard the cry, then the bang and neighing, and ran over to see our ambassador lying on the ground. Someone was leaning over him."

"What did he look like?"

"It was dark. . . . When he saw me he ran off. I fired and knocked off his top hat."

"Baron Cobenzel," interjected Kungurtsev, "is a marvelous, fantastic marksman. There are legends circulating about his art."

"At what distance did you fire?"

"I don't remember precisely. Ten paces or so, maybe fifteen."

"And for all your legendary art you couldn't hit a man at ten paces?"

"It is demeaning to have to defend myself to you," said Cobenzel, "but everyone knows that I never fire at live targets. No sooner do I aim at a person or an animal then my hands start shaking. I simply cannot pull the trigger."

"How did you go hunting with the deceased prince and Baron Hohenbruch?"

"Your knowledge evokes respect, but I was there only as a spectator. In my whole life I have never shot a single duck or hare. I have never once fought a duel. Or rather, I have only fought with sabers."

"You could kill someone with a saber?"

"I served in the cavalry. In battle I had to. . . ."

"What about sticking a pig, for example?"

"In any case, I have slaughtered chickens on campaign."

"So you're incapable of shooting them?"

"What do you want from me?" Cobenzel blazed up.

"I want to understand why you took your pistol along."

"To fire in the air if bandits attacked. Even I find it strange that I was able to fire at that man. There was something about him. . . ."

"You didn't get a good look at him, though."

"Nevertheless. . . . In short, I knocked off his top hat."

"And where is it?"

Ivan Dmitrievich took the black top hat brought to him by Nikolsky—it was the kind torch bearers wear at rich men's funerals—and poked his finger through the bullet hole. The bullet had struck nearly at the top and passed clean through. The edges of both openings, burned by the white-hot lead, were a brownish yellow.

"I picked this up there, too," said Nikolsky.

Ivan Dmitrievich saw Hotek's familiar wallet with the Hapsburg eagle embossed on the leather—the same eagle as on the carriage. He opened it. Inside lay some letters and calling cards. Feeling shy about digging in another man's wallet, Ivan Dmitrievich carefully felt it from the outside and then squeezed it between his palms. There was nothing hard in it. The key from the prince's trunk, the snake-key found under the Edenic apple in the ink device, had vanished. But he had seen Hotek put it there with his own eyes. He placed the wallet in his pocket.

Ivan Dmitrievich took a step toward Nikolsky.

"Was it you who found it?"

"Yes, it was lying on the ground."

"You didn't open it?"

"What are you implying!"

"You didn't find a key? One like . . . a circle—a snake holding its own tail in its mouth. That wasn't there?"

"Word of honor, there was nothing else."

Kungurtsev took out his tablet and began writing feverishly: "A snake biting its own tail. What is this? A symbol of eternity? Or a hint that the ambassador's suffering was his own fault? An amazing night. Why was it I who ended up at the center of events? Is this a punishment or a boon? A coincidence or logic? The Austrian ambassador is on my sofa. A death's head hawk moth. Masha in her little robe against a painting in the spirit of Callot. April 26, 1871, 6:22 in the morning."

"By the way, Baron," Ivan Dmitrievich asked as nonchalantly as possible. "Did you dress as you were leaving the embassy or did you set out directly looking like that?"

"It's not summer yet." Cobenzel shot him a look nearly of hatred.

"But perhaps you were so alarmed by the ambassador's long absence . . . . You were wearing your coat? And hat? Where are they?"

"I took them off in the front hall. Why do you care?"

"When we carried the ambassador into the apartment," Nikolsky interjected, "you weren't wearing a hat."

"Evidently I dropped it in the entryway."

"And when I went outside and saw you, you had no hat either!"

"A plot for a story," Kungurtsev wrote rapidly. "Baron C., a brilliant marksmen, never fires at living beasts. He violates this vow given in his youth one time and loses his superhuman art forever after."

Ivan Dmitrievich put the wallet on the table and picked up the top hat again. For half a minute he twirled it in his hands and nonetheless could not resist the temptation: with a sudden movement he planted it on the head of Cobenzel, who was taken by surprise. The top hat fitted him just right.

Cobenzel tore it off and flung it into a corner.

"You're taking liberties!"

"Forgive me, for God's sake."

Before Ivan Dmitrievich could continue, that very moment, Hotek moaned and opened his eyes.

"Your Excellency!" Forestalling the doctor, who had hurried out of the adjoining room, Cobenzel was the first to lean over the sofa. "It is I! Do you recognize me, Your Excellency? Tell me who attacked you! Did you see him?"

He asked in German, but Ivan Dmitrievich understood everything perfectly, although he could barely wish his neighbor the baker good morning in the language of Schiller and Goethe.

"Your Excellency . . . ."

Hotek lowered his lids without answering.

"He's not going to tell you anything," said Masha.

She emerged from the bedroom wearing her black silk dress with the poufs, in which, as Kungurtsev had long ago noted, every word she said sounded especially convincing.

"Why?" Cobenzel turned toward her.

"He doesn't want to talk."

"Why not? Why do you think that?"

"I don't know," said Masha quietly. "But it seems to me the ambassador recognized the man."

"And so?" Cobenzel pressed her.

"And so he doesn't want to say his name."

Cobenzel squatted back on his heels near the head of the sofa. He seemed ready to grab Hotek by the shoulders and shake him to dislodge the answer from him.

"Your Excellency, who was it? One word, Your Excellency! Did you get a good look at him?"

Hotek again made an effort to separate his swollen eyelids: "Yes . . ."

"Who was it? Who?"

A minute of silence, then Hotek whispered:

"An angel . . ."

Masha gasped, Kungurtsev the atheist and the doctor exchanged understanding glances, Cobenzel moved away from the sofa rubbing his temples, and Ivan Dmitrievich swept into the vestibule and dashed out onto the landing, where at his appearance agitated voices fell silent at once. Sopov and Sych ran over to join him immediately and three pairs of boots thundered down the staircase.

"That's our Lecoq!" Kungurtsev winked at his wife. "I'm afraid his career will be over at this."

He looked at Hotek, who was lying motionless, indifferent to everything, and from his face you'd be more inclined to assume he had encountered a devil.

"Why have there still not been any officials?" asked Cobenzel.

Kungurtsev gestured helplessly.

"I don't know."

"What is going on? Can you explain this to me? Where am I? In the capital of a friendly state or the enemy camp?" exclaimed Cobenzel.

"Everyone will be coming soon," the doctor reassured him. "Don't get upset."

Kungurtsev removed the student coat from the hook and brought it to Nikolsky:

"Get dressed and go home."

"Under no circumstance," said Masha firmly. "Petya is staying with us."

"Darling, do you realize the threat posed to us by the presence of a person suspected of the murder of the Austrian military attaché? He must leave this minute!"

"Over my dead body," said Masha.

Nikolsky was silent. He didn't care. He had gradually drunk up half the bottle of Cahors opened for Hotek, but nothing had helped. The dead man's head he had stolen from the anatomical theater and thrown away near the Three Giants tavern gazed at him from the dusk outside with its formaldehyde-scorched eyes. There was no running away from that gaze.

II

They left the droshky around the corner and let the coachman go. Helping each other up, Ivan Dmitrievich, Sopov, and Sych climbed the fence surrounded the Preobrazhensky grounds and, unseen from Millions, past the barracks, alongside the still deserted parade ground with its white lines drawn clearly in lime, ran toward the gates. From there they had a good view of the entire street in front of von Ahrensburg's home. With a running start Sych was eager to go farther, but Ivan Dmitrievich held him back by his collar:

"Where are you going?"

Now they needed to stand there and wait for the person to appear who had taken the key to the trunk. If he took it, that meant he knew what this key could open and where. It was better not to enter the house. He might be there already and abscond through one of the windows on the courtyard. This way he would come out by the same route he took in.

These are the words the tavern keeper who gave Ivan Dmitrievich the jar of pickled agarics had overheard: "Death to your prince," whispered the man, who had leaned toward his mate, who knew about the trunk, the bell pull, and the creaking doors. "Death to him if he doesn't tell us where the key is." The tavern keeper had misheard the second half of what he said and decided von Ahrensburg was already murdered.

"Ugh, no saber or revolver!" Sych worried.

Neither he nor Sopov knew who they were watching out for here, but they didn't dare ask. One time Sych had inquired and received his final answer: "You'll see when he comes."

The question was, when? In two hours? An hour? Five minutes? Before nightfall? Ivan Dmitrievich tried not to think about the fact that this person might have managed to get inside the house before they'd taken up their position. He stood by the gates, hidden behind a stone pillar, waited, and fiddled around in his pocket, in the tobacco dust, with the Napoleon from the Church of the Resurrection. It felt warm and familiar.

Approximately the same size as a particular spot. The

mark of Cain, which in legend appeared on the body of every murderer in the same place through which he had deprived his victim of life. Thus, in any case, Ivan Dmitrievich had been informed by his father, who had served as a copyist in a district court. He had found it easy to believe. His papa had sat in the court his entire life, but he had never looked a genuine murderer in the face. In those days, no one ever killed anyone in their small town. Somehow things never got as far as blood and thunder. Even when the opposite ends of town went head to head and bloodied the ice on the pond, though they complained cruelly, broke arms and legs, and smashed heads, everyone managed to survive. From time to time the highwaymen in the neighboring forests started up and robbed, grabbed purses, naturally, however even they were wary of taking a mortal sin on their soul. Now even there things were different, and here, in Petersburg, so much the more. Sometimes Ivan Dmitrievich thought his father had been right. In the old days, the mark of Cain did appear, but nowadays it didn't. The Lord God's heavenly stamp, which he had used to make his mark, had worn down because he'd had to use it too often.

"It's late," said Sopov with doubt in his voice. "They've already been here."

"He doesn't care about that," replied Ivan Dmitrievich.

Imagine, passersby! It was quieter in the afternoon. A respectable gentleman could ring the bell, enter the house, sweet-talk the valet, and then strike him on the noggin.

"Ivan Dmitrievich," whispered Sych with sudden inspiration. "I thought of something! We should put a hat by the front steps and a brick under it. We could use my cap! That swine, he wouldn't be able to resist. He'd kick the cap and go lame. Then we could—"

"Be quiet," ordered Ivan Dmitrievich.

Although it did occur to him that this childish ambush with the hat could be put to good service. Too bad he couldn't go out from behind the fence.

A light gray shower was sprinkling down. Not even rain but mist. In the moisture-soaked air, Ivan Dmitrievich's side whiskers fluffed out. He kept the front steps of the prince's house and the adjoining section of the street under surveillance, watched the sparrows peck the muck left from the embassy, gendarme, and Cossack horses, and listened to the wheezy breathing of Sych and the calm breathing of Sopov behind him. Behind the barracks the soldiers were washing up, snorting and splashing water on each other's naked backs. A water carrier drove down the street, and the barrel attached to the side clattered for a long time. A rooster crowed in someone's kitchen, dogs barked, smoke from chimneys spread low over the roofs, not rising any higher because in that kind of weather there was almost no draft, and the green spring firewood burned slowly and listlessly in the stoves. The crows clamored. As always in spring and fall, when the trees are bare, the crows' cawing, not muffled by the rustle of foliage, was particularly loud, tiresome, and annoying. A baby started crying in the next house. The porter, scattering the puddles, wielded his broad wooden shovel rimmed in iron with a soul-rending sound. The day was beginning, ordinary life was flowing, and it did not seem at all incredible that the death of Prince von Ahrensburg was the result of just this life with all its coincidences and confusions rather than any other important life for which this one was merely a pediment.

Suddenly Sych, who had pressed his eye to the gap in the fence again, turned a deathly pale face toward Ivan Dmitrievich.

"This must be who we're waiting for."

Ivan Dmitrievich glanced around the pillar. Hurrying down the street, heading in a businesslike way toward von Ahrensburg's house, was Lewicki.

III

First to jump out onto shore was Shuvalov's adjutant with the Koran under his arm, and behind him, Pevtsov.

"Rukavishnikov!" he called.

But Rukavishnikov was not to be found on the footboard. In the mad race he had fallen off somewhere along the way.

Two seagulls were perched on the water behind the Italian schooner's stern. Dawn was breaking.

"We got here in time," said the adjutant looking with some regret at the smoke pouring from the stack.

He sympathized with the emissaries of Garibaldi who had had their revenge on the Austrian prince.

"I think it would be improper for me to be on this vessel," commented Shuvalov, getting out of the carriage.

"I'll go alone," Pevtsov volunteered.

"What do you intend to do there?"

"For starters, I'll have a talk with the captain."

"Do you know Italian?"

"They all understand French quite well. If they don't start pretending, we'll come to an agreement."

"Maybe you'll take one of them?" Shuvalov nodded at the Cossacks who had already rushed up and were standing at a distance, holding their horses by the bridle.

"No, Your Excellency. Here we'll do better without a fuss, delicately."

"Captain," Shuvalov ordered. "Give the lieutenant your revolver."

Pevtsov took the weapon.

"Loaded?"

"Yes, sir."

"What about me?" asked Konstantinov.

"If I need you, I'll call. For now, stand here."

Returning the empty holster to the Cossack captain, Pevtsov stuck the revolver in his waistband, under his tunic, and started clambering up the ramp. The Napoleons taken from Konstantinov lay in his pocket.

A head wearing a sailor's beret with a pompom appeared over the side.

"Ho! You pilot?"

Pevtsov was enraged. A blue greatcoat, epaulettes. . . . You had to be an idiot to take him for a harbor pilot.

Five minutes later he was sitting in the captain's cabin, leaning back against the partition between a copper crucifix and the portrait of a stern gentleman with a lipless mouth. When asked which of the crew had spent the previous night in the city, the captain, an elderly man with sad Southern eyes who was disturbed by the surprise visit, replied that both yesterday and the day before yesterday all the sailors given shore leave had returned to the ship by midnight.

"Do you have any passengers?" Pevtsov inquired.

The captain shrugged.

"No one wants to sail to Italy, though I put an advertisement in the newspaper. We have two marvelous cabins, and the price is reasonable. When we sailed here from Genoa they were occupied by a Turkish diplomat, Yusuf Pasha, and his family. They were quite satisfied with the journey."

The mention of Turks, who along with the ill-starred Kerim-Bek had vanished forever, it seemed, from the list of possible murderers of Prince von Ahrensburg, put Pevtsov on his guard, but he decided not to bring up that topic for now.

"Are there Russians on the crew?" he asked.

"Madonna mia! Where would we get them?"

With an imperceptible motion, the captain extracted a squat bottle with a little sealing wax left on the neck and two faience mugs.

"Actually," he went on, pouring the marvelously aromatic rum in them, "I do have one Negro stoker on the ship."

"Are you mocking me?" Pevtsov pushed the mug away. "What Negro?"

"From Ethiopia, signor officer. He says they have the same faith as you Russians. Should I call him in?"

Pevtsov shook his head. That's all he needed, Ethiopians.

"Are there Poles?"

"No. True, Dino Cielli's mother was born in Poland."

"Who is he, this Cielli?"

"You don't know Cielli?" the captain was amazed.

"I have not had the honor."

"I was in Calcutta, and they know Cielli there. Oh, Cielli! The eleven best steamers in Genoa—that's who Luigi Cielli is. The *Triumph of Venus* isn't even the very best. Far from it! Although I will say without boasting, in calm weather—"

"Get to the point," Pevtsov cut him off.

"Here he is, in front of you," said the captain, pointing to the portrait. "My owner, Luigi Cielli."

"But you gave a different name, as I recall."

"Yes, Dino. That's his oldest son. The heir. His father sent him with me to gain experience. His mother's a Pole. When she was a young woman she dressed in men's clothing to fight the Russian tsar and fled to Italy. Luigi abducted her from a convent. She is a woman of extraordinary beauty, a Venus—"

"Yesterday," Pevtsov interrupted again, "one of your men attacked a policeman in a tavern. I have to find the bandit. Please be so kind as to assemble your entire crew on deck."

"Signor officer, there is some misunderstanding here. A mistake! At least tell me what this scoundrel looks like."

"Every last one of them," Pevtsov repeated. "I have to look myself."

He purposely did not name the criminal's features, although Konstantinov had described him thoroughly. They could easily hide him somewhere in the hold. Then try finding him.

The captain shrugged and went out. Under the floor the engine was knocking louder and louder. The vibrations made the surface of the rum in the mugs contract in even, barely trembling, concentric circles. After his sleepless night, they were as hypnotizing and stupefying as if he had sipped the drink itself. Naturally, there was a temptation to lie down, but Pevtsov fought it off. He was still belching the prince's sherry, drunk before its time.

On deck a whistle sang out. Noise, trampling. It sounded like dozens of men running. But when he came out on deck, Pevtsov counted just nine sailors. Not one among them with a beard.

"This is everyone?" he asked.

"The Ethiopian stayed by the firebox," the captain reported, "and Dino is sleeping in his cabin. We're not going to wake him, are we?"

"Everyone here immediately," ordered Pevtsov.

A couple of minutes later the Ethiopian appeared—beardless, obviously, since Negroes can barely grow whiskers. He walked across the deck, wiping his sweat, breathing in the cold air with pleasure. A thought flashed: what if this detective, this Putilin spy, were lying? Could Putilin himself have insinuated him here? Where was there anyone here with a beard? But his doubts were instantly forgotten the moment the captain brought in Dino Cielli. The owner's son was a hardy, insolent fellow with a blond beard. He looked around him with displeasure, and he had a parrot sitting on his shoulder.

"Please walk toward the side," Pevtsov told him. "Closer."

And he shouted down to Konstantinov: "Is this he?"

"The very one!"

"And do you know this man, Monsieur Cielli?"

He shook his head.

"Oh, you snake!" Konstantinov raged, standing at the edge of the berth. "You don't admit it?"

"Monsieur Cielli, show me your hands," Pevtsov requested.

"Take a good look, the snake!" Konstantinov shouted below. "Don't turn away!"

The confrontation was a success. Dino stepped hastily away from the side and put his hands behind his back with a challenge, as if to ask, Well now, and what are you going to do to me? He even attempted to whistle a vivacious Neapolitan tune, but his lips were trembling and he couldn't. His unease was transmitted to the parrot, which ruffled up and began clawing angrily at his shirt.

"Even the bird realizes you're nervous," said Pevtsov gaily. "I must conduct a search in your cabin."

"Just a minute, signor officer! We need to talk alone. I want to tell you . . . Let's go!"

Again they descended to the captain's cabin. His suggestion that they sit was met with a refusal.

"I'm listening," said Pevtsov.

"Signor officer," the captain began, pressing his hands to his chest. "Dino is a rascal, yes, but he's not a bandit. He's just a proud boy and he stands his ground. At his age I was proud, too, but I now have five children. Answer me as if this were confession: is the case serious?"

"There is none more serious."

"And that man on shore, is he a general?"

"Something like that," Pevtsov nodded, not going into detail.

The captain grabbed Pevtsov's hand.

"I beg of you, have pity on my children! Don Luigi will never forgive me if I surrender his son!"

"Unfortunately, I'm powerless to help you. You will have to postpone sailing."

"Tell your general you were mistaken."

With these words the captain made the same imperceptible movement he had half an hour before when he had extracted the bottle of rum from somewhere, as if materializing his notion of it in the air. A light clanging broke out, and Pevtsov felt the left pocket of his greatcoat suddenly grow heavier. He put his hand in and pulled out a heavy purse.

"Yusuf Pasha paid me in gold," said the captain modestly. "By the way, he liked our rum quite a lot. You shouldn't refuse it."

Trying to determine by its weight the price this Italian had set for him, Pevtsov hefted the purse a few times in his hand and then flung it on the table, saying, "I am a Russian officer!"

The purse dragged heavily across the bare tabletop, struck the partition with a jangle, squirmed, and fell still. One gold coin fell out and rolled across the table.

"I see you are an honest man. If only our king had such officers! Your emperor is lucky," said the captain, moving cautiously toward the door. "All right, do your duty. I'll go stop the engine."

He slipped out of the cabin in an odd kind of way, sideways, but Pevtsov was not paying attention because he had seen the coin that had just fallen out of the purse. He was sick to discern on it the familiar goatish profile.

Left alone, he grabbed the purse and tore it open. There were another ten pieces just the same. . . . Damn!"

Pevtsov rushed toward the door. Locked! His memory brought up the click of the lock that he had heard out of the corner of his ear a minute before. He drummed on the door with his fists.

"Open up! Open up. I have something to tell you!"

No one responded. The pistons struck more and more crushingly and the rum in the mugs splashed onto the table. The berth's log deck shuddered and floated slowly by in the porthole.

Pevtsov tried to open it, but he couldn't get the better of the securely tightened thumbscrew. He grabbed a footstool, squinted so his eyes wouldn't be cut by shards, and smashed it into the window. He poked his head out. Right by his head he heard the ramp being thrown back and the spray reached his face. He licked his salty lips. There was already a sazhen and a half between the ship and the berth, and the icy water churned and foamed below. He was afraid to jump!

Konstantin and Shuvalov's adjutant were running up and down the edge of the mooring, waving their arms, opening their mouths without making a sound. They were looking up, at the deck, and didn't notice him.

"Hey!" shouted Pevtsov. "I'm here!"

No, they couldn't hear. His voice drowned in the splashing of the water and rumbling of the engine.

That was when he remembered the revolver. He fired once, twice. Aha, they saw him! But what could they do? It was too late! Without a pilot, without a parting blast of the horn, the *Triumph of Venus* put out to sea.

IV

Glancing out the window, Ivan Dmitrievich whistled softly the way you call dogs: fyu-fyu!

Lewicki halted.

Again: fyu-fyu-fyu!

Now he realized where the whistling was coming from, noticed Ivan Dmitrievich behind the column, and headed toward him with a fashionable smile and foppishly waving his walking stick.

"He's actually smiling, the swine!" whispered Sych.

"Fool!" said Ivan Dmitrievich. "Don't you recognize one of us?"

"Thank God you're here," said Lewicki, approaching with him some wariness. "At first I was going to drive by your house. We were separated so unexpectedly last night—"

"Where did I send you yesterday?" Ivan Dmitrievich cut him off.

"Where you sent me, that's where I went."

"And what wind blew you to the Yacht Club?"

"A fortunate one, Ivan Dmitrievich. If I hadn't turned up there, you and I wouldn't have understood anything. You don't know who sicced the gendarmes on me, do you? We parted so suddenly that I didn't have time to explain."

"Who was it?"

"Hohenbruch. Have you heard of him?"

"Baron Hohenbruch?"

"He's no baron! His father spent his whole life in Prague selling kneidelach. He purposely told Lieutenant Colonel Foch all about me. Well, you know, that I'm not the least important person in Poland, so to speak, and might have an interest in war between Russia and Austria."

"And what use was that to him?"

"That's what I thought, too. Why? Why did Hohenbruch need the gendarmes to suspect me of murdering von Ahrensburg? Our relations are quite friendly, we trust each other. Why play such a dirty trick on me? Last night I'm lying there and suddenly it's like being struck by lightning. That's what it is, I think! You see, Ivan Dmitrievich, he wanted to divert suspicion from himself."

"Had anyone really suspected him?"

"I had," said Lewicki. "I'd suspected him. Or rather, I suspect him now."

"You do?"

"Nature has not shorted me on analytical capabilities, and Hohenbruch has had more than one opportunity to convince himself of this at the card table. He realized I had grounds for suspecting him."

Ivan Dmitrievich continued to keep one eye on Millions, but he was listening carefully to Lewicki, who was recounting under his breath how a few days before he had been at the Yacht Club, where Hohenbruch had approached him and asked him whether he, Lewicki, could set it up so that when they played as a threesome he, Hohenbruch, would lose and their third partner would win. Lewicki wondered at this unusual request, but said yes, he could. Why not render his friend this small service? Especially since the third person to sit down at the table with them was none other than the deceased von Ahrensburg. They started playing. In the end, Lewicki broke even, Hohenbruch, with his help, lost, and the prince, accordingly, won a dozen French Napoleons d'or and was as happy as a child, since usually he was not lucky at cards. He rose from the table in excellent spirits. They went to the buffet, and on the way Hohenbruch said, "By the way, Prince, I received those Napoleons d'or from Yusuf Pasha." They started talking about some rifle whose patent Hohenbruch had either sold to the Turks or was planning to, and von Ahrensburg was unhappy about that and said, "You're harming my reputation, and I'm going to oppose you decisively!" Laughing, Hohenbruch replied, "Unfortunately, Prince, you can't challenge me to a duel because my father sold kneidelachs."

"What happened after that?" asked Ivan Dmitrievich.

"They drank some Champagne and went home."

"Did they clink?"

"How's that?" Lewicki didn't understand.

"Glasses. I'm asking, did they clink glasses?"

"I don't remember."

"Did the Prince return the Napoleons?"

"Yes," Lewicki suddenly remembered. "That completely slipped my mind. He dropped them on the table in front of Hohenbruch, the whole dozen, and said, 'Take your dirty money. I'm going to oppose you decisively!' Later, of course, he regretted it and changed his mind. He was basically stingy, the prince."

"Aha." Ivan Dmitrievich nodded. "Why do you think Hohenbruch killed him?"

"Ivan Dmitrievich, you amaze me," said Lewicki with a familiarity that he would not have got away with any other time. "Why, one asks, did he lose those Napoleons? He wanted to gain the prince's favor, take advantage of his good mood, and win him over to his side, so that he wouldn't oppose him. Instead, he suffered a fiasco and . . . I think it's perfectly clear."

"When the three of you were playing, did you in fact break even? Or might you have pocketed a coin or two, eh? Have I guessed right? Hohenbruch set the gendarmes on you, and now you think you're going to set me on him?"

Ivan Dmitrievich frowned and glanced at his secret agent. No, it was not for him to judge. Hadn't he done the same thing when he had pointed Pevtsov at the lieutenant and now sent Pevtsov himself to the *Triumph of Venus*? Yes, it was bad. But what could you do?

"All right." He clapped Lewicki on the shoulder and shifted his gaze back to Millions.

The sun was already rising over the rooftops. Ivan Dmitrievich looked at the wet pavement in front of the front steps to the prince's house, where in a transparent ring, holding hands, unlucky Boyev and Kerim-Bek, the Strekalov husband and wife, the brave lieutenant with the bitten palm, Counts Shuvalov and Hotek, Barons Cobenzel and Hohenbruch, and his, Ivan Dmitrievich's, own agent with the Jagellonian crown on his bald head circled. Russian émigrés, Polish conspirators, Italian Carbonari, Turks in red fezes rushed, a multitude of shadows, and in this incorporeal circling, in this file of phantoms, turning pale in the light of day, a man entered, calm of step, wearing an official's greatcoat with a fur collar and a sable cap with a nice new trunk in his long apish arm. When they had chased him to the harbor, his kerchief-concealed face had seemed horrible, but now Ivan Dmitrievich saw before him an ordinary face with little piggy eyes and a red, bare chin that needed no shaving.

"Pupyr!" Sych exhaled.

All of a sudden he felt a long-forgotten pain spring to life in the shoulder that had been battered by the boat and fill his soul with malicious delight.

"That's Pupyr?" Lewicki couldn't believe it. "Ivan Dmitrievich, is that he?"

"It is. . . . He's here, our angel."

Lewicki crossed himself:

"Lord, I was sitting next to him yesterday in the pastry shop. Baron Cobenzel and I stopped in at the pastry shop on Nevsky to drink a cup of chocolate, and he went there, too. Cobenzel left, and he followed. Only he was wearing a top hat."

"Chocolate, you say?"

"Yes, Ivan Dmitrievich, I don't drink coffee, it makes my heart pound. Word of honor!"

Sopov pressed up to the gap in the fence, and Sych began dashing about feverishly, searching for something to arm himself with. Crouching as if he were under fire, he ran toward the barracks wall, where the fire gear was hanging, and grabbed an axe.

Pupyr strode pompously, unhurriedly. His face looked mildly offended, his little blue eyes were ransacking the street and the windows of the neighboring buildings and latching onto passersby for too long. Then he climbed the front steps one at a time, shifted the trunk from his right hand to his left, and rang.

Sopov cautiously drew his saber from its hilt.

Ivan Dmitrievich took a look at the glinting blade, trying to decide which was more reliable, a saber or an axe, and said to Sych, "Give that over!"

V

The water was boiling under the propeller, the wake ran off to the east, bubbling up and subsiding, and was lost in the fog, which had already hidden the palaces and prospects of the Palmyra of the North from view. Seagulls were shrieking and wheeling above the clutches of foam breaking up in the hope of seeing among them the white belly of a fish deafened by the blades.

Without stopping, full steam ahead, the *Triumph of Venus* passed Pilot Island. Here lived the Petersburg pilots, here is where they boarded the ships in order to guide them past the sandbars of the gulf, but the captain decided to do without an escort. Relying on instinct, orienting himself by the color of the water, he himself guided the schooner. He had to slip past Kronstadt before the customs commandant was informed of his escape.

The captain had calculated events correctly. Shuvalov's adjutant was already racing to the telegraph office.

The Ethiopian stoker was throwing coal in the firebox shovel after shovel. The pistons pounded faster and faster, the arrow on the pressure gauge crept past the red line and pointed dangerously to the top of the scale. Whistling fountains of steam struck from under the valves, and the joints of the pipes and nipples hissed.

The captain frowned and tried not to look toward where the gloomy stone edifices of the Kronstadt forts were looming up. Fifteen years before, during the Eastern War, the British squadron of Admiral Napier had shamefully retreated under fire from their weapons. He imagined he saw movement there and divined the black cannon muzzles on the quay. Actually, even without that he might go to the bottom if the boilers failed to withstand the pressure and blew up.

In the heat of the moment, Pevtsov had fired all his bullets into the air, something he now regretted. With his revolver, barricaded in the captain's cabin, he might have withstood a siege until the nearest port and drawn the customs agents' attention with his shots. What if the Italians decided to drown him, to throw him into the sea? The cabin's window was located on the side opposite the Kronstadt bastions. Smoke from the stack was pouring down and clinging to the water.

While Shuvalov was composing his dispatch, while the adjutant was looking for the telegraph operator, while the key was clicking at the other end of the cable that went across the sea bottom and the dots and dashes were being translated into Russian, they awakened the commandant, who the night before had sat up over his papers past midnight and half-awake had only a vague notion of why they had to catch the Italian merchant ship. In short, while the mighty will of the Chief of Gendarmes was embodied in the small sailor-signalman, in his fingers, which had pulled the wet line in order to throw up a signal up the flagpole—"Check your engines and stand at anchor"—the moment slipped. The *Triumph of Venus* was already sailing in sight of the Kronstadt forts and speedily leaving their cannons' range.

Noticing the signal, the captain ordered more speed, and Dino Cielli himself went to help the Ethiopian. Frightened by his mother's stories of the horrors of tsarist despotism, he was afraid of ending up in Siberia over the fight he'd started in the tavern and promised the captain that he would take all responsibility before his father. His mother had said that in Siberia they gave exiles to white bears to tear apart.

Pevtsov, trying to move the massive table, which was firmly attached to the floor, toward the cabin door, distinctly pictured one other possibility for his own fate: the Italians setting him down on a desert island.

The signal went unanswered, after which the commandant ordered a warning shot fired. They fired blanks, but even that had no effect. The commandant, an old seaman who had sailed under Nakhimov's flag, cursed and lashed out at the gendarmes, who in his opinion had no reason to exist on this earth. The duty officer listened with cautious satisfaction to these treasonous speeches. Once again they loaded and once again they fired, and again without the slightest result. The damned Italian was still sailing full steam ahead. Meanwhile,

Shuvalov's dispatch prescribed the use of all available means, up to and including live fire, to detain the ship, and the commandant, who was dead-set against firing at the merchant vessel, grudgingly ordered the small caliber battery readied for battle.

Meanwhile, the *Kinburn,* an examination vessel called upon to note and write down in a special shipboard journal all the ships abeam of St. Petersburg, lit out in pursuit of the impudent Italian, which did not respond to their request and proceeded with a thievishly lowered flag, but the three stripes on its stack gave it away—red, white, and green.

One charge landed astern, another to starboard, and spray lashed through the broken porthole in the captain's cabin. A third landed far ahead of their course, and another two splashed weakly off to the side. The fortress artillery supported the *Kinburn's* forward cannon.

Hearing the cannonade, Pevtsov soberly assessed the situation. This father of five children was hardly going to be so rash as to ignore the arguments of reason spoken in the voice of the Kronstadt weapons. At any moment the mad knocking of the pistons would fall silent, the propeller would stop, and the anchor hawse would start its rumbling. It was time to prepare his arguments for his conversation with Shuvalov. To tell him, "You see what these people are capable of, Your Excellency! I was not so far from the truth."

But the salty wind kept singing with unrelenting force in the shards of glass poking from the porthole frame. Pevtsov was wrong this time, too. Her entire body shaking, the *Triumph of Venus* was moving westward. Pevtsov was flung first to one wall and then the other; the captain was maneuvering with as much art as if he had spent his entire life standing on the bridge of a military frigate and was accustomed to evading fire from shore batteries.

About fifteen minutes later, the *Kinburn* began to drop back, however its captain could not bring himself to turn his ship and fire a port salvo at the runaway. He felt awkward sending an unarmed merchant to the bottom, but it was getting harder and harder to aim from the forward cabin; they were moving crosswise to the wave. And from the bastions as well, despite Shuvalov's order, they were firing cautiously, more to frighten than anything else, and when a little Danish ship, the *Sekira Erika,* which was on its way to Petersburg with a load of smoked herring, appeared in the range of fire, they were forced to hold their fire altogether so as not to sink the innocent Dane by accident.

Another quarter of an hour later and the *Triumph of Venus* again entered a zone of fog. Pevtsov was biting his fists, and the Italians on deck were hugging each other and leaping for joy. Carefree children of the South. . . .

Chapter 15

The Gilt Worn Off

They led Pupyr away, and Sych solemnly carried off his chest. Ivan Dmitrievich was left with three things: a notebook with culinary receipts, a gold one-pound kettlebell on a chain, and a revolver with a long Gothic inscription and von Ahrensburg's monogram—exactly like the one on the silver cigarette case taken from the valet.

Pupyr had not had a chance to put his kettlebell in motion, but he had fired the revolver at Ivan Dmitrievich when he ran into the house first with the axe. The bullet passed high over his head and no one was hit, but Ivan Dmitrievich took advantage of that shot to give vent to his feelings and fetched Pupyr up on the back of his head with the blunt side of his axe. Sych, too, was anxious to pay him back for the boat and his family troubles, but Ivan Dmitrievich did not give him the chance.

While Ivan Dmitrievich was questioning Pupyr, Sopov brought Baron Cobenzel to the Street of Millions. First thing, the baron presented his hat, which had been found on the street in front of the gymnasium, and then inspected the hole left in the ceiling by the bullet and said, "It's easy to miss your mark. Revolvers of this system have a very powerful recoil. You have to aim at the feet in order to hit the chest."

At the same time it was clarified that the revolver had been kept in the dressing table not because the prince was afraid of anyone and always kept a weapon with him but for a completely different reason. It had been sent to von Ahrensburg by brother officers on the anniversary of some battle in which they had all participated. The prince had boasted of it to his acquaintances, including Cobenzel. Two days before, he had shown it and the Napoleons d'or won from Hohenbruch, and he had been very upset upon learning of its system's deficiencies.

Cobenzel and Lewicki were exchanging hushed words at the far end of the drawing room, and Ivan Dmitrievich, swinging the kettlebell on its chain, remained near the bay window. Pupyr was being led away by three policemen with bared clubs, and a fourth was walking along a little to one side. Next to him proudly strode Sych. Every so often he would shift the heavy chest from one hand to the other, but he had no desire to part with the trophy. Ivan Dmitrievich watched them through the dirty window and recalled the notary Gnetochkin lying in only his undergarments on the bank of the Neva with a shattered skull, the girl student Dravert whose ears had been torn over cheap earrings, the seamstress Darya Besfamilnaya, who one night had thrown on her squirrel coat and run to get the doctor for her sick daughter but returned without her coat or the doctor, who had seen the woman disrobed by Pupyr and been too frightened to go. The little girl had died.

Ivan Dmitrievich recalled the old chemist Zilberfarb, who had come to the police station every day to find out whether the medallion with the locket of his dead wife's hair had been found, and the seventeen-year-old cadet Ivanov, who after his encounter with Pupyr, when he lost a silver-plated copper medal, considered himself dishonored forever, confessed in a letter to the sovereign, and then put a bullet in his forehead. But for some reason most distinctly of all there arose before him the old woman Zotova with her blissfully mad face and the gray hair on her chin. Like Hotek, she had seen a golden halo around Pupyr's head and now for more than a month had been living in an insane asylum, believing that she had died and was now in heaven. He recalled people and faces, and if Prince von Ahrensburg and Count Hotek had fallen in line with them, that was just a coincidence, a minor particular in the life of a great city.

"Fine," said Hotek, approaching and standing alongside, "I allow that in the morning he was roaming nearby and might have seen Shuvalov give me the key. I also allow even that he heard to whom I, in turn, was supposed to entrust it. We were speaking outside and there were people clustering around."

Cobenzel was holding the little key in the palm of his hand. The serpent-tempter had bitten its own tail with such malice, it was as if he had failed to tempt Eve.

"But you must agree, Mr. Putilin, it is one thing to lure me into the toilet room of a pastry shop, knock me over the head, and steal that accursed key and quite another to attack the carriage of the Austrian ambassador in the very center of Petersburg. An ordinary street bandit, how dare you? I think he had someone behind him. Perhaps the same person with whose help he murdered Ludwig?"

"Pupyr says he did not try to kill Count Hotek at all."

"What do you mean? At whom did I fire?"

"At him, naturally. But he will swear that he had stretched the rope in expectation of some gain."

"And you believe him?"

"Who knows? Anything can happen in this life. In any case, he has not confessed to von Ahrensburg's murder. He says he bought the revolver today from some foreigner at the Apraxin Market, and he found the Napoleons this morning on Millions, near the prince's house. At this point, only one thing is beyond a doubt: he knew perfectly well where to insert that key."

"But how? Who told him?"

"Be patient for another couple of hours. I have to verify my conjecture. And for the love of God, forgive me that foolish stunt with the top hat. I had a similar case once. I saw the beaten path and could not resist the temptation."

"Well, at least explain," asked Cobenzel, "why you were so sure it was he and no one else. Have I understood you correctly?"

"Yes, it's he."

"Why did you know this?"

Ivan Dmitrievich gave Lewicki an order: "Go ahead, pull the curtains!"

It grew dark in the drawing room, he lit a lamp, put it on the piano, and blocking it with his back, swung the kettlebell on the chain as hard as he could. Cobenzel shuddered when he saw the even gold ring, the shining circle outlining Ivan Dmitrievich's head with a whistle.

Bronze Adam and Eve in the writing set tried even harder to cover their nakedness. Like an angel driving them out of paradise's garden, Ivan Dmitrievich stood by the piano and surveyed the drawing room; his field of battle was fifty square arshins.

Then he lowered his arm, saying, "There's the whole trick."

"Is it really gold?" asked Cobenzel when Lewicki had opened the curtains without being told.

Ivan Dmitrievich took out his pen knife and scraped the kettlebell with the blade. The gilt sloughed off, and under it was revealed porous black iron.

He recalled the Prussians firing the golden cannonball at Napoleon III. If it was anything like this kettlebell, it's a wonder the French emperor survived. There, in the eternally streaming ether, everyone knows.

Lewicki and Cobenzel got ready to leave. Escorting them out, Ivan Dmitrievich opened the notebook of culinary receipts as he went. He read about the fish pie and the kulebiaka with mushrooms and his empty guts growled loudly. What a swine! He tossed the notebook into the fireplace.

"I'll expect news in two hours," Cobenzel reminded him, shaking his hand.

But Lewicki was enjoying the fact that he was chatting as equals with Ivan Dmitrievich. Far from hurrying, he was dragging out the pleasure.

"The day before last, I remember, we were sitting in the Yacht Club over cards," he said. "Baron Hohenbruch, the deceased prince, and I. We started to play and then he asked me to deal him a card for luck. I shuffled the deck and threw out one card. And what do you think? 'It's the ace of . . . sorry, spades.' The prince said, 'Do it again!' I shuffled again—and again the ace of spades. It was fate."

"What kind of cards were they?" inquired Ivan Dmitrievich.

"Ordinary cards, the kind the Yacht Club provides. The king of diamonds is Julius Caesar, hearts is Charles the Great, clubs is Alexander of Macedonia, and spades is King David. I dealt out the kind we were playing with."

"You can't tell someone's fortune by playing cards."

"But"—Lewicki smiled—"before that I had passed them over a doorknob. The Gypsies say, that way you *can* read playing cards."

Glancing at his delicate, seemingly as boneless as worms,

fingers, with their long phalanges, the fingers of a professional cardsharp, it occurred to Ivan Dmitrievich that he could pluck any card out of a deck. He couldn't tell whether Lewicki was lying or telling the truth, and if it was the truth, had the ace of spaces, promising death, fallen out by accident or not?

"And what about the prince?" asked Ivan Dmitrievich. "Was he very distressed?"

"Not a bit. 'Thank God,' he said, 'I am healthy, have yet to suffer any ailment, and in my youth it was foretold that I would die in my own bed.'"

"I heard that prediction from him, too," confirmed Cobenzel. "Maybe that's why Ludwig distinguished himself with such valor on the field of battle. He attacked Italian batteries mounted."

"And it came true." Lewicki sighed.

"Meanwhile, the rifle Hohenbruch sold our military department with the help of von Ahrensburg and you," Ivan Dmitrievich asked Cobenzel, "I hope you don't have to aim it at the feet in order to hit the head?"

"Well, that depends on the distance. But since you said that, that means you know I was present at the trials. When they asked me my opinion, my counsel was to adopt it. The model is very fine. In such cases I do not act against my conscience, especially since my family has been linked to Russia since the time of Ivan the Terrible."

"Wasn't it you who gave the soldiers testing the rifle vodka to drink?"

That caught Cobenzel off guard.

"The thing was, I couldn't talk Hohenbruch out of it. Not that that changes anything. The model is truly fine."

"But how did he contrive to sell it to the Turks as well as us?"

"Oh!" said Cobenzel respectfully. "There are no secrets from you, Mr. Putilin. I myself learned of this only last evening. How did you come to know?"

Ivan Dmitrievich did not reply, giving Lewicki a sidelong glance, but he had the sense to bite his tongue without being told.

"I understand, Mr. Putilin, an official secret. I was also dumbfounded when Yusuf Pasha informed me of this news. I must admit, I even thought that death had relieved Ludwig of the need to untangle himself from an ambiguous position. However, after I thought it over, I arrived at the conclusion that this was nothing more than a bluff on Hohenbruch's part. . . . It seems I'm keeping you. Shouldn't we talk more afterward?"

"Add five minutes to that two o'clock," suggested Ivan Dmitrievich, "and continue."

He already knew that this damned rifle, like the situation in the Balkans, had absolutely nothing to do with von Ahrensburg's murder, but he wanted to clarify something else for himself. He wanted to understand whether the prince's death had been fortuitous or there had been something in his life that had promised his death here and now.

"An agreement had been reached with Hohenbruch," Cobenzel began his story, "to adapt a certain number of muzzle-loading weapons according to his system. If they are adapted, he is due a percentage of the principal. And based on the hints Hohenbruch made to me, I had come to the conclusion that he had decided to blackmail officials from your War Ministry. To give them a choice: either he received a percentage or else he sold his model to an army that in the future could be an enemy army."

"The same system? Isn't that prohibited by the contract?"

"Hohenbruch convinced the Turks that the model had been so significantly improved that it could be considered new. Given his forcefulness, he might even have been counting on a small advance. However, all this was a gamble of the first water because he had not made any improvements in his model. I know that for a fact. So that Ludwig had nothing to worry about. More than likely, Hohenbruch had initiated him into his plans. But I think Ludwig told Prince Oldenburgsky everything. I can imagine them laughing. Such a witty manner of stirring up your military officials, and then to lead the Turks . . . ."

"Hohenbruch and the prince were drinking Champagne at the Yacht Club and laughing," interjected Lewicki. "At first the prince was unhappy, but then he laughed and said, "I can see right away that your father sold kneidelachs."

"Yes, very gay," said Ivan Dmitrievich.

The threesome went outside and at the front steps went their separate ways. The sun was warming, and the drying paving stones were giving off steam. Before Ivan Dmitrievich could take ten steps he noticed Konstantinov running down the street. One of his eyes had watered up completely.

"Ivan Dmitrievich!" he shouted from a distance. "The Italians have sailed off with the captain!"

"What do you mean sailed off? Where?"

"To Italy. He boarded the ship alone and they locked him up in a cabin and sailed off. And he has my coins."

"I wish someone would sail off with me," said Ivan Dmitrievich wearily after a pause, "to Italy."

He gave Konstantinov the promised reward—the Napoleon d'or brought in by Sych—and told him to go home. The air was morning fresh and clear. Through the usual city din his ear barely discerned the distant rotund sound of cannon fire rolling in from the sea, from Kronstadt. "They're firing cannons from shore," thought Ivan Dmitrievich, "ordering the ship to halt." He felt not the slightest twinges of conscience. That was all right, that meant the time had come for Pevtsov to suffer for his fatherland, too, just like the lieutenant, Boyev, and Ivan Dmitrievich himself. "The sheep on his right hand . . . ."

Later, when the bell tower of the Church of the Resurrection came into view, in the distance, he had almost a physical sensation in his fingers of that desired thread that had only to be tugged so that Harlequin's costume, already dulled, would suddenly fly to pieces and fall at his feet in a flurry of motley colored rags.

II

Ivan Dmitrievich turned into a gateway, and before him opened up a courtyard framed by firewood thawing with the approach of spring and squeezed in by the unstuccoed brick walls of rooming houses. This is where he had sent Lewicki the previous afternoon.

In the middle of the courtyard, among the sheds, latrines, and trash bins climbing out in clusters from under the store and some lumber awaiting removal, there jutted up a two-story annex made of blackened logs that was listing to one side and shored up by long poles up against the timbers. Here lived the person on whom the fates of Europe depended. That short, emaciated man who had left his Napoleon d'or with Savosin the sexton at the Church of the Resurrection. The candles he'd bought had burned down long ago, melted away into dry waxy puddles. Now he was no longer protected by their flame.

Slops struck the front steps, the clinging stink of cat attacked his nose from every crack. A girl of about five whose sickly pale face looked like it had been rubbed in flour and who was dressed in tatters was singing a lullaby to a log wrapped up in a blanket. Ivan Dmitrievich held out five kopeks to her and she grabbed the coin and vanished without a sound, like a cat.

The steps had rotted out. The only way you could climb them was by hugging the wall. Following the instructions of the prince's driver precisely, Ivan Dmitrievich ascended to the second floor, pushed on the burlap-upholstered door, and found himself in a tiny room with a slanted ceiling. Dirty boots were lying across the threshold and their owner was lying on a cot fully dressed. The emaciated man with the ginger stubble on his wan Petersburg face was asleep. Had it not been for Pevtsov and his plans, Ivan Dmitrievich could have come here long before. What a helper!

Ivan Dmitrievich saw a table made of unpainted boards, a chair with a seat of bast, and a tin washbasin in the corner. On the table was an empty half-shtoff, an onion peel, and a pile of salt directly on the tabletop.

He walked over to the sleeping man and shook him by the shoulder.

"Hey, Fyodor! Get up."

The prince's former servant Fyodor, who had been driven out by von Ahrensburg for drinking, reluctantly opened his swollen eyes.

"What do you want?"

"Get up, I'm from the police."

Silently, somehow not looking very surprised, Fyodor sat up on the cot, yawned, and shuffled his bare foot over the floor in search of his boots. He pulled them right over his bare feet, without any leg wrappings, and then found a crust of bread under the onion skin on the table and stuck it in his pocket. Removing the wash basin from its nail, he took a long drink from it and spat out a cockroach that had evidently drowned there long ago and ended up in his mouth with the water.

"Pfah! Cuirassier, damn you!"

"Who?"

"The cockroaches. That's the heavy cavalry," Fyodor explained with an equanimity that astonished and outraged Ivan Dmitrievich more and more. "The bedbugs are the light cavalry. The prince served in the cuirassiers before. In the morning he'd get up and say, 'Theodore,' he'd say, 'the Uhlans attacked me in bivouac!' He meant the bedbugs. And he slashed cockroaches with his sword. Once he had people visiting and he argued with them that he could cut a running cockroach in two with his sword just like that. I brought one in from the kitchen and let it go. And what do you think? Clean in two."

As he told his story, Fyodor dragged a crushed lambswool felt hat out from under the bed and started straightening it on his knee.

"Chopped it in two and flew into a rage. 'Theodore,' he shouts, 'bring me another and I'll cut off its whiskers!' And he did. And the cockroach lived. His friends wagered him a hundred rubles. A dashing gent he was! But tightfisted. In the fall someone swiped the knocker from the front door and he filed a complaint with the governor general himself. But that knocker wasn't worth a pin. They poured me a mug of beer for it, that's all."

"You swiped it?" asked Ivan Dmitrievich.

"What for?" Fyodor denied it without blinking. "I have my own just like it."

You'd think it would have cost him nothing to confess that sin now. What was a knocker compared to killing a man? Why didn't he?

"Oh, a fool I am, a fool to have come here," said Fyodor. "Fool, I couldn't help myself. I had the half-shtoff hidden there, so I came."

"But how did you know people would come looking for you?" Ivan Dmitrievich was amazed.

"How couldn't I?" It was Fyodor's turn to be amazed. "That's what the police are for, I dare say."

"No, I was asking something else. How do you think I found out about you?"

"Well, you don't have to be a Solomon exactly."

"Fancy that!" Ivan Dmitrievich took offense. "You think it was easy to figure out?"

"If I'd taken the half-shtoff and used my God-given legs . . . ." Fyodor sighed. "No, first I had a drink and then I went to bed."

Ivan Dmitrievich raised his voice.

"Don't try to wiggle out of this! Tell me how you found out!"

Fyodor merely waved his hand, as if to say, Why all the carrying on? He put on his hat and his threadbare coat with the ripped pocket.

"Let's just go, all right?"

They went down the stairs; he to one side, Ivan Dmitrievich to the other. The little girl popped up again out of nowhere and walked weightlessly between them over the rotten steps, unafraid of falling through, and clutched her little log to her breast.

"Hey, Zinka," Fyodor asked her, "Did you feed your baby or have a wet-nurse?"

"You gave me a sweet," the little girl said softly.

"That's right," Fyodor agreed, "I did. But now I don't have any. The sweets are gone."

He stroked her fine hair and went outside. The girl walked all the way to the street with them.

"Yours?" asked Ivan Dmitrievich.

"Mine are in Ladoga." Fyodor shook his head and turned around. "Go home, Zinka. Your mother's looking for you."

Standing on tiptoe, he suddenly crowed like a rooster, rocking his whole scrawny little body comically. The little girl burst out laughing, and her little white face shone like a beacon in the gap of the gateway. She was gone when they turned the corner.

Once again Ivan Dmitrievich returned to their interrupted conversation.

"So how did you find out I knew about you?"

But this was of no interest to Fyodor.

"You see you asked about the knocker," he recalled. "What you should ask is how many times they docked my pay. And what for? I'd tell you but no one believes it. And they drove me out owing me a month's wages. Aren't I a human being? Don't I have a wife and children in Ladoga who want to eat and drink? And they're not little logs, after all, like Zinka has! The prince took me in, unschooled, so he could pay me less. But in one night at the club he could lose a thousand rubles. He had a whole chest full of money. He said I ruined his frock coat. It wasn't me! It was a crow. I can't answer for a bird. Over there on Nevsky the statues are all shat on, but you get your pay properly, I dare say. Right?"

"That's not my concern," said Ivan Dmitrievich. "I'm from the detective police, I catch murderers and thieves. How do you think I caught you?"

"You came and I was sleeping."

"But why did I come for you? Rather than someone else?"

"It's my sin," Fyodor reasoned fairly, "so you came for me. Who else is supposed to answer for my sins?"

His patience was wearing thin, but Ivan Dmitrievich controlled himself.

"Fine, your sin. But how did you realize it was yours?"

"It doesn't take a great mind."

"But no one else figured it out!" Ivan Dmitrievich lost

control. "Only I did."

"They said I broke their china cups," Fyodor continued. "I did, I'm not arguing that. But were they really Chinese? Germans made them. They just looked Chinese. The dragons had dog's ears. . . . And the day before yesterday I came on the up and up, sober. Thus and so, I said, Your Excellency, for the month I served you, you owe me ten rubles, or else I'll petition the sovereign. And he grabbed me by the scruff of my neck and tossed my mug out the door. With a boot to the rear, too. What's there to say! I drank some vodka at the tavern, and whether you believe it or not, I was sober as a judge, my whole drink burned up in the insult."

Stopping, Ivan Dmitrievich grabbed him by the collar and pulled him closer.

"How did you find out that I knew you . . . Oh, to hell with it!"

"What's that? Come on, you know how."

"Yes, I do. What about you?"

"How could I not know about myself?"

"Maybe you think someone told me?"

"That's it!" Fyodor grinned crookedly. "It's clear as day, he ran to the police early, in the morning."

Ivan Dmitrievich gave him a shake.

"Who is 'he'?"

"He," said Fyodor. "The gentleman."

"What gentleman?"

"My old master. The prince."

"The prince?" Ivan Dmitrievich was dumbstruck as his eyes were finally opened and he realized that before him was perhaps the only man in the entire city who had not heard about von Ahrensburg's death. Then why had he taken the Napoleon d'or to the church?

"Why are you choking me?" said Fyodor hoarsely, stretching his scrawny neck. "What are you grabbing my shirt for? I'm not holding back. I'm telling you everything the way it was."

They moved on.

Ivan Dmitrievich kept sneaking sidelong looks at his companion's face—the despondent morning physiognomy of a first-rate cock that was illuminated now and then by the last glints of the decisiveness he'd felt the day before yesterday. He could stop worrying about him running away, and he didn't need his revolver. Ivan Dmitrievich didn't ask the policeman they encountered to escort them.

"I'm sitting in the tavern," Fyodor narrated without his former energy, inasmuch as the time had come to move from causes to effects, "and this fellow in a top hat takes a seat next to me. Says he's a torch-bearer. Come to wet his whistle after a funeral. Well, one thing leads to another, and I tell him about my insult, just like I did you. He snorts, feels around the table, and says, 'If he won't give it, we'll take it ourselves!' I say, 'How? Bless you, good man!' He says, 'Do you know where the prince keeps his money?' I say, 'In a chest, but I don't know where the key is.' He asks, 'Did you ever see the key?' 'Yes,' I say, 'it's a snake in a circle, biting its own tail.' He says—"

"I understand," Ivan Dmitrievich cut him off.

"What do you understand?" Fyodor reared up. "What can you understand inside my soul? I just wanted my ten rubles. My hard-earned money! Pay for a month and let them dock me for the cups. Not a drop more! I'll buy treats for the children, I thought—and go to Ladoga to see my wife. Fat chance! I visited my woman that afternoon and told her everything. She's a good woman, a cook for an officer off the Fontanka. Pevtsov's his name. Wears a dark blue greatcoat. . . . My woman says, 'Tomorrow I'm going with the lady in the lord's carriage to look at the dacha, and I'll take you through the gate,' she says. 'They've got that face of yours on a list there. But no policeman would dare stop my carriage,' she says. 'They creep before my master like grass!' Before night the devil'd messed me up with this half-shtoff. Fool that I am, I fell asleep."

"You promised to tell it as it happened," Ivan Dmitrievich reminded him.

"Uh huh. We went over to Millions. The torch-bearer says, 'My heart aches for you, friend. I don't need a kopek of the prince's money!' I pulled the door—it was open. Myself, I'm shaking, I don't even feel my feet under me. We go in—and straight to the pantry. As soon as the prince leaves for the Yacht

Club, the new servant skips out for a snooze. Right away. Then we go into the rooms. We look all around, but no key. The chest's sturdy, the lid's copper. You can't pry it open with the poker. Mmm hmm. . . ."

"We start waiting for the prince. I'd have been happy to run away. It was too much! The torch-bearer doesn't let me. So we wait for the prince. We go into his bedroom, pull off the bell rope and tie him up. Some sheet in his mouth so he won't yell. We ask him, 'Where's the snake key?' He's shaking his head, 'I won't tell you,' he says. A hard master! I take two gold coins out of his table. I look and the torch-bearer is dropping the rest in his pocket. I say, 'Thief! What are you doing?' But he's brutal, he grabs the prince by the throat and says, 'Where's the key?' Then he throws a pillow on his face. I get scared, I grab the torch-bearer by the arms, and he gives me a kick, something clatters, and I whisper, 'Let's run! The servants are up!' And we ran away."

"You ran away together?" asked Ivan Dmitrievich.

"No. I went in one direction and he the other."

"What did you take from the prince?"

"I said, I took two gold pieces."

"That's all?"

"Yes! I don't need other people's money."

"Why did you take one to the church?"

"When I started buying the children treats," Fyodor explained, "I asked the shop man, 'For one coin like this, how many ruble notes would you give?' He and the owner talked it over, and he says, 'Ten.' Exactly as many as the master owed me. Well, I thought, I don't need anyone else's money. But you can't give it back! So I brought it to the church. I set some candles and ordered prayers for the prince's health, so he wouldn't be sick. We were a little physical with him. . . . Did you catch the torch-bearer already?"

"And how!" said Ivan Dmitrievich.

"Damn thief!" Fyodor cursed. "And you know he was nicely dressed. He should be sent to hard labor, the thief. . . . What's going to happen to me? Eh?"

Ivan Dmitrievich was silent and frowned.

"I dare say I'll get a hundred lashings," Fyodor supposed. "No more, likely. No reason. If not for me, the master might have expired under that pillow. Isn't that so?"

"He did," said Ivan Dmitrievich.

Fyodor, who had pulled his bread heel out of his pocket, suddenly crossed himself very quickly with small movements of the bread, then he stuck it in his mouth, bit down, stopped, and started chewing, slowly and crookedly moving his jaw, as if he had in his mouth not bread but a piece of resin from which he had to pull out his stuck teeth.

They were standing in front of a shop door. "Schoolbooks and School Maps Store," Ivan Dmitrievich read.

"Wait here," he told Fyodor, and he pushed the door open.

Behind the counter sat the owner, and on the other side two boys were examining the continents hanging on the walls and drowning in blue. They were whispering over some eighteen kopeks, but their faces were like pilgrims' who after their long travels had crossed the threshold of the long-sought shrine.

Ivan Dmitrievich walked over to a big map of Europe with the different colors for empires, kingdoms, and republics. For some reason, on all of the maps like this, Russia was a dark green, the sultan's realm a brighter green, and the lands subject to Franz Josef were marked in bright yellow, and Italy was the color of a fallen oak leaf, as if eternal autumn reigned there. After checking that all four capitals were where they should be, Ivan Dmitrievich looked out the window. Oh, Lord! That's all he needed! He had been prepared to see an empty front step, but no. Left unguarded, Fyodor had not even thought to run away and was obediently sitting on the stoop. His head had sunk between his knees, and his felt hat was lying on the ground.

"I'm from the police," said Ivan Dmitrievich softly, leaning toward the owner. "Where is your service entrance?"

He made his way through the alley to the parallel street, hailed a cabbie, and went home dreaming of hot tea with lemon and sugar and without any herbs, damn them all.

Simultaneously he was thinking about how today, under the weight of the evidence, Pupyr would admit to the murder of von Ahrensburg and name his accomplice. Sych and Konstantinov would go off to catch that ninny Fyodor, but they wouldn't. What can you do! That was what his agents were like. In short, trusted.

His wife met him in the vestibule. His son came galloping in with his butterfly, which now flapped both wings.

"All it took was hammering in one nail," said his wife, not boasting, but quite the opposite, apologizing for stealing these laurels from her husband and not letting him show himself to be a genuine father.

"Did you sleep last night?" asked Ivan Dmitrievich.

"How would you like me to answer? What would be nicer for you to hear, that I worried and didn't sleep or that I slept like a log?"

"Well, if I have to choose between my male vanity and your health, I choose the latter."

"Then believe that I slept."

"And in fact?"

"I dozed off a little just before dawn," his wife admitted.

Ivan Dmitrievich kissed her. Embracing him, she took the umbrella off its hook with the other.

"Are you sorry you didn't take it?"

"Oh, very sorry."

"Will you listen to me from now on?"

"I will, I will."

"Please, Vanya," his wife requested, "never answer me like that. Just say, 'I will.' When you say, 'I will, I will,' that means you only want me to leave you alone. I'm right, aren't I?"

Ivan Dmitrievich kissed her again and went to wash up. Vanechka pattered after him, rolling his butterfly in front of him. Both of its wings were flapping up and down, up and down.

III

A couple of weeks later, Ivan Dmitrievich was told to appear on the Fontanka for an interview with Count Shuvalov. He appeared at the reception half an hour early but was shown into the study half an hour after the appointed time. This time Shuvalov behaved with great politesse, coldly and aloofly, as if that night on the Street of Millions had never happened. Ivan Dmitrievich read clearly from his face that none of it had happened, not Boyev and Kerim-Bek, not the lieutenant, not the Strekalovs, not the shredded letter and the claimant to the Polish throne, to say nothing, naturally, of his ultimatum, his despair, and the hook from Shuvalov's uniform that had popped off and clicked like a hailstone on the window glass. Nor had there been a bellowing Count Hotek, either, naturally. No one had been planning to turn the murderer-ambassador into the ace of trumps in the big game, and the *Triumph of Venus,* like a ghost ship, had vanished with the first rays of the rising son. A mirage, a bad dream about which in the morning, upon awakening, you cannot say whether you dreamed it just now or years ago.

In service, Ivan Dmitrievich reported to the capital's chief of police, who reported to the head of the police department, which was, in turn, under the Ministry of Internal Affairs, but Shuvalov's arm was stronger and longer. Putilin? And who was he anyway? A nobody, a pitiful detective. The rogue, the poseur, how dare he arrange that monstrous performance? As a result, all of Ivan Dmitrievich's bosses took a deep breath and agreed that Mr. Putilin had to be removed from his post as chief of detectives. He was blamed for Pupyr's rampage, which he had not stopped in time.

In addition, even the press had weighed in with a verdict of its own. Although no articles ever did appear in the newspapers about von Ahrensburg's murder, the *Saint Petersburg Gazette* did publish a tiny item about his death, without indicating any causes, and the liberal *Voice,* without Shuvalov's knowledge, ran a bizarre allegorical article about a foreign diplomat who had perished tragically and a certain guardian of law and order, also nameless. The latter, as the article's author asserted, had known in advance of the crime being planned but had undertaken nothing so that he could catch the murderer quickly and obtain two orders: one Russian; the second from the sovereign of the power represented by the murdered man. The article was signed with a pseudonym, which many considered a form of authorial coquetry. The style, the passion, the mordant precision of the wordings, and the political audacity pointed unambiguously to Pavel Avraamovich Kungurtsev.

The fact that von Ahrensburg's former servant, Pupyr's accomplice, had fled and not been caught could have been one of the charges brought, but it wasn't. Racked by conscience, Fyodor turned himself in.

"There, you see," said Shuvalov, when Ivan Dmitrievich had familiarized himself with the issue of *Voice* hot off the press, "your affairs are in a bad way. You could simply resign, or you could . . . You could open an investigation."

Pevtsov's sinister shadow loomed up behind Shuvalov. He acted as though he didn't care, but from time to time his sunken eyes bored into Ivan Dmitrievich with hatred, and the latter couldn't help but shrink under that gaze. Pevtsov had become noticeably thinner and his uniform hung on him like on a scarecrow. On the other hand, a lieutenant colonel's epaulettes gleamed on his shoulders. Ivan Dmitrievich knew that the Italians had landed him on some desert island where for a week he had lived on algae and rotten fish that had washed up on shore. When he was picked up by Estonian fishermen, Pevtsov could not utter a word. He just cried and looked at his saviors with a madman's eyes.

"Measures like this seem rather harsh to me, though," Shuvalov went on. "I feel sorry for you. I think that with a certain good sense on your part you might well count on the post of Haymarket inspector, even senior inspector perhaps. Agreed?"

"I'm endlessly grateful," replied Ivan Dmitrievich. "I shall never forget Your Excellency's kindness."

He bowed and went to the Haymarket.

They had taken away his official horses, and cabbies no longer argued over the honor of driving the former chief of detective police, especially for free. Ivan Dmitrievich adapted to going to work on foot. Occasionally he would meet the Strekalovs on his way, an unusually amiable couple. The wife was walking her husband to the Department of Surveys, the spouses walked arm in arm, supporting each other with that diligent devotion one usually finds between old people living out their last days in final, almost heavenly love. At first they still nodded to Ivan Dmitrievich reluctantly, but later they began pretending they hadn't noticed him. This was understandable. After all, people always like to think that they are obliged for their happiness to themselves alone, not to anyone's outside intervention. Every true man picked the keys to his rose all by himself, and any woman is insulted to think that it all happened with her differently.

Actually, many people now failed to notice or recognize Ivan Dmitrievich. True, there were those who did not abandon him in his misfortune. Sych, for example, also became an inspector at the Haymarket, only a junior one, and Konstantinov, even under the new chief of detective police, remained Ivan Dmitrievich's trusted agent.

Epilogue

Five or six cups of coffee were drunk that night, and only crumbs remained of the rusks in the rusk basket. The cock had crowed long since and dawn was starting to break. Safonov slammed his notebook shut, and taking a blissful deep breath and cracking his entwined fingers, he barely managed to speak out of his yawn-twisted mouth.

"Ye-e-es, we've sat here good and long."

At that moment, something shuddered in the bowels of the large clock hanging on the wall, which throughout the night he had glanced at time and again through the veranda's open doors. The next moment, the clock emitted a muffled warning rumble. Safonov looked at it with venomous surprise. It had not struck once before, even at midnight, and now all of a sudden it had woken up, rumbled, and was ponderously and powerfully counting off twelve full-weight strikes. At the same time, the arrows on it pointed to five forty-four. Outside, in the garden, the trunks of the apple trees still stood out distinctly on the dawn's early light.

"Yes, I forgot to warn you," said Ivan Dmitrievich softly and gravely, "that clock is adjusted so that it strikes only once every twenty-four hours. At the very minute my wife passed away."

"And do you wake up each time?"

"It's the old man's lot, usually by that time I'm no longer asleep," replied Ivan Dmitrievich, twisting his right side whisker into a tail.

All her life, his wife had tried to train him out of this habit, but her life ran out first.

He rose and suggested to his guest a walk to the riverbank to admire the sunrise. Safonov had no objections, and they descended into the garden, where there was a gentle and, because the air was so still, especially strong and pure smell of dewy greenery. Invisible, the birds vociferated in the leaves. As he passed by one of the apple trees, Ivan Dmitrievich, like a good husbandman, broke off a dried branch and asked Safonov to break off another he himself could not reach.

Safonov carried out his request, having caught himself thinking that the world around him seemed less real than the one left behind in his notebook. Things there weren't like they were here. There, in the name of love, people confessed to crimes they had not committed and saw what did not exist and failed to notice the obvious; there, legends, dying, vanished without a trace instead of drying up like mummies for all to see; there the truth was still blinding in its nakedness and the bearded lady was a much more common phenomenon than the murder of a foreign diplomat. That world had vanished forever, but from it there emerged and was now offering Safonov an apple found in the grass, while simultaneously wiping it off with his jacket hem, the master of this paradise, a cunning but honest man with ginger side whiskers, a seeker of the truth, defender of the innocent, connoisseur of the female heart, and lover of salted mushrooms.

They resumed their walk.

"Once we get our fee, I'll put on a new roof, fix the fence, and dig a new well. After my death, you know, I'd like to leave my son at least some money," said Ivan Dmitrievich as he walked. "How do you think you'll spend your share?"

"I'll put it in the bank to earn interest."

"That's sensible. Do you have a bank account?"

"I will if you and I write this book. It should be a success."

"From your lips to God's ears!" responded Ivan Dmitrievich.

He strode ahead. Looking at his broad back and thick mane, Safonov asked, "How is your stomach these days?"

"My wife died and all that passed immediately. You saw for yourself. I drink cups and cups of coffee and eat everything at once. But I miss her so! I could howl like a wolf."

"Did it happen long ago?"

"The year before last. She loved this spot, so I buried her here."

They came to the end of the garden, and then a path wound among the thickets of dog rose. Soon they came out at the Volkhovo and sat down next to each other on a bench dug into the earth amid tall weeping willows. Safonov was chewing on the apple.

"The willow is my favorite tree," said Ivan Dmitrievich.

Then he recounted how he himself had made this bench and placed it here, near the river precipice, so that he could mourn sometimes over the flowing water. There was another just like it at his wife's grave.

"I like it here," he said. "I come here after dinner. I sit and watch the river and read Victor Hugo."

"You like Hugo?"

"He was my wife's favorite writer. She was always reading him out loud to Vanechka when he was little."

"By the way," Safonov remembered, "wherever you find Hugo, you find Charles Dickens, too. You were showing me a quotation from him that you wanted to use as an epigraph for the chapter about the murder on Millions. The woman there was lying on the sofa and dreaming all sorts of rubbish."

"Because she was lying in an uncomfortable position," Ivan Dmitrievich clarified, interrupting.

"What is the point of the epigraph?"

"That the artificiality of a situation engenders monsters."

"I thought the dream of reason did," Safonov grinned.

"Your idea is a special case of mine," commented Ivan Dmitrievich. "After all, the dream state is artificial for the reason. But do you understand the point of the second epigraph? 'An envoy arrived mute and brought a letter unwritten.' Do you remember?"

"Well, in this case the word 'envoy' in and of itself brings up several associations. Hotek comes to mind and his letter to Strekalov."

"That's all?"

"I think so," said Safonov, having decided not to delve into the metaphysics.

"That's too bad. I was hoping you would help me word it. Otherwise I feel there's something here, in this riddle, connected with von Ahrensburg's death, but I can't put it into words."

"Oh, just forget it!" said Safonov with a wave of his hand. "Finish your story instead."

"What's that?" Ivan Dmitrievich was surprised. "You mean I didn't? What else do you need? The murderer was caught. The guilty, including I myself, were punished."

"That's just the point! As far as I know, the last few years you headed up the detective police of Saint Petersburg continuously. This means I have to explain to our readers how you managed to turn Shuvalov around. Or will that be a separate story?"

"It's not a story at all. It's all very simple. Six months after the events on Millions, murderers and thieves inundated Petersburg and people were afraid to leave their homes at night. The only island of peace and order was in the center of the city. . . ."

"Haymarket?" Safonov guessed.

"Exactly. There was no getting around it. They had to appoint me chief of detective police again. It was from that post that I retired this spring."

Safonov made a sour face.

"What, you don't believe me?" Ivan Dmitrievich smiled.

"I confess, I don't. I'm afraid your readers won't believe it either. They're not fools. If you're counting on fools, you should asked someone else, not me, to be your assistant."

"In that case, cross out the last few pages in your notebook and write that Shuvalov forgave me."

"Oh no, that's just as unlikely. Peter Andreyevich was not the kind of man to forgive things like that."

"Then," Ivan Dmitrievich suggested after half a minute's pause, "let's cross out the whole second half of this story. Let's stop at the episode where I accused Hotek. Let him be the murderer. Then we'll go on to write that the Chancellor Gorchakov promised Franz Josef not to make the incident of the envoy-assassin public, and in exchange Vienna supported his demands for retracting the conditions of the Treaty of Paris so humiliating for Russia. Napoleon III had foisted that accord on us after the Crimean War. According to one of its articles, the hardest for us to swallow, Russia was forbidden a navy in the Black Sea."

"I remember." Safonov nodded. "We read it in grammar school."

"Well, there you are," continued Ivan Dmitrievich. "In that same year, 1871, Vienna supported Gorchakov, and that article of the agreement was withdrawn. Our battleships once again appeared in Sevastopol, which came in very handy inasmuch as six years later the war with the Turks began. Shipka, Plevna, General Skobelev on his white horse, Gurko in San Stefano, remember? However, without a navy we could not have won. The Bulgarians would have remained in the power of the Sultan and his desperados. Boyev's homeland was liberated in part thanks to me. My perspicacity—"

"Stop!" said Safonov. "This is no good either. Tell me what actually happened."

"I don't remember."

"How nice! And who does?"

"No one. Too many years have passed!"

They were sitting at the edge of the cliff, and swifts were drawing lines in the air right at their feet. The sun had not risen yet. Under the whitened sky the river's surface looked matte, and an osier bed swirled like a fog on the opposite, flood-plain bank. The moored ferry there was dark.

"All right , we'll admire the sunrise tomorrow. Let's go to bed," said Ivan Dmitrievich, yawning.

Safonov tossed the apple core in the river and waited for the splash, and they started back—through the dog rose thicket, through the apple orchard, and to the house with the veranda, where they had another entire month to spend in each other's company.

Dear Reader,

Thank you for purchasing this book.

We at Glagoslav Publications are glad to welcome you, and hope that you find our books to be a source of knowledge and inspiration.

We want to show the beauty and depth of the Slavic region to everyone looking to expand their horizon and learn something new about different cultures, different people, and we believe that with this book we have managed to do just that.

Now that you've gotten to know us, we want to get to know you. We value communication with our readers and want to hear from you! We offer several options:

❖ Join our Book Club on Goodreads, Library Thing and Shelfari, and receive special offers and information about our giveaways;
❖ Share your opinion about our books on Amazon, Barnes & Noble, Waterstones and other bookstores;
❖ Join us on Facebook and Twitter for updates on our publications and news about our authors;
❖ Visit our site www.glagoslav.com to check out our Catalogue and subscribe to our Newsletter.

Glagoslav Publications is getting ready to release a new collection and planning some interesting surprises - stay with us to find out!

Glagoslav Publications
Office 36, 88-90 Hatton Garden
EC1N 8PN London, UK
Tel: + 44 (0) 20 32 86 99 82
Email: contact@glagoslav.com

Glagoslav Publications Catalogue

- ❖ *The Time of Women* by Elena Chizhova
- ❖ *Sin* by Zakhar Prilepin
- ❖ *Hardly Ever Otherwise* by Maria Matios
- ❖ *The Lost Button* by Irene Rozdobudko
- ❖ *Khatyn* by Ales Adamovich
- ❖ *Christened with Crosses* by Eduard Kochergin
- ❖ *The Vital Needs of the Dead* by Igor Sakhnovsky
- ❖ *METRO 2033* (Dutch Edition) by Dmitry Glukhovsky
- ❖ *A Poet and Bin Laden* by Hamid Ismailov
- ❖ *Asystole* by Oleg Pavlov
- ❖ *Kobzar* by Taras Shevchenko
- ❖ *White Shanghai* by Elvira Baryakina
- ❖ *The First Oligarch* by Michel Terestchenko
- ❖ *The Stone Bridge* by Alexander Terekhov
- ❖ *King Stakh's Wild Hunt* by Uladzimir Karatkevich
- ❖ *Depeche Mode* by Serhii Zhadan
- ❖ *Saraband Sarah's Band* by Larysa Denysenko
- ❖ *Herstories, An Anthology of New Ukrainian Women Prose Writers*
- ❖ *Watching The Russians* (Dutch Edition) by Maria Konyukova
- ❖ *The Hawks of Peace* by Dmitry Rogozin
- ❖ *Seven Stories* (Dutch Edition) by Leonid Andreev

More coming soon...